PRAISE FOR ANNE BUIST AND *MEDEA'S CURSE*

'A harrowing and thrilling read, this mystery will keep you on the edge of your seat.' *Buzzfeed*'s Great Australian Books from 2015

'An intelligent, well-paced thriller.' Adrian McKinty

'Forensic psychologist Natalie King is not your average heroine nor is *Medea's Curse* a predictable by-the-numbers thriller…An intelligent, thought-provoking tale.' *Courier-Mail*

'A gripping ride of crime and tension, with a Lisbeth Salander-like lead roaring through danger and intrigue at a million miles an hour.' *Adelaide Advertiser*

'Crime novels and thrillers depend on strong investigators whose idiosyncrasies make them distinctive and attractively flawed. Melburnian Anne Buist has ticked these boxes with her creation, Natalie King.' *Herald Sun*

'Buist has used her twenty-five years' experience in perinatal psychiatry to good effect in her first psychological thriller… King is a lively new character with a good mix of appealing characteristics and interesting flaws.' *Sydney Morning Herald*

'Buist brings her considerable experience as a perinatal psychiatrist to bear in this novel, giving it authenticity and gravitas.' *Daily Telegraph*

'Will stay with the reader long after the last page is turned. A brilliant read.' *BookMooch*

'Handles its issues compassionately, builds tension well and has a fascinating, flawed protagonist.' *AustCrime Fiction*

ALSO BY ANNE BUIST
Medea's Curse

Anne Buist is the Chair of Women's Mental Health at the University of Melbourne. She has over twenty-five years' clinical and research experience in perinatal psychiatry, and works with protective services and the legal system in cases of abuse, kidnapping, infanticide and murder.

Professor Buist is married to novelist Graeme Simsion, and has two children.

annebuist.com

ANNE BUIST
DANGEROUS TO KNOW

TEXT PUBLISHING MELBOURNE AUSTRALIA

textpublishing.com.au

The Text Publishing Company
Swann House
22 William Street
Melbourne Victoria 3000
Australia

First published in 2016 by The Text Publishing Company

Book design by Text
Typeset by J&M Typesetting

Printed and bound in Australia by Griffin Press, an Accredited ISO AS/NZS 14001:2004 Environmental Management System printer

National Library of Australia Cataloguing-in-Publication entry
Creator: Buist, Anne, author.
Title: Dangerous to know : Natalie King, forensic psychiatrist / by Anne Buist.
ISBN: 9781925240887 (paperback)
          9781922253514 (ebook)
Subjects: Suspense fiction. Forensic psychiatrists—Fiction.
Dewey Number: A823.4

This book is printed on paper certified against the Forest Stewardship Council® Standards. Griffin Press holds FSC chain-of-custody certification SGS-COC-005088. FSC promotes environmentally responsible, socially beneficial and economically viable management of the world's forests.

For Graeme, Daniel and Dominique

'Mad, bad and dangerous to know.'

LADY CAROLINE LAMB,
OF LORD BYRON

PROLOGUE

I have examined my life; but examining murder is another thing altogether.

The hospital door is ajar and I catch a glimpse of the uniformed officer stationed there. There have been no charges, not yet. But soon the ICU physician will take his head out of the chart where he has plotted my electrolytes, heart rate, blood pressure and fluid balance, and will decide that the morphine and pain are in equilibrium. Then Natalie's detective friend will arrive armed with recording devices, reciting my rights. They believe that they know. But they are wrong. Natalie thinks she is my equal, with her intuition and her single-minded search for the truth. She believes that if she searches she will find the answer that she wants to see.

We are all guilty of wanting to see our world in a particular way, at least for brief periods of time. Who hasn't looked back at a wedding or graduation photo and marvelled at the innocence and aspirations, at odds with the later reality in all its different, perverse forms?

I have allowed myself to be blinded for too long. I no longer have that luxury. The time to make decisions is running out; but the decision will be mine not theirs.

I have examined my life. I have reflected on what childhood experiences might have driven my parents and their choices and I know my own strengths…and those areas I was likely to avoid delving deeply into. How then, can I justify avoiding so much? How could I not have seen what was happening when I understood the *why* so well? How could I have persevered in my ignorance, now to have deaths on my conscience?

Impossible, unforgiveable. Eighty per cent of juries have made up their mind after the opening address, and do not change their view. No defence attorney's arguments could possibly be as compelling as the simplest of statements from the prosecutor:

How could he not have known?

She watched the needle prick the vein in her hand and wished it hurt more. Pain—real pain, rather than the deadened reality of the last weeks—would have been welcome. Or had it been months? The man with the needle told her she was going to sleep; she had been doing a lot of that. The bitch nurse who talked to her like she was retarded put her notes on the trolley and walked off. The male nurse, still smelling of a recent cigarette, smiled at her. In her mind she smiled back, though she doubted her lips moved. The facial expression she saw occasionally when she caught sight of herself in a mirror was wooden, her hair hanging dull, the red highlights washed out; she couldn't recall when she had last used a brush. She had barely recognised the face as hers. Her brown eyes appeared enormous, her cheek bones too prominent, her slender body wasted. The line of silver studs in her ear was the only hint of any kind of attitude.

The blood in the syringe confirmed Needle-man's expertise. She closed her eyes as the anaesthetic took over, her last image the small white cubicle and the steel trolley of equipment, the anaesthetist turning to retrieve the mask. She felt him place it over her face as the psychiatrist, a tall lean

Indian man whose name she had forgotten, checked dials and picked up the paddles that he would apply to the right side of her head. When she woke up, only a few minutes would have passed. She would be in the recovery room, as she had been twice already this week. She would have a headache and her memory would be hazy. If she was lucky, for a period of time she would forget where and who she was. The decisions she had to make. The things she needed to leave behind.

'How are you feeling, Natalie?'

Declan's look of concern had acquired a tinge of hope. The creases around his eyes seemed less compressed than they had on his recent visits. She had washed her hair and was wearing a clean T-shirt, not the grubby green one that had doubled as a nightie for most of the last two months. It wasn't her usual bolshie sub-Goth style but it was a step in the right direction. And she was sitting upright in a chair. In his office, at the front of his house, surrounded by polished surfaces, brocade curtains and antique furniture.

'Hamilton Depression Scale score of eight?' She shrugged. 'I'm cured.'

A slight exhale, but he was still watching her carefully as he ran his hand through what was left of his hair.

'Don't worry, they stopped zapping me when I asked Vijay Venkatasubramani for a date.' Not a date exactly, but she thought she'd keep things nice for her supervisor.

She saw Declan smile before he was able to stop himself. 'It was probably more that you could recall his name.'

'Have you met him? At least there isn't anything wrong with my taste.' She knew she was avoiding what she was here to talk about. Knew Declan would be wondering if she even remembered the last conversation, when he'd come to see her in hospital. Speaking as friend and mentor, rather than as her supervisor.

She did remember.

You didn't choose this illness Natalie, but you have a choice about how to manage it. Right now your lifestyle isn't working. I know it's not fair, but to stay well you have to make sacrifices.

That meant giving up the stressful work that energised her; the late nights; the alcohol and wild sex in favour of a quiet life. Early nights, a balanced diet and a stable relationship.

Could she? Maybe.

Alcohol wasn't such a big thing for her, and in the short term she wasn't contemplating any kind of sex. But the band, the music that made her feel alive—that would be harder.

And her job? Impossible to give that up. Right now she didn't need the money, but she needed the sense of purpose. And she was good at it. It had taken her five years of medical school and five years of specialist training to get to where she was. She wouldn't throw that away.

'I asked the hospital manager for a six-month leave of absence,' Natalie said. A compromise. 'To decide what I want to do.' And to avoid running into Liam O'Shea until she knew she could handle it.

Declan nodded, pouring tea from a faded bone china teapot. No wine today. He was being careful with her.

'I thought I'd move to the country. Maybe try out research.' Declan raised an eyebrow. He knew of Natalie's fraught relationship with academe. But all he said was, 'Anywhere particular in mind?'

'Little spot west of Lorne on the Great Ocean Road. I

5

used to holiday near there when I was a kid. Fresh sea air and not too many people. Not now the summer's over.'

Declan rubbed his chin. 'It's a long way from Melbourne.'

Natalie shrugged. 'A two-and-a-half-hour ride. I can come up once a week to see you and my Monday patients. And Geelong's only an hour away.'

She'd done a cursory search of the university department in Geelong, which boasted Associate Professor Frank Moreton as the sole psychiatrist with any academic standing. She remembered him vaguely from some lectures he'd given on somatisation; how people's early childhood and personality could influence the type of illnesses that afflicted them. He was British, from memory. Good looking but way too self-important. A few of the female registrars had been conned, but good looking and arrogant was not her style. Not since Liam, anyway. The new Natalie King was going to do yoga every morning and be in bed sipping herbal tea by nine each night. Alone.

The concern was still there in Declan's eyes when he wished her well.

Natalie packed up her Ducati, carefully covering Bob's cage so the ride wouldn't strip out all of his feathers. As relationships went, this was one of her more successful. Since a patient had asked her to take care of the cockatoo and then gone AWOL, Bob was one of the few predictable elements of her life.

She took the wide new freeway that led to the winding coast road. A chill blew off the cool grey ocean, and there were long sections of sweeping curves with no traffic. After she'd left Lorne behind, the houses on the hills to her right were lost among the trees. The only light came from her bike, sending eerie shadows across the road.

When she arrived at Separation Creek, fog hugged the meagre street lights and the houses—mostly built on stilts to deal with the steep hillside, probably all weekenders—were dark. She slowed the Ducati. *Keep on after the last house,* was the agent's instruction. *You won't get lonely will you?*

She only found the driveway after the road disappeared into a dip and she knew she'd gone too far. Slower on return, she caught sight of the track between two gum trees shedding bark like snake skin and gunned the bike up the steep incline. She cut the engine as she roared into the carport, which was empty except for a stack of wood.

'How do you feel?' Poor Bob. He sounded like he wasn't feeling well.

Natalie foraged for the key and opened the door, then grabbed his cage and headed up the staircase.

'You could have been a star,' Bob muttered unconvincingly. Why did the damn parrot have to misquote Dylan?

She forgot him as soon as the stairs opened into a huge living area. Floor to ceiling glass doors led to the balcony; beyond, the moon was just visible through the sea mist, the wide expanse of the bay below largely hidden apart from splashes of white surf.

Natalie threw open the doors. The sounds of waves crashing in the distance and a gust of cold salty air greeted her. It couldn't have been more different from the warehouse in Collingwood where she had lived for the last two-and-a-half years, wedged between a printer's office and a brothel. Her new home backed into a thickly wooded forest. Only a few lights twinkling on the distant hills opposite suggested any civilisation at all.

If isolation was what she wanted, she'd certainly got it.

She was woken by a screech, like a train going through a tunnel. Several trains. Natalie was out of bed clutching a knife before she even remembered where she was. There was more screeching; too loud to be just Bob. The bright light streaming through the doors was dazzling and she had to squint to make out what the problem was.

Bob was marching up and down the far banister periodically letting rip. Six very large white cockatoos were lined up along the balcony. Another two were fighting over an empty feed container surrounded by cracked seed hulls. They eyed Natalie with minimal interest, even as she opened the door to join them. Bob flew to her shoulder and bit her ear.

'I don't think you're going to be lonely here Bob,' said Natalie.

Would she be? Or worse? Natalie looked at the blade in her hand. It had been over six months since the attack, and the Worm was now in prison awaiting trial on child-porn-related charges. But his intent when he came for her had been clear, and she'd escaped more through good luck than good management. And it had left a mark: she slept with a knife now.

It was only six-thirty. She tried meditation for ten minutes then abandoned it for coffee and the view.

By nine she was on the road, to make a ten o'clock appointment in Geelong. She'd told Declan she'd take it easy, and she intended to. But she knew she needed something to focus on. The arrogant associate professor had said he'd be happy to see her, and some low-key academic work would be perfect. Stimulating enough; nothing to get her into trouble.

Frank Moreton's office was easy enough to find. The department of psychiatry was sign-posted in the hospital foyer. But the secretary's desk showed no evidence of any recent activity. Behind it, a door was propped open with a pile of journals. Natalie peered cautiously into a large room. Three dormant computers in carrels. No paperwork or personal touches. Two office doors, one open and the other closed, at the other end. Natalie was debating whether to try the far door when she heard a chair scrape. A head appeared above a carrel.

'Yes?' High cheek bones and cropped black hair above prominent ears. Behind red-rimmed hipster glasses, wide-spaced eyes suggested a Chinese heritage.

'I was looking for Professor Moreton.'

'Is he is expecting you?' An educated British accent.

'I'm Natalie King. Prof Moreton suggested this time.' Natalie kept a careful neutral smile in place.

There was a fleeting expression of impatience before a reluctant smile. 'I'm Wei.' An androgynous figure rose. About the same age as Natalie, and a willowy five centimetres taller. Skinny jeans. No visible waist or bust—probably male, Natalie decided, although close up it looked like he was wearing mascara and nail polish, so she wasn't putting money on it. Wei looked at the bike helmet in Natalie's hand, seeming equally uncertain how to categorise her. Natalie had changed into an unusually demure dress, so the confusion was understandable.

'You can leave your gear here. Frank's in his office.' Wei tilted his head backwards, towards the closed door, then sat down and went back to his computer.

Natalie recognised Associate Professor Moreton immediately. He stood up, smiling. As she had recalled, he was good looking. Maybe even exceptionally good looking. A little under six foot and solid. Not overweight, but filling the room with his presence. Blue striped shirt with sleeves rolled up to expose a smattering of fine dark hair; silver-blue tie. Pretty, she decided. Boyish, with dark hair that curled over his collar and long eyelashes. He was wearing a wedding ring.

'Dr King.' He took her extended hand with both of his, smiling playfully, and held it. Pulled back an instant before it became too much, too long.

'Natalie.'

Frank went to the door and stuck his head out. 'Wei? Would you mind getting us some coffee?' There was a slight formality to his speech: a British childhood that had given way to some Australian broadening of vowels, was Natalie's guess. He'd been in Australia longer than his research assistant.

Natalie didn't hear Wei's response.

'So, Natalie, you're interested in research?'

Not really, but that probably wasn't the ideal comeback. 'Looking at possibilities.'

'You said in the email that you were interested in PTSD?'

It had been the only overlap between his publications and her interests. 'I was thinking childhood abuse as a risk factor for post-traumatic stress disorder and postnatal depression.'

'Excellent! We have an obstetric ward here and I'm sure we could set that up easily.' He was outlining some of his own research when Wei returned with plunger coffee and a surly expression. When he left he banged the door loudly behind him.

'We might get you a scholarship,' Frank continued, oblivious, pulling mugs from his shelf, 'but it wouldn't pay anything like your clinical work.' He sat back in his chair, at ease, eyes not leaving her.

Natalie nodded and took the coffee he poured; luckily she liked it black and unsweetened.

'But,' Frank leaned forward so she could see the flecks of green in his irises. 'I could easily get you some clinical sessions to top up your income.'

'How about I try out the research first?' asked Natalie.

Frank smiled. 'Of course. We...I...look forward to it.'

He made no move to touch her. Why did it feel as if he'd patted her hand?

At that moment a pretty blonde woman Natalie recognised breezed into the office and stopped dead when she saw who Frank was talking to. She was obviously pregnant, probably early third trimester. Her skin had the glow that women get when the hormones agree with them, and she exuded a kind of satisfaction; her life was apparently on track. Her outfit was tailored, in a pale blue that offset her eyes, with whimsical lace at the sleeves and hem. Feet in strappy heels, light blonde curls framing her face. The blue eyes narrowed as they moved from Frank to Natalie.

At that moment something Declan had said flashed into Natalie's mind. Something about what she was making sacrifices for, but she lost the thought with the final realisation.

Alison was not happy to see her.

Natalie was more attractive than I expected her to be. I like beautiful, striking women, women who make a statement with their presence; life is too short to bother with the others. And women like me. Really like me. Alison, for example, was interested in me from the first time we met, even though I was married at the time. I take care of myself, and women appreciate that. Italian designers, fair trade coffee; a balanced intake of omega three.

I could tell that Natalie was a man's woman. I hadn't expected that either. Ten years or more in the medical course and specialist training, trying to prove they belong, is rather at odds with developing an alluring manner. Desperate and lonely is more common—supposed professionalism shrouding fear and lack of imagination. She was not as opinionated as I had been told to expect, either. Perhaps my colleague got it wrong about her, or she was just on her best behaviour.

She wasn't as confident as she wished to seem, but of course women rarely are, not in both aspects of their life. If they are beautiful then they fear they aren't clever enough. If they are intelligent, they worry about their looks. And she isn't young anymore. Thirty-three and single. The biological clock was evident behind the uncertain look back at me when she entered, the casual glance at my ring finger.

I understand, of course. Age and women and the whole children thing. I didn't think much about it until I had my career well established. I had the male advantage, could bide my time and play the field. But then, I became tired of the endless small talk and bored by inane smiles. Tired of games.

I wondered, when Natalie arrived in my life, at the similarities between her and my first wife. A similar look, the same sharp intellect, but with an underlying insecurity. If I believed in fate, I would have read much into Natalie's sudden need for a sea change. But I didn't ask. When she came into my office I saw Reeva; and I was missing Reeva.

'Natalie. What a surprise.' Not a pleasant one, judging from Alison's expression.

Frank had stood up and was looking at them with a coy smile; probably his way of dealing with tension. Natalie had the impression he'd be happy to let her and Alison slug it out rather than get his hands dirty.

'You know each other?' he asked.

'We were interns together.' Alison's tone was tense.

'We were just finishing up talking about possible research projects,' said Frank, his smile now almost provocative.

'How interesting.' Alison's lips were stretched tight, her eyes wary.

Frank turned to Natalie, smiling. She wondered whose reaction he was testing. Or was she reading too much into the scenario? She wasn't completely certain that shock therapy hadn't messed with her judgment along with her short-term memory.

'We have an appointment to get baby photos,' Frank said, adding '...via ultrasound,' as Natalie shot him a bemused look.

'Yes of course.' She stood. 'I've got plenty to think about.

Maybe I'll email you?' As she left she turned to Alison. 'Congratulations. I had no idea you and...Well, you look great.' She didn't wait for a reply. Academe was probably not a good fit for her anyway.

Natalie and Alison hadn't been close friends in their first year working as doctors. But the end-of-year revue—a hospital-themed spoof of *The Rocky Horror Show*—had meant nightly rehearsals together, along with Alison's fiancé, Oliver.

It was in the last rehearsals that things started to derail, with Oliver's suggestion he could down more vodka shots than Natalie and still be under the legal limit.

'Fighting words,' Natalie said with a giggle. She'd been giggling a lot lately; completely out of character.

Next day, despite the hangover, she didn't seem to be able to stop talking.

'Jesus Nat, what have you been smoking?' asked Tom, her on/off boyfriend and the drummer in her band. He was still pissed off at her for coming on to one of the groupies the week before; it had seemed a good idea at the time.

'You know I don't take any of that shit.' She hadn't gone home the night before the revue. Just a couple of hours sleep on the X-ray table next to the emergency department. Too much to do.

Like the backdrops.

'Pretty wild, hey?' she said when someone commented on them. The colour enlargements of scenes from the emergency department had cost her most of a week's wage. It was possible that she had gone a little overboard with them.

She'd held it together until after the performance, which

felt brilliant. There had been lots of laughs, and that was what it was all about. Unwinding after a year of almost unbearable pressure.

She had vague memories of Alison looking pissed off with Natalie's after-party performance of Alison's big number from the show, along with the pelvic thrusts the song called for. But Natalie hadn't made Oliver leave with her afterwards; or at least she didn't think so. Her mind hadn't been able to hold onto any one idea long enough to consider consequences.

Afterwards she would never be able to put together exactly what happened. A splash through the moat around the National Gallery and a wild drive along the coast road, a stop somewhere for a skinny dip. Oliver had given in to exhaustion long before her and she had no idea how he got back to Melbourne. She returned two days later—via the police station. She gave them Tom's number and it was Tom who called Declan.

In the whole horrible mess that followed, including a four-week inpatient stay, Declan's role changed. No longer just the therapist who had helped her recover after a motorbike crash at sixteen, he became more like her minder.

That was her first bipolar episode. Not her last. None since had ever been so out of control, though.

At the time she thought she would never speak to Tom or Declan again. Later, after the lithium kicked in and Natalie realised just how the night shifts had destabilised her, she came to thank them, albeit grudgingly. She hadn't thanked anyone for her diagnosis, and still railed against it at times. But as a psychiatrist, she was now well aware how sleep deprivation could trigger manic episodes.

In the end, the only ones among her colleagues who

really knew how far off the rails she'd gone were Alison and Oliver. Oliver wasn't going to tell anyone because he was just as embarrassed as she. And Alison? Eight years later in Frank's office, her tight-lipped smile told Natalie she hadn't forgotten—and she sure as hell wasn't forgiving.

The next morning there was an email from Frank. She figured it would say, *On reflection...*or *It doesn't look like I'll be able to fit you in after all.* She left it while she filled Bob's feed container—indoors where the local flock wouldn't harass him—grabbed a towel and wandered down to the beach.

The water was still warm enough but there was an icy chill in the early autumn air when she resurfaced. It felt good—she needed the wake-up, needed to think about her other options. She had the triggers for her depressive episode mostly in hand: medication—tick. Calmer lifestyle—tick. But the assault in her warehouse the previous year by the man she called the Worm was still giving her nightmares. And there was Liam.

She knew she couldn't avoid him forever. He was running the prosecution case against her patient, Georgia, charged with murdering her three children. It was due to go to trial in two months. Natalie wanted to avoid testifying but suspected Liam was relishing the idea of a cross-examination. Liam O'Shea, with his deadly Irish brogue and cocky smile, the black curl that hung over one eye. She dreaded the reminder of what had been between them. Something she had hoped would become a distant memory still felt raw.

When she got back she made herself a coffee and sat out on the balcony with her laptop to read Frank's email. Then read it again.

Frank was welcoming her on board. Almost effusively: *It'll be wonderful having a fellow psychiatrist working here.* He'd already lined up some sessions in the acute ward whenever she wanted to start. There was no doubt he was keen.

She doubted his wife was so enthusiastic. But Alison was remembering the old Natalie. Declan said she had to change her lifestyle in order to stay well, and that was what she was doing. She didn't know how her life would end up looking, though. Husband, family...the white picket fence—Alison's ideal?

Natalie couldn't quite picture herself with a domesticated suburban new-age guy. And she didn't want to think about Eoin, who had died in the motorbike accident that nearly crippled her at sixteen, still wanting everything. Or Liam, who she wanted and couldn't have.

She went to get dressed to meet with her new supervisor.

Nine a.m. and no one had bothered turning on the lights. She understood that research didn't have the urgency of clinical work, but surely Frank's team should be here by now?

'If you're looking for Frank,' Wei's voice echoed out of the darkness, 'he does a teaching round Monday mornings.'

Natalie hit the light switch. 'Where is everyone?'

'Everyone?' Wei squared his glasses. 'I am everyone. PA, RA and general dogsbody.'

Natalie took a moment to process this in the context of the deserted space, and Frank's list of publications. 'But there were more of you once, right?'

'Eight of us when I started.'

'Research money ran out?'

'I'm finishing the tail end of the final five-year grant,

writing up the last papers. After that...' He indicated the door.

Natalie nodded. Her clinical sessions could pay for her time with some research on the side if she wanted; the funding wasn't such an issue for her. But poor Frank. And there was an uneasy sense of loneliness about the space. She had pictured a vibrant group exchanging ideas and inspiring her.

'Why are you here?' Wei looked at her suspiciously.

'Thinking of doing some research.'

'Well you'll have to do it on your own.' Wei zipped up a satin jacket. His eyes had a line of kohl under them today. 'Why here?' he said. 'Why now?'

Questions Frank hadn't thought to ask.

'A change of scene. I have a touch of PTSD. After an assault.'

Wei's expression softened fractionally. 'Maybe,' he said, watching Natalie carefully, 'you'll turn out to be another whizz-kid medico.'

'I've never written a research grant.' Natalie shrugged. It wasn't like that would stop her, even if Wei wasn't going to be much of a help. '*Another?*'

'Frank's first wife was the grant queen. Sadly, his second isn't.'

First wife. And one that Alison couldn't match on the work front.

'Reeva, you understand,' said Wei, 'was responsible for the grant that got this lab up and running. She was brilliant.' Wei's tone left no doubt about his admiration for the absent Reeva.

'They're divorced?' Natalie asked, wondering how research grants could be part of the alimony.

Wei had turned back to the computer. 'No. She died.'

Reeva was not beautiful. At first I didn't think she was attractive enough, truth be told. Nose a little too prominent, eyes a fraction too close. And worse, it bothered her. I like women who are confident in their femininity. Who aren't surprised to turn heads and would not question that they deserved such attention.

Once a girlfriend caught me looking into a mirror and called me vain: rolled her eyes and sang a line from the Carly Simon song. But I was not looking just at myself; I was looking at us as a couple. If I was guilty of vanity, it included her. While attractive enough, she was, regrettably, also stupid. An arts degree from a minor college that she kept mentioning as if it proved something, but her stupidity was mainly about human nature. She underestimated me and overestimated her own power. Thought that being young and attractive was enough. It isn't. We looked good together, but that was all.

When I glanced into the mirror at Reeva and myself, I saw something she gave to the relationship that was beyond the superficial. It radiated out of her. She may have lacked the showy confidence that men would want to be with her,

but there were depths to her self-esteem, not beset with questions about her worth as a human being. It was a look that developed in tiny steps and I watched her as if she was a bud developing. Her delight, quickly tempered, when I asked her out on the first date; the hesitancy in her when it became clear I wanted her to share my bed; the steady glow that each encounter added, until that point when she finally knew I was the one. When the mirror showed us as *almost perfect*.

After a restless night, Natalie managed a full hour of something that approximated meditation, though it was more mindfulness mantra and enjoying the sounds of the water breaking, the smell of salt, the cold air rustling her hair, than blank mind. She had read that it was possible to come off medication altogether by managing your circadian rhythms and meditating daily. She suspected that this also required giving up a desire to live life on the edge, and she had a long way to go before she'd be ready to accept that. Mindfulness was living in the moment and here the moment was a wonderful place to be. Bit quiet, maybe, but that was what she was after. She could do this.

After a herbal tea—if she was going to be health conscious she might as well do it right—she went for a jog along the road behind the house that wound through the national park. No one else was about, but the birds were alive and active, and several koalas observed her with interest from the trees. The road finally turned south and back to the main road by the ocean that in summer was cluttered with tourist buses. As soon as she could, she cut down to the beach, the run harder but worth it, the sand and water bringing home

the lesson of celebrating the present time.

She'd been running for over an hour when she decided it was time to head back along the main road. It was a mistake. The pack of bikers riding past her took her back in an instant to living with Tom and always being on the edge of something dangerous. One rider wobbled as he was showing off and made her think of Eoin, just before the fatal crash. A lone man at the café, sitting watching her, made her heart accelerate even as her pace slowed. And all the good of an hour's meditation was gone in an instant.

After a month of her new life Natalie had lost track of the days. Each seemed to roll into the next. She was spending nights alone with Bob playing guitar and reading, and days at 'work'—still waiting for ethics approval to come through before she could start any research. The drawn-out process added to her feelings of depression. It was so safe and predictable; it made her feel like she was edging closer to the black hole that had swallowed her only weeks earlier. She remembered the days before being hospitalised. Taking all the pills out of their bottles, counting them. Calculating their effect, the risks if her calculations were wrong. Hated her weakness and found herself shaking now as the memory taunted her. She'd played Passenger's *Let Her Go* on repeat in the darkness of her warehouse for weeks but she wasn't entirely sure she had completely let Liam go, even though he'd never been hers in the first place. Now even Bob quoted her version of some of the lyrics. Jesus, she had been sick. What had she been thinking? Passenger? Really?

Now, looking in the mirror, she wasn't sure she even recognised herself: had she really bought this top with *flowers* on it? Who the fuck was she?

At least she found the work easy. She was already well into the second chapter of what would ultimately be her thesis if she continued, but it was a big if. She hadn't started clinical sessions—her income-protection insurance would last for another couple of months at least—but the lack of patient contact, apart from her Mondays in Melbourne, was taking its toll. The lab was empty except for the uncommunicative Wei and the silence wasn't helping. She was deeply bored.

'Free for a drink before you go home?'

Frank's smiling face tilted past the door frame. He had the ability to smile innocently and provocatively all at once. He played it, she figured. Emphasising the long eyelashes and dimples when he grinned a certain way.

The computer clock said 6.30 p.m. She remembered Wei leaving earlier with a stunning blonde woman who'd looked at her curiously, but they'd disappeared without introductions. She'd thought she was alone but here was Frank smiling a cub-scout grin. They'd had coffee at least once a week in the month since she'd started; three times last week, now she thought about it. She had the impression he was lonely. Probably not getting much at home, with Alison in her third trimester.

'A drink? Not sure that's a good idea.' Actually she was completely sure it wasn't. A drink after work was different from a coffee date. Particularly if he was sensing her sexual frustration.

The last time she was in Melbourne had only made it worse. It was great Tom and the rest of the band wanted her back singing while they did a stint along the coast, but it turned out Tom was no longer a friend with benefits. He'd awkwardly announced that he'd moved in with Maggie, the bartender at Natalie's Collingwood local. Shit, why was everyone settling down when all she wanted to do was burn the speed limit on her Ducati and shag someone silly?

Frank sat down next her, scratching his head and avoiding eye contact. 'I didn't mean...' He sighed. 'Sorry that was stupid, wasn't it? But there aren't too many people I can talk to right now.' His eyes, now resting on her, said the rest.

'How about Alison?' Natalie probably sounded harsher than she intended, as she broke eye contact. Married men? *Not again.* Particularly since she already owed this man's wife.

'Not a good idea at the moment.' Frank's expression now was bordering on plaintive Labrador.

He'd piqued her interest. Why *not at the moment*? Natalie closed down the computer. It wasn't as if Bob and the cockatoo contingent were missing her. Anyway, this was work. Her supervisor: a colleague. And she owed Alison: she'd lend Frank a sympathetic ear and direct him back to his wife. 'One drink.'

The bar was nondescript, wedged between a pub and an upmarket steak restaurant. Probably aiming for clientele that no longer existed in a town hit with business closures and high unemployment. The after-work crowd was thin, the guy behind the bar periodically checking out his Twitter feed, and the female server was disengaged. From Natalie anyway. Frank rated a double-take and a smile.

Natalie watched her supervisor struggle to start and felt as though she was with a psychotherapy patient.

'Do you know about Reeva?'

'A little.'

'I know there's no reason to be anxious, that it was all just one of those random things, but...'

'You'd better back up. I know she was your wife, and a researcher, and that she died.'

'A brilliant researcher.' The light was dim but Natalie was sure his eyes were glistening. No wonder he couldn't talk about this with Alison. He was still grieving. Maybe this was how she could make it up to Alison; help him move on.

'What happened?'

'I don't know. One moment she was fine, a bit tired of course, went to bed early and then never woke up.'

'Why *of course*?'

Frank looked puzzled. 'Tired you mean? Nothing out of the ordinary. Just the pregnancy.'

Natalie stared at him. *Pregnancy?* 'How many weeks?'

'Thirty-nine.' Frank was looking down into his glass of wine.

'So the baby?' Natalie's voice was little more than a whisper.

'We lost him too.' Frank looked up so slowly it was as if there was physical pain in the action. 'He was...I'd felt him move right before she went to bed.'

'Oh Frank, that must have been...' Been what? There were no words for this.

'Both being doctors, I think makes it worse. Like we...I... should have been able to do something.'

'It's hard to sit with the feeling you've failed.' Natalie knew this all too well. She'd spent months wanting to go back and tell Eoin not to get on the bike that last time.

'And now Alison thinks I'm neurotic.'

'It's natural for you to be worried.'

'Yes, but it isn't just me. She thinks we're all neurotic. But my...mother had lots of miscarriages and...we just want this baby...and Alison...to be well.'

'How many weeks is she, Frank?'

'Thirty-six.'

Natalie automatically put her hand over his. 'Only a month, Frank. It isn't the nineteenth century, maternal mortality's around one in ten thousand.'

'Talking with you helps. I appreciate it.'

In his look she read more, but dismissed it. The shock treatment; she still wasn't herself.

Georgia Latimer arrived on time at Natalie's Punt Road rooms. Furious.

'You want me to go to prison, don't you?' Georgia, fully made up, looked younger than her thirty-eight years. Blonde hair brushed the collar of her white cashmere top. Her jeans were tucked into long brown boots. She made an unlikely defendant to three murder charges.

She'd read Natalie's report.

'It's not up to me Georgia. I think you are very troubled, but—'

'But you think I killed my children, don't you?'

Natalie pondered this. There was still doubt. Georgia continued to deny it. The pathology wasn't conclusive. And Georgia's self-harm, the cutting, had happened before the first of her children died: it could have been the only outlet for her anger.

'I'm neither jury nor judge,' Natalie hedged.

'I'll never agreed to a guilty plea.'

Natalie nodded. This had always been the dilemma for Georgia and her barrister: try to convince the jury that all the children died of natural causes, an improbability that might be explained by an undiagnosed genetic problem. Or try for a lesser sentence by agreeing to plead guilty to infanticide. In which case they needed to use mental illness as a defence strategy.

Seemed like the Office of Public Prosecution—Liam's office—wasn't playing ball on the latter. And her mental illness would not be enough to defend a murder charge.

'Do you believe Paul influenced me?'

'I know you tried to make me think that.'

'Because he did!' Georgia banged the window hard, the wooden frame shaking. She was crying.

After she had reined in her fury, Georgia started again. 'I've been having this dream,' she said. 'I couldn't ever quite remember it. Just that I'd wake up and feel...'

The silence stretched out and finally Natalie, looking at the time, prompted her. 'Feel what?'

'Ashamed,' said Georgia, so softly that Natalie couldn't be sure she hadn't missed something.

'Ashamed of what, Georgia?'

'I remembered then, you see.' Georgia turned around, leaned back against the window frame, pressing her flushed cheek against its cool glass. 'It was before Genevieve was born. Before I was pregnant. Just a look, nothing more.'

Natalie waited and as Georgia described the scenario, she tried to picture a younger Georgia and Paul. She had met Georgia's husband once.

'I was having lots of problems with my periods. Cramps and bleeding. The doctor had started me on another pill to see if that helped. But Paul walked into the bathroom and I hadn't disposed of the pads. The look...' She shuddered and looked at Natalie. 'I didn't want to ever, not ever, see that look again. I felt so...ashamed.' Georgia smiled suddenly. 'But why on earth should I have been?'

*

'Did you suggest formal psychotherapy?' Declan was pouring tea again. At least it wasn't Morning Dew, a herbal brew the organic food shop in Lorne had foisted upon her. They said it would improve her morning meditation and in a roundabout way it had. She chose meditation as a way to avoid drinking tea that smelled of dog piss on cut grass. Neither had yet led to spiritual enlightenment.

'It's only a month.' She caught Declan's look. 'Anyway, Frank's far too narcissistic to ever admit he needs real help.'

'So it's informal?'

'Absolutely. Like…like peer support, I guess. Frank's got a lot on his shoulders. He's trying for a new grant, a big one, and without Reeva, Wei thinks they have at best a fifty-fifty chance. If he doesn't get it, he'll lose his one researcher at the end of the year.' And her, if she was to stay even that long. It seemed unlikely. Her Monday patients made her feel more alive than at any time in the empty research lab.

'Peer review has its own rules and obligations. Being vulnerable in front of your colleagues creates its own issues. Have you thought about why he's chosen you?'

'Yes.' Natalie took a sip of tea and grimaced. 'No chance of a dash of bourbon I suppose? Okay, I was joking. Just all this healthy living is…'

'Natalie.'

'I said yes and I meant it. I mean I really thought about it. Have you ever known me not to take your wise counsel?'

She put the cup down. 'This is how I see it. Frank is your average narcissistic academic; better looking than most and knows how to use it. He's also a little fragile, defences low because he's been skating on the skirt tails of wife number one and isn't sure he's up to the task by himself.

On top of this, he lost her and his son and remarried almost immediately after. It fits with his take on the world—that is, he needs to be adored. Alison would be good at that. She got her second-year registrar position despite a screw-up with a patient, because she burst into tears. The surgeon was probably afraid she'd go him for harassment, but she followed him around like a puppy for the rest of the rotation.'

Natalie paused, checking Declan was following. 'Trouble is, now Alison's pregnant and needing Frank. And he's still traumatised by Reeva's death.'

Declan smiled tightly, lining his pens up on the desk. She tried to interpret the obsessional defence but couldn't see what his issue was. Her own mental health? Okay, she rated her mood as about four out of ten most days, but that wasn't zero.

'So no way in hell is his ego going to survive scrutiny by someone like you, Declan. In me, he sees someone younger and less experienced and he's used to charming women. He thinks I'm a pushover and you can't blame him.' She gestured at her bland top and navy skirt. 'I'm dressing like Miss Krabappel these days.'

'And are you a pushover, Natalie?'

'For a charming older married man?' Natalie's eyes glinted. 'Now that ain't any mistake I'm going to make twice. I'll get him through until he's a new dad and then relinquish the responsibility with pleasure.'

Declan looked down. If she thought there was doubt there, it was trumped by her certainty that she had Frank in hand.

Reeva was pregnant almost immediately. I was not enthusiastic. We had decided to wait, at least until after the American conference where our preliminary data was to be presented.

'I'm as shocked as you,' said Reeva, the brilliant physician. She pointed out that she had been on the pill since she was eighteen. 'I thought it would take months just to start having periods.'

It hadn't.

I didn't lose my temper. But I ended up going to the USA alone—she was in the third trimester and there had been some complications—and the meeting was not the same without her. She had the flair and warmth that the Americans seem to like. She also had a great mind. At least until her hormones rendered it little better than gorgonzola cheese in the heat.

I missed her, too, the core of her that was mine. I missed her from the moment she turned inward to focus on the baby, however natural that might have been.

And of course I knew the ripples the pregnancy had set in motion. How could I not? I felt the ghosts from my nursery like a cold breeze over my skin. They insinuated themselves into my life as if greedy to take hold and score points. They were there when I caught myself criticising Reeva again for being unduly anxious, when I heard the lilt of my grandfather, Antonije, in my voice and when I felt the safety in the remoteness of my father as I pulled away from her.

When Reeva died, I cried. I missed her and all we could have been. I wanted her back, if only for a moment, to say I wished I had done things differently.

'You have impossible standards,' she had said and she was right. But by then we were estranged and she no longer confided in me.

I cried for the loss. I wondered, as I looked at Natalie, head bent over the articles piled on her desk and spilling onto the floor, what would help me heal.

The house had no television or landline, but it did have reasonable mobile reception, and Natalie was able to use the internet. There were two mentions of Reeva Osbourne's death, both in the Geelong paper. One, a paragraph at the time it occurred, reported 'no suspicious circumstances'. The other was a half-page about her life, as celebrated at the funeral. There was a picture of Frank turning towards Reeva's grief-stricken parents. Two women to his other side, faces away from the camera, were not named. Neither of them was Alison.

Just one of those terrible tragedies. It was unusual, in the first world, for a woman to die late in pregnancy. The dangers tended to be very early, with an ectopic, or during and after labour. Had Reeva gone into early labour and not been able to call anyone? Unlikely.

Natalie kept googling, whether from boredom or morbid curiosity she wasn't sure.

Frank lived outside of Lorne. Quite a way out. A rural property called Mount Malosevic that had its own website. The gardens were featured on the home page, full of sculptures by local artist Antonije Malosevic. She was pretty sure her school, years ago, had organised an outing to it; she'd wagged to go off with Eoin instead. In the small print she found Antonije Malosevic was Frank's grandfather, deceased five years ago. A year before Frank married Reeva. Two years before she died.

So Alison, as second wife—second pregnant wife—was also living in the house Frank had shared with Reeva. Natalie squashed a sense of unease. She was being ridiculous. If you had a grand family house worth millions, why wouldn't you live in it? Alison would adore being lady of the manor. In her intern year she'd talked more about where she and Oliver were house-hunting than about her patients.

So Reeva had died out of town, but in easy reach of an ambulance. What else could have killed her? Pregnancy puts pressure on blood vessels so if she had a pre-existing weakness there was a much higher risk of rupture. In that case, she probably never knew what happened. A nice way to die, but the timing sucked: it was about forty years too early. And it was rare, so Natalie could confidently reassure Frank that the chance of Alison also having the same problem was infinitesimally low.

She thought of Georgia suddenly, and how even the experts had misunderstood the stats about the likelihood of more than one child dying in a family. If there was a genetic factor at play, it was more likely a child would be at risk from natural causes rather than less.

But Alison and Reeva weren't related. There wasn't really much risk, just anxiety. Both Frank and Alison must be experiencing understandable, reactive anxiety and it would pass. If Alison didn't get postnatal depression; she'd have to be at risk, remote from family and with her high expectations of herself.

They were going to call the child Harry. Frank had let the name slip. Alison had needed to know its sex; she wanted to buy the right colour clothes.

Natalie should have left it there. She had no reason to ring Damian. But the hours of silence stretched out before her and Tom said that Damian had turned up to one of their gigs asking for her. He'd texted and left messages on her answering machine a few months ago that she never returned. Telling her the results of the Hardy case; letting her know he'd got the promotion to homicide he'd been working towards.

Homicide wouldn't have investigated Reeva's death, she was pretty sure, but Damian would have access to the coroner's report and the pathology findings. And what the hell, she needed a shag.

'Detective Senior Sergeant McBride.' He answered on the second ring. The calm voice of reason and stability. The thought made her wince and immediately want to drive the wrong way up a one-way street. Speeding and naked. After the shag, perhaps.

'I'm told this is the line for desperate and dateless.' There was dead silence. Stupid. Dateless then didn't mean dateless now.

'Natalie?'

'Afraid so.'

Damian laughed. She let out her breath, realised only then she'd been holding it. She needed to get a grip. He asked her about the band; she told him she had some gigs coming up in Lorne and Apollo Bay.

'And are you?' he said.

'Am I what?'

'Dateless. And or desperate.'

'Right now I'm looking at grey ocean as far as I can see and the only red-blooded males are a fifteen-minute ride away in Lorne, where most of them are underage. If I had better eyesight there might be a tanker out there with a prospect.'

Damian laughed again. 'Send me the band dates and I'll try to come.' Solid Australian accent. Nothing like Liam's brogue.

'Are you married?'

There was a silence. Of course he was married.

'You still seeing O'Shea?'

They'd never advertised it, because of Liam's wife. But Damian wasn't stupid.

'No.'

'Then I'm not married. Least not...' he paused, 'as of ten days' time.'

'Divorce coming through?'

'Yep.'

'I'll text you the times. And Damian?'

'Yeah?'

'I need a favour.'

Reeva had died in January three years earlier. The coroner returned an open finding, but not because the pathologist wasn't able to establish cause of death.

Reeva was a healthy thirty-nine-year-old Caucasian woman in her first pregnancy. The foetus, a near-term male child, was developmentally normal. When Reeva was found by Frank Moreton, bringing a cup of tea at 8 a.m. as he always did, she was cold and pale. He tried to find a pulse but knew quickly it was too late. She'd been dead at least five hours, too long for the baby to have survived.

All her organs were in good condition. No placental rupture, no aortic tear, no bleed into her brain. Her protein levels didn't suggest pre-eclampsia; the cervix was not dilated hence she hadn't been in labour. Temazepam was present in low levels. In the police notes the prescribing doctor, obstetrician Sam Petersen, confirmed Reeva had a normal pregnancy and that sleep difficulties were common. She had attended all her appointments with her husband and had the standard screens and ultrasounds. The only problem was her blood sugars: Reeva developed gestational diabetes by the time she was twenty-eight weeks. But that was not uncommon, even in someone as slim as Reeva, with no past or family history. For two months prior to her death Reeva had been self-administering insulin. On the night of her death something had gone wrong; post-mortem sugar levels could be unreliable, but it appeared that they had been catastrophically low. Reeva had made a lethal miscalculation with her insulin injection.

The coroner had left the verdict open because there was inadequate information to decide whether it was accident, suicide or a post-mortem artefact.

But Reeva had been a brilliant physician. Surely an accidental overdose was out of the question?

'It's hard to describe how I felt.' Frank was halfway through a glass of red wine before he even tried. Natalie waited. At her insistence, they were at the Wye River pub so she could walk home. It would be a twenty-five-minute drive home for Frank, but that was shorter than his commute to Geelong. She'd also insisted he tell Alison they were meeting. She wasn't sure he had.

'I just knew. It was like her life force simply wasn't there, and it made no sense to me. None whatsoever.'

'You were in shock.'

'Yes, I suppose I was. But I also...' He shook his head.

'Also what?' She saw a flicker pass over his features before the well-worked smile returned.

'I think I stayed in shock for at least a week, until after the funeral anyway. Longer really, because it wasn't as if the house was empty and there was any need for me to do anything. My mother and sister live there, we have staff...' He looked briefly apologetic about his lifestyle, misreading what had caught her interest. It was what he hadn't said, what he was carefully covering up, that made her pleased she was on low-alcohol beer. This might not officially be psychotherapy, but if she was going to help him resolve his issues—and thereby help Alison live happily ever after— then she needed to be aware of his defences.

She couldn't afford to be pulled in too deeply. Which might not be as easy as she had thought. He was a compelling mixture of needy little boy and arrogant game player. She often enjoyed the latter—Liam had been a stimulating adversary. But the neediness disarmed her. Patients were often needy, of course, but she knew when to back off, when to put up the boundaries. How did it work with a supervisor who, theoretically, was the one holding the power?

'It was back at work where I missed her most,' he continued. 'My team was wonderful, don't get me wrong, but...'

'Reeva was exceptional.' Natalie caught herself. Luckily Frank hadn't noticed her tone. Where did poor Alison fit, Natalie wondered? Second best? Rebound? For the first time she thought how much Frank really did need to see someone. Perhaps she could convince Alison to get him to go to a therapist, alone or together. Maybe he subconsciously thought the after-work drinks could go on indefinitely. Her discomfort increased. The bored part of her looked forward to these meetings; they made her feel useful. And if she was honest with herself, it was flattering that a professor had chosen her to confide in. Part of her knew he thought she was as clever as Reeva...and smarter than Alison.

She needed to talk to Declan, though he would only tell her that Frank needed a therapist. *Just until Alison has the baby.* She could hold him together that long, surely?

'She could light up a room just by walking into it. Everyone always knew she was there.' Frank's fingers were white from his grip on the glass. 'I had to pack her photos away. Alison thought I was being morbid.'

'Did your family like her? I can't imagine it was easy for her living with her in-laws.'

'Everyone liked Reeva. She was...'

'Exceptional, yes.' Natalie took a breath and went for the jugular. 'So that must make it almost impossible to express how angry at her you are.'

Frank's expression didn't change but his stillness gave him away. Stillness and a very slight twitch in the corner of his eye. 'You aren't trying to analyse me are you Dr King?' He smiled, but was there warning there too. Natalie felt nervous suddenly. What the hell was she doing?

'I'm not suggesting it's logical.' Natalie looked at Frank. 'But unexpected deaths are hard to deal with in patients. It must be worse...if it's your wife. And you weren't able to help.'

'It's been some time.'

Meaning don't go there. Because...he could deal with it...or because his rage was dangerous? Natalie wished her head felt clearer. She hated that she wasn't as crisp, able to pinpoint what was going on as she normally could. Would she ever get back to normal? She didn't dare think about changing her meds. Too soon.

If Frank hadn't dealt with his grief, Alison was under enormous pressure. Perhaps she felt she had to make up for all that he'd lost with Reeva: maybe she felt the anger Natalie was certain was there under Frank's surface charm. Did she think it was directed to her? And what if Frank's anger was about more than just the loss of Reeva?

When Reeva died I was furious. Natalie got that right; but then she's quite an astute psychiatrist. I wouldn't have selected her otherwise. I wonder if she will guess the rest of it; there is something terrier-like about her. If she sees herself as a rival to Reeva she isn't likely to roll over and let a ghost win. Unlike Alison.

Reeva shouldn't have died, and she really shouldn't have killed my son in doing so. I was surprised at the extent of my reaction. I had apparently made a connection to this unborn being, this foetus with half my genes. I had felt him move, watched him on the ultrasound, made out facial features; we had joked, before those last weeks when things changed, that he was going to take after her grandfather. Neither of us had met him, but in photos he looked like Yoda from Star Wars. I didn't mind; with Reeva's genes and mine, my son would have had a formidable mind. I resented that loss of potential and possibility. I don't like waste. And when I saw him cold and pale in the forensic morgue, he didn't look like Yoda. He looked just like me.

I stood there looking at him until one of the attendants told me they were closing. I felt a flash of intense rage. The attendant went scurrying away and I saw security staff milling as I exited.

I was told my father was prone to rages and that as a child, I too could be rendered frozen with fury. Once I refused to speak or move until my mother returned the toy she had confiscated. She tried waiting me out. For two hours I didn't move. When she returned the toy I thanked her, politely, and we have never mentioned the incident since. I had just turned four. She never took a toy from me again.

I doubt if any of my colleagues see that in me now. The benefits of reflection, of understanding what makes us who we are. It ensures our feelings are more manageable. I was a good student of the intricacies of human emotions long before any formal study; I had to be. From the time Wendell died when I was ten, I was the man in the family. Or I was at least until Antonije arrived in England to bring his daughter and grandchildren back to Australia.

In fact I haven't lost my temper once since I was ten. Natalie's suggestion of current anger was as much an educated guess as anything she detected in my demeanour. My early years taught me to be British: stiff upper lip. From Vesna, my mother, I learned not to trust. But after that there were other lessons, lessons of privilege and responsibility.

'With money,' Antonije told me, 'comes power.'

He might have added responsibility. Those with power need to make decisions. Even if they are difficult ones.

It was still dark on Monday morning when Natalie set out on the long haul back to Melbourne. Too early for even Bob to bother commenting. By the time she reached the Westgate Bridge the peak-hour traffic was lined up, but the bike cut through it and she parked easily at the legal end of Lonsdale Street.

Jacqueline Barrett was already in her office, black bob sleek and perfect, coffee brewing in the dripolator. Not the pristine lawyer's office Natalie would have imagined for her: there were files over the desk and floor and the only print on the wall was her degree. Hanging crooked.

'Milk?' Barrett said, adding it before Natalie could respond. 'I hope the coffee hasn't been on the warmer all night.' Her killer heels lay beside the desk and she padded across the room in stockinged feet to deliver what looked like a cereal bowl of pond water—'European breakfast cups,' she explained—before sitting on the other side of the desk. She rummaged among the files there, frowning, looking up when a harassed-looking young woman entered.

'Photocopier wasn't working. Had to use the one downstairs.' The girl gave them each a sheaf of paper and scurried out. Natalie recognised her own court report on Georgia Latimer.

Jacqueline threw her copy down on the desk. 'This isn't exactly helpful.'

Natalie didn't bother saying helpful wasn't her brief. Understanding her patient was. She had laboured over every word, reread it before she left her stilt house. Murder charges, three. Georgia's children Genevieve, Olivia and Jonah.

'Georgia says she's pleading not guilty,' said Natalie.

'Correct.' Jacqueline sounded matter of fact about it, but there was an edge to the upbeat tone. 'I asked her to consider a guilty plea. I might have persuaded her, if we'd been able to change the charges to infanticide.'

'The judge wouldn't buy it?'

'Not in light of the vociferous opposition from the Office of the Public Prosecutor.'

Natalie looked again at her summary. Her view was that if Georgia had indeed killed the children a legal defence of insanity was not viable: Georgia knew the difference between right and wrong.

But that didn't mean she had a squeaky clean bill of mental health. She definitely dissociated—Natalie had seen it herself. There were indications of a personality disorder. Then there was the early childhood abuse, which had made her vulnerable to manipulation, specifically by her husband Paul.

If Barrett was stuck with a not-guilty plea, Natalie thought, her worst nightmare was expert testimony suggesting Georgia was mad enough to kill but sane enough to be convicted. Which was pretty much the thrust of Natalie's report.

'You know one expert witness is saying she had

44

dissociative identity disorder and *if* she did do it, is not guilty due to insanity.'

'Wadhwa? Yes.' Natalie and Associate Professor Wadhwa had disagreed about Georgia's diagnosis, but that wasn't the only reason she thought he was an idiot. He also had no idea about the law in this area. 'My understanding is that's highly unlikely to be accepted by a jury.'

Jacqueline looked irritated. 'I know. We aren't calling him. The prosecution is.'

This was news, but it made sense: if Barrett was running the tragic-accident line, Wadhwa's testimony about Georgia's problematic mental health would be much more useful to the other side.

As would Natalie's.

'I'd rather just not call you either.' Barrett seemed to echo her thought.

'Then don't. Fine with me.'

'But the prosecutor seems to know you've been seeing her.' Liam O'Shea. Yes, he did.

'And if I don't call you, he will.' Jacqueline crossed her arms. 'I'd rather have you in my tent. Try and minimise the damage.'

'Could I decline because I'm her treating doctor?'

'No,' said the lawyer. 'You might get away with refusing to produce your private files...?'

Natalie pictured the expression on Liam's face if she did that. 'No,' she said finally.

'All right. Well, what I need to know,' said the lawyer, 'is what you'll say if you're asked about the husband's influence. Is O'Shea going to be able to float a scenario where Georgia kills the babies because of something in the relationship with Paul?'

45

'It will depend on the specific question,' said Natalie. She'd thought a lot about this. 'Georgia's sexual abuse was when she was very young, she has no memory of it. The abuse that left its mark was the lack of emotional nurture. She needed Paul for that: which meant she was likely to be jealous of the children receiving it instead of her.'

'So what? She wouldn't be the first mother envious of her daughter.'

'Her daughter wasn't even two. What you're talking about is a different form of maternal envy: adolescent child, menopausal mother, and the loss of vitality and potency as the new generation takes over. In Georgia's case the children were seen more as immediate threats—rivals for Paul's attention.'

Jacqueline's face said this wasn't the answer she wanted to hear. 'Look, we're all influenced by one thing or another.' She drummed her fingers impatiently. 'What about this for an idea? All this is nonsense. She had a bad start in life, I get that. But you and Wadhwa are trying to make that out to be the cause. So she's narcissistic. So what? We all are, a bit, but we don't go around killing our kids. How about the poor cow was just plain unlucky?'

'She dissociates.' Natalie was firm. 'You can't get away from that. The question is, to what degree. And whether, as another personality, she could have committed murder. I don't believe she has other personalities. But a murderer working on Paul's behalf? Paul definitely influenced her, but she's still culpable.'

'Our expert has some excellent statistics about how many women there are with abuse histories worse than Georgia's, and with the sort of personality disorder you describe. And they don't have a high rate of murdering their children.'

Natalie nodded. 'I'm not saying she did,' she repeated. Thinking statistics could say whatever you wanted them to in a murky area like this.

'He cried?'

'Like a baby.' Natalie had had a week to work through Frank's reaction before coming to Declan for advice. But at the time, she hadn't known quite what to do.

'I'm pretty sure it was therapeutic though. He'd pulled himself together by the time I packed him off home.' After a long hug. The discomfort she felt then had been mingled with something else. Subdued desire? A small boost to her ego, which had taken a hit since Liam left? Now the memory of Frank's brief outburst of affection just left her feeling guilty.

'He needs real therapy Natalie. There's too much opportunity for games with you.' Declan didn't miss much. If possible he was paying even closer attention than usual.

She bristled. 'You don't think I can handle him.'

Declan measured his words carefully. 'It's not an issue of what you can handle.' Pause. 'Because it isn't formal therapy, you won't be able to call him on things, not in the same way.' Another pause. 'And it puts you in an awkward position.'

'But it also gives me some power,' said Natalie. 'Which might be advantageous, who knows? I might have a job for life.' In research, not as his counsellor. 'I made him promise to talk to Alison about it.' But there was something else. Something in the midst of his tears that had been guilt or anger, something she couldn't place.

'Will he?'

'I doubt it. Alison needs a hero. Not that she isn't tough.

Just that, well, she is thirty-eight weeks now and she has a real baby to think about. I suspect at this point she'd just tell Frank to man up.'

'I think I'll just be grateful they aren't having a girl.'

'Because?'

'In a moment of profound gratitude Frank might want to name her after you.'

Natalie felt her mouth drop open. In all the time she had known Declan this was the first joke he had ever made. But on reflection she thought that maybe he hadn't meant it as one.

She looked at the text from Frank, unsure what to make of it. Bring an extra helmet? She hadn't even known he knew about the bike. Wei must have said something.

Bob's new friends were eyeing her in frustration. One cocked his head, raised his crest and let out a shriek. Bob being fed indoors was not making him happy. Bob on the other hand appeared content as he announced, 'You're an unknown,' and his head disappeared into the seed container.

Was she excessively indignant at Declan's inferences? Perhaps *the lady was protesting too much*? She shook her head. Frank didn't have the attractive edginess of Liam, nor the prosecutor's passion. He wasn't her type, and the sea change had yet to alter her that much.

More critically, she just didn't get the vibe from him. Which, given her state of sexual frustration, had to surely mean he either had the wrong pheromone mix for her or he really was happily married, despite being simultaneously grief-stricken, and not looking to stray.

Or her antenna was faulty; she felt uncomfortable that the latter might be closer to the mark. Her mood hovered around four out of ten, neither depressed nor manic. But her trademark sharpness, the essence of self; she had almost forgotten what that was like.

She thought again about Declan's comment, and felt he was trying to get her to see something without telling her. The comment suggested he thought Frank might be idealising her. Which didn't quite fit with her take—that Frank thought he could manipulate her.

Frank made no reference to the text when he stuck his head into the researcher's room and issued a blanket 'Hello, everything okay?' She just nodded, leaving Wei to pull an ear plug out, squint and shrug.

Natalie had already logged on and found a long email from the ethics committee with a series of inane questions about her project that had to be answered before the cut off for submissions at 5 p.m. She was going to be battling to make it. One of the recurring complaints was use of the *modified absolute*. Really? What even was that?

Wei had warned her. 'They like to feel useful. And to impart their ideas.'

Great. She was back at school with a bunch of power-tripping pedants. She had just finished the last of the changes with five minutes left to run copies over the road to the main section of the hospital when Frank turned up at her door.

'Are you still all right to give me a lift?'

'Are you sure you're up for it?'

'As long as you don't mind me looking like Danny Zuko.'

Natalie frowned.

'John Travolta? In *Grease*? Alison dusted the leather jacket but it looks sadly dated.'

At least he had told Alison. She looked forward to telling

Declan this piece of information.

'She dropped me here on her way into Melbourne to see her mother,' said Frank. 'She'll pick me up at Wye River on her way home. If we're still on?'

Natalie rarely took passengers; Liam had been her last. She tried not to think about this as she handed her spare helmet to Frank.

He was a lousy pillion. No instinct. There was a sense on every corner she was going to lose him. She slowed down; better to arrive late than to deliver him back to Alison with chunks missing.

When they arrived at the pub he was blowing on his hands, his face several shades paler than normal. Scarfed and gloved, Natalie felt guilty she hadn't told him to rug up. The little-boy-lost routine made her feel more motherly than anything else. Maybe she'd run that past Declan too. Or maybe it was better buried, along with the question of why she was continually comparing him to Liam.

Natalie found a table by the window while Frank bought drinks. It was dark outside but the night was clear enough for her to see the water in the bay, stretching out towards Separation Creek like a shimmering blanket.

'Corona for you.' Frank placed the beer down in front of her, then a bottle of red wine with two glasses next to it.

'You planning a long night?'

Frank shrugged. 'I'll stay for dinner and Alison might have a half glass. You can always have some and come back for your bike tomorrow.'

Natalie planned to stick to the one beer, then go home to meditate and learn how to cook curry. Could you call it cooking if the can said just add chicken?

She watched Frank sink the first glass. Waited. There

was plenty of time to elicit the information he'd been keeping to himself.

'I thought about what you said last week.'

Natalie nodded encouragement.

'And you were right.'

So far, he was just trying to please; she wasn't going to give him anything to show she was pleased. Not yet.

'I mean how can you be angry at someone who's dead, right?'

'So why are you, Frank?' Anger, they both knew, was a normal part of the grieving process. Sometimes projected at the doctors or paramedics who had been unable to save a loved one, occasionally for good reason. But ultimately the anger was at having been *left*. So the pain and anger were all the worse if the loss happened in the middle of an unresolved argument or if there was a suggestion that it could have been avoided by something either of them could have done. In Frank and Reeva's case all these seemed possibilities.

'It just shouldn't have happened.'

'*Shouldn't* Frank? You've done enough medicine to know the world isn't like that.'

'But...' He looked miserable. He sighed, swilled some red wine in his glass, sculled it and refilled. 'She was fit and healthy, there was no reason for her to die. Okay, she was an elderly primigravida, but everything had been going fine.'

'No complications at all?'

'Not unless you count the diabetes. She enjoyed being pregnant. It was only in those last few weeks...'

When he didn't continue Natalie prompted him, asking what had happened near the end of Reeva's third trimester.

'She wasn't sleeping well. Irritable. But that was to be expected.'

'What did they say was the cause of death?' She asked offhandedly but was watching for his response. He winced.

'Hypoglycaemia most likely, though post-mortem blood levels are...unreliable. She developed gestational diabetes but it had been fine. She was a physician for Christ sake, she knew what she was doing.' There was anger in his voice now; she was getting closer.

'They think she mixed up the units?'

'She must have, but for the life of me...' He shook his head. 'This is a woman who could account for every milligram of her lab materials. Balanced books for her grants that would put an accountant to shame.'

'You said she wasn't sleeping,' said Natalie. 'Could that have affected her judgment?'

'I suppose. The temazepam.'

An explanation, but barely credible. He wanted more: the sedation theory wasn't enough to assuage his guilt. And Natalie still felt she didn't know enough. There was something he wasn't telling her.

'Why weren't you sleeping together that night? As in sharing a bed, I mean.'

There was the tiniest tightening of his lips, his eyes refused to meet hers. 'As I said, she wasn't sleeping. She didn't like keeping me awake so she insisted on using the spare bedroom.'

It sounded reasonable. But Natalie knew he was lying. Why? And about what?

'Alison has been having sleeping problems for some time too,' I said to Natalie. We hadn't been having sex for months either, but I was hardly going to tell Natalie that. Not yet, anyway.

Alison was a mistake. I'm not often guilty of such misjudgments but as she approached the end of the pregnancy I knew it wasn't going to work. Everyone turns a blind eye at times to the obvious and if I had I been pushed on the point, I could have articulated my knowledge of our innate incompatibility. It wasn't buried so deep that it was driving me subconsciously in directions that I wouldn't choose to take.

I knew I was miserable. Knew that Alison, while prettier in a girlish way than Reeva, was no match for either of us intellectually; and that no matter how and when I looked into that mirror with her at my side, the picture was never going to be perfect. But I also knew I was, for the time at least, stuck. My family has never been conventional but I was not going to leave a pregnant wife.

There was also the small matter of our child, another boy. Would he look like me? More crucially, would he have my mind? Would he have the kind of potential I would want to shape? I needed to extinguish the ghosts in my own past so I could find a way to be the sort of father I wanted to be. I had some hope, on the better days. When she wasn't haranguing me about moving to Melbourne (*or any city for that matter! You have a US grant. Why can't we live in New York or Boston?*).

I understood it was hard for her living with my family, separated from her own; she was less understanding of the pressures I was under, but I was prepared to overlook that, in the short term at least. I didn't love her as I loved Reeva; would never love her in that way. But I felt guilty about my first wife and I was unable to make it up to her. Alison became a substitute.

'Don't lose patience with me,' she said, faking a smile. 'All pregnant women get hormonal.'

I didn't bother replying.

'Even Reeva I bet.' Her voice had risen an octave.

'You don't need to make a scene, Alison.'

She bit her lip, tears welling in her eyes. I sighed, and hugged her.

'I'll be a good wife, honestly,' she said. I hoped she wasn't dripping mascara on my shirt. 'And a wonderful mother!'

'I imagine so.'

Alison looked up at me, uncertainty in her eyes, unable to tell if I was serious. Mostly I was bored with the conversation. 'Maybe you should stay with your parents for a while.'

She looked stricken. 'Why?'

'They'll look after you, make you feel...I'm at work a lot, and I know it's hard for you here.'

'It's my home, now.'

I didn't think our marriage would last. But I did not want to be heartless; I thought perhaps once the child was born there would be a solution we could come to. I had been considering options.

I was dreaming a lot more, and possibly because of Alison's disturbed sleep patterns, I was waking and recalling the nocturnal imaginings. I had lots of dreams when I was young. The artistry of my genes played out in the rich colourful imagination of my nights.

According to my mother, as a child I would sometimes wet myself with my nocturnal terror. I rarely remembered the dreams and nightmares in the morning, just the fear. It is still there, hovering at the edges of my subconscious; but I have no intention of exploring what it is in my past that my wives and their pregnancies have stirred up.

Instead I said to Natalie, 'Pregnant women don't sleep well.'

She has an empathetic smile. I am sure she uses it with her patients to good effect. But it was the warmth of her skin as my hand covered hers that gave me more comfort.

When Alison arrived at the pub, Natalie was still toying with a half-drunk Corona, no closer to solving the mystery of what Frank was feeling guilty about. He retracted the hand that had patted hers and then lingered, and beckoned to his wife to join them. Natalie looked up. *Fuck:* Alison's expression made it clear that Frank hadn't told her who was giving him the lift. Or why, presumably. Alison had seen the guilty withdrawal of the hand. What the fuck was he playing at? Bolstering his fragile ego? Afraid of being usurped in Alison's affections by the baby, and showing his wife he had alternatives? If murder had been legal Natalie would have considered it.

'Natalie...'Alison started to speak, then stopped herself, re-grouped and tried to pretend that she had known all along Natalie would be there.

'Hello, Alison.' Natalie waved her beer. 'I'm just finishing. I'll leave you two to your dinner.'

Alison looked hard at Frank, before turning to Natalie. 'You live near here?'

Natalie nodded. 'Just up the road.' She watched Alison carefully. She looked tired and pale. Probably a five-hour round trip to Melbourne this late in pregnancy wasn't a good idea.

'Can I get you something to drink?' Frank asked, and disappeared to get water.

'You always meet here?' Alison said pointedly. Here, close to your house, was what she meant. And do the two of you ever go back to your house was the question they might get to. Alison was not one of those women who was prepared to turn a blind eye.

'Just a couple of times,' said Natalie. She looked for Frank who seemed to have vanished. 'He's anxious about you. Just needs to talk about it.'

'And he chose you?'

You, for Alison, held memories of a scantily dressed boyfriend-stealer.

'I'm the only psychiatrist working for him. I understand...' She was about to say grief. Stopped herself. 'New parents.'

'*You* have children?' If Alison was having difficulties picturing it she could get in line. Natalie didn't add that generally the new parents she saw had murdered or abused their children before she ever met them.

'I think we're capable of dealing with parenthood together,' Alison went on. *Without your help* implied.

Natalie stood, leaving her beer unfinished. 'I know you will. Frank will be fine. He's just anxious because of Reeva.'

As she left, she thought she heard Alison mutter *bloody Dr Perfect* and thought of the millions of ways she so was not. It was only later she realised Alison was not referring to her.

Friday night Damian was drinking a Crown Lager at a corner table in the Lorne pub, watching her. When she turned to him he raised his beer in salute but remained seated.

Damian was looking good; good enough to remind her how long it had been since she'd let her libido loose. Her meds clearly hadn't taken her desire away entirely. She still hadn't dropped her antidepressants, as suggested by Declan, who was worried they would send her into a high. She'd been more worried about the despair that lingered at the edge of her thoughts. But tonight she felt a lifting of spirits. She watched Damian for a moment, wondering if she'd make him come to her. She didn't want to rush it, realising she felt nervous. It was not a feeling she was familiar with in this context. She was used to having men like Damian for breakfast. Was this the depression, the ECT after-effects or...Frank?

Natalie turned away, her grip tight on the beer bottle. She closed her eyes and counted to ten, willing her nervousness to dissipate. Pictured herself on stage singing. She'd been preparing herself for it all week: she wanted that part of herself back. It was the same part that would help her manage whatever happened with Damian.

His legs stretched out under the table in faded blue jeans. On top he wore an open-neck shirt with a white T-shirt underneath. Brown hair, short enough for the forces, but well barbered with a little extra on top. A solid one-eighty-five centimetres, muscle and only a hint of good living. When he smiled under her scrutiny she weakened. He watched her all the way as she sauntered over. It had taken her two hours to dress; something that normally would have been a routine fifteen minutes. She had never quite got used to herself in a blonde wig, but the tight black partly sheer top showing her navel ring and the short black leather skirt that barely covered her butt embodied the wild part of herself. The rock chick that Natalie wanted to embrace. A silver band on her arm covered the tattoo that had been a result of a previous hypomanic episode. But it was the over-the-knee fuck-me boots that Damian seemed to be currently enjoying.

'So it's DSS McBride now, I believe?'

'Off duty for the weekend.'

She sat down beside him, aware how much a stranger he was. 'Are you missing the wonderful windy Welbury?'

'Now living in the bustling burrow of Brunswick,' he replied after a pause.

'Enjoying homicide?'

'Enjoying isn't the first word that comes to mind.' He smiled. 'But it's what I always wanted to do.'

'Too much TV as a kid?'

'No, too much DV.'

Natalie took a sip of her beer. 'Father?'

'Yeah. My mother baited him. He was fine with my stepmother.'

'Very un-PC.'

Damian shrugged. 'He shouldn't have hit her. Just seemed like half the time she wanted him to. Confusing for a kid. Guess I had to go into the police to save women. Or end up a psychologist like you, trying to understand them.'

'Psychiatrist.' Natalie took another sip. 'How did you know about O'Shea and me? Or did you just guess?'

'I'm a cop, remember.' Natalie raised an eyebrow and he added: 'I know the guest house owner in Welbury.'

Natalie looked away. Liam and she had clocked up quite a damage bill there. 'Shit.'

He looked intently at her. Her voice had betrayed her. 'It didn't end well,' she acknowledged.

'Still recovering?'

Was she? Maybe. 'How about you? How long?'

Damian involuntarily rubbed his empty ring finger. 'Five years married, a year apart. Divorce just came through.'

She looked at his mouth, wondered what he'd taste like. Definitely in need of recovery sex. Both of them. Perfect.

It took her a couple of songs to warm up. Shaun, the keyboard player, was kind to her, picked the easy ones, letting her get a feel for the stage again. By the first break she was starting to feel alive again, in a way she hadn't in months. Damian brought her a beer backstage, told her the audience, though small, were loving her. It felt good to be attractive, however guarded they both were. He let an arm slip loosely over her shoulder at one point and there was a rush of warmth in the feeling. Part of it was a remedy for loneliness, she knew. Being independent didn't mean she didn't want a partner. She just couldn't picture anyone in the role who wouldn't stifle her.

She let loose in the last bracket, the loud raunchy songs she did so well. But with the applause she became acutely aware of being watched. Not just by Damian at the back, trying not to look like a cop and failing badly. It was the gaze of the men on the front table that had her wondering. What was Frank doing there, and who was the dark intense young man in the shadows sitting next to him?

Damian picked her reaction. He asked about it later but she kept it vague. Something stopped her identifying Frank, whose first wife's autopsy and coroner's report Damian had provided. The questions he would inevitably ask were unanswerable. She was still wondering why Frank was there and who his companion was. And where was Alison?

She was most likely reading too much into it. Frank lived locally after all. He could eat there every Friday night for all she knew. He would be bound to know a lot of the locals. Something about the other man nagged at her, but she hadn't got a good enough look. Just an impression.

It was conceivable that Frank hadn't recognised her, but her instinct said otherwise. Would he mention it if she didn't? She thought of him sitting behind her on the bike, of the hug. If he was checking her out, as a woman rather than a colleague, that would require some thought.

Maybe it was her preoccupation that made Damian hesitate. Earlier she might have grabbed him, put a bit of tongue into her kiss and left no doubt of her intentions. Now she let him peck her chastely on the cheek and say he'd catch her soon. She watched him leave without looking back. It left her feeling restless, aware of the despair hovering at the edge of her thoughts. Maybe he was the type of guy who didn't have sex on first dates. If a date was what it had been.

Natalie's stage persona was quite a surprise. Perhaps not to Alison, but as my wife was no longer interested in evenings out I was spared her reaction. I had already heard at length about Natalie's role in the hospital revue; Alison seemed to think it cast Natalie in a bad light.

Alison does not understand men.

I am not usually attracted to women who are so overtly sexual. If this had this been our first meeting, I might have categorised the singer as someone to fuck, should the opportunity arise, and move on from. But I knew Natalie had interesting depths, so I continued to put her in a category all of her own: *to be determined.*

It was annoying to run into Jasper. Predictable, perhaps. Being unemployed he seems to have nothing better to do with his time than hang around in pubs. He has it in his head that he can use his very tenuous links to me whenever it suits. I will keep my thoughts about that to myself for the moment.

But his head has been filled with nonsense by his mother and, while I was willing to buy him a drink, I decided to leave without speaking to Natalie. Better that Jasper didn't know the link to her. Better that he stayed away from me and my family.

My family has always been close.

'You're so old fashioned,' Reeva teased.

'This is suffocating,' Alison screamed.

To me, it was just natural. When family systems came up in my studies I was genuinely surprised that all families were not like mine. It wasn't until I was well into psychiatry that the complexity and diversity of families—including my own—was clear to me.

Both Reeva and Alison spoke of bland sibling rivalry. Squabbles with sisters, disdain for younger brothers. But Mala is so much younger—in our early relationship I was her protector. Vesna was sick throughout the pregnancy, both physically and mentally. Before Mala was born there were nights I was farmed out to my paternal grandparents, when I would sneak down the stairs to the place I couldn't be seen but where I was able to hear the litany of their complaints, the reasons Vesna shouldn't have got pregnant, the reasons Wendell should never have married her.

Had I been, say, two years of age when Mala was born, a temper tantrum would have been expected. But as it happened her arrival was a distraction from my father's death. She was a beautiful baby thanks to an emergency caesarean, her features unsquashed. She had a pointed chin and huge eyes and when they opened she seemed to stare right at me. From the moment she could crawl she followed me. Then I was always there for her, shielding her from the impact of Vesna's paranoid view of the world.

So Mala adored me, Vesna didn't know quite what to do with me but treated me like a rather strange creature that had turned up unexpectedly, and my father was dead. And Antonije? My grandfather knew I was his heir, and heirs mattered to Antonije.

Heirs matter to me, too.

When I returned home after my night at the Lorne pub, Alison was waiting for me. Alison and the son she carried. My son.

'You went to see her didn't you?'

'Alison you're tired, go to bed.'

I went over, kissed her gently on the forehead.

'Are you sleeping with her?' It was barely more than a whisper.

'No Alison. She isn't my type, truly.'

Alison grabbed at my hand. I brushed her wet cheek and sighed.

When the band dragged themselves out of bed at eleven, Natalie had already been awake for three hours and gone for a jog. She hadn't felt like it. After a largely sleepless night, partly because she had been up drinking with the band, partly because Tom and Maggie in the next room had made a lot of noise, she woke to a wave of depression. She had promised herself not to give in to it, so she crawled out into drenching wet mist. Ran harder to keep herself warm.

She was onto her second coffee when Shaun played a loud riff singing *Well I woke up this morning*, and joined her. Once they had all surfaced she convinced them to walk into Wye River for brunch at the café.

They were seated at the back on a long wooden table, facing plates piled high with eggs, bacon, tomatoes and thick slices of toast when Frank walked in alone. He saw Natalie and gave her a small smile. Dressed in dark trousers and a black polo neck he looked a little like Liam. She squashed the idea and tried to think calming thoughts.

'An admirer?' Maggie teased her. Natalie wondered if Maggie felt she had been treading on her toes. Another man other than Tom in Natalie's life would be good for them both.

'My boss.' Natalie watched him order at the counter and didn't have to wonder for long whether he would come over.

'Natalie.' The smile included a twinkle in his eyes. He bent over and kissed her cheek.

'Frank. The band,' she said by way of introduction. Frank didn't bother pretending he didn't know. 'Shaun, Gil and Tom. And this is Maggie.'

'Did you enjoy last night?' Tom didn't miss much.

'Yes I did,' said Frank, pulling over a chair that he angled between Natalie and Shaun. 'I didn't know Natalie had another life.' His look suggested otherwise. 'Sadly though, I won't be able to make Apollo Bay tonight.'

Was this a game, making sure she knew he was following her movements? Part of her was annoyed, but the part of her that was flattered worried her more.

'Is Alison okay?'

Frank leaned back. 'Alison? She's fine. Just not getting much sleep so she goes to bed early.'

'And doesn't eat lunch?' Natalie saw Maggie look at Tom, who shrugged.

'How long have you guys been playing together?' Frank asked as the waitress delivered him a coffee. She smiled at him; a smile for a regular. Or else just because he worked hard at being charming.

Shaun finally answered; there had been some changes along the way. Tom and Natalie were the only original members.

'Ever thought of going professional?'

There were three answers at once. Only Natalie said no.

'I write my own stuff,' said Shaun. 'Natalie does too on occasion.'

Frank looked at Natalie. She couldn't quite pinpoint

what it was about the look that differed from how Damian had looked at her the night before. Or how Liam used to undress her with his eyes. More intellectualisation maybe.

'I'd love to hear them sometime.' Now that was something Liam would have said. *Shit*. She was doing it again. It was something anyone would have said.

Natalie focused on her plate

'We're doing a few gigs down here in the next month or two,' said Gil, probably the only person at the table not aware of the undercurrents.

'I look forward to them,' said Frank.

As soon as she saw Damian there at Apollo Bay she wondered about the rules of second dates. The band ribbed her, but it felt good. More to the point it felt safe, not something she usually chased after. But right now whatever was going on with Frank was too complicated to dwell on. She needed some simple light relief and was not going to let the opportunity go if she got another chance.

'How about closing with "Fucking Perfect"?' It was how Damian was looking to her at that moment and there was a sadness in the song that she also detected in him; he'd been hurt.

Shaun grinned under his blue-banded straw hat. 'Hope that doesn't mean we have to find somewhere else to spend the night.'

'Not if you don't mind some extra noise.'

'Can't be any worse than Tom last night,' Gil said, fiddling with his bass tuning. Tom had the grace to look away. He looked happier than she'd ever seen him. She felt happy for him; she hoped her brief surge of anger was about growing old and not about jealousy. She squashed it. Damian had to be interested if he'd turned up two nights in a row. Her instinct couldn't be that far off, could it?

He was seated at the bar and as she came over in their break he offered the guy on the next stool a free beer to vacate it. The guy looked her up and down and grinned. 'Good taste, mate.'

She shimmied herself onto the seat and her skirt rode up. There wasn't much distance to go.

'Man might be right,' said Damian.

She loved feeling his eyes on her, wanted to punch her fist in the air and say fuck off to the blues. Right now she didn't care if she needed a man to help her do that. She had been low long enough to know every moment of feeling good needed to be savoured. And she did feel good, just wasn't sure it would last. With Liam the sense of him never being hers had added to the adrenaline, but ultimately got in the way. The chance that Damian could be hers terrified her. She was shooting holes in any picket-fence fantasies as fast as her mind conjured them up.

He accepted the invitation to come back with the band for drinks. As she'd come with Shaun she went back in Damian's Camry, a sound family car with room for kid seats. She hated it. At least it was full of litter and wet towels.

'You been swimming?'

'Surfing.'

'Really?' He was on the right coast.

'Bit rusty. Welbury's landlocked, obviously. And Caitlin wasn't a beach person.'

'Your ex?'

'Yeah.'

Bob let out a screech as they opened the downstairs door. Damian looked startled.

'Hello to you too, Bob,' said Natalie coming up the stairs. 'This is Damian, he's a cop.'

'Call the cops!' Bob strutted, yellow crest up.

Damian laughed.

'You're in luck,' said Natalie. 'He likes you; hope you enjoy "Hurricane".'

She dragged him out onto the balcony, still hot and wired from singing. When the rest of the band arrived they could make themselves at home without her intervention.

'Drink?'

He shook his head. 'Just water. I'm driving.'

She went inside and poured herself a bourbon and then a scotch into another glass. Returning to the balcony and closing the door, she offered him the second. He looked quizzically at her. 'There are some rules I don't play games with, Natalie.'

'What? Oh, drink driving. Nor do I.' She kept her eyes steady, arm still outstretched. She watched as her intent dawned on him, a softening of his features, a brief flash of vulnerability. He took the drink and immediately put it down on the table. Stepped in closer, close enough for her to be able to smell him. She was wondering about how he tasted, the feel of his chest under her fingers, whether he was the athletic type or a gentle giant. Imagined him taking her; whether he would enjoy watching her. In the look they shared she knew his imagination was somewhere in the same vicinity.

He went to speak but she shook her head and pulled him towards her. Lost herself in their kiss, desperate to reconnect with the inner core of a life she had been missing. His hands moved down over her butt, his breath drawn in as he found it bare. Her hands fumbled with his shirt buttons, feeling the roughness, the maleness of the lightly haired torso that was so different from Liam's.

When the band arrived he was temporarily distracted, until she moved his hand down to be sure she kept his attention. She doubted exhibitionism was usually his style but his enthusiasm suggested but he'd built up as much frustration as she had. It made up for the clumsy speed and mutual lack of familiarity.

He was taller than Liam, more of everything but somehow softer. The balcony rails were an awkward height and she was grateful in the end that he didn't let her go as she came. She might have tipped over the edge at the final moment.

Later when the band had disappeared they stood naked beneath overcoats, watching the waves together, before she took him to her bed.

They went again, slower this time, more considered, still new to everything about each other but without the frantic need that had driven them on the balcony. She fell asleep in his arms, her last thought a vague wondering about whether his feet hung over the bed end.

'Fuck.'

Damian tensed beside her. 'I'm sorry. I thought you...'

Natalie looked at him and frowned. 'Forgot to close the blinds.' The clock showed 7 a.m. In the early morning light, he looked every bit as good as he had the night before. He tentatively put his arm around her.

'So you didn't mean...?'

Natalie laughed and turned her head to kiss him. 'No, don't panic, I'll take fifty per cent of the blame.'

Damian seemed perplexed.

'*Neither* of us remembered a condom. And it's been a while so I stopped the pill.'

Damian looked tense. *Shit*. Men.

'It's fine. I'll just have to go to a chemist and get the morning-after.'

This didn't seem to help Damian's state of mind. He put his other arm under his head and looked at the ceiling. She felt a twinge of uncertainty. Surely he didn't have an STD?

'You don't have to bother,' he finally said.

Natalie remembered Declan's non-joke about Frank naming his child after her. 'Oh yes I do.'

'I'm infertile.'

Natalie stared at him. 'Oh Damian.' She watched the many nuances that flashed across his face as she put the pieces together. 'With Caitlin. Was that...?'

'Yes.'

She didn't say anything, waited for him to continue.

'Our chances of getting pregnant without intervention were something like one in a million. I wasn't keen on intervention.'

'I'm sorry.'

'Yeah well I guess I just have to live with it. Better you know in case you were intending anything more than a casual screw.'

'No, that wasn't why I was sorry. I was sorry it broke up your marriage.'

'She got what she wanted. The happy couple are due to be parents at any moment.'

'She left you for someone?'

'In time-honoured fashion, my best mate.'

'And I suppose it's him you miss?'

Damian finally smiled. 'Actually I miss the sex. Until last night anyway.'

'The upside of not having enough little swimmers,' said Natalie climbing astride him, 'is that we can think of something else to do instead of racing to the chemist.'

I watched her from my car as she entered the café. There is something mesmerising about her, an inner vitality that draws me to her. I love how her nostrils flare when she thinks she is losing the game, how she comes back batting. She wants me to know she is onto me. Or so she thinks. But this is my territory, both physically and metaphorically. I have been playing these games to survive since I was a child.

Now I am playing them with Alison.

'What do you mean you're supervising her?'

'She wants to do research. It's what I do. You may recall we have a large gap in funds; Dr King doesn't require funding immediately and she may be able to help us put together some smaller grant proposals. Her academic record is outstanding.'

'Academic record?' Alison's laugh when she was angry had a harsh sound, most unfeminine. 'You mean she'd sleep with anyone to get what she wanted?'

I had perhaps exaggerated. Her referees spoke primarily of her clinical acumen. Her referees I noted, were all men, except for the manager at Yarra Bend forensic hospital.

'And she just happened to find you?'

'Yes.' I am, as I have said, a patient man. I put the paper down and looked out across the manicured lawn to the lake: the magical kingdom Antonije had brought us back to when I was ten. 'Don't do this, Alison.'

Alison burst into tears and took off to the bedroom, slamming the door behind her. I'd give her a half hour then go and give her the reassurances she was after.

'Trouble in paradise?' Mala went to the drink cabinet and poured herself a gin and tonic.

'Is it terrible of me to have some empathy with Henry the Eighth?' I asked.

'Oh God. Not another four, please.' Mala's hand trailed over my shoulder as she rounded the couch and sat next to me. 'Of course, it was the third wife who gave him the son.'

But the third wife died in childbirth. Almost like Reeva.

I shook my head. 'I'm just tired.'

'Hardly a wonder, brother dearest.'

I frowned. 'Mala I know you loved Reeva, but...'

'Reeva had chutzpah.'

And Alison...'It's just the pregnancy. She'll be fine.'

Mala didn't look convinced. I turned away, watched my mother leaving the boathouse that she used to paint in when she was well, to hide away in when she wasn't. Vesna glided, I thought; long black-grey hair flowing behind her. As if the path she walked on might break into a thousand pieces at any moment.

'She's stopped taking her pills.'

It took me a moment to register that Mala was watching Vesna too. I didn't respond.

'It wasn't fair of me to be mean about Alison.' Mala stood by the window. 'Vesna isn't exactly the perfect mother-in-law.'

'She doesn't need half the pills she's on.'

Mala turned and regarded me silently before speaking. 'I know they're mostly sedatives. But un-sedated…there's no telling what she might say.'

Or do.

'You talked about shame in the last session,' Natalie began. 'I wonder if you remember any times you felt like that when you were a child?'

This early period in her life was where Georgia had got her scars. Opening them, a little at least, was the way to help her understand herself and make changes. To date, Georgia had been too ready to give the answer she thought Natalie wanted. Or more likely the answer that would serve her in court.

Georgia's expression was flat. Her denial about life after her trial—the most likely outcome—was breaking down. Her sleep was poor and she'd made a manic return to the gym six times a week. And no makeup today. For once she looked older than her years, a normal tired housewife rather than the Stepford version.

'It was Virginia's favourite phrase.' Virginia was Georgia's aunt, the woman who had mostly raised her. '*I'm so ashamed of you.*' Her tone was biting and her face screwed up in a parody of the disapproving parent.

'That must have been hard.'

Georgia shrugged. Easier to cut off from the importance

of people and emotions than to re-experience the intense vulnerability she had felt at the time.

'Can you think of an example?'

Georgia waved her hand dismissively, then stopped, her hand mid-air slowly coming back to her mouth.

'What did you just remember?'

'It was nothing.'

Georgia needed it to be nothing now. Natalie suspected it hadn't been at the time.

'Tell me anyway.'

Georgia frowned. 'Just an image, from nowhere really.'

'Describe it.'

'I was in the kitchen. I think I must have been helping Virginia cook.'

Natalie waited.

'I suppose I must have dropped the eggs on the floor. I think she turned and bumped me. Or maybe she'd told me not to touch them and I'd been trying to help.'

'Do you remember how you felt?'

'I can just see those eggs on the ground. At least two, yolks smearing and mixing with the whites. I can remember the stickiness of the egg white on my hands.' Georgia absentmindedly rubbed her fingers along the neat crease of her trousers.

Natalie, watching her patient relive the episode, half-expected her to dissociate. A little at least. Some of what she'd seen in the past had been for show, but some had been genuine.

'She made me hold out my hands and she hit them with a wooden spoon.'

It wasn't the pain that had upset Georgia. Something else.

'I just kept looking at the eggs. It sounds stupid.' She shook her head, her ice-blue eyes meeting Natalie's. 'I somehow believed that I'd killed a real chick. We had some at kindergarten and we'd petted them and next day they were all dead. But this felt like I had done something even worse. Something...' her head dropped towards her lap as she whispered, 'something wicked.'

For a moment Natalie just stared. Was it this scenario she had recreated as an adult, only with her children instead of eggs and chicks? *Identification with the aggressor.* A defence mechanism developed to shield oneself from immense fear and pain. And shame. Using anger and self-righteousness she'd learned from Virginia to cover what she really felt.

'How old were you Georgia?'

Georgia sighed. 'I don't know. Four I suppose.'

So maybe a year at most after her mother was imprisoned for murdering her father, and after a series of foster care placements before she was uprooted to live with an aunt she had never met and who hadn't wanted her.

'Do you remember anything else?'

Georgia shook her head. But she didn't look up.

'You were there standing with sticky hands, looking at the eggs. Did she make you clean it up?'

Georgia started trembling. Natalie watched it start in her patient's legs and work through her body until finally she was rocking, teetering, on the edge of her chair. Teardrops splashed onto her hands; later Natalie wondered if it was this sensory trigger that took her back. Certainly she was revisiting some intense memory, perhaps several, from her first difficult year with Virginia, before she turned into the perfect child who never again risked her aunt's wrath. As Natalie moved closer, knees touching, hand steadying her,

Georgia cried deep sobs that moved like tidal waves through her body. She cried out that she was terrified of the dark, begged to be let out of the cupboard. In a final recreation of trauma, as Georgia reached the same depths of despair she had experienced so many years ago, her bladder gave way and she wet herself.

'It was the most primitive experience of humiliation I have ever witnessed,' Natalie told Declan later that afternoon. She had declined the tea. She was riding back to the coast when they finished and didn't want to have to stop.

'Genuine?'

'Absolutely.'

'A critical turning point in therapy, then.'

'For what it's worth. I won't get to see her in prison.'

'Perhaps you won't need to. She's made an enormous breakthrough, reliving a trauma without the same ending. If you're right about her husband manipulating her to satisfy his own needs, it's for the first time in her life.'

'That's assuming the new ending was better.'

'Was it?'

Natalie nodded. It hadn't been easy remaining calm with her trouser legs soaked in urine—she'd been kneeling at Georgia's feet before she noticed the accumulating puddle—and reassuring Georgia at the same time. She asked her secretary to dash to the nearest Target for two pairs of tracksuit bottoms and some underwear: staying with Georgia was one of the greatest feats in her career to date. The woman had needed a mother in that moment who was above all else kind—one thing Virginia had never been. Natalie couldn't give her the unconditional love of a mother, but she could respect her and honour her pain. This would normally be the beginning of a long process of resolution in therapy. Prison, however, wasn't renowned for kindness. The best that could happen there was that Georgia would grow old in relative peace; find the pain diminished without being triggered by relationships.

'She went a deeper shade of crimson than I thought was physically possible,' said Natalie. 'And when I looked into her eyes...' It was hard to explain. The pain and despair seemed like those of a three-year-old. 'She thanked me, but then after she changed her clothes, the veneer was back up again. As if none of it had happened.'

'Your attitude towards her has changed.'

Natalie was startled. Declan was right. When she had first seen Georgia she viscerally disliked the woman. 'I guess...I understand her a bit better now. She's no longer trying to manipulate me, and she's allowed herself to be vulnerable. She has antisocial traits, and it doesn't excuse what she did, but mostly she's a damaged child who uses narcissistic defences.'

'Is she living alone?'

'Yes.' Georgia had been out on bail since before Christmas. Natalie knew instantly what Declan was thinking and looked at him. 'You think she's at risk?'

'Narcissists live in a world where they, or perhaps their partner and relationship, are perfect and special. Georgia's shown you how good she is at denying that anything other than perfect exists, certainly denying the importance of emotions. It is a long way to fall from that fantasy world of perfect to reality. Especially the harsh true glare of her particular reality. She won't know how to ask for help— vulnerability is failure, meaning she's unlovable and thus rejected. So yes, she's at risk. But perhaps not right now;

unlike Virginia and Paul, you didn't reject her.'

Uneasiness seeped into Natalie's mind. Reject her? Not as such. But what about her report? And what might happen when Liam interrogated her on the stand?

She didn't see Frank all week. He was in Canberra according to Wei, romancing the national medical research funding body. He was flying back on Thursday but Natalie assumed he would head straight home; Alison was, after all, now thirty-nine weeks. She assumed wrong. The text came through after he landed: *see u @ W.R at six*. She contemplated cancelling, recalling Declan's unease with the relationship. He'd only been partly reassured by Alison's interrupting their last session, and Natalie's interest in Damian.

But Natalie didn't cancel, precisely because Alison was thirty-nine weeks. Frank's anxiety would be at its peak from now until delivery. At least, that was what she told herself. She didn't think it would convince Declan. Truth be told, she wanted to see Frank not because of any attraction he held for her but because she was sure he had lied to her about Reeva.

What had happened the night of her death and why hadn't he been sleeping with Reeva? Natalie wasn't going to rest until she worked out why, and exactly what happened to the exceptional Dr Reeva Osbourne. She was almost certain Frank knew, or at least knew more than she did, about how the events leading to Reeva's death had unfolded. A knowledge he hadn't seen fit to share with the police or the coroner.

She arrived at the pub before him and ordered the beef casserole with extra fries. Closest she came to cooking casserole was heating a can, and frozen fries just lost something. She wondered if Frank or Damian cooked. She doubted it.

She was looking at a plate of steaming meat and vegetables—greens as well as the essential carbohydrates—and was trying to recall when she had last eaten anything containing this much B12 and folate, when he walked in.

'The traffic getting out of town was unbelievably bad.' He looked tired and distracted.

'Hope you don't mind me eating.'

'No, of course not. I'll just stick with the wine. I can always get something at home.'

'Alison might have preferred you to go straight there.'

'She's being…it's a difficult time.'

And you seeing me isn't making it easier, Natalie wanted to say, but instead took a mouthful of food. When he didn't continue she swallowed and asked, 'Why do you think that is, Frank?'

'She doesn't like it when I'm away, but then when I'm there she complains I'm fussing too much.' Frank didn't seem to think both could be true, or that Alison might want something in between and that it wasn't an unreasonable expectation. Then Natalie remembered how Alison had been at the last meeting, and thought she probably wasn't making Frank's life particularly easy.

He went on. 'I've been thinking maybe she should stay with her mother.'

Really? 'Why?'

He wasn't touching his wine. 'We're a long way away from the hospital.'

'What, an hour and a half?' Natalie looked at him with no attempt to hide her frustration. 'Frank, first labours take longer than that. And worst-case scenario? She delivers in the back of the car.'

'Yes of course, you're right, I know.' His smile waned.

'Is there anything else, Frank?' She tried for a softer tone.

'What do you mean?'

'Like anything else that is reminding you…triggering memories of what happened with Reeva?'

For a moment he stared, and she felt that he was looking right through her, that he had somehow briefly been transported elsewhere.

'No, no. Just that Alison's so close. She saw her obstetrician today. He's happy. I rang him myself to be sure.'

'Then stop worrying.'

He smiled, the boyish smile that took years off his age. 'Did I tell you that you look really hot as a blonde?'

I understood that it was Alison's insecurity that made her fearful I would be attracted to someone else, and it wasn't without basis. But her attack strategy, accusation oscillating with slobbering remorse, was unattractive. And tiring.

'You're meeting with her again.'

Alison has a talent for stating the obvious.

'Alison, she is doing a PhD with me. Given I haven't funds, I'll be lucky if I can keep her. And I need someone smart to write research proposals.'

'That's what Wei does.'

'Wei isn't a doctor.'

'Like Reeva, you mean.'

I really did try hard not to lose my patience. 'You should stay with your parents. Until after the baby.'

'So I won't get in the way of you screwing the bitch?' Alison's face was blotchy with tears. If her obstetrician hadn't assured me her protein was fine I'd have wondered about fluid retention.

'Over the last eight months I have found methods of relieving sexual tension that do not require the services of Dr King, or anyone else for that matter.' Though the thought of the good Dr King taking over from Mrs Palmer was appealing.

'It's your baby.' She said it as if it hadn't been her screaming biological clock that had brought us to this point.

'And your choice.' I didn't wait for her to burst into tears. I left and locked myself in the study. I truly did not want to do something I might regret.

Natalie woke at 3 a.m. just as the phone stopped ringing. A local number. The voicemail—Frank's voice, indistinct—just said to ring. She replayed it, tried to make sense not of the words, but the tone. Then she got it. Shock.

It wasn't Frank who picked up when she rang back. It was a vague-sounding woman who said she'd give it to someone else. It was a few moments before an authoritative voice identified itself as Sergeant Mark Pengana. 'Who am I talking to?'

'Dr King. Professor Moreton left a message for me.'

There was a pause. 'One moment.' She could hear the murmur of voices but they were muffled, probably by his hand over the receiver.

'Professor Moreton wonders if you could come.'

'Why?'

'I think you should just come.'

She googled a map as she dressed. Straightforward, but it meant a dark ride along unfamiliar winding country roads with a turn at the end that could easily be missed unless Sergeant Pengana had blue and whites outside with lights flashing. At least she'd only had the one beer, a few hours earlier. What on earth was going on? Pengana may have assumed she was Frank's GP. If he did need a doctor, she was badly equipped. She packed a bottle of her own diazepam, another of quetiapine. She could at least sedate someone. After all, Pengana was a cop. It wasn't a medical emergency that had brought him to Frank's house.

Which meant what? And what on earth would have made Frank think of calling her? Her senses were on full alert. Everything about this felt badly wrong.

At Lorne she slowed, not quite to the legal limit, and turned left, away from the ocean into the Otway Ranges. The road to Mount Malosevic meandered around the hills behind Lorne, through the dense foliage of the national park. The sky above was heavy with cloud, and even if it hadn't been the moonlight would have struggled to penetrate the canopies. Confronted by the unknown at each corner, she was concentrating on the road because not to do so was to risk losing the bike. But it was hard not to let her mind drift to the situation she was heading to.

As a forensic psychiatrist—until recently at least— she was well aware of the bad things that could happen. Images of Alison, her face taught and tense, flashed before her. Angry, tearful, but…Alison was healthy, early thirties. Maybe a little old for a first child but not dangerously so. She'd just been to see the doctor and been given the all clear. If she went into labour, she was essentially full term.

But if Alison was okay, why would Frank ring her? It certainly wouldn't have been Alison's idea. Shock treatment might have meddled with Natalie's intuition, but not on this. The clear ultimatum in subtext from Alison was *Stay away from him or else, you bitch.* Maybe she'd goaded Frank into violence. Natalie would not be on board with supporting Frank if he was the perpetrator of DV.

The strong smell of eucalypts penetrating the layer of mist was the first thing Natalie was aware of when she slowed her bike down at the huge wrought iron gates of Mount Malosevic. The sign at the entry gave visiting hours but also acknowledged the original designer, Antonije Malosevic; Frank's grandfather. The driveway went for nearly a kilometre. In daylight, presumably, it gave the visitor a sense of approach, of natural context. Now in the silent darkness with the light in the distance, the impression was of oppressive solitude.

It wasn't until the final turn that the mansion appeared, and there was no doubt in Natalie's mind that the dramatic reveal was intentional. Rising out of a shimmering moat and rock walls with cascades of climbing plants was a wall with long, narrow windows reminiscent of mediaeval arrow slits and, judging from the glow above it, a ceiling of glass. Every light in the house, it seemed, was turned on, ensuring it appeared as a beacon to passing planes.

Or passing cops. There was one standing out the front by a divvy van: no lights on. A couple of other cars were parked in a lane heading to what she assumed was a garage. The policeman straightened his shoulders and hat and frowned at her. He looked about twenty.

'This is a crime scene,' he told her. It sounded like he had been wanting to use the line for years. 'I'll have to ask you to leave.' He tilted his head to get a better look at her bike before he remembered his role, and frowned.

Natalie pulled off her helmet and tossed her hair behind her. She could see the constable wasn't expecting a woman. 'I'm the doctor,' she said casually, all the time wondering *what crime?* 'I spoke to Sergeant Pengana.'

The constable did a double-take. She saw red hair at the base of his cap as he pulled it down harder. 'Um, yes of course, I thought we were expecting Dr Taylor?'

Natalie had no idea who Dr Taylor was. Local GP?

'I'm Professor Moreton's...colleague.'

Constable Red Hair seem to decide that this was one outside his pay scale. 'Wait here.' He disappeared through ceiling-high front doors that looked like half an oak tree was used to form them. Maybe a whole one.

There were murmurs in the distance. Shadows flickered and for a fanciful moment she felt menace in the ice-cold wind that swept across the drive. She shivered, and was pulling her jacket tightly around her when Constable Red Hair emerged and invited her inside.

The wide hallway opened out into a spacious living area. A wall of glass merged with the ceiling, which was also glass for its first metre. In daylight, she imagined, you'd be able to see right along the coastline—Point Lonsdale in one direction, Portland in the other. Except that the Otway Ranges would get in the way. At the other end, a huge canvas hung in mid-air beside a spiral staircase that ascended to the balcony. Later she was unable to recall anything about the painting except that it had made her catch her breath with the sense of a surge of electricity passing through her. She dragged her eyes away from it, aware of a light outside: through the huge window on the far side of the house, there was a lake with some kind of boathouse beside it. A lit window sent streaks of light across the lake towards her. She could make out a lone uniformed policeman standing on the jetty and a small row-boat moored to it.

In the room in front of her Sergeant Pengana was

standing: around forty, at least partly Indigenous with a richly toned skin and broad nose. His black hair was greying at the temples and his frown suggested he'd be greyer before the night was over. Behind him on a sofa, Frank Moreton sat with head in hands. He didn't look up. There was a woman on either side of him; each of striking appearance. The three together might have been doing a photo shoot for *Vogue*. The older of the two was about sixty; Natalie took her to be Frank's mother. She had long black hair streaked with grey and was dressed in a flowing white robe—either a kaftan or a nightie, Natalie couldn't be sure. There was an ethereal quality to her, as if she didn't quite belong in the world. She looked at Natalie but her gaze was glassy. As if she had just been woken or hadn't bothered to find her specs. One hand was on Frank's knee but it was hard to know whether she was comforting or drawing strength from him.

On the other side of Frank was a woman about her own age with long blonde hair done incongruously in pigtails. Natalie fancied that, dressed differently, she would be stunning. She was wearing a long pale blue silk top and baggy trousers and here, too, it was unclear whether it was bedroom attire or boho couture. Natalie thought she looked vaguely familiar, then realised she was the woman who had come to meet Wei at the lab some weeks earlier without introduction.

Opposite them a thin woman in her forties lay back in a chair with her eyes closed; on the arm of the chair sat a dark-haired man with a craggy face and a grim expression who watched proceedings furtively. Both wore jeans and jumpers. At their feet a pyjama-clad teenager was biting her fingernails. The staff?

Frank hadn't registered her arrival. The slim blonde

looked her over, her expression too guarded to interpret. Natalie hesitated and then walked towards the police sergeant. 'I'm Dr King,' she said, extending her hand. 'What happened?'

Pengana took her to the kitchen.

'What happened?' she repeated.

'Professor Moreton went to check on his wife. Found her unresponsive. Tried to revive her.' He cleared his throat. 'Unsuccessfully.'

Natalie knew what it felt like when time stood still. She'd had an odd dissociative experience once on antihistamines. This was a little different, though. Now it was if everything around her faded away, the pots and pans and hanging utensils no longer part of her reality, instead a slideshow of images flashing through her head. Alison prim and proper, Alison looking uncomfortable as Rocky-Horror Janet in her underwear, Alison crying, laughing...Living. The last picture seemed to sear itself into Natalie's memory: Alison accusatory, bitter and angry, and Natalie felt overwhelmed with shame.

Sergeant Pengana shifted uncomfortably.

The blood had drained from Natalie's face. She pulled out a kitchen chair and sat down.

Alison was dead. Natalie had failed her totally. She looked at Pengana. 'The baby?'

He shook his head.

For one horrific moment she pictured Declan pontificating, suggesting she had fantasised about being Alison, just as he had once mused about her putting herself into the shoes of Lauren, Liam's wife.

No every pore of her body screamed. Frank was not a replacement for Liam, not at any moment, ever.

Natalie felt the tears coursing down to her chin. Alison couldn't be dead. She was about to live the dream. *Have the baby and live happily ever after.* And what were the odds of one man's two pregnant wives both dying at thirty-nine weeks?

She waited until her breathing steadied. 'Do you have any idea what caused her death?'

'Mm.' Pengana scratched at a light chin stubble. 'We do.'

The downward intonation didn't leave much opening for expansion. Nor did Pengana's squint as he pulled out a notebook. 'Did you know the deceased?'

Natalie ignored the question. 'Is it being treated as suspicious? Has Frank...?'

Pengana clicked his pen. 'The family are waiting for a lawyer to arrive.'

This wasn't good. Or maybe it was. Better safe than sorry. 'Can I speak to Frank?'

'Certainly, but please do so in the living area. At least until the homicide squad have spoken to him.'

Homicide. Her stomach dropped and she felt an urge to ring Declan. Could this much madness be so well hidden? She'd been starting to question things about Reeva; what had she missed?

Pengana took her name and details, including when she had last seen Alison, and let her return to the living area. She went directly to Frank, kneeling down in front of him. His head was still in his hands. 'I'm Natalie King. I'm a doctor. I work with Frank,' she explained to the two women.

The older woman focused briefly then looked away with a fatuous smile. The pigtailed woman smiled minutely. 'I'm Frank's sister Mala.' She nodded to the older woman. 'Vesna, our mother.'

Natalie's smile was sombre and brief. 'This is obviously…a traumatic time.'

Vesna gave her a tight smile, suddenly focused. 'Would you like a tea?'

Natalie was about to say no when Mala intervened. 'What a good idea. Gordana?' The woman opposite returned the gaze with a sullen expression and pushed the younger girl with her foot. The sullen expression did not alter as the girl leapt up, using the request as an opportunity to escape.

'You say you work with Frank?' said Vesna.

Frank didn't appear to be listening.

'Yes,' said Natalie, 'Research. I'm a psychiatrist, though.'

Neither Vesna nor Mala was giving much away, but it was hard to assess anyone for the first time in circumstances like this.

Mala seemed to sense Natalie's unease. 'Frank found Alison. Out in my grandfather's boathouse.' She shook her head, as if she still couldn't quite believe it.

'She had been quite hysterical you know,' said Vesna. 'What on earth was she thinking, making Frank tramp out there to check on her?'

Frank. 'Had anyone else checked on her?' Natalie had asked before she realised how it would sound. But everyone appeared too distracted to worry.

'It's freezing out there. She shouldn't have been there.' The dismissive tone suggested there was no love lost between these women and Alison.

'We couldn't persuade her to stay in the house,' Mala added, leaning into her brother to comfort him. 'Lord knows Frank tried.'

'Can I do anything to help? Frank?'

Frank lifted his head. His skin looked curiously pale,

perhaps the light, and though he looked dazed, he also seemed years younger. All of them in fact had remarkable complexions; even Vesna looked like an older sister rather than their mother.

'She's dead.' There was bewilderment in his voice, but also something else she filed away to reflect on later. She thought momentarily of Anders Breivik, his cool calm in the dock after he had murdered all those children in Norway. If Frank had killed his wife and child, his acting was at award level. And his psychopathy just as profound.

Natalie took his hand as much for her own comfort as his. Their eyes locked. She heard the door from the balcony open. Voices. She looked up, recognising one immediately.

Damian was staring at her. And he didn't look happy.

'When were you going to tell me, Frank?'

Alison had insisted she wanted to sleep in the boathouse.

'Come back inside Alison, you're being irrational. It's cold.'

Alison hugged herself, arms resting on her distended abdomen. She had been crying and her eyes were puffy slits. Her skin was mottled in the lamp light. 'I've had enough of you and your family.'

I *had* told her to stay with her mother. Now she was here for at least the evening. Perhaps tomorrow I could drive her back into town. Alison's parents had become increasingly distant with me as the pregnancy had progressed. Or, more pertinently, since Alison had become increasingly irrational. I understood it was because they had Alison's interests at heart and were too over involved to see the situation in perspective.

'You can have our bedroom and I'll take the spare,' I said calmly. The spare room Reeva died in.

'The bed here is fine.' She tried the defiant-little-girl look. It must have worked in the past but she had failed to register that it had never done so with me. She didn't know what else to try. We are all creatures of habit. Even though I knew it was pointless I reiterated my previous position. 'There is nothing between Natalie and myself. This…situation has been stressful for us both. I needed someone to talk to.'

There were fresh tears. 'Of all the women in the world why did you have to pick her?'

Of all the woman in the world I could have picked Angelina Jolie. We were talking about what was practical and who had skills, but my wife wasn't capable of being rational.

'I could hardly have been expected to know you two had history.' This wasn't entirely true. I had noted when reading Natalie's CV that her intern year had been at the same hospital as my wife.

'But I told you, that first day!' Alison had started to shiver. She sat on the couch bed and pulled the quilt over herself. The boathouse had been my grandfather's studio. It was never intended to accommodate someone overnight, or at least not in winter. The large windows onto the lake offered little insulation but at least were well sealed from the wind gusting around the wooden structure.

'If you hadn't kept on about her'—and Reeva, Mala, my mother, the internet's ten tips for expecting fathers and any number of other tedious topics—'I wouldn't have been under so much stress, would I?'

'I'm the one who's pregnant!' Alison screamed at me. Or had that been Reeva?

I didn't lose my temper. I greeted this type of ridiculous behaviour, as always, with silence. I turned and went to the gas heater. It took several minutes to get going; it wasn't even possible without a long match, now the pilot didn't work. It had probably been years since we'd last used it. If she insisted on being irrational I needed to do what I could for the wellbeing of Harry. Harry. I hoped he took after my side of the family and not the Cunninghams or, and it was hard not to shudder, the British prince that Alison found appealing. Really? I had given up arguing about the name; it wasn't what was going to be on the birth certificate, and my family and I were certainly not going to call him Harry.

'I know,' she said finally. She sounded surprisingly calm.

When I stood after lighting the heater and glared back at her she gave a look of triumph. 'What is it that you imagine you know?'

They were waiting for the arrival of the crime-scene officers. And the funeral director. Natalie frowned at this—surely it was too soon to confront the family with funeral details?—then realised that, Alison's death having been reported to the coroner, the hearse was required to deliver her body to the morgue for an autopsy. Involuntarily, Natalie found her gaze being drawn to the boathouse. Alison was still there. Natalie still couldn't work out why she had been there in the first place. Frank could barely string two words together and Damian was ignoring her.

As the CSOs unloaded equipment and descended on the boathouse, she had plenty of time to wonder what she was doing there, and why Frank had called her. But the Moreton-Malosevic family's lawyer arrived and sequestered herself away with the family, and the police finally acknowledged Natalie's presence.

The family were in shock, none more so than Frank. Vesna was reacting defensively and Mala had taken on the role of holding them together. Natalie had the feeling she had done it before. With Vesna, particularly, there was a sense that Mala was the parent. The staff, too, looked to

Mala to take charge. In other circumstances perhaps Frank took control but with the loss of a second wife and child, no one was expecting too much of Frank. The police were polite, deferential, but only to the family's grief. Damian didn't look like a newbie. He wore the homicide mantle like a glove.

'I'm just going to speak to the doctor,' Natalie heard Damian tell his colleague, who was about to take statements from the staff. Damian walked over to her. Took her firmly by the arm and led her into a room on the other side of the hallway. She picked it as Frank's study: books lined the walls and the desk was covered in paperwork.

'Care to explain what you're doing here?' She couldn't quite make out his expression in the light of the sole lamp, except that he was working hard not to give anything away.

'I work with him. He called.'

Damian waited.

Time to turn things back on him. 'Did you recognise his name when you got the call?'

This produced a reaction. 'Yes. As it happens I was down at my mate's, local detective'—*hoping to see you* was the unsaid implication—'and he said I could tag along.'

It was her turn to wait.

'So you were working for him, and you were curious about his first wife. Please tell me you had *no* idea that his second was going to die. I'm already going to have a difficult time explaining why I was asking for the first coroner's report two weeks *before* the second wife dies in suspiciously similar circumstances.'

'You can say I mentioned Frank and Reeva and thought her death unusual. That you wondered about the case. Coincidence, nothing more. I'm still registered as a forensic psychiatrist so it could have been a semi-official discussion. If anyone notices, which I doubt.'

'You avoided my question.'

'No, I confirmed the circumstances. As to the question…' Natalie thought about how she'd failed Alison. Again. 'I was an intern with Alison. I'd like to help.'

Damian raised an eyebrow. 'I could see that.'

'He's in shock. I wasn't referring to helping Frank.' Though he would need it and she would offer it and maybe she could help him. But it was Alison she owed.

'How did…Alison die?'

Damian hesitated.

'I know Frank, he confides in me,' she said softly. 'If you and I work together I can tell you if I think he's guilty. More to the point, why he did it.' Well, she hoped she could.

'I thought you guys were hung up on confidentiality.'

'If he was my patient, yes,' said Natalie. 'But he's my supervisor, and then only in an informal way.' Even if Frank had been a patient, if he was also a serial killer of wives then she had a duty of care to any future wife—theoretically anyway.

She watched Damian process the information. She thought of his steadiness with her. Remembered that even sex with her after a drought hadn't entirely enabled him to drop his guard. An introvert, a man who would be hard to read when he chose to hide his feelings. Unknowns there. But she doubted they would be as surprising as Frank's depths.

Could she work with Damian? She wasn't sure she wanted to.

He ran a hand through the short spikes of his hair. 'This has to be completely confidential.'

She nodded.

'Faulty gas heater.'

She would have gone to sleep and not woken up. There were worse ways to die. 'And...the baby too?'

Poor Alison. Natalie turned away, didn't want Damian to see her vulnerable. Grief, she told herself, not depression. Loss of two lives, one not yet lived and the other cut far too short. But whatever this feeling of vulnerability was, she didn't want it. Not before a man she was sleeping with, it gave away too much power. And her need for sex already did that.

When she looked up Damian nodded, expression grim.

'So it...Could it have been an accident?'

'Yeah, but two wives? Both pregnant?'

They looked at each other. Georgia Latimer came to mind: surely this wasn't a coincidence? What Oscar Wilde had said about losing parents was even truer for wives. One—unfortunate. But two? Careless at the very least.

It was seven in the morning before Natalie made it back to the stilt house. Bob and his friends were waiting.

'Champion of the Universe!' Bob serenaded from the gutter.

'Not sure they agree Bob, but keep on trying.'

She made herself a coffee and drank it slowly. Tried to make sense of what had happened. Alison was dead. Frank's marriage had been under pressure; she knew also that unresolved grief for Reeva, as well as Alison's antipathy towards Natalie herself as Frank's confidant, had added to the tension. She wished she had done something differently. Wasn't sure what.

Natalie stood up suddenly and flung her coffee cup. 'Fuck!' It smashed against the wall, sending Bob screeching across the patio in alarm as the dregs formed Rorschach blots. 'I will not fucking get depressed over this,' she screamed, and went to change into running gear.

Five kilometres later she was feeling better, her head clearing. She had not caused this and had not missed anything. But if there was something to find, if Frank had thought even for a minute that he could play her, then he was going to find out he was wrong. And if he was a victim of an improbable but not impossible double tragedy, then he deserved to be innocent until proven guilty.

Natalie broke the news to Wei.

He stared at her. 'Poor Mala.'

Mala? Wei saw her frown and shrugged. 'She came back from Oxford you know, when her grandfather died. Then Reeva. The house is cursed. I'll go and see if I can help.'

'I'll lock up,' Natalie assured him. And she would. After she'd searched Frank's office.

She had no idea what she thought she might find, just that she needed to know everything she could about him and Reeva. She hadn't slept, but one night surely would be okay? Tonight she'd take extra quetiapine. And a dose of lithium after missing this morning's. Maybe more antidepressants? She wanted to ring Declan and swear she hadn't done anything to cause this, but that she couldn't walk away. She really had tried to find a quieter life.

Frank's cabinets were locked but the key was in his top drawer. Everything was labelled. All his research articles and grants, patient files from research projects with data de-identified but keyed to a code, to be accessed if needed. Wei's CV was also there. She took a quick look. He'd studied at Oxford, which was presumably where he'd met Mala.

She had probably asked Frank to give him a job. Frank's CV was impressive, and there was a file full of newspaper articles and DVDs of television appearances. In two of the articles there were photos of Frank with Reeva. In the first they were looking at each other rather than the camera, but it was clear she was an attractive woman. Slim; slight build like Natalie's. Blonde, though, like Alison. She exuded an aura of confidence and calm. A certainty about her place and her future.

Natalie felt a surge of mixed feelings; a foreboding sense of the unknown hazard just around the corner, that even someone as smart and worthy as Reeva hadn't been able to prevent. It seemed such a waste. A meaningless waste of potential. But there was also another feeling. In the other photo Reeva was pregnant. Natalie folded it away quickly.

The desk was no more personal. A workplace that still had traces of Reeva but no strong sense of her presence, no hint of the hold she still had on Frank nor the answers Natalie felt she would offer, if Natalie just knew where to look. The only slightly incongruous item in the room was a small bar fridge containing a bottle of white wine, another of champagne, and two chilled glasses. A celebration that had never happened—and if it was for Harry's birth, never would. There was a small leather bag in the bottom; Natalie opened it to find it empty. She couldn't remember ever seeing Frank with the bag. Maybe a present he had no use for; but why in the fridge?

Closing up Frank's office in frustration, she moved on to look in the empty office next door. Again there were rows of cabinets with research articles and grants. All had handwritten tags in a neat bold pen. She quickly excluded all the reference articles—unlikely to provide anything of interest—but one cabinet appeared to have neither labelled reference articles nor grant applications. The tags were scribbled out. Natalie paused, and took her time with each file set. These were articles too, and at first she just thought they had yet to be filed. But some dated back ten years and while there was overlap with the ones Frank had, these were all Reeva's. Had they been together that long? Certainly Frank was not a co-author on the earliest papers. His name didn't appear until six years previously.

Natalie checked every paper for co-authors and research subjects. Nothing struck her as unusual until she had closed all the cabinets and was heading for the door. The topics. She turned around and went back to check. Reeva had an extensive research record: all her publications were on cytokines, inflammatory response and cancer. Some of the later papers, with Frank as first author, covered depression. She double-checked through the research grants and found the same.

So the file containing articles on half a dozen rare medical disorders seemed to be an anomaly. Had Wei or Frank misfiled them? Some of the disorders might have been genetic but as far as she knew they weren't inflammatory— the type of disorders that Reeva researched. Taking out the unnamed folder she went through it slowly. There were a range of articles, and a handwritten sheet at the back. Reeva had a list. Some, such as Parkinsons and MS, had a line through them. Others were annotated: *Unlikely* or a question mark. She saw schizophrenia and bipolar among the list; the former crossed out, the latter questioned. That felt too close to home. She had no idea what Reeva had been trying to work out. She took a photocopy in case it was important.

Reeva died in the guest bedroom. I came in and found her at 8 a.m., just as I told the police, with a cup of black tea for her in one hand. It remained there untouched as they took her away, strapped to the stretcher. I watched as she disappeared from my life. She had been dead for hours. I found Alison much earlier, perhaps only minutes too late, but still not early enough to save her or my son. The hypoxia would have affected his intellect even if I had been able to revive her.

I could imagine a jury thinking that, as I lay there unable to sleep, in the warmth of the master bedroom, I was planning the rest of my life without her. Is that what the prosecutor would say? That I got out of bed and pulled on some warm clothes to go down and check that she had died, rather than to make sure she was all right?

The police have been polite but distant. I can see they think this is too much to be written off as bad luck. I can't blame them, though it would be reassuring if I could believe one of them might actually understand statistics. Improbable things do occur. But these are the sorts of men I would expect to see in the police. Most criminals are, after all, not particularly smart;

police are not paid well, and their jobs are unstimulating for the most part. These are much the same as the ones who took my statement after Reeva died. This time they are edgier. This time they are looking at me as if I am a killer.

My lawyer, a feisty Vietnamese woman, is protective. She is barely five foot tall and next to the policemen she looks mildly ridiculous, as if playing at being a grown-up.

Yes, I have told her, my fingerprints will be on the gas heater. I lit it for Alison, an act of kindness. Yes, we had argued; what couple doesn't? I wonder what Alison told her parents, what they will tell the police. I feel that it should be me that breaks the bad news to my in-laws but I have already mixed up names. I think I sound as if I am drunk and they have taken a blood sample, but it is hours since that drink at the Wye River pub; even then I doubt if I was over 0.05.

What will Natalie tell them? That my marriage was troubled? That I made an inappropriate comment, for which I immediately apologised? Maybe. She will feel sorry for me no doubt, but she will wonder. Even if she does understand statistics. Will she want to know about my relationship with my mother, and how that has affected my relationships with my wives? Whether I have a deep-seated, unresolved murderous rage towards the woman who bore me which is now projected onto any woman who attempts to take over her role as the family matriarch?

She will, of course. And then I suspect she'll tell the tall cop who is...what? Her boyfriend I suppose. I saw how he looked at her in the pub that night. If he isn't yet he certainly wants to be. He isn't, of course, smart enough for her, but she will work that out.

Will she work me out?

Only if I let her.

The church was already full when Natalie arrived. A thin, anxious man was ushering people along the sides of the pews to jostle for a position where they could see. The screen at the front behind the lectern, on which pictures were rotating, was large enough for everyone to catch a glimpse. Natalie wondered who chose the photos. Not Alison's mother, surely, given there were several of Alison in Rocky Horror undress. Oliver was by her side. White Y-fronts, thought Natalie, hadn't done anything for his porcelain skin.

She recognised herself in one shot and hoped no one else did. Except Damian. He and his homicide partner were on the other side of the aisle. She saw him smile at the photo of her in a bodice, stockings and suspenders. Today she was wearing the dark grey suit jacket she had bought but refused to wear for her final psychiatry oral examination. She felt as uncomfortable in it now as she had then. At least she'd paired it with jeans, though. It would have been too hard to change at a church after arriving by bike.

From the side, ten rows back, she was able to survey the congregation. Alison's family were in the front. Damian had been given permission to help with the case and interviewed them. Alison had been anxious. *Not herself.*

'And,' Damian told her, 'they think he did it.' But were too polite—or shocked—to say so.

The Cunninghams looked shrunken and faded, older than they should have. Alison's mother, Lally Foster-Cunningham, had been a model once but it was hard to see her beauty now. Luke, Alison's brother, looked grim in a charcoal suit. A lawyer, she recalled. Probably too early in the grief process for recriminations, but they would come. Luke walked over to Frank, seated between his mother and sister, and they conversed briefly.

There were a number of doctors she recognised, some from her year, some not. According to the memorial booklet with her graduation photo on the front, Alison had finished her general practice training while Natalie had been doing psychiatry. She had met Frank in her psychiatry placement, but of course there was no indication of whether he had still been married then.

There were a lot of tears but at least there was no tiny second coffin. Harry was to be buried with his mother. Alison's old school friends, now professional women, told stories with practised delivery. The sobs didn't erupt until they were collected by other women at the end, all regressing to schoolgirls again in their little huddles. Stories of Alison's childhood from her brother with accompanying video clips; stories of her medical training told by the doctor who had played Columbia in the doomed Rocky Hospital Horror.

Natalie felt curiously detached from it all; she felt they had missed the essence of Alison in her last year or so. Perhaps that turmoil was not the stuff of funerals. But it was disconcerting, and difficult to reconcile Alison as she had last seen her with Alison the netballer, Alison the winner of the dermatology prize, goofy teenage Alison in braces. Even Frank's brief farewell failed to evoke a woman who'd had a lifetime meticulously planned.

Frank looked depleted, almost crumpled, although his trousers had the usual crispness and his shirt and tie were in order. It was the creases in his face, a sagging she hadn't ever noticed before, that made him look older. At the end of the ceremony she gave him a quick hug and nodded to his family. He held her hand, reluctant to let it go, but was soon herded away.

She offered her condolences to the Cunninghams, who looked blankly at her, then went to make a rapid exit, wondering why she had come. She avoided funerals. They reminded her of Eoin, and that she hadn't been able to attend his, over half a lifetime ago when she was in intensive care. Before she could escape, Columbia—the program said her real name was Marcie, though Natalie had no recollection of this—cornered her.

'Well that was pretty bloody depressing.'

Natalie nodded. Marcie looked like she'd been crying. She pulled out a packet of tissues and offered Natalie one.

'I only saw her last week. Seems unreal.' Doctors didn't find sudden death any easier than anyone else.

'How was she?'

'Looking forward to having it all over. I mean the pregnancy.' She started sniffing and wiped her nose.

'I got the impression she and Frank weren't getting on so well.' Natalie looked around self-consciously. No one was paying them any attention.

'I don't think he was the easiest man to live with, reading between the lines.'

'No?'

'She wouldn't say much but I got the impression pregnancy wasn't much of a turn-on for him. They both just wanted it over.'

Over. Natalie felt a shiver go through her.

'She thought it would improve after the baby?'

'Hell yes. I certainly hope so.'

For the first time Natalie realised Columbia-Marcie was pregnant. 'Congratulations.'

'I'm a bit spooked, to be honest. Still got three months to go.' One of the doctors Natalie recognised as a surgical registrar from her internship joined them and put his arm around Marcie. Natalie reiterated her congratulations to them both and excused herself. It wasn't just funerals she avoided: reunions had their own issues.

'Didn't think I'd see you here.'

Natalie swung around, knowing who it would be before she saw him. This was a reunion she really didn't need. Memories of the art gallery moat flashed through her mind.

Oliver was looking good, but then he always had, Y-fronts aside: man most likely to succeed, doctor most likely to make professor—or a million dollars—first, the husband and son-in-law everyone wanted. His skin was still porcelain though there were fine lines around his eyes; blond hair, complete with dark tips, was still swept back behind his ears and over his collar. The blond version of Frank: Alison's taste hadn't matured much. Natalie had heard he was an obstetrician. It would fit. Perfect job for a man who fancied himself as a ladies' man but was at heart a misogynist. He was wearing a bowtie.

'You were back on speaking terms?' Oliver offered her a cigarette.

'Yes, but more by circumstances than anything else.' She shook her head at the packet and watched him light up and lean his head back to expel a long, heartfelt drag.

'Family still don't speak to me. I hid up the back.' He took another drag, looking around awkwardly. 'Do you know what happened?'

'Accident with a gas stove.'

'Definitely an accident?'

Natalie looked at him, wondered if this was old guilt at play; like *if I hadn't been a cad, she and I would be happily married* type guilt. She looked at his left hand; it had a wedding ring. She doubted he had pined long for Alison. 'There'll be an inquest.'

Oliver's eyes darted to the last of the crowd leaving the church.

'So, had you been in contact lately?' asked Natalie.

'What? Ah, no. I haven't seen her in years.' He dropped the half-smoked cigarette, stepped on it and smiled at her. 'Got to get back to my patients. Nice seeing you. You look good.' He kissed her on the cheek, and she stared after him, wondering.

She had rung Jacqueline Barrett when the subpoena arrived at her Punt Road rooms.

'It's part of discovery. The prosecutor's office is entitled to see your records.' The lawyer seemed to cover the phone and start barking orders to someone else.

'I don't want to give them up.'

'You've changed your mind? Is there something prejudicial against my client?'

Natalie rubbed her temples. 'They're private confidential patient records. I'm her treating psychiatrist.' And Georgia was finally, against all odds, beginning to trust her.

'Then lodge an objection.' Barrett gave her the details and hung up. She appeared to have more important things to focus on.

Natalie could have mailed the objection, but after the funeral she had to go right past Liam's office. She was tired of allowing the thought of Liam to spook her. Fate could decide if she was about to face her nemesis. It would certainly be better to get the personal feelings out of the way before they faced off in court.

Carol, Liam's secretary, was at the front desk, her toothpaste teeth brighter than ever. They arranged themselves into a knowing smile as Natalie handed her the paperwork and turned to leave.

'Can you wait here?' Carol said sharply, walking off down the corridor, past Liam's office. Natalie let out her breath. The door was open; he wasn't in. A minute later Carol returned. 'Miss Perkins would like a word. Last office on the right.'

The door had her full name on it. Someone with short blonde hair and a long fringe falling over her eyes, presumably Tania Perkins, was sitting on the desk talking on a landline.

Natalie stood in silence waiting for her to end the call. It seemed to take forever.

'Dr King?' Tania said after finally hanging up and waving her in as she pushed her fringe behind an ear.

'I'm sure she'll answer to Natalie.' The voice came from the right, on the other side of the room. As she stepped reluctantly inside, almost as if compelled, Liam was leaning back in the chair, watching her. There was an instant of fear, then anger flared up before she got it under control.

She didn't look at him, afraid that the next feeling would be longing. Their affair hadn't ended well: her fault. Faced with a choice between what was right for her patient and her patient's child, and her own relationship with Liam, she had chosen the patient.

'We got a copy of your report,' said Tania. She took a seat by the table and indicated another for Natalie, who hesitated before taking it. 'Can I clarify? You are saying she doesn't dissociate?'

'I'm not here to discuss the report.' Natalie tried to block Liam out. Tried to stop minding that she was dressed more conservatively than he had probably ever seen her.

Tania picked up the objection document. 'We want your records.'

'I'm treating her. It's not in her best interest.'

'What about the best interest of her surviving child?' Liam's voice was cool. Irish accent barely detectable.

'That isn't my concern.'

Liam leaned forward in his chair, a lock of black hair falling over his right eye. The longing feeling was there, far too strongly for her liking. 'But it is ours.'

'Does she or does she not dissociate?' Tania was not about to let it go either.

'I never said she didn't dissociate,' said Natalie, cursing herself for being sucked in. 'She dissociates, just not into separate personalities.'

'Could she have committed murder while doing this dissociation thing?'

Natalie stifled her irritation. 'Not in my opinion: not without some premeditation.'

'So she killed them?'

'She says she is innocent.'

'But what do you think?' It was Liam this time, edging forward on his chair, almost close enough for her to feel his leg against hers.

'I don't know.' She let her breath out as Liam sat back.

'What about her husband?'

'I only interviewed him once,' said Natalie. 'I believe they have, or rather had, a close enmeshed relationship, but how much he knew I don't know.'

'She knows the difference between right and wrong?'

'Yes.'

'Not psychotic?'

'No.'

They were both looking at her.

'I intend to go ahead with my objection.' Natalie, watching their faces, couldn't read anything in them. She turned and left as fast as she could without actually running.

I have relived the funeral in my dreams.

In the past, dreams disturbed me nightly but until Reeva died I had forgotten about them. Now my wives and their deaths are also fragmented inclusions in my reliving of my childhood, unanswered questions about death still gnawing at me when I awake.

I was not close to Wendell. There was always a remoteness to my father that I now put down to his British upbringing, the years at boarding school and nannies prior to that. His own mother had died when he was young and I don't think his stepmother ever had maternal feelings. But I knew Wendell loved me and he had been a reliable presence, whereas Vesna blew hot and cold, sometimes smothering and then absent. Wendell had that English eccentricity that Australians like to laugh at. I picture him in an odd collection of clothes, including a waistcoat even in summer that may, for all I knew, have been the height of fashion. He liked ice cream, I remember that vividly. His stepmother would tell him he was too old for it—he mimicked that disapproving voice when he and I were alone.

In my reliving of his funeral I am always alone, or at

least cut off from anyone around me. The minister is smiling gravely; is it his white robes that seem to dazzle me as the coffin disappears into darkness? I always wake then, with a sob. I have no memory of the graveside and what happened there, or indeed anything until Antonije arrived to save me. I was only ten.

This funeral is the third in five years: first Antonije's, then my two wives, taking with them my two sons. I felt the waves of animosity toward me despite Mala's attempts to shield me. She positioned me with Vesna on one side, herself on the other. The Cunninghams were still in shock; only Luke has thought beyond this event. I could see it in his eyes, the same look the tall policeman, Natalie's friend, gave me.

It is understandable. How could they not wonder, even if the methods and cause of death were different? But in the look is also the bewilderment. What could my motive possibly be? This in the end will save me from anything other than irritating scrutiny in the next weeks. I am a wealthy man in my own right. Divorce is simple and without risks. No cause need be provided. Reeva and Alison had money of their own, and while they would have had some claim to my income, the estate is in a trust. And I am a generous man. Why would I not want to support my child?

I didn't view the child. Couldn't bring myself to do so. I knew I needed to look ahead, not back.

As I walked down the aisle after the service I looked up and caught Natalie's eyes; locked for a moment before she looked away. The policeman was watching us both. Interesting. Even more interesting was what I saw in Natalie's glance. She doesn't know yet, but she is the one person who might be able to understand. And I want to be understood.

Natalie needed every minute of the two-hour ride to de-stress. The mindfulness techniques were useless; she needed more practice. Instead she replayed the conversation with Liam over and over in her mind, hating herself for the accompanying physical longing. She thought about putting the dose of her antidepressants up again. But this felt like grief, not the black falling through space that had engulfed her when she was in the grip of her depressive swing. She hoped.

She reached the Great Ocean Road and stopped the bike. Gave herself five minutes to regroup, take deep breaths and remind herself of all the ways Liam was bad for her. Ahead of her the road hugged the coast, to its right, set back a short way from the sea, the Otway Ranges were shrouded in mist. Though she'd never been to Britain, she imagined this was what the Lake District or Scottish highlands looked like in parts. She went back to mindfulness, concentrated on this moment and these surrounds, far from Melbourne.

Still feeling flat, but less like taking her bike over the edge of the road where it gave way to rocky cliffs, she kick-started the bike, waited for a line of cars to pass and pulled in behind them. A slow drive back was probably wise. She was soon lost in thought, watching the cars disappear ahead.

Natalie didn't notice the car behind her until it was square in her rear-vision mirror. A hotted-up silver Commodore V8. Its lights went on and she took that to mean he thought she was holding him up. Natalie briefly considered flooring it so the driver behind her could see real power—on the corners the Ducati would have it for breakfast—but instead slowed and pulled as close to the edge as was safe. She didn't trust her reaction times with the medications she was on.

The car maintained its position, a little too close for comfort. Irritated, Natalie waved it past. No response. Great—a V8 driver too frightened to pass because the stretches of straight were too short. She pulled over into a rest stop. The silver Commodore pulled in after her. One foot on the ground, Natalie looked back, all senses now on alert. The windows were tinted and she could only make out a sole driver in Ray-Bans. He revved the engine and edged a little closer. No one she knew. Just a local having fun?

Plan B. She opened the throttle so fast the bike jerked forward and nearly lost her. The Ducati flew down the straight section and she barely eased back at the corner, leaning into it so low she thought she wouldn't be able to correct. She saved it—just—but lost valuable time and the Commodore was now back right behind her. Far too close for safety, and she was the one at risk, not him.

Two more corners in a similar fashion but this time she gained time, only to see him in her mirror bearing down along the straight, lights on high beam.

On the third corner her line took her to the centre of the road, narrowly missing a car on the other side—the blasting of the horn was as much for her as for the V8 driver who also came dangerously close to collecting it.

Catching her breath, heart racing, Natalie slowed. If she was going to come off the bike she'd rather it was at lower speed. The V8 was now so close its lights filled her mirrors entirely. If it hit her, she wondered if she would be able to think fast enough to roll. Doubted it.

A sheer drop loomed on her left. The car now edged level with her as the signpost indicating the town perimeter flew past. The driver edged over again and his passenger window wound down. She looked over. Saw the driver draw one hand in a cutting motion across his throat. The car moved even closer, this time leaving her no choice but to move over. Half a metre and she could make out rocks at the bottom of the twenty-metre drop.

Ahead the road widened and another rest stop appeared to the left. One car was parked there; she prayed they didn't open their door. Without warning she accelerated and swung left, hoping the car driver would pull in too. He did. But with less room to manoeuvre he slowed to avoid the parked vehicle while Natalie passed it with only a few millimetres to spare and jerked sharply back to the road.

It only gave her a few seconds, but she flew into town ahead of him, hit the brakes hard at the first intersection and spun her bike to the right, straight up the side street. She started to slide, but by this time her speed was slow enough and her leathers tough enough that it looked more like a spectacularly staged arrival than a stack, the bike landing first and Natalie shortly after.

Just as two constables, one of them Constable Red Hair from the night at Mount Malosevic, were stepping out of the police station.

*

'You what?'

'I'll explain later,' said Natalie. 'Could you just tell these police officers that I'm normally a safe driver and that they don't need to arrest me?'

The phone conversation between Damian and the Lorne police wasn't as short as she had hoped. In fact the constables were still looking as unimpressed as when they had jumped back inside thinking the bike might take them out. A sergeant who had joined them was no happier. Didn't the imprimatur of a homicide DSS count for anything? Seemed not.

After much discussion they reached a compromise. They wouldn't charge her if Damian personally came to pick her up. That meant she would have to cool her heels in their company for an hour. At least he was already heading this way, coming from Melbourne following the funeral.

Damian barely looked at her when he arrived, showing his colleagues his badge and disappearing behind closed doors. After fifteen minutes he returned, picked up her helmet and threw it at her. 'Let's go.' His expression softened a little when he saw the state of her leathers. They'd done their job but she'd be needing a new pair. The bike was still on its side where she'd dropped it. About to get in his car, Damian turned and saw she hadn't moved. 'Don't tell me you can't pick it up?'

'Not a hope in hell.'

Damian shook his head, muttering something that sounded very like a sexist insult as he walked over and heaved on the Ducati. It was hard enough even for him. The bike possibly hadn't been her smartest purchase. She'd certainly overestimated her capabilities: mania had its obvious up, but also its down, sides.

She hit the starter, revved the engine and jumped out of the standing position possibly a little faster than was wise. Right now she was feeling pleased to be alive. She was still in one piece when they got back to her stilt house and she let herself in, leaving the door open for Damian to follow.

'Start explaining.' The speed she'd just been travelling at probably hadn't improved Damian's mood. 'And don't imagine for a moment that because I'm in homicide I don't think dangerous driving is a problem.'

Natalie had pondered this all the way back. She thought of her pursuer's cut-throat action. Who was he? Did he know her? She'd been too busy trying to survive to get a plate number, and the cops had clearly thought she'd overreacted. Had she?

'I've got some PTSD. The motorbike accident years ago, the assault last year...This guy was seriously tailgating me and I overreacted.'

'Not a great defence against trying to kill two cops.'

'I wasn't trying to kill them. I just took the corner too quickly, because...'

Damian looked like he couldn't decide whether to get himself a beer or get the hell out of her life. The latter might have been wiser. Natalie pulled a Little Creatures out of the fridge with one hand and grabbed a bottle of red with the other. She jiggled them.

He went for the beer and took a seat in the armchair watching her.

'Call the cops!' Bob announced, watching them from the veranda. Natalie opened the door, braving the elements to fill his seed container. Several other cockatoos joined him and she poured more seed into a bowl at the other end of the deck.

'Better get it fast Bob.' Natalie doubted the local crew would stick to their end for long.

'Now tell me what really happened Natalie.'

'I wasn't kidding.'

'Just PTSD?' He watched her, seemed to be debating whether to tell her something.

'I've got bipolar disorder.' The words surprised her. She never told *anyone* about her illness. 'I've been on antidepressants and I'm going a little high.' Not exactly true, but she was feeling mostly better, until Alison died and she met up with Liam, anyway. She was already dismissing the Liam encounter. Maybe she was going high. The Commodore incident hadn't upset her, and now she was feeling like finding the arsehole and bawling him out.

Now Damian surprised her. 'I know.'

'What?'

'Well, I knew you were depressed. When I checked the band out—months ago, I mean—your drummer told me you were in a downer and that was why you wouldn't respond to my messages. I was referring to what happened today.'

Natalie stared. She wasn't quite sure what she was most stunned about; that he didn't seem to care about her mental illness, or that he thought she wasn't telling him the whole truth.

'The cops were heading out on a call about a drag race when you nearly collected them,' said Damian. The car they'd narrowly avoided must have called it in.

'Look, it was no biggy, okay?'

Natalie stood up and waved at the more adventurous cockies that were narrowing in on an assault on Bob's food container. With the glass between them they ignored her. She put her wine down and lit the potbelly stove. The assault had just made her hypervigilant, that was all. There was no reason for anyone to be after her now. It was just a jerk thinking he was tough. She didn't want Damian worrying about her—or worse, Declan. Last thing she wanted was more medication. She just needed to forget it.

'It isn't anything, really. I was overreacting.'

His look suggested he still didn't entirely believe her.

Since it looked like he'd be staying, she pulled some meat out of the fridge and threw him a barbeque spatula which he caught in the hand not holding the beer. 'Can you use one of these?'

'I'll manage.'

They'd been cautious with each other since the encounter at the crime scene. One brief phone call, and they hadn't spoken at the funeral, just nodded over the rows of heads. And this episode hadn't endeared her to him. But by the time they'd both changed into comfortable clothes and had a couple of drinks on the balcony, Natalie was reminded of the ease she felt in his presence. He was looking more surfer than cop having changed into a windcheater and the long shorts some men wore even in the winter chill.

'Can we talk some shop before we drink too much?'

'Maybe.'

'What's happening with the investigation into Alison's death?'

'Your professor is well qualified and well connected. No one wants him arrested unless we have a clear case.'

'What do you have?'

Over steak and salad and another beer, Damian outlined the evidence. As suspected, the cause of death was carbon monoxide poisoning. The gas heater was old and hadn't been serviced. Frank's and Alison's fingerprints were the only ones on it.

'The pilot system wasn't working, hadn't been used for years,' said Damian. 'Hence why Frank said he got it going for her when she couldn't.'

'So it blew out?'

Damian shook his head. 'It was windy, but not indoors. It does heat the place up quickly; one possibility is that she turned it off because it was too hot and didn't do it properly, or tried to turn it back on later and couldn't, and mixed up the position of the switch and let it run. The windows were sealed so there was very little ventilation. And there was a lot of soot in the heater, which meant there was more carbon monoxide circulating than there should have been.'

Natalie tried to picture this. It was feasible that the Alison she had last seen had been tired enough to make a mistake. Or that it was just bad luck with an outdated heater.

'The Malosevic place is pretty amazing, I have to say,' Damian said. 'Huge. Have you ever been in the grounds?'

Natalie shook her head.

'They do charity events in summer. String quartets on the lawn; opera in the park. I've never seen a tree house that big, stables that don't look like they've ever had a horse in them, a maze...There's even a pet cemetery.' Damian shook his head as if mystified about why anyone would waste their money like that.

Alison had spent her last day there, indoors, apart from meeting Frank at the Wye River pub. Where Natalie had been with him—something Damian didn't seem to know. Natalie was concentrating on what he was telling her, and it was only much later she realised she hadn't given him this information. Damian seemed to think Frank and Alison had had dinner there. Frank hadn't mentioned he was expecting Alison: hadn't he said he would eat at home? She was fairly sure she hadn't seen Alison in the car park. She'd had probably been in the shadows checking them out. She wouldn't have seen anything to worry her. Natalie tensed. Except the goodbye kiss; but she'd turned her cheek quickly. Nothing in that, was there?

Damian had Alison's phone and her electronic diary. The team were going through all her recent contacts to get an assessment of her mental state. Suicide was obviously being considered as a possibility, as it had been with Reeva. Could Frank have driven both his wives to the same end? Natalie felt her own black hole at the edge of her consciousness and dismissed it.

Six people other than Alison had access to the heater and boathouse. The first, Frank, admitted he was there trying to convince her to come back to the house.

'Did he say why she was there?' Just like Reeva, sleeping separately.

'He said they had fought.'

'Over what?'

'He indicated that he felt her pregnancy was getting her down, that she was irritable because she wasn't sleeping. He had wanted her to stay with her mother because she hated the isolation and it would be closer to the private hospital where she wanted to deliver.'

'What did the others say about the argument?'

'The three staff are dumb, deaf and blind. Drago and his wife Gordana the chef, anyway. She smelled like a brewery so she probably didn't notice anything useful. Drago has been with the family since he was a child; his father worked for Frank's grandfather. He wouldn't tell us what they had for breakfast. A strong case of Serbian amnesia.'

'The girl's their daughter, right?'

'Yes. Senka. She works there too. She knows something, we just haven't got to it yet. I'm questioning her tomorrow down at the local station.'

'And Vesna and Mala?'

Damian finished the last of his steak, and pushed the plate away. 'Was it the first time you'd met them?'

'Yes.'

'Impressions?'

Lots. Some ephemeral, like a trace of memory long since buried. Others were clearer, and it was only these she was prepared to share. For the moment.

'People handle shock in different ways. This family is educated and upper class. I say that deliberately, because that's how they see themselves. They aren't Australian in that sense. Frank has a trace of a British accent and according to his LinkedIn profile that was where he went to primary school. Mala's profile says she went to Oxford, but she'd arrived here as a baby. I couldn't find anything about their father but I'm thinking he was probably a Brit. Their grandfather was some sort of minor Serbian royalty. They're privileged.'

'Why's that relevant?'

'They called a lawyer because that is what they would do. Not necessarily because they're guilty.' There were other things she'd observed in her long wait in their living room that informed her observations. Their clothes, certainly, but more their demeanour. She had thought Mala's poise, like her mother's, was part of how they saw themselves. Just a little above everyone else.

'There is something else, which may or may not have a

bearing on what happened.'

Damian waited.

'Vesna's not well,' said Natalie, closing her eyes to picture Frank's mother. 'And my guess is it's psychiatric, possibly with a physical component.' There was a waif-like aspect to Vesna she had seen in some cancer patients. 'In any event, she's taking sedatives.'

'You're sure?'

'Yes, and quite high doses if it's benzos. But I'm thinking anti-psychotics. She was spacey. Couldn't quite focus, might even have been a little thought-disordered. Without knowing more I can't be certain.'

'Thoughts on Mala?'

'Smart, but...' Natalie tried to make sense of the pigtails versus the taking control. 'I'd say somewhat innocent. Like she's been shielded from anything difficult. By Frank, by the Malosevic millions, I guess.'

'And Frank?'

Her impressions of Frank? 'Complicated.'

Damian raised an eyebrow. 'Because of your personal relationship? If that's an issue I want to know now. I don't want this case compromised.' Meaning he didn't care about what she did? Or was he just trying to be cool?

'I don't have that sort of personal relationship. He has been using me to work through his grief over his first wife's death; he could hardly talk about that to Alison.'

'But he could talk to you? How did Alison feel about that?

'I think,' said Natalie slowly, 'it was hard being in Reeva's footsteps.'

Damian thought about this, then said, 'We've called this Operation Blue.'

'Why blue?'

'Officially? Because it's on the surf coast. Sea and sun and all that.'

'Unofficially?'

Damian grinned. 'Short for Bluebeard.'

Mala was worried. She didn't say anything, but she didn't need to.

'There is no evidence. It doesn't matter what they might think,' I told her.

She smiled; when she does she reminds me of our grandmother. She has Lyuba's eyes, large and wide set, but in the old photos the eyes were always cloaked in sadness, even those that were taken once they had arrived in Australia. My grandmother had a difficult life, and some things can't be fixed once they are broken. That is how I think of Lyuba: broken.

Mala's eyes are full of surprise and promise, of mystery and the impossible.

'They'll drag everything up again. Reeva. The media.' She wasn't tense; not really worried. Except perhaps for our mother.

'You can hole up here as long as you like. They can't get to us. Or why not go away? Take Vesna on a holiday.'

'And leave you to go through it alone?' she scoffed. 'Hardly.'

'I could find someone to come and keep me company.'

'I'm sure you could, but would that be wise?'

I patted her hand and she put her head on my shoulder. 'We should all go away, when this is done,' she said.

'You know I have work commitments.'

'I know they can wait.'

'Perhaps,' I conceded. I was tired, very tired. I couldn't recall the last time I had had a holiday. A real one, not interrupted by pregnancy symptoms or grant applications.

'I wonder...' Mala waited until she had my full attention. 'Senka is still seeing Jasper.'

I knew where Mala was going. How could I not have wondered myself what Jasper knew or thought he knew: what his mother had told him or let him believe.

'Don't worry about Jasper,' I said. Mala had felt me tense. 'I have him in hand.'

Frank was already there with a glass of wine in hand when Natalie arrived. He had a Corona as well. She poured herself a glass of water and joined him.

'You look like shit, Frank.'

His smile was little more than a flicker. They sat in silence, watching the only other diners, a couple with a newborn in a capsule under their table and a toddler who was being given a free rein of the entire room. Frank huddled over his glass, with his back to them. She watched him tense as the toddler joined them, confident in the belief that everyone in the world wanted his company as much as his parents. Frank clearly didn't.

'Do you want to get out of here?' Natalie shooed the child away; it looked at her in astonishment, smile turning to wail. 'My place isn't far.'

Frank drove in silence. She wondered about the wisdom of her invitation but it was hard to turn her back on the grief that was etched into every pore of the man's being.

'You have a choice of beer,'—Damian's—'scotch or bourbon. And my cooking, I'm afraid. Pasta with...' Natalie rummaged in the cupboard. 'Tomatoes.'

Frank just nodded. She poured him some scotch and put a saucepan of water on to heat.

'Have the police been difficult?' Natalie sat down on the chair beside him. Outside it was dark. She could hear the waves in the distance, the soft regular sounds of the nights when the wind wasn't creating havoc in the national park behind the house.

'They're just doing their job.'

They sat in silence for a while. She said quietly, 'Do you want to talk about what happened?'

He nodded, though she wasn't sure he had heard her. His mind seemed to be tuned into some inner torment. The one she wanted to access.

'It was an accident.'

Natalie didn't respond; she tucked her feet up underneath her. Frank finally looked up.

'Do you believe me?'

An interesting question. How to answer? It wasn't so different from being with a patient, managing the balance of interest and reserve. But Frank wasn't her patient; and he might have murdered his wives. Right now it was hard to believe that he was anything more than a grieving husband who needed a friend.

'I guess you must be feeling that no one does,' she said.

'I understand if you don't,' he said, not fooled by her sidestep.

'Tell me what happened.'

'I dreamed last night of my father's funeral. I hadn't had the dream for months but I suppose it's been triggered. All this death.' He put his head in his hands.

'You were young when your dad died, weren't you?'

Frank nodded.

132

'So tell me about him.' Natalie walked over to the stove to tip the pasta into the boiling water. 'It might take your mind off things. Five words or phrases to describe your relationship with him.'

'Wendell?' Frank frowned. 'Five words?'

He didn't appear to know the Adult Attachment Interview. But then he was a biological researcher, not an attachment theorist. A small advantage.

'Yes, just the first random ones that come into your mind.'

Frank shrugged, looked like for a moment he would resist. But she stood watching and waiting and he finally replied. Long enough to have considered his answers, but not long enough to have worked out what she was really after.

'Fun, responsible, remote, I guess. Sporty: it was the one thing we did together, you know, he'd come to my football matches and we went to see Arsenal once. Was that four? Umm…disappointing.'

There was the sense Frank was going to say something more, then stopped. Had he been her patient she would have waited him out, but the polite smile suggested she was close to losing him. 'Fun. How come dads get to be fun? Did you know that's how their children bond to them? When they play with them.' Natalie had turned away, stirring the pasta before putting the lid on and turning it down. She let him relax again as she pulled out two bowls before she asked, 'In what way responsible?'

There was only the briefest pause. 'British thing. Oldest son and so forth.'

Was this the moment? Natalie took a breath. She sat down on the sofa next to him, knees to her chest. 'How did he die? He must have been young. Was he sick?'

Frank stared out the window. 'Car accident.'

'That must have been awful. At least if he's sick you get some warning.' Natalie felt genuine sorrow for him. He'd had a lot of losses. She wondered if, rather than adding up, they multiplied. 'Was anyone else...was it just him?'

'No,' said Frank. 'He ran into another car after going through a red light. He was drunk.'

'Shit.' Natalie leaned forward and put her hand on his. 'I'm so sorry.'

His head turned slowly, eyes glistening with tears meeting hers. 'He was on the way home from seeing my mother. Mala had just been born. I was with him in the car. I escaped without so much as a scratch.'

Time passed as she sat there and tried to absorb some of his pain. She didn't notice his hand continuing to hold hers, or his fingers absentmindedly brushing along her bare feet. Later, when the pasta had gone well beyond *al dente*, he added, 'The woman he killed was eight months pregnant.'

She was speaking too fast. She took a breath and sat down, mindful that Declan was assessing not just the content of her speech but her mental state. At least she could truthfully tell him she was compliant—not just with the medication but also her exercise and meditation regime. True, he thought she was off her antidepressants; she needed to get around to telling him she was still taking a Zoloft in the morning. Or had it been two recently? Time to get off them.

'You think Frank killed his wives?' Declan finally spoke. His grip on his pen looked like he might break it in half.

'I don't know, of course,' said Natalie. 'It isn't like he's confessed or anything. But I'm almost wondering...'

'Wondering what?'

Natalie bit her lip as she reflected. 'The grief is genuine I'm sure,' she said as much to herself as Declan. 'But over whose death?'

'I felt you were wondering about something more than that.'

'Yes. But I don't quite know how to explain it.' Her mind went back to her house, Frank's grey pallor in the dim light. How comfortable she had felt with him. 'He opened the door to his father, then seemed surprised that I went with it. Or...maybe it just the particular question I asked, inspired by the AAI.'

'The AAI was designed as a research tool, not for clinical purposes. And certainly not for forensic use.' Declan had more time for analytic theories than tool development.

'I know, but the question about the five words, about the early parental relationship, it was also designed to catch people off-guard. And unless you've studied it, which he clearly hasn't, you don't know that the words themselves don't actually matter.'

'So what did you make of what did matter? The examples to support the words?'

'I think they were genuine reflections of his parental relationship. Disappointing was the most interesting one. In general he was light on detail. Fitting a narcissistic personality style—he is quite grandiose, likes to be the centre of attention...' Natalie thought about him surrounded by his adoring research staff. 'Stemming from a dismissing, avoidant attachment. There wasn't much time or nurture given to emotions when he was little. Disappointing fits, in that his father didn't measure up. He certainly disappointed Frank by dying, and in the circumstances he did.'

'And the fact that a pregnant woman was killed by his father?'

'I don't know. It's too...like he was delivering me something on a platter.'

'A lie?'

'No.' Or at least she didn't think so. 'But did he tell me knowing I could find out? Letting me know it couldn't drive him subconsciously?'

'Does he know you're dating a policeman?'

Was she? Sex, yes, but dating?

'No.' She stopped. 'Possibly.' She thought of Frank holding her hand, his hand on her foot. She had been so absorbed in his grief that she hadn't thought it was anything more than his seeking comfort, like a child.

'If he's playing me,' she said suddenly, 'why was he stupid enough to make a pass at me before Alison died?'

Declan looked slightly agitated. 'Natalie, you need to send him to see a therapist. Whether he is...responsible for these murders or not...being involved isn't healthy for you.'

'It's too late, I am involved.' Natalie sounded harsher than she intended. 'When he told me I looked hot—was that to pull me in, or let me know that once he got through this he would be available? What do you think?'

Declan put the pencil down with a clatter. 'Natalie, you are over involved. You're too close to this.' She waited. After a moment he sighed. 'Okay, yes, that's possible. If he has a strong narcissistic structure he would want an adoring woman in the wings. He would also probably consider himself infallible, so that a mistake wouldn't be any real risk to him.'

Declan looked like he regretted the outburst. Maybe she had got it wrong: maybe it wasn't her that Declan was concerned about. Frank being a colleague seemed to be really getting to him. Maybe Declan was over involved too.

Natalie returned to her Collingwood warehouse after seeing her Monday patients. It felt odd returning home; neither there nor the stilt house by the sea felt quite like a place she belonged. It was about not being comfortable in her own skin, she supposed. Trying to be something she wasn't had left her feeling lost.

She had organised to meet Damian around the corner at a bar called Naked for Satan. He wanted to buy her dinner, she wanted to eat tapas and hear about the afternoon's interview with Reeva's parents. In particular, the answers to the questions she'd asked him to cover.

'The Osbournes are pretty well off,' said Damian. 'Leafy suburbs, old house on the outside, all glass and stainless steel renovations on the inside. Colin, Reeva's dad, is a senior manager with Toyota.'

'A salesman?'

'Was. Still more down to earth than your professor; got the impression they didn't have much in common.' Damian paused. 'I asked him how he would have sold a car to Frank.'

'And?' Natalie was impressed with the question. Not one she would have thought of.

Damian grinned. 'He's good. Said that to sell to Frank he'd make sure Frank did all the talking and thought it was his idea.'

'How about her mother?'

'Conned.' Damian swallowed a bite-sized morsel and winced.

'Don't like anchovies?'

Damian shook his head and took a swig of sangria.

'Did you ask about a family history of mental illness?'

'Yes. And yes. Reeva's grandmother had postpartum psychosis. Is that relevant?'

'Might be.'

'There was something more interesting though.' Damian waited until he had her full attention. 'Gail Osbourne says that at the wedding, at Mount Malosevic, she overheard one of the guests say she wished Reeva better luck than her predecessor. Might mean nothing.'

'But it does mean we need to find out about our good professor's previous love life,' said Natalie, licking the oil off her fingers. 'He was thirty-six when he married Reeva. He must have had one.'

'According to her parents they had only been going out for two or three years prior to that.'

'So there could be several girlfriends before her, but it sounds as if this particular one would have been local. Want to make a bet?'

'About what?'

'About her profession.'

'You think she'll be a doctor?'

'No,' said Natalie. 'I think that's exactly what she won't be.'

I shouldn't have been surprised when we ended up talking about my father. Funerals had been on my mind, after all. And it wasn't as though I wanted to talk about Alison. My mind had been in a fog since first seeing her lying so still under the covers. Her face such a healthy pink colour, it hadn't occurred to me that she was dead. I stood in the doorway and looked at her lying there, and it was her stillness that alerted me to the problem before I thought about the gas.

I didn't hurry. There was no point really. Except to turn off the gas and open the windows so as to not to succumb to the same fate. I put my hand to her abdomen. Only a week earlier I had seen an elbow and foot jut out as Harry squirmed. I felt tears, hot on my cold face, and wished for all the things that could not be, things that death, this death in particular, put an end to.

I came alive, the fog lifting with Natalie's barely disguised attempts to get me to talk. Women have always found me attractive. My female teachers were often inclined towards leniency, some even inclined to spend spare time with me. It was useful at times, though I never found older women particularly appealing. Miss Sandrine Williams was only five years my senior when she decided to initiate me into the adult world. She thought me quite gifted. She was not; but I did very well in history that year. She also thought I showed great promise, which I did, but not in history.

Wendell Moreton was not much of a ladies' man in my memory but in photos he is handsome enough. Vesna thought him sufficiently charming to let him sweep her off to the other side of the world. She told Mala and me that he was smart and hardworking and ambitious, which I suppose was true. He held a diplomatic post at one stage; he could have been someone important. Instead he became a dead drunk.

But I had other, better male role models; my grandfather was considered something of a demi-god by women. In photos the younger Antonije was handsome, certainly, but it is the twinkle in his eye and a certain bravado in his stance that jump off the page. In my favourite photo he is with my grandmother just after he had rescued her from the Ustaše at the end of World War Two. A bear of a man, with rifles and ammunition strapped to him, she little more than a child. Lost and clutching him as her saviour.

Of course he saved me too. At the end of the whiteness and sobs of my memory, he is there. I picture him as he was in the photo but in real life he was older—and would hardly have been wearing a partisan outfit—in 1982 when he arrived in England to bring his daughter and her children home.

My own father disappointed me; curious that I used that word with Natalie but it was true at many levels. Mostly Wendell was dead and unavailable, but Antonije stepped into the role effortlessly. We never went to an Arsenal game, but I did spend hours in the boathouse talking to him as he painted, sometimes with Mala painting next to him or posing for him. She did that even when she was very young. And I suppose I watched his succession of girlfriends: Lyuba had died long before I was born and he never remarried. How could I not come to the conclusion—in this house of women who adored me and with my role model adored by women—that this was my destiny too? It wasn't anything I ever really questioned. Girlfriends were just never a problem.

But I was a problem for them. All young men, are, I imagine, are a little heartless if they can get away with it. I have to say I am ashamed of some of my behaviour. I wasn't always as polite as I should have been. I embraced good manners in my thirties.

I had previously imagined Natalie would be most interested in my mother but I am sure we will get to that. As it happened, discussing my father gave me opportunities to have her ponder the dark depths of my psyche. She is a worthy combatant. Different, more street savvy than my very focused first wife. And of course far more knowledgeable about psychopathology than Reeva, whose brilliance was in the twists of DNA, cytokines and inflammation. In the end Reeva's lack of knowledge was her undoing; and Natalie's knowledge may in turn be hers.

'I'm having dinner with him.'

'Where?'

'I don't need a bodyguard.'

'He's a suspect in two murders, Natalie. I'm not taking risks on a third.'

'He only bumps off wives—Bluebeard, remember?'

Damian was silent on the other end of the phone.

'Okay, okay. I'm in town and so is he. We're eating at Huxtable in Smith Street.'

'Is it purely coincidental that it's about a hundred metres from your warehouse?'

'No. Means I can walk there. And no, he isn't invited back afterwards.'

Another silence.

'Cross my heart.' She could tell he only half-believed her, but the restaurant was too small for Damian to turn up and not be noticed, so he'd have to lump it. She could look after herself. Or so she told herself when she woke in the middle of the night drenched in sweat and gasping for air.

*

Frank had suggested the restaurant, which indicated to her immediately that he had done his homework and wanted her to know. If he knew her better he'd have suggested Huxtaburger—the takeaway joint opposite, but still. It meant he was either indicating an interest—or a warning. And it left her edgy, in an alive way that she hadn't felt with a man since Liam. Whatever else could be said for Frank, he was intellectually stimulating. She had taken less quetiapine too, it was true, but she needed to be on alert and she didn't want the sedation. She promised herself she'd take extra that night. It would have the added benefit of helping her sleep through any nightmares.

Frank was in charm mode. Dulled at the edges just now, of course, and his smiles were no more than fleeting, but his focus was on her, totally. Even the young waitress with the short skirt didn't get a second look, and she was trying. He let Natalie talk and made it easy for her. The slight nod of encouragement. The suggestion he could block out two possible murder charges and two dead wives, just for her and her inane chatter about how she had ended up buying a Ducati—minus the mania that drove the particular choice. He seemed to know she'd been in an accident. Or maybe people who didn't ride motorbikes just assumed all motorbike riders ended up getting scraped off the road at some point. He almost got the history of her accident and Eoin's death out of her until she changed the topic.

But the brush with the subject of past loves gave her the intro she was looking for. 'How about you? There must have been a long string of heartbroken nurses and doctors before Reeva?' She didn't look at him, didn't want to risk giving away that she had an agenda.

'No one serious. I was too busy.'

'Would they have said the same?' This time she smiled, teasing him with her look, but leaving him no doubt she had his measure.

He held her look. 'Probably no different to the trail you left behind.' He paused. 'So I imagine.'

In the pause she thought of Liam. Her hand gripped the glass, smile still in place. 'Relationships suck.'

Frank raised an eyebrow and she reminded herself that the new Natalie wouldn't say something like that. And the old Natalie wouldn't be sitting in a trendy bistro eating crab noodles and tempura eggplant fritters. Particularly dressed in a floral skirt, even if the flowers were dark and nondescript; even if she had at least paired it with her leather jacket.

'Ahh...can be fraught,' she amended lamely.

'First loves fall the hardest, don't you think?'

She stared. 'Yes, I guess they do.' She twirled her fork in the noodles. 'Tell me about yours.'

'Nothing remarkable. Just too young to settle down. I went off to medical school and she didn't. I went out with a dozen or so others, but no one was special, not until Reeva. A couple of psychiatry registrars, now colleagues.' He took a sip of wine. 'I could tell you a story of two, Gillian Lang and Victoria Moore, though maybe I'll save that for my memoirs. Change names so I'm not sued.'

Natalie vaguely recognised the names; Gillian was an academic specialising in eating disorders. Victoria was in private practice. From memory they were both attractive; one blonde, one brunette.

'Gillian worked with one of your colleagues,' Frank continued. 'Jay.'

She frowned.

'Jay Wadhwa.'

Great. Frank looked smug, showing he'd checked her out. She certainly hadn't given Wadhwa as a referee. No, Frank was smug about something else. She replayed the conversation. Yes. He'd told her something, then headed her away in the direction he wanted to go; any direction except the one she had been looking. And it suggested he'd really checked her out if he knew about Eoin.

'I haven't seen my first love since I was sixteen. Half a lifetime ago.' She looked directly at Frank. 'Do you see your first love around?' He had, she thought, believed he could tease her with his knowledge and then thought she wouldn't linger there. He was wrong. He took time to answer.

'She's still there in Lorne as far as I know. An artist. Probably what attracted her to me; she mistakenly thought I was going to be another Antonije.'

There couldn't be that many female artists of the right age in Lorne.

He lingered over their farewell, waiting, Natalie was sure, for an invitation. When he kissed her cheek and whispered thank you into her ear she almost issued one; another drink and she was sure she could get closer to his core, to understanding how he thought. She recalled the maternal impulse she'd felt before and wondered how the need to care for him gelled with finding him appealing as a potential partner. When he looked at her, the Natalie that woke drenched in sweat, the one whose loneliness swamped her in moments of despair, felt that he could be the answer to everything. But it was Damian's words that she thought of as she pulled away, squeezing his hands.

Missing her normal life, she decided to stop off at her usual pub for a Jack Daniels to help her sleep—Vince the owner and his son, Benny were both there; Benny greeted her warmly but Vince rolled his eyes.

'Figured you'd be turning up.'

'And how did you figure that Vince?'

Vince inclined his head to the right. 'He's come in a few times.'

Liam was sitting in the same corner he had been on their very first date, which had actually been a meeting about a case. Guinness in hand, just like then too. She was tempted to down her bourbon and turn on her heel. But he'd think she was running—and she would never let a man, least of all Liam, think that. So she walked to his table and stood there waiting.

'Can we talk?' Liam wasn't smiling.

'There's nothing to say, Liam.'

'How about your objection?'

'I'd prefer to deal with that through the court.'

Liam looked at his drink, contemplating his next move. Natalie watched him warily. They hadn't left on the best of terms. She had threatened him with blackmail to save a patient he was prosecuting. He wasn't to know she'd never have gone through with it.

'We have unfinished business,' Liam finally said.

Natalie downed her drink so she could leave, but his look stopped her. It said *you owe me*. And she did. Out of the corner of her eye she caught Vince's disapproving stare.

'Okay,' said Natalie. 'I'll hear you out. But let's not put a show on here. My place.'

She turned without looking back; he knew the way, barely a hundred metres from the pub. She didn't hear him behind her and left the door open, using the time to steel herself. She figured it wasn't going to be pretty.

He took his time. Perhaps five minutes, but it felt like fifteen. His tread was soft on the stair, and standing at the top in the lamplight he looked good. Far, far, too good. He didn't make any attempt to come in further, watching her like a cat about to pounce. Natalie smiled tightly, stepped towards him, challenging him to do his worst.

'First things first,' Liam said softly. 'No one blackmails me.'

Natalie winced, but didn't speak. Too late now to explain, and it wouldn't have satisfied him anyway.

'And just so you know, it was totally ineffective,' Liam continued. 'Your stalker did his worst—Lauren knew about our affair within a week of that particular conversation.'

Which meant Natalie had never had anything to blackmail him with.

Natalie groaned. 'Oh Liam, I am so sorry. I never wanted that.' She took a breath. This did change things. Why had he gone along with what she'd wanted?

'You threatened it.' Liam had stepped closer, anger in the tone of his voice and the tension of his shoulders. 'But you see Dr King, *I* can sleep straight at nights because I, unlike you, did not compromise my integrity.'

Natalie stiffened.

'The facts of the case pointed to the person who pleaded guilty,' Liam continued. 'I did my job.' He paused. 'Did you?'

He went on, eyes narrowing, 'And you *dared* to bring my personal life into the equation.'

Natalie took a breath. 'I didn't get off scot free, if that helps.' Months of depression. Shock treatment. 'I would never have told her.'

'Justice,' said Liam, 'is my job, not yours.'

She wondered if Lauren had thrown him out. Whether

147

he saw his kids at all—because it had always been about them more than his wife. It wasn't as if Natalie had been his first indiscretion.

There was another pause. Some of the tension in him seemed to ease subtly.

'You're looking good, Natalie.' He leaned in closer. To her irritation she felt her heart race, felt the desire for him as strong as it had ever been. He leaned down to her ear. 'Have you missed me?'

Missed him? She hadn't thought of anything else for six weeks. But no way in hell was she telling him that. 'I think you should go.'

'One drink?'

'No Liam, bad idea.' She couldn't risk going there again. Sacrifices, Declan had said. Liam was one of them.

'I bought you some bourbon.' He held up the bottle, but it was the way he amped up his Irish accent that made her stomach drop.

She didn't answer. She had already had an evening of verbal sparring; she no longer had the energy to think about her behaviour or analyse anyone else's.

She could hear her own heartbeat pounding in her ears. Liam didn't move, stood on the last step, watching her. Why was he here? She didn't want to think about it; was aware only of a rekindling of the longing she had tried to bury. His anger had made him all the more dangerous, and impossibly, all the more attractive. The curl over his eye, the cocky stance, the whole sense of him being comfortable with himself and his place in the world. Was this why she had been drawn to him, because he could take it up to her, because he'd liked her just as she was?

She looked at him now, wondered in those seconds

where his anger had gone, whether the longing she read in his look was tempered by other, darker, emotions.

It was Liam who moved first. Or at least that was what her memory told her later. But she moved too, any hesitancy disappearing in the moment of his first step. They sank into the kiss, her last rational thought being that she'd worry about the aftermath tomorrow.

He tasted of liquor and she wondered how much he had drunk, whether he had needed it to break down the barriers that led to her door, and why now after so long?

Against her his body had none of the gentle hesitance of Damian's, nor the soft privilege she sensed in Frank's touch. It was a body she knew and missed, wanted though she knew she shouldn't. She moaned gently as his hands moved over her, felt his need of her as strong as hers was for him.

He pushed her hard against the wall. Whispered, 'You are such a bitch' in her ear before kissing her again, a bruising, intense kiss that she returned with just as much force. In those moments she forgot all the pain of the past months, all her hard work, the tentative steps to be a different person, to try a relationship with someone that was good for her rather than someone who was dangerous at every level.

Sex with Liam was intoxicating, an addiction. She laughed when, in the rush to run hands over each other, her boring floral top ripped down the front. Felt alive with his touch, an electricity surging through her that the gentleness of Damian couldn't hope to compete with. Liam was, she was certain, every bit as aroused as her; he took her, pushed up against the wall, her legs wrapped around him, finishing with them both exhausted on the floor.

But he didn't wait as their breathing eased back to normal, or linger to savour the feeling of skin on skin. He was standing up almost immediately, clothes on before she even rolled over.

'Now,' he said, not looking at her, 'we're done.'

He succeeded, she thought later. If it was revenge he was after, he got it.

She didn't sleep, just stared at the ceiling. Feeling the humiliation burn in her gut. Thinking of how she was destined, like Frank, not to live happily ever after.

I may have underestimated her—not an experience with which I am familiar. People by and large are both gullible and predictable. She is neither, nor is she the type to which I am usually attracted, apart from her intellectual capabilities. There is a brittleness to her, an unknown territory. Perhaps I'll be able to use this to my advantage if necessary. I have more than enough to occupy my thoughts, yet I find they keep turning back to her.

The challenges with her are far more edifying than the tedious discussions with DSS McBride. I waited in a poky room that smelled faintly of urine while Mala was interviewed. We had a moment together as she passed the baton (personified by our lawyer, Amy, who insisted on being present). Mala, hovering in the doorway, out of earshot, rolled her eyes. 'All the usual questions.' She paused, squeezed my hands, looking at me carefully. 'I tried to be helpful.'

'Meaning?'

'They wanted to know what I thought.'

I nodded. 'Which is?'

Mala sighed. She had her hair pulled up into a bun. Her

serious look, but I doubt if it made her any less distracting to the two male cops. 'I'm sorry. But I do think Reeva more than likely killed herself. Alison?' She shrugged. 'An accident I guess.'

'They didn't ask about Vesna?'

'Only about how she got on with your wives.'

'To which you answered?'

'Honestly. She's not the first woman to have issues with her daughters-in-law. Don't worry, I don't think she's in their sights.'

Mala was told she could go, and she elected to wait for me in the café around the corner. My turn. The focus was, predictably, on the night Alison died.

'What were you fighting about?'

It was the hormones, she was irritable. Nothing serious. All married couples fight. She hadn't been sleeping. Neither Alison nor Reeva slept well. Or any other woman at thirty-nine weeks pregnant. The uterus rests on the bladder; they need to get up frequently.

'Isn't it a little strange that you were not sleeping in the same room with either of your wives the night they died?'

As above. The same questions, the same answers, occasional objections from Amy.

'Did you love your wives?' 'You remarried quickly.' 'Had you grieved for your first wife?' I caught a trace of Natalie in that question coming from DSS McBride. He was polite, hadn't moved into bad-cop mode, not yet. None of them had, all hedging around me, my status, my lawyer. To say nothing of the absence of proof.

DSS McBride leaned back in his chair. This was the second time I had been asked to visit the Lorne police station. Amy told me I didn't have to, but what's the sense in antagonising them? My wives died in tragic accidents.

'I'd just like to go through this with you again.' He looked apologetic but I wasn't fooled. 'Can we start with that morning?'

Now this was a shift. Previous conversations had started with our meeting at the pub. The police assumed I had been eating there with her and I hadn't dissuaded them of the belief. They had assumed we had arrived together. Not that I had lied; they just needed to ask the right question. I imagined that now they had got Senka to talk. She didn't have her father's sense of family duty. They had no interest in the mundane details of life as an academic. But I made sure I told him in absolute detail of the day. McBride managed to maintain concentration, which is more than I could say for his overweight sidekick.

'And after you left Canberra?'

'I met one of my researchers for a drink at Wye River pub.' If he knew where I was going he showed no indication. But then he would have steeled himself to look blank. Perhaps I could test that. 'You've met her. Natalie.' I paused, but he just kept taking notes. 'I rang her and she was there later that night,' I continued, annoyed that he wasn't showing me simple courtesy.

'Yes. Dr King,' he said, still not looking at me. 'You were there at the pub how long?'

I told him, told him Alison met me and we went straight home.

'So how did you get there?' DSS McBride asked.

'My own car, I had left it at the airport.'

'So you didn't need a lift?'

Obviously no. I smiled.

'So why did Alison come if you weren't eating there?'

'We changed our mind.'

DSS McBride didn't bother hiding his disbelief. 'And when did the fight with your wife start?'

'Immediately.' I smoothed the crease in my trousers.

'And remind me, what was it about?'

'I had been away. She thought I should have sent someone else to Canberra rather than going myself.' He still wasn't looking at me. Thinking of fucking Natalie perhaps. I imagined she might be entertaining. 'Though choosing to keep my appointment with Natalie...Dr King...That didn't help.'

This got his attention. He didn't see the smile but it was there, deep beneath my concern.

'Would you like to expand on that, Professor Moreton?' His eyes are hazel, nondescript. Flecks of green. Steely in their focus now, though.

'Alison didn't like me talking to Natalie. She was... insecure. But I had been very anxious about Alison's pregnancy. After Reeva I mean, and Alison wouldn't allow me to talk about Reeva so Natalie...understood. Being a doctor I mean.'

The fat cop sat forward in his seat, wide awake now. 'Sounds like things were pretty tough at home. Must have been tempting to pass time with this Natalie. Another doctor, right? Hot is she?'

I watched DSS McBride's mouth tighten. This was almost enjoyable.

'I haven't really noticed. But my wife was in the same year as her at med school. She apparently had a *reputation*.'

I would have liked to see McBride's response but he was back looking at his note pad.

'I mean, yes, she's attractive. But I was worried about my

wife, detective, not thinking about having an affair.'

'Were you? Poking her?' The fat cop was no sophisticate.

I winced. 'No detective, I was not. Nor was I having sex with her in any shape or form.' I was looking at McBride when I added, 'You only have to ask her if you don't believe me.'

Georgia had lost weight. She was intense and anxious, pacing the consulting room. But apart from that, Natalie was impressed by how well she was holding it together.

'Are you self-harming?'

'Sometimes.' Georgia stopped for a moment. 'The mindfulness techniques work for a while but then I keep thinking how unfair everything is.'

'Unfair in what way?'

'Every way.' Georgia slumped in the chair. She looked depressed and despairing. 'Who would choose to change places with me? With any part of my life.'

She had a point. But all of Natalie's patients could say the same. Abusive childhoods, domestic violence, mental illness. 'It is about your future now, the choices you make,' Natalie said. It was as true of her own life as Georgia's.

'I'm not going to have a choice am I?' Georgia looked at Natalie pointedly.

'Nor do I,' said Natalie evenly. 'When I'm sworn in I have to tell the truth.'

'Psychiatrists' truth seems to be rather subjective.'

'It's not an exact science.'

'Then how are you so sure you know what happened?'

'I'm not.' Natalie looked at Georgia, wishing she did know.

'Well, what do you think happened?'

Natalie pondered the answer to this. It wasn't as if she hadn't thought about it. 'I think your reality is blurred, full of mixed emotions. That your children crying and needing you, rather than adoring you, stirred up a hornet's nest of unresolved longing and need.' And of terror at being seen as not good enough, and the shame of failing.

Georgia looked away. But Natalie could see tears in her eyes. She waited.

'Paul loves me,' she whispered.

'Despite everything, she's still hopeful. Delusional almost.'

Declan nodded gravely. 'She may need it to keep going. Literally, perhaps.'

'She continues idealising Paul because otherwise their whole life together was a sham?'

'Remember she has a disorganised attachment so her defences are primitive and chaotic: idealisation, which you have noted with Paul—and devaluing. There isn't a middle ground for her.'

'Then is she likely to devalue him at some stage?'

'She has held onto him as a narcissistic extension of herself for a long time. If he isn't perfect then she can't be either.'

'I wouldn't call her a perfectionist.'

'Not in the way it is commonly used, no.' Declan finally gave in to a fight he had been waging since she arrived. He opened the bottle of wine and offered her a glass. She declined but was unable to read his response. 'The anxious perfectionist is about controlling her environment to help herself stay in control. Georgia? Georgia is about the perfect relationship.'

They didn't talk about Frank but Declan urged her to get him to a therapist before she left. She thought it curious; Declan usually waited for her to bring a topic up. What was so different about Frank?

Perfect relationships, thought Natalie on the long drive back down the coast.

Narcissists wanted to be adored. Georgia's problem was that babies weren't big on providing that sort of positive feedback, or at least they didn't show it in ways that stoked the ego, which had been Georgia's problem. And Frank... *Dr Perfect* Alison had muttered under her breath the last time they met. What if she hadn't meant Natalie, but Frank? Maybe he was anxious that the baby wouldn't be perfect— perhaps his narcissism couldn't accommodate anything less. Was this what he and Alison fought over? Reeva too, given that they had also ended in separate bedrooms.

The scrap of paper she had found in Reeva's work file listed disorders with possible genetic transmission. If it was to do with her own pregnancy rather than her research, she was worried about some genetic disorder in Frank's family... Perhaps his father could have had some condition Frank was afraid would be transmitted to his child. Damian had given her the obstetrician's records for both women. The tests he'd conducted—Downs, neural tube disorders—were common, especially in older mothers. She tried to think of a recessive disorder Frank's father might have had; something Frank could be a carrier for. Some of the Mediterranean blood disorders, like thalassemia? It seemed farfetched, but she texted Damian asking him to check.

The Bentley—an ancient green relic—crawled cautiously to the bottom of Natalie's drive and the driver unwisely attempted to make it all the way up the steep slope to the door. It took three attempts, and reversing out was going to be entertaining. The man in the driver's seat was wearing a cap, so her guest was presumably the woman in the back, hidden under a broad maroon coloured hat.

The chauffeur, who looked a lot like Drago, stepped out and opened the rear door. A slim bare ankle in flat grey leather pumps slid out, followed by a stick-thin figure, clad in a long black and burgundy dress, part flapper outfit, part kaftan. In her running gear Natalie was going to be at a disadvantage, and if the guest had been Mala she would have assumed that was the point. But it was Vesna, altogether a greater unknown than her daughter.

'Jesus,' she muttered to herself, 'Does Frank's mother think I'm going to be wife number three?'

'You're a complete unknown,' Bob duly contributed.

Vesna, standing on the doorstep, looked startled but didn't comment.

'Vesna. What an unexpected pleasure.' Natalie took the older woman's hand and it felt as though there was no blood flow. Vesna turned and beckoned the chauffeur without saying a word. Instead of following, he went to the boot of the car and filled his arms with flowers.

'From my garden and hothouse.'

Natalie stared. Flowers. Maybe Vesna really did think she was Frank's girlfriend.

'You shouldn't have.' This was what you said in normal

polite society wasn't it? Rather than *You've got to be fucking joking?*

Vesna was already ushering her man upstairs and there was little Natalie could do but follow.

Drago deposited the flowers on the table and withdrew.

Vesna looked around rather as if she'd been put down suddenly on a different planet. Perhaps she didn't leave Mount Malosevic often. Question was: why had she now?

'Tea?' Natalie put the kettle on, somewhat at a loss.

Bob paced his perch in bemusement and finally announced 'Call the cops!' to Vesna's alarm, before flying to the back of a chair.

'He thinks he's Bob Dylan,' said Natalie.

'Really? How...' Vesna was unable to find a suitable adjective.

'The flowers are lovely,' Natalie told her again, 'but you really didn't have to.'

'I like to.' Vesna's hand rubbed along the silk dress on her thigh. 'Mount Malosevic is far too big for just us.' For a moment Natalie wondered if she was actually going to invite her to stay, then she added: 'The flowers need to be enjoyed by more than just my family.'

'You must have lots of visitors seeing the garden.'

'Yes, but strangers. I had thought by my age I would have grandchildren to share it with.'

This family certainly didn't mess around. Natalie decided she'd respond to this as a psychiatrist rather than a future daughter-in-law.

'The last few years must have been very difficult.'

'Difficult?' Her eyes widened. Her lips formed an o.

'The death of your father, then Reeva and Alison.' More than ever, Natalie would have liked to see a toxicology report on this woman. Alcohol? Benzos? Antipsychotics? She tried to check out Vesna's pupils, wondering about opiates, but the irises were so dark it was hard to see where they finished and the pupils began.

'You must be wondering why I am here.'

Natalie let this go.

'Do you like my son, Dr King?' The sudden steeliness in the voice jolted. The woman was sedated, yes, psychotic at times maybe. But not in the dependent regressed manner that had been apparent on the night of Alison's death. Less medication today, perhaps. Or no Mala keeping her in check.

'I don't know him well, Vesna. I feel sorry for him.' If he didn't kill his wives.

'People have always been envious of us, you know,' Vesna said. 'You wouldn't believe the mail, the phone calls. People you know can be quite...cruel.' She looked at the tea Natalie had poured her but showed no inclination to try it.

'I've been exposed to people's cruelties all my life, so I'm used to it, but it's a mother's role to protect her children. He was such a solitary boy, kept so much to himself. He wouldn't talk to me really. Didn't want to worry me.'

What, Natalie wondered, did Vesna think she needed to protect them from now? Natalie, presumably. But what did she think Natalie was going to do?

'Envy drives people to want to tear down those who are successful and better off, you know. I've seen it firsthand.'

'I'm not a threat to Frank, Vesna.' Not strictly true. 'Just a confidante.'

Vesna looked her up and down. 'We stick together, the Malosevics. We always have and it has got us through.'

'Did Alison and Reeva ever truly become Malosevics?' Natalie didn't expect an answer; the woman was paranoid, though maybe with good reason. Google had revealed that her mother had been in a Balkan concentration camp, and then died when Vesna was young. Reason enough not to trust the world.

'Never.'

Natalie was surprised by the firm immediacy of the response, accompanied by a quick look down and to her left that made her wonder what the older woman was hiding. And what 'never' covered.

'Reeva,' Vesna said, 'was concerned only with her career.' She sneered. 'All those papers and science. There is no beauty in science.'

So it was only Frank, not Vesna, who was after more doctors in the family.

'I knew she wasn't caring for him enough because the sleep problems he had as a child came back. Worrying again.'

'And Alison?'

'Alison.' Vesna shook her head, lips pursed as she stood up to leave, tea still untouched. Natalie waited but Vesna had said all she intended to say on the topic of Frank's second wife.

She paused by the flowers as she left. 'Lilies,' she said, 'for purity.'

Purity? Vesna couldn't be talking about her. The desired characteristic of Frank's next wife?

'White carnations,' Vesna continued, 'for good luck.'

She paused at this bunch, fingers running down the edge of the holly leaf that was providing an artistic green contrast. A prickle drew blood but she didn't react, just smiled and turned to Natalie. 'And holly for protection.'

'Protection?' Natalie was looking at the droplet of blood, then drew herself away from it to look into Vesna's vacant eyes. 'From what? Or should I ask...whom?'

Vesna put her finger to her lips and sucked it. 'It isn't wise to trust anyone, in my experience, other than family. You, I think, would be especially unwise to trust Eliza.'

The perfect partner. Do we ever know what we really want? Perhaps. Less so what we need—until we find it.

Evolutionary theory directs us to someone who looks like our own family, for familiarity; it says the prototype is etched in our young minds, formed from those we loved and trusted, of our perfect other. Even if the childhood itself wasn't perfect, the imprint is still there and we chose our partners to fit this pattern. Again and again, good or bad. Unless we choose to alter it.

My partners have not really had a great deal in common, apart from physical attractiveness, which in my twenties I over-valued at the expense of other attributes. Now I know the greater importance of intelligence. The template for these qualities is there within my own family.

Reeva scored high on intelligence, lower on beauty. Alison was a sad compromise on both. Eliza would have been another disappointing compromise, had I ever thought of her as a future partner. And she has become very tiresome.

Natalie isn't classically beautiful but she is more

striking than Reeva, and petite, so she would represent an improvement. I find increasingly that I am drawn to her. I am prepared to see what the future brings.

She wasn't hard to find. There were three artist's studios in Lorne and one of them was owned by Eliza Carson. The door was locked but through the windows Natalie could make out large bright paintings of local birds. She made a note of opening times and planned to come back.

She was too early to meet Frank so she wandered into one of the other galleries.

'Can I help you?' The man's smile revealed a gap between his front teeth. Short, stocky and, she thought, Turkish. Olive skin and a hint of a stubble.

'Possibly. You don't have any of Eliza Carson's work do you?'

The smile faltered and he shook his head, pointing back to where she had come from.

'Anything by Antonije Malosevic?'

Again he shook his head, waving his arms theatrically. 'Of this, I dream. You like his work?'

'I haven't seen any,' Natalie confessed.

The smile was back as he pulled out a large coffee table book titled *Malosevic's Magic*. 'He is very well known, and not just here. All over the world.'

Natalie was the first to admit she knew nothing about art. She turned the pages, at first flicking to get a sense of his style—broadly, was he Rembrandt, Van Gogh or Pollock? Almost instantly, however, she had to turn slower, to try and make sense of what she was seeing. None of her three reference artists was helping. These pictures were almost all black and white, with sometimes startling use of a single colour in an unlikely place. When she looked closer she realised that they were mostly portraits of one to three people, all young women, sometimes posed in what she imagined to be the gardens at Frank's house.

'Those ones are from the series *Memories*,' said her Turkish man. 'The most famous. After *Family* of course.'

'*Family*?'

He nodded vigorously and flipped to the end of the book. There was one photograph: it looked like the painting she had seen in the living area at Mount Malosevic.

'That,' he said, 'is the only one ever seen from that series.' He leaned in towards her and though she wasn't sure why, lowered his voice. 'Other than by the *actual* family of course.'

'So what's meant to be so special about *Family*?'

The man waved his arms again, beaming. 'Malosevic himself said they were his best pieces, which says something. That one...' he pointed to another page. A girl who Natalie thought was probably a young Vesna was standing by a lake. 'That fetched a record price for an Australian painting when it was auctioned in London just after his death.' He mentioned a sum, in hushed tones suggesting he wasn't quite sure it was true.

Natalie took a closer look at it; there was no doubt he had captured a sense of a poignant fragility that might disappear at any second. But it conveyed something else too, as had the work she had seen at the house. Something that left her uneasy.

The Greek restaurant in Lorne where she was meeting Frank was a short walk. *Not* a date, she had told herself and Damian, who hadn't answered several phone calls and had then been short with her when he did pick up. Could Damian have known about Liam? Only if Liam had told him. She felt a coldness in the pit of her stomach. Perhaps that had been part of the revenge plan. Poor Damian; he had a history of relationships where the women screwed other men.

'You always lived here?' Natalie asked over dip and fried cheese, though she knew the answer.

'Ever since my father died. Mala was only a baby and my mother...didn't cope well.'

'Depression?' Or psychosis? Maybe this was the beginning of the pills and being spaced out.

'Grief, depression,' said Frank. 'She's had a hard life.'

Natalie waited expectantly.

'Her mother died when she was a child. She adored my grandfather, but he expected too much of her.'

Natalie pondered that *too much*. 'She cared for him?'

'Yes, and posed for him. Growing up we would be stopped in the street by people who recognised her from Antonije's work.'

Natalie wondered how much of a childhood Vesna had had, with her mother dying young. 'She came to see me. Your mother.'

Frank put the piece of bread he had just run through the tzatziki down on his plate.

'Brought me flowers,' Natalie continued. If Frank thought this was odd he wasn't showing it. Nor did he look worried. What had he told Vesna about her? Maybe she had made her own assumptions? There hadn't been much time between his wives; perhaps Vesna was assuming he'd continue in the same vein. Natalie felt a moment of discomfort. Frank had been 'seeing' her before Alison died.

'How are your mother and sister coping?'

'As well as can be expected.'

'Does your sister work?'

'She runs the Malosevic Trust.'

He saw her look and continued. 'My grandfather wanted to support young artists, and left a trust for scholarships to be awarded from the interest. It also funds the upkeep of the house and grounds and the functions that are held there.'

'So you kind of live in a museum?'

'In a way, I suppose. Mala has always had a passion for it.'

'You don't paint?'

'Me? No, a talent that passed me by.'

'Mala isn't married?'

'No. She…there have been relationships but I think it's hard to find anyone to fill Antonije's shoes.'

'So it's not your father who was the big influence.'

'No, she never knew him; Antonije raised her.'

'Not your mother?'

'Vesna, yes, of course she did too.'

Natalie helped herself to some charcoal-grilled lamb from the platter that had arrived. 'Are you close to her?'

'We have always been a close family. Probably because we've had to be. We've had our fair share of tragedy.'

'So play the game with me.' She smiled, aiming for

beguiling. 'Five words for your relationship with your mother as a child?'

'As a child? Loving. Responsible. Tiring. Caring. Can I pass with just four?' His smile was all boy-scout, thinking he was better at this than her.

'Responsible. You said that with your father too.'

'Yes I did, didn't I? But for totally different reasons.'

She let the pause hang.

'With my father it was about learning to be responsible, with my mother I felt I was responsible.'

'Which was tiring?'

'At times. She wasn't well when I was growing up.'

'She seems even now...fragile?'

'She isn't as fragile as she appears, but yes. Doesn't always manage life well.'

'This must be difficult for her. Did she like Alison?'

'Yes, but she was worried; she doesn't trust readily. And it seems she was right.'

Right to not trust Alison? Or that fate was capricious? Natalie had the sense Frank was managing the conversation, had been prepared for it, which suggested he worried about Vesna. Or what Vesna might say.

They ate in silence for a moment then he said, 'I've thought of a fifth word, a phrase really, it popped into my head. *Alice down the rabbit hole.* It was a little like that. My mother can be rather unexpected.'

'She told me to beware of Eliza.'

'Oh dear.' Frank didn't miss a beat. He took a bite of his bread, chewed and swallowed. Playing for time? 'I'm afraid my mother never liked poor Eliza.'

'Girlfriend?'

'Many years ago, yes.' Taramasalata dropped onto the

table and Frank took a moment to wipe it carefully with his napkin. It was, Natalie mused, the first time his attention had strayed from her since they had sat down to eat. He was capable of being very intense, to the point of being almost too close, too interested. But she—and others, she was certain—let him get away with it. Perhaps it was the angelic face. Hard to imagine anything but good intentions lay behind it.

'She lives in Lorne,' Frank added, his eyes returning to meet hers.

'So why would your mother think I had something to be concerned about?'

The smile never wavered. 'As I said, my mother never liked her, didn't think she had enough *class*. It didn't end all that well.'

Natalie wanted to ask what he meant by that but she had the feeling he would just hedge around it. In any event, better to hear it from Eliza.

After dinner they walked out to the carpark and Frank took her hand. For a moment Natalie thought he was going to kiss her and wondered what she would do. Then she thought Frank used this intense look with everyone, or everyone he wanted something from. In the end his lips brushed over the skin of her hand as he bowed his head and thanked her for her company. She was left wondering what a real kiss would have been like.

'Do you have a list of all the GP training rotations?' This was the third person Natalie had been put through to. 'I need to chase up the doctors that came to do psychiatry in Geelong. We're having a reunion.'

Lame, but the administrator didn't care one way or another.

'Online. Look under *Training*, then under speciality.' The phone went dead.

It only took a few minutes to navigate. Alison Cunningham. Her final term before qualifying as a general practitioner; six months in Geelong. The start date was seven months before Reeva died.

Damian was waiting for her the next night; he'd let himself in with the key she kept hidden.

'If you're planning on staying you'll have the crowd. We're on tomorrow tonight at the Lorne pub.'

'If that means we're sharing I guess I'll manage.'

She looked at him sharply. He looked tired. Long hours on this case and getting nowhere. And he was juggling another case as well, so the travel alone would be exhausting. No looks of recrimination; the guilt was all hers. She decided not to tell him about Liam. Even though Damian and she didn't have anything official going—and although he'd work hard on hiding it—it would hurt him. And she hadn't exactly invited Liam around, nor did she expect to hear from him again. Except in court.

Over fish they cooked on the barbeque, both rugged up against the cold, he brought her up to date. She sensed she was getting a sanitised version. Because he didn't trust her, or because he was a stickler for protocol, she couldn't be sure.

'I found the old girlfriend,' she finally told him.

'How?'

'Frank was evasive so I don't think it was information he was keen to share, but his mother helped things along.' She explained the odd visit. 'Paranoid personality, by the way.'

'Dangerous?'

Natalie watched a pair of kookaburras perched on the balcony eyeing off the heat rising from the barbeque. 'I don't think so. Not easy to live with, probably vicious if she thinks you're after her...'

Damian raised an eyebrow. 'How vicious?'

'Verbal. I think.' But she couldn't be totally sure. In her own house with Vesna the atmosphere hadn't been as malevolent—but it hadn't been comfortable either. At Mount Malosevic, where both of Frank's wives had died, the presence of Antonije seeped through the crevices.

'Are we talking about the girlfriend?' Damian paused with tongs in mid-air. A kookaburra edged closer. She imagined that in winter, without the tourists to feed them, times were lean.

'No, Vesna. My guess is that her mother, a concentration camp survivor, was beset with anxiety and well-founded paranoia. So she modelled the fear of the world for Vesna, but she also was unable to deal with Vesna's emotions, escalating rather than containing. When she died Vesna must have been only six or so, thus confirming how unsafe the world is.'

'And dads can't make up for it?'

'Not hers. Too into himself would be my guess. Neglectful, or maybe very critical. Wouldn't be surprised if there was more between them, too. Sexual maybe. She used to paint with him; she was probably never good enough.'

Damian paused, taking in the information. Cops probably found the sick stuff even harder than psychiatrists. 'So the girlfriend?' he asked finally.

'Eliza Carson.'

Damian's pause this time was long enough for the kookaburra pair to execute their assault. They swooped from opposite directions, taking a flathead tail each, straight from the grill, and Natalie had to duck.

'Lucky I wasn't hungry.' Food had lost its appeal over the last day or so and she feared she might be getting depressed again. She'd finally stopped the antidepressants but the risk she still needed them gnawed at her. As much as she hated taking pills, the fear of the black abyss at the edge of her consciousness was greater. It wouldn't take much to trigger her bipolar. She wasn't exactly experiencing the stress-free life style Declan had prescribed, and the lithium she was still taking was better protection against the highs than the lows.

Damian took the remaining fish off the barbeque and they adjourned inside.

'Her name came up in Alison's diary.' He had clearly thought before telling her this gem. 'Eliza was the last person Alison called before she went to meet Frank at the pub.' He put the fish on plates and she added the bowl of salad greens she'd dumped out of their plastic bag into a bowl on the table. She hadn't thought to buy any dressing. '…Where he was with you.'

The tone of the voice said everything his words hadn't. This was what was behind the tension then. Not Liam.

'We'd been meeting there once a week,' Natalie replied. 'And I didn't see her.'

They ate in silence until he finally gave her a piece of information she had asked for.

'Frank wasn't lying about the woman his father killed. She was pregnant.'

Natalie nodded, unsurprised. Frank wouldn't lie about something he could so easily be caught out on.

'But there is an interesting twist,' said Damian. 'Her baby survived.'

Natalie stared.

'She was still alive when they got her to hospital and they did an emergency caesarian. A boy.'

I knew we'd get to my mother. Psychiatrists have been blaming mothers for most of the last century. Of course we have moved onto the concept of epigenetics now; the interplay of genes and environment, and can include a good deal more than just mothers in the list of potential abuses. Natalie is curiously old fashioned in her tendency to overvalue psychodynamics as causal of our life problems. She should have asked about family history; but then I suppose that's harder to drop into conversation.

Mothers are meant to give unconditional love. Vesna gave love as best she could; just always with strings attached.

'Would you mind getting Mummy...' The refrain from my childhood. But I never minded. Her smile was reward enough. 'My little man', she'd say, and 'our little secret'. But nothing I ever got her was enough to take away the ever-present anxiety that followed her wherever she went.

I daresay Natalie's preoccupation with psychodynamics is a consequence of her accident. Too much time to contemplate one's own mortality at such a young age. At ten, after my father's death, I was too young to think along these lines, and my sleepwalking was a temporary solution from the unconscious.

Genes are clearly the driving force in our lives. Identical twin studies show glaring similarities between subjects, even those raised apart. Genetic abnormalities such as Down syndrome have massive impacts. Environment has an effect, no doubt. But subtle differences in rearing between siblings can hardly account for the disparities that often exist between them.

In any case, there are far too many permutations and combinations to imagine. Mala never met Wendell, who raised me for ten years, yet we are in many ways similar. Smart, ambitious, family-focused. The common factors are genetic.

Natalie's genetics are interesting; perhaps we will be able to discuss it some time. I wonder if she knows who her biological father is. Not the man who raised her, it seems. Perhaps that's why she asked me about my father first. Her own unresolved issues.

After the band had left the next day, Natalie sat drinking coffee, looking out at the mist rolling in over the sea and thinking about Frank and his family. Smoothed out in front of her was the piece of paper on which she had jotted down his home phone number the night Alison died.

It took until the end of the second coffee before she rang. It was a young girl, Senka presumably, who answered.

'Is Mala there?' Natalie asked.

Senka didn't bother replying; the phone clattered in Natalie's ear and then there was silence until a minute later a voice came on.

'Mala Malosevic.'

Interesting. Not Mala Moreton. Still, a famous name might be more than enough reason to change. And she had never known her father.

'This is Natalie King.'

'How uncanny!' There was a light musical laughter. 'Please tell me you're free for brunch.'

Natalie's phone slid through her fingers. She caught it just before it hit the floor. 'That is...a bit freaky.'

'You were thinking the same? Vesna would say our fates

have aligned. Is Apollo Bay too far? There is a café that does a good breakfast.'

Mala offered to pick her up but Natalie elected to ride. The Great Ocean Road was a dream for motorcycles and fast cars, particularly out of season. The Ducati made easy work of the terrain. The absence of traffic meant Natalie could take racetrack lines, braking hard into corners and then accelerating hard out and along the straight sections. No V8 in sight.

She was there first, getting seated on the upstairs veranda behind plastic curtains zipped at the edges but still not able to completely stop the wind from whipping under them. She left her leathers on, and a heater above her meant any exposed body was adequately warm.

Below she saw a silver sports car, top down, park opposite. The roof glided into place as Mala stepped out in a full-length fur coat, scarf and hat. Straight out of *Dr Zhivago*. Impossibly exotic, but today felt cold enough. Certainly in a convertible.

Mala took off the fur and shook out her hair. Her cheek was cold against Natalie's as she brushed a kiss on both sides, continental style.

'Sometimes I think winter here is never going to end,' Mala said breathlessly, nodding to the waitress who was offering them coffee from a dripolator jug.

'You look well prepared.'

'This?' Mala handed the coat to the waitress, who looked as if she was unsure what to do with it. Under the coat her clothes were plain but expensive: a green silk shirt and well cut dark trousers. 'Courtesy of my time at Oxford. English weather is so dismal.'

'What were you doing at Oxford?'

'A post-doc in art history,' said Mala. 'Though I never finished it.'

Natalie smiled, encouraging.

'I came back for my grandfather's funeral,' she said. 'Then stayed for the wedding.'

'Frank left it late, didn't he?'

Mala smiled. But something in her eyes said *I know where you are going with this*. 'He was busy with his career.' She turned to the menu and called the waitress over to order.

'You didn't go back? To Oxford?'

'No. After Antonije died there was the estate to organise, then the wedding and then...I felt Frank needed me around.'

'Reeva dying must have been a shock.'

'It was,' said Mala. 'They say, don't they, that things go in threes? Perhaps now our bad luck has ended.'

Threes? Antonije, Reeva and Alison? Or Eliza, Reeva, Alison? Reeva, Alison...and her?

'Your mother visited me,' said Natalie. 'I thought I'd ring because I wondered...I had the sense that you were all a bit cut off up on the hill.'

'Cut off?' Mala laughed. 'Oh, I never feel like that. Frank thinks I must miss Oxford and London but the truth is I found them rather boring.'

London and Oxford boring? Natalie couldn't imagine it; she hadn't travelled further than New Zealand, but maybe that was the problem.

'I don't like *old*,' Mala explained. 'And England is stuck in another century. Now, New York—things happen here.'

'Very different to the north Lorne hinterland.' Though a little too much was happening there.

'True,' said Mala. 'But there's time.'

'You're waiting for...?'

Mala's perfectly sculpted eyebrows lifted. 'You're not trying to get me out of the picture are you?'

Natalie inwardly cursed herself. 'I'm sorry. Of course not. I meant, I wondered what kept you here. Myself, I'm finding country living a little...dull.'

Mala seemed amused. Or pleased to have the upper hand. 'I was waiting for Frank to be the happy father. But it wasn't meant to be.'

'Was he happy with Alison?'

Mala looked up from the long fingernails she was checking. 'You knew Alison. What do you think?' Her words were polite but Natalie detected a challenge.

'I think why and how people choose their partners is a bit of a mystery.'

Mala laughed. 'You are so right! I knew I was going to like you.'

'You didn't like Alison.' Natalie was careful to inflect her tone down; this wasn't a question.

'Alison was neurotic.' Mala giggled, then seemed to remember Alison was dead. She straightened her face. 'She had listeria hysteria, ever heard of it?'

Listeria was a bacteria: she'd never heard of it causing hysteria.

'Poor Alison. Gordana used to serve up every meal with a touch of some forbidden food, you know, the ones that can damage the foetus. Gordana thought it was nonsense and no amount of Alison laying down the listeria science would convince her otherwise.'

Poor Alison indeed. Mala might not feel isolated at Mount Malosevic but Alison surely had. 'What do you think happened to Alison and Reeva?'

Mala took a long sip of coffee. 'Do you mean did my

brother kill them?' She held Natalie's gaze without wavering. 'No, he didn't. Personally, I think they both suicided.' She put her cup down. 'Do you like Frank?'

Vesna had asked her the same thing. Did she? 'Yes,' said Natalie. 'And I feel rather sorry for him at the moment.'

'You don't look like the pitying kind.'

'Meaning?'

'The sort that swoops on a man in need to mother him.'

Natalie thought of the strangely motherly feelings Frank had evoked. 'I don't think any of my exes would have said so, no.' Tom would have said crazy, actually. Liam? Liam would have said wild, energetic and unpredictable. And in the end, dangerous.

'You wouldn't believe what it was like after Reeva died.' Mala sat back to let the waitress deliver the breakfast orders. 'The hospital CEO gave him a casserole. Offered to come around to cook it.' She rolled her eyes. 'His research team kept turning up at odd times just to check out he was doing okay.'

'Wei?' For a moment Natalie had forgotten that once Frank really did have a full team.

Mala let out a peal of laughter. 'Hardly! Though poor Wei probably does fancy Frank, too.'

'I thought he came here as your...friend.'

Mala shrugged. 'I think he thought it'd be easier to get a gender reassignment here. Or at least that Australians would be less judgmental about it. I don't think he finds it easy being BC.'

BC? Was this a new way of saying bisexual or transgender? Mala saw her confusion.

'British born Chinese. He was brought up in Cambridge, but his father was straight out of the old country.'

They spent a moment in silence, eating.

'So...after Reeva died, was Alison on the scene?'

Mala dipped a strawberry into her breakfast yoghurt and licked it slowly, eyes on Natalie. 'She was his registrar.'

So Mala was evaluating her as the potential wife number three. The same MO. On the scene before the death and now moving in. Natalie could hardly blame Mala for thinking this. Time to direct the conversation elsewhere. 'If I worry about Frank,' Natalie said in between mouthfuls, 'It's as a psychiatrist. I feel the need to care for my patients.'

Mala's eyes glinted. 'You feel like Frank is your patient?'

Natalie felt his lips brush over her hand and had to stop herself rubbing the spot. 'Not exactly. But he is...grieving at the moment.'

'Yes, I suppose he is.' Mala looked hard.

'He'll survive though,' Natalie said. 'You could go off to New York.'

'I could.' Her tone suggested otherwise. Natalie wondered if she would stay and care for her grieving half-sister or half-brother in similar circumstances, or they her. She rather doubted it. But then her mother wasn't Vesna.

'How is your mother holding up?'

'Vesna?' For a moment Natalie almost thought she caught a glimpse behind Mala's facade. Anger? Pain? She wasn't sure.

'Frank described his childhood as a bit Alice in Wonderland.'

'Really?' Mala laughed as she reflected on the idea. 'Yes I suppose it was.'

'How?'

'How? There was one time when...' Mala paused; Natalie had the impression that she was used to thinking on her feet. 'Vesna is troubled, you understand. She tries. One time she packed us into a taxi, I must have been five? Frank came along though I can't imagine he wanted to. He's ten years older than me and teenagers don't generally want to go places with their mother and little sister.'

But he would have felt responsible.

'And she took us to the circus. In Melbourne. The taxi drove to Geelong, then we went by train and it was supposed to be exciting and wonderful, but Drago's father ended up picking us up because she lost her money, and the circus was not a big one but some little pokey thing with horrid clowns and soggy hot dogs.' Mala regarded her fingernails. 'That was Vesna. Misplaced enthusiasm that ended in tears.' She looked up. 'We couldn't ever trust her.'

'But Antonije?'

'Antonije was always there. He was our hero.'

Natalie thought that, in the words of the old song, heroes often failed. She saw the smile on the edge of Mala's lips and had the curious sense that Mala knew exactly what she was thinking. Which spooked her even more. *If You Could Read My Mind.*

'I tried analysis for a while,' said Mala. 'So did Frank. We are smart people, we have worked through it. It's hard to let go of your heroes, I get that. I think Frank's wives have struggled with the notion more than Frank or me.'

But Frank didn't have an idealised mother, so perhaps that's why he had at least tried marriage.

'Hard for you to find a man to wear Antonije's shoes, though,' Natalie said softly, watching Mala closely. Mala didn't waver, moved her hand over Natalie's where it rested on the table.

'What makes you think it's a man I'm looking for?

184

Mala's other hand went to Natalie's thigh. In Mala's eyes there was more of a challenge than attraction. But Natalie was left feeling she would have gone along with it if Natalie had taken her up on the unspoken offer.

The day she took us to the circus she had intended to escape. She didn't say anything but I could tell in the shake of her hand, the furtive smile at me and the triumph as she looked back at Mount Malosevic receding through the back window of the taxi. She'd tried before. Pregnant with me, she had escaped Antonije's kingdom to strike out on her own, only to be dragged back as a grieving widow with a newborn. She watched Antonije cast his spell over us and was powerless to stop it. She wanted us to adore her as we did him but she was too twisted inside with pain and fear to bring us joy as he did. To have Antonije smile at you was to have the sun come out; you were safe and invincible, delighted and delightful.

On the way to the circus that day she talked incessantly, the nervous talk of a person on the edge. Mala was excited, thinking of lions jumping through hoops and aerial artists flying through the air. I didn't say a word, torn and uncertain, the words from my father's funeral still echoing in my ears.

I didn't want to be the man in the family. I wanted Antonije to be. It was his castle I wanted to be mine one day, not the cluttered house of Wendell's childhood—a house full of musty smells and dim lights, where the pipes creaked and the water was lukewarm. Most of all I didn't want to be responsible for Vesna. Vesna, with her fears and ideas that never quite worked. Vesna of the smothering cuddles that were for her reassurance rather than to soothe either me or Mala.

'It will be an adventure,' said Vesna, eyes darting around, wondering probably if Antonije was in the shadows.

'What sort of adventure, Mummy?' whispered Mala.

'The best sort,' said Vesna. 'We'll have lots of fun food and watch TV and...'

'Fairy floss?'

'Yes, lots of fairy floss...'

But she couldn't find any, and the hot dogs were cold. She took us to the airport hotel in a panic about misplaced money, though I suspect Antonije had already cancelled her account. Mala cuddled up to me for comfort. By then Antonije was already on his way. When Mala and I got into the back of the car to sit next to him, neither of us looked to see Vesna's expression. And after that time she never tried again. I imagine Antonije and the doctors got her better in hand.

It was the next weekend before Natalie was able to visit the Carson Gallery. If Frank knew she had met up with Mala he hadn't mentioned it. But when he cancelled their usual meeting she wondered if it was pique.

She passed a parked silver Commodore that reminded her of the one that had harassed her. It was the middle of the day and not far from the police station but she felt uneasy anyway. Damian had left early, called back to Melbourne for his other case. He'd told her they had interviewed Eliza and found that she and Alison occasionally had coffee. The last phone call had been to say Alison was running late. Alison had visited her before meeting up with Frank, on the night she died.

'She denied that Alison was anything more than tired and irritable and looking forward to having her baby.' Apparently Eliza had also denied any problem with the Malosevics, although she considered Vesna an 'uptight bitch'. Actually she thought the whole family had tickets on themselves, and she wasn't alone there.

Damian added 'How did you know she wouldn't be a doctor?'

'Because,' said Natalie, 'he didn't marry her.'

'Lucky for her.'

The gallery was open and doing a modest trade from weekenders and occasional tourists. Like the pictures she had already seen, the art was vibrant and local, a mix of birds and other animals, as well as some beach scenes.

Eliza was a trim brunette in her early forties, hair long and fringed, in jeans and a T-shirt. She looked up when Natalie came in. Natalie debated how to approach her but to her surprise Eliza was the one to take the initiative.

'You're the shrink singer aren't you? I've seen your band. You're not bad.'

'Thank you. But...the shrink bit wasn't on the billboard last time I looked.'

Eliza's features seemed too small under all the hair; her eyes fixed on Natalie in a way that made her squirm. 'Small town,' she finally said. Her eyes said she was lying, and more, that she knew Natalie would pick it and didn't care. One love: Natalie's serve.

'Can you tell me anything about Frank?'

Eliza hadn't expected that. It took her a moment to regroup. 'Why should I?'

'You were Alison's friend, I'm guessing. Did Frank know?'

'I haven't had anything to do with the Malosevics—Alison aside—for years.'

'So why was Alison the exception? Worried about her safety after what happened to Reeva?'

'Why are you interested?'

Natalie hesitated. 'I owe her.'

Eliza laughed. 'Well there's one for the books. Pity

Alison isn't still alive to hear that.'

Natalie stood her ground under Eliza's scrutiny. 'Okay,' the other woman said finally, standing up and going over to the door. The gallery had emptied of potential customers. She turned around the sign saying *Back in five minutes* and locked the door. 'Let's get a drink.'

Eliza led Natalie out the back into a bright kitchen cluttered with dirty dishes and knickknacks. It opened into an observatory where they took an open bottle of red wine. Sun filtered in through the glass ceiling, partly shaded by the huge tree. A painting of the tree sat unfinished on an easel.

'You first,' said Eliza as she poured. 'Was Alison right that Frank was hitting on you?'

Natalie shook her head. 'Not really, though to be honest, he's...well he likes to be surrounded by women is my guess.'

'You didn't think to send him home?'

'I didn't take him to mine.' Not until after Alison died, anyway.

Eliza shrugged. 'I figured Alison was overreacting.'

'Was she worried about other things?'

'Alison was worried about everything.'

'Her safety?'

'No.' Eliza swilled her red wine. 'She didn't know them like I did.'

Natalie watched Eliza. It looked like she wanted to talk but didn't want to be pushed.

Eliza put down her wine and stared at Natalie from under her heavy fringe. 'I grew up here. The Malosevics came from a different time and place. They make their own rules.'

'The Serbian influence? Vesna was born here and Frank in England.'

Eliza laughed. 'We used to call Mount Malosevic little

Serbia. Haven't you noticed? Even now the staff are all straight from the old country. Yugoslavia, Serbo-Croatia, whatever. Antonije was allegedly some war hero. When Antonije was alive he was king of the castle, and they all jumped. I think he wanted lots of children so the family could take over the region, but things didn't go according to plan.'

Serbo-Croatia. Allegedly. Natalie filed a thought away. 'What did Alison make of them?'

'She was a bit of an innocent; I thought she needed a friend who wasn't so starry-eyed.'

'Starry-eyed about what?' Natalie was starting to show her frustration. Eliza somehow managed to go around points without ever getting to them.

'Alison wanted the white wedding and the happily-ever-after. She didn't believe in the past tainting the present, didn't see shadows beneath the surface.'

'Did Reeva?'

'In the end, yes, I think she did. I only ever saw her once, maybe a month before she died.' Eliza took a large gulp of wine. 'She came into the gallery like you just did. Told me I was lucky.'

'Lucky?'

'I presume she meant that I had got away. I had the impression that she was thinking of leaving.'

Leaving! With Frank's son and Frank's research grant. Men killed over less. Natalie recalled thinking Frank had been feeling guilty about Reeva, something he hadn't disclosed. What if Reeva intended to leave and that enraged him enough to kill her? Was it narcissistic rage that she was still sensing beneath the surface?

'Why would she have come to see you if she didn't know you?'

'Probably to see if what she'd heard was true.'

'Which was?

'That I was a witch, I suppose. Who couldn't be trusted.'

'Vesna? Why would she say that?'

'Because after her golden boy dumped me I had a baby. Unfortunately everyone assumed it was his.'

'Was it?'

'No.' Eliza looked directly Natalie. 'Jasper is not Frank's son.'

'Do you believe her?' Damian asked her over dinner. Bob was sitting on the back of his chair viewing the array of red meat with disapproval.

'In general or about Frank's fertility?'

'Either.'

Natalie took a sip of the white wine he'd brought. Surprisingly good. 'She's hiding something, I just don't know what. On balance, I'm inclined to think she jumped the next guy who came along to shove it up him and his arrogant family.'

'Is she still carrying a grudge?'

'Befriending Alison to then murder her? She didn't strike me as a psychopath but she was guarded. Hell hath no fury.'

'There's something else?' Damian sat back watching her. Natalie looked at him. For a cop he was very in tune with where others were at: her last cop boyfriend hadn't been the intuitive type.

'Did you get sexual vibes from Mala?'

Damian looked startled at the change of direction, then grinned. 'Jealous?'

'No. *You* might need to be.'

'You mean...?'

'Not sure,' said Natalie. 'But she did try a line on me.'

Damian drummed his fingers on the side of his glass. 'Wouldn't have picked it,' he finally said.

Nor had she. Maybe Mala was bisexual. But it could have been something else altogether. Natalie had a feeling that Mala had used the manoeuvre to distract her, she just couldn't work out from what. Wondered if Mala was protecting Frank. Or Vesna. It seemed they all had secrets to hide.

Bob woke her with his train impression. Even though she'd put him in the carport he sounded like he was outside her window. She groaned. The clock said 2 a.m. Bloody hell. Possum? Whoever said it was quiet in the country? Damian was snoring. 'What the...?'

She put her feet in the small of his back and pushed. 'You go.'

Damian rolled over but she pushed him again.

He returned a minute later. 'You'd better come see.'

'Is Bob okay?' Damian had already disappeared again.

The carport light was on. Bob had flown up to a low branch of a tree next to it. A pile of feathers decorated the carport floor near his stand. He was no longer attached to it. She frowned. 'Bob, come to Auntie.'

'Auntie?' Damian crossed his arms, grinning at her.

'I can't come at Mother.' She walked closer to Bob.

He hopped up to a higher branch.

Damian burst out laughing. 'Bird seems to have ideas of his own.'

'Call the cops!'

'Bob!'

'Champion of the Universe!'

193

Natalie shook her head. Just what she needed at 2 a.m. She went upstairs, got a container of seed and returned. 'Bob you can come now,' she said jiggling the food.

Bob marched up and down the branch watching them with interest. She was about to give up when he flew down to her shoulder. She grimaced as his claws broke her skin. She should have put a shirt on.

Rubbing his head, she said, 'Now just what happened to you?' and clipped his chain on, moving him over to his stand.

'That,' said Damian, 'is a very interesting question.'

'Did a possum or something attack him?' Natalie looked around, not sure how a possum would have managed to unclip him.

'Not something. Someone.'

Natalie looked where Damian was pointing. Her bike. Someone had slashed the tyres.

'Shit.'

Eliza was not quite seventeen when I met her, in her final year at school and a little younger than me. She had come to one of the open days at Mount Malosevic with her school art class, her skirt hitched up over spindly legs and a white shirt with one extra button undone, revealing an extra two inches of creamy white breast. Pert breasts, with nipples that showed through her clothes. I knew as soon as I saw her that I was going to find a way to touch and taste her intimate parts. The knowledge gave me a delicious sense of power: she, with her innocent smile, had no idea of what I intended.

She hung back in the studio with Antonije while her class was wandering in the gardens, breathlessly hanging off his every word. He winked at me, knowing what I was thinking. He invited her back to get some help with her school art project, knowing I would offer to drive her.

She was a virgin when we started dating and tiresomely insistent on remaining so. I had already had my own Mrs Robinson, and the offer of another, the heavy-hipped mother of a friend whom I had turned down in disgust. I was ready to induct girls of my own age into the delight of sex, but

Eliza was a good Catholic girl. Petting remained strictly above the waist.

I was a patient man, prepared to wait, and besides, there were girls at university available to fill my more immediate needs. Eliza was always there on the weekends I returned home as I waited for my patience to be rewarded. The boathouse was my favourite place but she was always fearful that someone would walk in on us, so the first time I saw her body it was after I had managed to ply her with a good deal of alcohol and dared her to swim naked. She was slender, only the slightest hint of curves, long hard pink nipples and soft lips covered in golden hair that, had she allowed me, I would have buried my face in. But even when she was drunk, Eliza's fear of sinning was tediously strong.

There was a time much later, in the boathouse where she would open herself up, ready and willing.

But by then I didn't want her.

'Vesna's quite paranoid. It must have shaped Frank's narcissism but I can't quite understand how.'

'Paranoid personalities don't all look like Charles Manson,' said Declan, pouring tea. It was still afternoon and Natalie would be riding back to the coast. 'They project anger but it's fear that drives them. There's shame too, but unlike the narcissist they've buried the fear so deeply—they're so bent on revenge against anyone who shames them—their own shame is undetectable.'

'Get them before they get me?'

'Yes, essentially. They are so deeply fearful of their own insignificance that to be hated is better than to be forgotten. With Vesna, it may have come from her parents' experience in the war; but it suggests that perhaps to one of them—her father, I should imagine—she felt she was a source of disappointment. Now in all her relationships she fears that if anyone really knew her then they would reject her as deeply unworthy. Wicked, even.'

'Wicked?' Natalie felt again the piercing coldness go through her that she had experienced standing outside Mount Malosevic.

'For the paranoid,' said Declan, 'the world is an evil place.'

'So what if you have a mother like that?'

'A profoundly disrupting experience for a child. The safe haven doesn't feel safe herself, and the child of course cannot differentiate between real danger and the mother's psychic ones.'

'Shouldn't that make Frank paranoid too?'

'That's one possible result. But he was also exposed to the godlike grandfather. As a boy, that might have had a different impact; it gave him someone powerful to identify with.'

But it suggested a fragility beneath the surface, however deep. 'What would happen if his narcissistic sense of self was threatened? Could he become paranoid?'

'It's common for different defences to work at different times and in response to different threats,' Declan said, his look telling her he knew exactly where she was heading. 'The paranoid also struggles with envy. They might be committing adultery or thinking of it, and yet have intense delusional jealousy if their partner is the one who is having an affair.'

So, what if Frank thought Reeva, and maybe Alison, was going to leave him?

Jealousy. There were other possibilities: Vesna herself, for one. She was disturbed, whereas Frank was functioning: a job and friendships. Then there was the unknown quantity of Eliza. Any jealousy there would have been worked through long ago though, surely?

The sudden chill made her shudder this time. She wondered if it was contagious, watching Declan's hand unsteadily return his cup to the saucer.

'I've been given two weeks.' Damian looked frustrated.

'To do what?'

'Find something concrete. Or we close down the investigation, treat it as an accident.'

'We're narrowing in on something, I can feel it.'

'Really?' Damian was onto his second beer. Neither of them had made a move towards dinner. 'About as close as the local cops are to finding out who slashed your tyres, I'd say.'

Natalie didn't want to go there; she'd convinced herself it was kids, refused to link it to the silver Commodore. She tried to get her thoughts clear. 'We know how they died, so the choices are accident, murder or suicide.'

'That's really narrowed it down.'

Natalie ignored his sarcasm. 'If Frank was involved it wasn't because he was psychotic. He may be narcissistic and his motives warped, but he would have to have a motive. 'We know or think we know that both Reeva and Alison were unhappy by the time they were about to deliver. Why? Reeva was looking up gene tests, maybe thinking of leaving him. Maybe Alison threatened the same.' Hopefully not over Frank's meeting with her.

'So the man doesn't believe in divorce?' Damian absentmindedly rubbed the finger where his ring no longer sat.

'He doesn't believe in being left,' said Natalie. 'Too great a blow to his ego. He owns them, they can't leave him, only he can choose that.'

'Like with Eliza.'

Natalie nodded. 'The added twist is that they are threatening to take his child. Which adds weight to why

Eliza got away; Frank presumably knew Jasper wasn't his.'

'So better to kill the child than let someone else bring it up?'

'Maybe. It happens all the time when couples separate, the murder-suicide thing—if I can't have them neither can you.'

'You don't sound convinced.'

'I'm not. Frank's father killing a pregnant woman may be a factor that goes towards explaining a murderous rage. It's really at his father for leaving him, but mixed up with Mala and the car-accident woman's child living when it was his father he wanted.'

'Enough to kill?'

'Maybe.'

'Anyone else in the family have motive? Or madness?'

Natalie gave him a smile. 'We could easily be just seeing the tip of Vesna's paranoia.'

'Mala?'

'Avenging her brother's honour?' Natalie shook her head. 'The Malosevics may think they are god in this region, but that's a very long bow to draw.'

'Where does Reeva's gene thing fit in?'

Natalie pulled out the piece of paper she had been trying to make sense of all day. Without her textbooks she was relying on the internet and her memory from medical school.

IEM? Not a clue. Next was SSD. Still no idea. Porphyria—okay she knew that one, a rare inherited disorder—and MCL. Some type of chronic lymphoma or leukaemia?

Then there was a list of autoimmune diseases. SLE she knew as lupus; sarcoidosis and Hashimotos were standard med student fare; antiNMDA rang a vague bell. All this group were in brackets; Natalie decided that this meant

Reeva had thought them less important.

After that was BPAD: bipolar affective disorder wasn't autosomal dominant or recessive, but those who'd been diagnosed often had family histories dotted with similar diagnoses, or undiagnosed outliers of the self-medicating variety: the alcoholics and suicides. Not that her family history did. Or at least the family history on her mother's side, which she all she knew about.

Could Frank's family have it? Grandiosity and narcissism were possible indicators and Frank had them in spades. So had his grandfather by all accounts.

BPAD was underlined. So was the final item: HD. Huntington's disease?

Lyuba had died young. Huntington's was an autosomal dominant disorder affecting men and women equally, so fifty per cent chance Vesna would have it if her mother did. Symptoms, including psychosis, depression, promiscuity and aggression didn't appear until middle age. Suicide occurred either as a consequence of the depression or at the fear of what lay ahead.

If Vesna was suffering from Huntington's it might explain her mental state. Was this what Reeva found out? That Vesna had a genetic disorder? Vesna was at best paranoid and Huntington's could start like that. She had no involuntary movements that Natalie had noticed, though. Perhaps they were controlled by the medication. Vesna was old for the usual form, but there were variations. Huntington's could be tested for—Frank and Mala might have had the test, might know. Had Reeva asked?

Natalie wondered what it would feel like, already pregnant, thinking there was a fifty per cent chance that the child you were carrying had a disorder that would have such a profound effect on them. In this context finding out there was a family history of bipolar would have been a welcome relief: it wasn't directly transmitted and it was thought that life events might affect whether it ever even appeared. Natalie would never know if her own bipolar would have surfaced without the serious accident in her teens or the night shifts of her intern year.

Natalie stared at the paper. Some of these could be tested in utero with an amniocentesis, but not others.

Reeva was a physician. If she had known there was a risk, she would have had her foetus tested. Natalie's sense of the woman was that she was pragmatic, that she probably would have had an abortion if the test was positive. So why hadn't she had the test?

Damian repeated his question. 'The gene thing?'

'If it is Frank killing his wives—and that's a big if—it might be about his genes not being perfect and he's projecting this anger onto his wives.'

Damian looked at her blankly.

'What if, for some reason, Reeva, and maybe Alison, found out about a genetic disorder that ran in the family and wanted a test? Let's assume for this argument that Frank is in denial but they've seen evidence his mother could have the disorder. Or grandmother. Maybe this is part of his attraction to doctors, a subconscious desire to be saved, or at least cared for.' Add in the impact of his father's death, when Frank survived the same accident. Doctors were powerful. They had the power over life and death, or so it might have seemed to a child. Enough to sow the seed. 'His wives were both doctors, and Reeva was a very astute one. He is a narcissist, unable to admit to his own weaknesses. The attraction to doctors, and why he became one himself, may revolve around the subconscious desire to find a cure.' If he had Huntington's then he might already have symptoms of it: grandiosity was not uncommon among sufferers.

'According to Sam Petersen, both women only had the routine Down syndrome testing.'

'That's all he knew about.' Natalie was typing into Google as she spoke. She paused to read the information on her screen. 'Reeva was interested in disorders that had psychosis as a symptom; Vesna, presumably. Hence if Frank had the gene, she was worried her child would have a fifty per cent chance...Yes, here it is.' She pointed to the screen. 'Huntington's is one that can be tested in pregnancy. The test's been available for some time, certainly when Reeva was pregnant.'

'I'm still not following you.'

'Didn't Petersen say Frank went to the appointments? The one he couldn't attend with Alison he rang up to check on. Alison and Reeva wouldn't have had a chance to ask in private.'

'So she went somewhere else.'

'Yes.' Natalie put the paper down. 'And another thing— wild card.'

'Yeah?'

'The boy who survived the car crash that killed Wendell Moreton thirty years ago. Do you have any idea where he is now?'

When I think of my childhood it is in fractured halves: one of worry and impotence as my father left me to the paranoid anxieties of my mother, the second dominated by the golden ideal of male power. I gravitated naturally, under the circumstances, towards my mother's father, who had in every practical sense become my own father.

Antonije was charismatic, charming and funny, handsome and generous. Though he could be cruel too, and at times I know Mala suffered, frustrated when she was excluded because she was too young—or because of her gender. It made her tougher, made her try harder and, with her quick mind and the beauty that was evident from an early age, she was eventually embraced by him, as much his child as I was.

I wanted to be an Antonije to my child, but a man on my own terms. Not as an artist but as something worthwhile. I had originally thought I would discover the cure of cancer; later the pull of understanding the mind was too great. I knew how influential a mother is in shaping confidence and personality, so my child needed to have the right mother, a woman who was not going to be like Vesna in any way. My mother did her best, I understand. I don't think she was ever the same after her mother died, in circumstances no child should have to deal with.

Reeva became irritatingly preoccupied with Vesna. When she found out about the manner of Lyuba's death and her fears reached such absurd proportions, it became increasingly evident that I had after all married my mother. I didn't share her conviction that Lyuba's illness was genetic— her experience in the camps was surely explanation enough. Lyuba had been there with her mother, rounded up because they were Romani. I know this only because Vesna told me; Antonije would not speak of it. My great-grandmother, I was told, had been a guest in the Gagro Hotel, the cellar where the Ustaše tortured their victims. Lyuba told Vesna her mother had been strangled with piano wire. She knew because in April 1945 when the Ustaše were torching the place, killing those left before they escaped the liberating partisans, Lyuba escaped and ran back to find her. She was lying with her dead mother when Antonije found her. Or so the story goes.

I didn't want my son to be exposed to the worry and impotence that Reeva's overt fussing would surely induce. Whichever way you looked at it, our son would have been at risk of mental illness from both sides of the family.

It was very disappointing.

'This is worse than working in a morgue,' Wei said. 'I never thought I'd say I was actually looking forward to going back to England.'

Poor Frank.

'You presumably didn't know Alison as well as Reeva?'

'Alison worked here also,' said Wei, not looking up from his computer. 'That is, until just before you arrived.'

This was news. Alison's earlier psychiatry rotation would have been clinical: confined to the wards. The move to research presumably happened after she got together with Frank. 'She was working on a grant?'

'She was going to.'

But probably decided the brilliant Reeva Osbourne was too hard an act to follow. Or else Alison found ethics applications as tedious as Natalie did. The committee had just asked for yet more changes to her proposal.

'Reeva worked right up until...didn't she?'

'Yes, it was horrid. One day she was here, next...' Wei gestured a thumbs down with both hands. 'Me? I'm sticking to cats.'

'And just totally well? No warning?' Natalie wasn't

expecting anything much from Wei but while she was waiting for Damian to chase up pathology labs for genetic tests, she wanted to do something to help make sense of Reeva and Alison's last days.

'She wasn't herself.' Wei shifted in his chair, rolling his shoulders.

'Worried?'

'I guess.'

Natalie edged her chair out of the adjoining carrel into Wei's. 'It wasn't your fault, you know. Reeva. You couldn't have done anything.'

'You can't help wondering, can you? She was...she didn't seem right.'

'In what way?'

Wei struggled to make sense of his memories. 'I don't know really. Preoccupied I suppose.'

Natalie pondered on Wei's observation on the way to her bike when Damian's text came: no amniocentesis results on either Reeva Moreton or Reeva Osbourne in any lab in Melbourne. He'd also checked Sydney, as she had made one trip there early in the pregnancy. Damn. If Reeva had organised a test, then she'd used a different name. Was she that paranoid? If she had been murdered, then it meant she had cause to be.

She was late; Frank had already ordered the dips and bread. Wye River had lost out to the Greek restaurant again. She wasn't planning on drinking, so the ride home wasn't a problem.

The way her stomach had been of late she wasn't sure she wanted to eat either—the case had been getting to her more than she liked to admit. She expected Damian to be at her house, so she planned to leave as soon after dinner as she could.

'Are the police still giving you a hard time?'

'They're just doing their job.' Frank's lethargy had gone; there was a new wariness, and beneath that, something hard to pinpoint.

'Wei is pretty gutted,' said Natalie.

Frank didn't appear to have Wei foremost in his mind.

'I remember…' Natalie was finding Frank hard to read, but pushed on anyway. 'That I felt you were feeling guilty over Reeva. Do you…feel that with Alison too?'

Frank put down his bread and looked directly at her. 'Reeva…it was different.'

Different? Because she was worried enough about a genetic disorder, fictitious or real to leave him? Or because he had loved her more?

'She was obsessed.'

'What about?'

Frank took a long sip of the wine. 'Reeva was someone who liked everything exactly right. By the end of her pregnancy she took it to a whole new level.'

Natalie waited. Gail Osbourne had told Damian there was a family history of postpartum psychosis—had Reeva's started in third trimester?

Frank's head disappeared into his hands. After a moment, to her shock, she realised his body was shaking with sobs. She knelt down beside him, hand on his arm and heard him whisper:

'I missed it. I'm a psychiatrist and I missed it.'

'Missed what?' But already knew the answer.

A minute passed. Frank finally looked up, looked at her for forgiveness. 'She was acutely psychotic.'

They were the only people left in the restaurant by the time Frank finished the whole story. It had happened gradually. Reeva had been a forceful, confident woman and it had taken a long time before Frank had started to query the hours spent on the internet, before he realised that the confident woman he had married was guarded and suspicious, keeping more and more to herself.

'Her family hadn't noticed?' Natalie asked.

'She hardly saw them. Phone calls, sure. But she was very good at hiding it. She knew we would think she was mad, and she wasn't going there. I thought at first that she was worried about the project, how she would manage motherhood and her career. I thought that's what she was doing, writing papers, getting ahead so she could have some breathing space.'

'But what was she doing?'

'I have no idea.'

Natalie frowned.

'I checked her laptop. She'd wiped her internet browser history before she...'

'Why did you check?'

'She wouldn't talk to me. We had had a very close relationship and the pregnancy changed it. At first I thought it was natural...'

'Did you talk to anyone about it at the time?' *Like you did with me about Alison?*

'We were writing up a grant. It was critical, something she was passionate about. But she wasn't managing and asked for help. So I spent more and more time at work, to let her go home early and rest.'

Would Reeva have seen that, or would she have read it

as lack of interest in her and the baby, and felt even more isolated?

'Did you tell the police?'

'No.' Frank rubbed his eyes. 'I didn't really put it all together and admit it to myself until months later. She wasn't the suicidal type, so it just never occurred to me. Then later...I felt guilty. Ashamed I'd missed it.'

Natalie nodded. It made sense.

The handwritten note—maybe Reeva had been worried about herself rather than her baby having a disorder. Damian had checked for amniocentesis results; he'd have missed tests done on herself. Or maybe her psychosis meant she had not been thinking clearly. Natalie had been looking for logical answers: psychosis spun an entirely different light on the situation—nothing had to make sense to anyone but the sufferer.

'Did anything she say suggest who or what she was suspicious of? The paranoia would mean she'd run or hide'— or threaten to leave him—'but not kill herself and her baby.' Unless she thought they were both doomed. If the psychotic thoughts had taken over and Reeva believed them to be true, then any action was possible. Andrea Yates had killed her five children because she believed they would go to heaven. The devil had told her so, and she had traded her own soul.

'I don't know. She wasn't talking to me and I foolishly gave her space rather than push it. Who's to say what went on in her head just before...' His voice broke and she moved to touch his hand in comfort. There were tears in his eyes as he looked at her: there was no doubt in her mind in that moment that he hadn't killed Reeva.

But if Reeva had suicided while psychotic, what had happened to Alison?

Alison didn't have a family history of mental illness. But she wouldn't let things go. She increasingly had the need for things to look 'right' with less and less idea of what 'right' was.

'Are you sure Vesna needs to be on all those medications?' she asked.

'I am not her treating psychiatrist, Alison.' I spoke occasionally to my mother's psychiatrist. I knew his rationale and had no issues with his treatment plan. Vesna was as well as she could be, given the circumstances. It wasn't Alison's business.

She might have let it go if it hadn't been for Eliza.

'I know,' Alison said to me that night.

I really doubted it.

'Eliza told me.'

'Told you what, Alison?' I didn't bother asking her why she was seeing Eliza. I knew Eliza would have been able to manipulate Alison with ease. She might not have been as intellectually gifted as my wife, but she was well ahead in native cunning.

When Alison was ashamed of something she always

looked away for a moment and then stared defiantly. She did that now.

'That mental illness runs in your family.'

I didn't react. This was all so tiresome.

'Why didn't you tell me?'

'I rather thought you were a doctor, Alison, and that you could see it for yourself. I have hardly kept my mother hidden.'

'Not just her,' Alison had screamed. 'Eliza told me about the paintings.'

'What paintings?' I asked, though I knew.

Eliza seems to think that enough time has passed that she is no longer under any obligation, that she is no longer at risk. She is, of course, wrong.

Natalie couldn't let go of the fact that Reeva, in suiciding, had killed her baby. She looked at the photo of Reeva she'd downloaded from the internet, certain she would have liked her. There was an impression of thoughtfulness about her, one that Natalie wanted to believe was solid.

'A family history of postpartum psychosis doesn't mean she had bipolar,' Natalie whispered to herself. 'Reeva isn't you.' But Natalie had visited her own dark place all too recently, and wanted to believe that somehow her core beliefs—and Reeva's—would triumph over anything that their disorders might throw at them. Her nightmares now included dead babies and more than once she had woken up drenched in sweat, with images of Alison before her eyes, and a gloomy sense of failure that took a coffee and a jog to lift it.

Had Reeva been psychotic? Possible; but it was unusual for the first episode to be in pregnancy rather than postpartum, when it could be triggered, in those genetically predisposed, by sleep deprivation and stress and maybe the dramatic hormone changes.

Rather than waiting for Damian to check, she rang the main labs.

'I'm sorry, I can't recall which lab I told my patient to use.' Enough to have the technicians go search. None had a record of DNA testing for Reeva Moreton or Reeva Osbourne.

Natalie looked at the note again. Reeva must have believed her child was going to have a genetic disorder, even if was via her rather than Frank. And Huntington's was right up there. But there was no evidence that Huntington's, or for that matter any other disorder, ran in the family. The belief itself must have been psychotic and Reeva as a result was too disorganised or too late to test. Or else believed she had something that couldn't be tested for.

'Did Reeva ever say anything to you about genetic testing?' she asked Wei over lunch, on a day Frank hadn't turned up to the office. She was trying to eat even though she wasn't hungry; her lithium was making her feel nauseous but if she didn't have food she felt bad until the levels settled mid-afternoon. Another month. Then maybe Declan could be persuaded to let her stop it and go back to one mood stabiliser only.

'Reeva? No.'

Natalie looked up at him. 'But she said something similar, right?'

Wei looked uncomfortable. 'Why is it you want to know?'

'Frank isn't coping well,' said Natalie. 'He is mystified about how both Reeva and Alison could have died. I guess everyone is. Reeva might have been psychotic.'

Wei nodded. 'She was not herself, but she never said anything about genes. Or her pregnancy, for that matter. She was a very private person.'

There was still something he was holding back. He

broke from the scrutiny of her look. After a moment he said quietly, 'But Alison did.'

Alison? 'What, when she was working here?' Just months earlier.

'Yes. That second office used to be Reeva's, then it was Alison's. She was chatty, friendly.'

'But she was worried about something?'

'It was more like very focused. Towards the time she left, more worried. Less open anyway. But I just thought...'

'It was the pregnancy.' Pregnancy got blamed for a lot, maybe not without some basis. From memory, pregnancy changed just about every hormone. 'Did she mention genes?'

'Yes, but nothing specific.'

Natalie gave up on her soup and tried some bread. 'She didn't use the same filing cabinet as Reeva did she?'

'No, she didn't have much to file, used my reference papers. But when she left I combined her files in with Reeva's.'

Natalie stared at him, saw how Wei had felt embarrassed because he was hiding something. The same look Oliver had at the funeral. The note had been Alison's, not Reeva's. And she'd found an obstetrician other than Sam Petersen—her ex-fiancé Oliver—to talk to.

Back at the research carrels, Natalie waited for Wei to leave before moving into the deserted office and firing up the spare computer. It was, she realised, the same one both Reeva and Alison had used, which had otherwise been redundant since the research team was disbanded. It didn't have a password.

Frank had said Reeva had deleted her browser search from her laptop. But she only had his word for that; Frank himself could have deleted it, if it had been deleted at all. But had either one thought to do it on the work computer?

Natalie clicked on the Firefox icon. Across the top were the bookmarked sites. Google with all the searches: most recent six months earlier. And a Yahoo icon that took her directly into Reeva's account, password already logged in and remembered. If she was paranoid, it hadn't been about anyone accessing her online data. Someone had opened it six months earlier—Alison presumably. Reeva had also, Natalie saw, copied some of the emails to her other account—a university one.

None of the other icons gave up Alison's email so Natalie went to the university website email access. Bingo. The user name came up as *amoreton*. Trouble was, it needed a password. Natalie thought about what she knew about Alison and typed in Mount Malosevic.

The site asked her to check she had the correct user name and password. Obviously she didn't. She went to the university website and staff email and clicked on forgotten password. What was the chance she'd know the verification question? She figured she had a one percent chance.

What is your mother's maiden name?

Natalie shook her head. Really? She typed in *Foster*, thinking of the *Vogue* pictures of Lally Foster in seventies swimwear that Alison had been so proud of.

Who is cute but not yet cuddly?

Natalie's fingers hovered over the keys. Typed *Harry* and was in.

It felt wrong reading Alison's emails. Too recent and too much like an intrusion, a violation of privacy. But at least there were none since she had left the lab. If she was still emailing afterwards, it wasn't from this account. In any case, there were none to Oliver. A few to medical friends, mostly social chitchat.

Reading Reeva's wasn't much easier, and there was a lot of junk to sift through. Checking the deleted emails, it appeared Alison, or whoever had delved here before her, had done that too. Alison would have felt it was her right to look. Natalie didn't, but she did have an odd sense of connection with Reeva, a curiosity about her, maybe a little of the jealousy Alison would have felt acutely. A benchmark of worthiness? And if so, where the hell did that come from? Using a dead woman to make herself feel better. Was it the depression, the ECT? Or Frank? Or worse, the lurking picket-fence fantasy?

Reeva's emails were brief, organised and efficient even though they weren't her work emails: presumably she used her university account for those. She'd finished work the Christmas before she died, using her email up until the day before her death, most likely accessing it from home. There was no discernible change in style. Just more saying she'd be out of action for at least a month. Surely if she had been psychotic, paranoid especially, there would have been a shift in wording and emphasis?

Natalie changed tack and moved to the most recent search list. Which would be Alison's. Genetic testing in pregnancy, organic causes of psychosis, recipes for paella, genetic causes of psychosis, the Bethlehem Hospital.

So Alison liked paella and was looking where she was going to deliver. Natalie hadn't heard of the Bethlehem, but she'd never researched private obstetric units either. But the others? This was *Alison,* not Reeva, doing the search. Natalie sat back and frowned. Okay, so Frank divulged his secret guilt about Reeva's psychosis to his second wife, which made sense. She'd then researched it? Maybe Reeva's paranoia hadn't been about genetics at all. The list of genetic

disorders must be Alison's. And she had no reason to be
worried that Reeva's psychosis was contagious—so it had to
be Vesna she was worried about.

Natalie clicked *organic causes of psychosis* on Alison's
search list, selected the Wiki link and recognised it
immediately. She pulled out the original list from the file.

IEM was inborn errors of metabolism. SSD an autosomal
recessive disorder of chromosome 6 which included mental
disturbance, among other difficulties that the Malosevic-
Moretons clearly did not suffer from. Porphyria was also
on this list and MLC turned out to be metachromatic
leukodystrophy, another autosomal recessive disorder with
an adult form. Again, it looked as if it became too severe too
early in adulthood to explain Vesna's disorder, if that was
what Alison had been trying to find.

She closed the browser and rang Oliver.

Oliver was in the delivery suite; his secretary took a message.
Natalie rode home wondering what he would be able to tell
her. By the time she was slowing to go through Lorne, her
mind had moved to Damian. Her sense was that he was
still wary of her, which was probably just as well. They had
eased into a comfortable enough relationship in which he
had replaced Tom as being the handy man in her life if she
needed one. She didn't think either she or Damian was really
ready for another relationship of the variety that hurt. She
felt vaguely uneasy that she hadn't told him about Liam, but
it wasn't as if that was going to do any good. It was a hiccup,
nothing more. And since Liam had shown what an arsehole
he really was, it was easier to be certain there wasn't going
to be a repeat.

Liam's memory of their last encounter seemed to be

different from hers, though. The text that said *I've missed you xxx* had come a few days after their last encounter and she'd thrown the phone across the room. Missed her? He'd said he was done with her.

Then: *We okay? A drink?* What did he mean, *we*? There was no 'we'.

She'd been smarting about the last text as she cruised down the main street and saw a young guy, maybe six foot, skinny, leaning against a silver Commodore watching her. Long shoulder-length dark hair pulled back in a ponytail. He was the spitting image of Frank.

'So she lied?' asked Damian. It was a chilly but windless night and they had elected to rug up and enjoy the balcony view of waves crashing onto the shoreline below. 'About him not being Frank's kid?'

Natalie reflected on her shattered certainty Eliza was telling the truth. Psychiatrists were, at the end of the day, a gullible lot it seemed. 'I think she wanted to believe he wasn't.'

'Maybe she didn't know, like there was more than one contender.'

'Possibly. She'd have to have a strong suspicion now.' So would Alison and Reeva if they'd ever seen him. And they surely would have.

'So Eliza cut herself off from the Malosevics because they wouldn't acknowledge her son?'

'Frank probably hurt her. She was young, remember.' Natalie warmed her hands around the mug of tea. 'And when they found she was pregnant maybe they threatened her.'

'Why? With what?'

'They wouldn't want her going after a slice of his birthright, I guess. Maybe not "threatened". Perhaps they paid her off.' This would account for her lying and reluctance to say much; she might have signed a deal.

'So,' said Damian, 'any chance, do you think, that Eliza or her son now thinks they deserve a chunk of the Malosevic estate?'

Eliza's pregnancy was highly inconvenient. Of course I offered to pay for the abortion. I even got her to the East Melbourne clinic but as soon as she saw the protesters with their 'pro-life' signs the Catholic guilt kicked in and she refused to get out of the car.

My patience had worn thin by this stage. We drove back in silence. I am sure she was fully aware of my displeasure. I was only days from end-of-year examinations and I needed to study. Fortunately I was able to hand over tissue duty to Mala, who, despite being a teenager at the time, was a skilled listener thanks to Vesna, who liked an audience for her conspiracy theories. Antonije took charge of the situation and ensured it was dealt with, and I was able to get back to my study.

But there is no Antonije now and I was aware of a feeling of déjà vu. From my father's funeral, the whispers that I was the man of the family now. McBride is becoming increasingly irritating. He seems to think he is Columbo, ringing up with 'just one more question'. And I can never be sure when I am going to return home and find him there. Yesterday he just wanted to walk around the grounds.

'Can't you do something about him?' asked Vesna. 'What does the lawyer say?'

We all watched his progress, from the living room, poking into bushes as if expecting to find a murder weapon. There isn't anything to find; he is wasting his time. But I wondered what morsel I could drop him about Natalie. Maybe I will try to get closer to her sooner than I had anticipated. People do strange things when they are grieving; she would understand.

Oliver rang the next morning. His guarded 'What did you want?' suggested he wasn't planning a long conversation.

'You said you hadn't seen Alison for years.'

'I hadn't.' Now defensive.

'But she rang you, right?'

There was silence. A sigh. 'Yes, but I'd rather no one knew. There's no point.'

Because she was dead and he didn't want to be called to a coroner's inquest—or worse, a murder trial.

'Tell me why she rang, Oliver. You owe it to her.'

'That's what she said too,' Oliver remarked dryly.

Natalie waited. Working as a psychotherapist in private practice had given her a lot of opportunity to perfect the technique. Obstetricians were more hands-on and rushed.

'She rang twice,' he said finally.

'When?'

'The first time? Shit, I don't know. She'd just found out she was pregnant. She wanted some information about amniocentesis. The risks.'

'And hospitals to deliver in?'

'No. It depends on your obstetrician what hospital you go to.'

'Where is the Bethlehem?'

'The Bethlehem hospital? Caulfield I think. But it's palliative care isn't it?' Caulfield wasn't far from Alison's family though, if she'd wanted to be close to them rather than Mount Malosevic. Maybe it had broadened its activities.

'Did she say why she was asking you? Or what she wanted to be tested for?'

'No, just asked broadly what could be tested.'

'And the answer?'

Oliver rattled off a list of what was most common; haemophilia, thalassemia, Ducenne's, sickle cell, polycystic kidney disease, Huntington's and Tay-Sachs. Only one overlap with the list Alison had hand written. The one with psychosis among symptoms.

'The second time she rang...' his voice caught. 'Was the day before she died.'

Natalie stared out over the ocean. 'Was she agitated?'

'No,' said Oliver. 'In fact she sounded fine. Tired maybe, and perhaps, I don't know, puzzled?'

'So why did she ring?'

'She said she couldn't talk about it with her family or obstetrician, that it had to remain private.'

'What had to?'

'She actually never told me, just wanted me to know her baby was going to be fine.'

'Are you sure? That's all she said?'

'Yes. I thought it a bit strange and then she died and... Well, I wondered.'

'Wondered what?'

'You're the psychiatrist. Don't people sound resigned

and at peace when they decide to kill themselves? After I heard...I wondered if she meant that her baby was going to be fine in heaven. I wondered also if she'd had the amnio and the test results came back.'

'Alison's baby was normal on autopsy, right?' she asked Damian over bacon and eggs—his. The smell made her queasy. Maybe she'd do the full health thing and become vegetarian. Lithium was unquestionably a lifesaver, but she wished the drug companies had worked on minimising the side effects.

Damian nodded with his mouth full. Egg yolk ran down his chin and she pointed to her own to give him the message to wipe it.

'Did they keep genetic material when they released the body for burial?' She couldn't bring herself to call him Harry.

'I think so. Why?'

'Have him tested for Huntington's. Come to think of it, get them to run a full genetic screen.' They wouldn't have done this as a matter of routine—not if he'd been normal in appearance. Genetic testing might have looked for causes of miscarriage, but Harry hadn't died because of anything related directly to him. *Miscarriages*. What was it about that that was niggling at her?

'If he's positive,' she added, 'I think we've found the cause for a second suicide.'

Damian's expression was hard to read, but it went something like *I'd rather be putting Frank away for murder*. Even if it meant the case was closed, it wouldn't be as illustrious a start to his career in homicide as he might have liked.

*

Georgia's lawyer rang to let Natalie know her objection had been knocked back.

'Is there anything in the files to be worried about?' asked Barrett. She sounded annoyed.

Yes. But too late now. 'Mostly shorthand no one will make much sense of.' Snippets of insights, questions relating to comments Georgia had made; a look into the head of someone accused of three murders. 'I didn't want them on public record mainly to honour the work that Georgia and I are doing.' To show her someone cared enough to do at least this for her. No one else had; her life was a litany of betrayals. When she finally accepted Paul's betrayal, however reasonable his actions had been by normal standards, she would have nothing. Natalie knew there were plenty of people wishing Georgia had just killed herself and saved the state the expense of a trial. But it didn't sit well with Natalie. Georgia hadn't chosen her childhood; she now had a chance to choose to live differently. Even if it was in jail.

'So this means I have to send in the records?'

'Yes. Tania Perkins is the bitch from hell, and for some reason she has a real bee in her bonnet about this case. You're instructed to send everything.'

Tania, or her boss? Natalie wondered.

'And,' Barrett added before she hung up, 'if you leave anything out, don't get caught.'

'I think we have an answer for what happened to Frank's wives,' Natalie told Declan. 'And if we don't the case will be closed anyway. All I've been doing is trying to find a motive. There isn't any evidence.'

'So your answer?'

'Not entirely satisfactory.' Natalie couldn't sit still. She stood up and wandered to the bookcase, trying to slow herself down so that Declan wouldn't interpret her restlessness as early signs of mania. She wasn't irritable or particularly energetic, nor was she feeling good. She'd dropped her lithium because of the nausea. She wondered when she could broach the subject of trying just the quetiapine again.

'Most likely? Reeva had a psychosis. Family history of postpartum psychosis. However, this started in pregnancy.'

'That's unusual.'

There was something in his tone she couldn't grasp; when she looked intently at him she realised he knew something she didn't. She thought of Mala's comments about her and Frank both dabbling in analysis.

'Frank wasn't ever in therapy with you was he?' she blurted out suddenly.

Declan took a moment to place his pen carefully on the desk before he looked at her. 'You know I can't answer that question.'

But if he did know something...

'In any event,' Declan continued, 'it is my role to help you make sense of the knowledge that you *do* have. Though I need to remind you that you are *not* Frank's therapist.'

'But even in unofficial peer support,' said Natalie, 'I have an obligation to ensure he is...safe don't I? Including to himself.' She paused, realising something that hadn't before crossed her mind. The death of two wives? It would hardly be surprising if an innocent Frank became depressed, despairing and worse, particularly as he was blaming himself for missing Reeva's psychosis.

She ran her hand through her hair. Dismissed the idea of him suiciding, at least on her current assessment of him, and went back to the timing of Reeva's psychosis. 'Reeva having antenatal psychosis. One of the less than satisfactory aspects, I agree, but if it's postpartum sleep deprivation that sets most vulnerable people off, then we know she already had that in her third trimester.' Because of the psychosis, Reeva could have threatened to leave Frank, which would give him a motive to murder her. But Frank as a murderer required an even further stretch of imagination.

'What about the second wife?'

'I think she found out about a genetic disorder. Maybe Reeva did too, and it triggered her psychosis.'

'A disorder on Frank's side, you are assuming?'

'Yes. I think Alison had just found out her near-term baby was positive for this unknown condition, and she couldn't face...'

Being less than perfect.

True, Alison did want the perfect everything around her. But the desire for perfection at a deeper, more primitive, psychopathic, level was more likely true of Frank. A psychopathy (if it existed) that was driven by grandiosity and by what he saw as his birthright. Alison's perfectionism was driven by anxiety about doing the right thing: the attempt to control her world and feel safe. In fact, Natalie could have seen Alison a year down the track as the president of a Huntington's support group—the 'perfect' example of how to manage a life catastrophe. Had she lived.

'But something about that doesn't sit well?'

Natalie selected a book from his shelf and walked back towards him. 'Two suicides? I guess shit happens. Maybe they both saw that any future child either had would be affected, one woman through a psychotic thought process, the other through a neurotic one.' And there was the fact that they were both living at Mount Malosevic. Natalie remembered the undercurrent; she thought of it as the ghost of Antonije Malosevic.

Declan interlinked his fingers. 'They were doctors. They would have known the odds. No more than a fifty-fifty chance it was dominant; only twenty-five if recessive and they were also carriers.'

But they would both have thought themselves unlikely carriers: the obstetric records suggested little in the way of significant family history, Reeva's grandmother's postpartum psychosis aside. She put the book down on Declan's desk. It was titled *Shame and Jealousy*.

'If I'm wrong about the suicides I have another theory,' said Natalie. 'Tell me about jealousy.'

'Jealousy?' Declan's fingers caressed the book cover. She detected a slight shake. Nerves? Early Parkinsons? Did he know something he wasn't able to share with her?

'There is of course delusional jealousy.' He opened a chapter and handed it to her. 'Includes erotomania, where the person believes the other is in love with them and can become enraged by anyone who gets in the way.'

'Enough to kill?' Natalie was familiar with this chapter. Delusional jealousy was in the end easy, because it was madness, a product of not being in touch with reality. It only required elucidation of the delusion, along with other symptoms to clinch the diagnostic criteria. From a legal point of view, there was no point in trying to understand it.

'Enough to be dangerous.' Declan leaned forward. 'You'll have seen these in the prison system, with diagnoses of schizophrenia primarily. Many, thankfully, thwarted by the concomitant cognitive decline before they actually cause harm.'

That wasn't likely in the scenario she was considering.

'What about in a narcissist or a paranoid personality? Possible killers when they are, or feel, rejected?' And who were responsible for their actions, as opposed to those in the grip of psychotic thought processes.

Declan leaned back in his chair, hands clasped. 'Rage is common in men. You'll recall the case of James Ramage?'

The last man in the state to use the provocation defence to fight a murder charge. The public outrage after he received only seven years for killing his wife resulted in the defence being abolished. A similar defensive homicide law was due for the scrap pile, too.

'He was almost certainly a fragile narcissist. Whether his wife taunted him or not is irrelevant, though she would have been unwise to do so. The rage of her leaving turned him murderous.' Declan paused looking at her intently.

Natalie had a distinct feeling he was hoping there was a particular lesson she was learning, but her mind had already moved in another direction. 'What about the paranoid personality?'

'It is about the fantasy of ownership, complete and to the exclusion of all others. And underlying it? It is a defence against guilt and shame. In the paranoid, a defence against being forgotten and insignificant.'

Better to be hated and hateful than considered insignificant. Eliza. She had not been considered good enough for the Malosevics. Then the shame of being a single mother, back then when it was socially unacceptable. Possibly. But what about the power of the jealous and paranoid mother to influence her son?

Eliza was out of our lives for many years. She went to an artist commune in somewhere like Byron Bay. I didn't think I would ever see her again. There was no need.

Then her mother died and left her a house, just off the main street of Lorne. Perfect, she told me, for an art gallery. She at least had the courtesy to ring. However it was bad taste to invite us to the opening. Mala went, perhaps out of curiosity; maybe she actually liked Eliza. I never asked.

'Colourful,' was her comment about Eliza's art.

The timing was inconvenient. I had just brought a new bride to Mount Malosevic. I didn't want Eliza stirring up trouble so I went to see her, naturally, to ensure we still had an understanding. She had aged well enough, though her hippie leanings had taken root and her hair was a natural mouse colour, long and uncut. She wore a hideous loose dress that did nothing for her figure, but as far as I could gather it was still slim enough.

'You look just the same,' she commented, which was true.

I didn't say anything.

'So the reason for your visit?'

'I wondered how you were doing.'

She laughed. A harsh sound from someone whose sweetness had long ago soured. 'No you didn't, Frank. You wondered if I was going to cause trouble.'

'Are you?'

'Me? Why should I do that?' Her look was all smirk and very unattractive. 'But perhaps you should decide how you're going to handle it if you bump into Jasper.'

She pulled a photo of a young man, out of her hand bag. I refused to take it.

'Why would I need to handle anything, Eliza?'

Georgia's trial had started. There was a picture of her on page five of the newspaper, with small insets of her three dead children. Liam was reported to have given a powerful opening that had left one juror in tears, although, the article went on, *Georgia Latimer appeared unmoved*.

The media had made up their mind. As with Lindy Chamberlain. Had Georgia even heard what the prosecutor said? More likely she had regressed into an inner fantasy world.

Two days later, the case made it to page three. This time the inset was of Paul and his surviving daughter Miranda. It looked as if it had been taken from an overhanging tree in a neighbour's house. Paul was feeding the eighteen-month-old with what looked like spaghetti bolognese. There was as much of the meal over the two of them as probably had ever made it into Miranda, and the smile they were sharing was heartbreaking in its innocence.

Paul Latimer broke down on the witness stand as he spoke of his love for Georgia and how his life had come tumbling around his ears when he read her Facebook page. He had been alerted to its alarming contents by a friend.

Liam was playing the Paul card hard. Natalie had met Paul, knew he would come across well on the stand. Jacqueline Barrett had an uphill battle if she intended to discredit him. But Natalie couldn't blame Liam. It was his job, and he was good at it.

Yet Paul hadn't understood the first thing about Georgia, and had been naively unaware as she murdered their first three children. Or else he had manipulated and controlled her, and had been too self-absorbed to see the consequences: maybe hadn't even cared. Or perhaps, as Jacqueline wanted everyone to believe, they were both just victims of bad genes and worse luck. Looking at Miranda, Natalie wondered uneasily what the future would hold for a little girl who had survived such a notorious mother.

'The baby was fine. No genetic abnormalities on the samples they'd kept.' Damian sounded matter of fact. 'And no tests I could find for Alison, blood or amnio, under her married or maiden name.'

What? She'd been so sure. 'They tested the foetus for Huntington's?'

'Yes. Negative.'

'Damn.'

'And the child, or rather the man who survived Wendell Moreton's accident? Now a researcher in the UK. It means we're closing down the investigation, Nat. It'll still be technically open until the coroner's findings, but no more man-hours.'

She felt uneasy. Because of the case, or because he wouldn't be staying with her anymore?

'I'll be there tonight,' he said, thoughts perhaps in the same place.

The band had a gig at Apollo Bay on Friday night, at Lorne on the Saturday. After that there were no more bookings apart from the regulars in Collingwood. If she wanted those she was going to have to negotiate with the band, and with Cassie. Part of Natalie thought these gigs might be the last time they played together. Once the thought would have eaten at her, unbalanced her sense of who she was. But she felt detached, even numb. The texts from Liam hadn't helped. She wasn't looking forward to appearing at Georgia's trial.

There was a chance that Frank would turn up at the gig. He had been hanging around her office a lot more, practising the Labrador look. She'd cancelled their weekly meeting on the pretence of being sick; in truth she was sick of trying to make sense of her intuition, which currently was not sitting comfortably with the facts. Frank had looked concerned, but it was the sort of concern that came just before a guy tried to get into your pants. Frank wasn't exactly predictable on this front, but she thought there was a good chance he'd be there to see her looking hot in a blonde wig.

She was wrong; there was no sign of him at either gig. But there was someone else more interesting. Eliza's son, Jasper. He was sitting at a table with another man she didn't recognise. Seeing him there made her realise Jasper had been there before in the audience—with Frank. What was their relationship like? The resemblance was certainly there; the eyelashes mainly. Taller than Frank, skinny in that young-man way that suggested he had yet to fill out. Maybe Eliza went for men with girly eyes, and Jasper's dad had that in common with Frank. Surely he knew who his father was.

If he didn't then he'd be in the same position as everyone else; doubting his mother's insistence that Frank was not his father. She thought of her own fights with her mother on the topic, how angry she had been in her teens.

'Your father dumped us. End of story.' That was all she was told. She had memories of him, fragments of him playing with her. She didn't think he had dumped them, and knew that it was probably wishful thinking on her part. Her instinct told her that her father was dead now, and she was at peace with that. But what about Jasper, still in his early twenties? Was he content with whatever story his mother had told, or was he an angry young man?

She forgot all about him in the second bracket. Halfway through the first song she caught sight of Liam at the back of the room and her mind froze. She lost the line of the song and the music was halfway into the next before, with Shaun's help, she picked it up again. Liam was talking to Damian, though his eyes were on her. When their eyes met, he raised his Guinness to her, smile sardonic, eyes betraying nothing. Damian was watching him. What the hell was Liam saying? She felt sick at the possibilities, sick that Liam had walked unannounced and unexpected back into her life. And sick that she had to work hard to stop herself shaking. Desire? Maybe, but with it a mix of anger and fear. She steeled herself, singing on autopilot. She *would not* let him intimidate her. Not him, not any man.

She contemplated staying in the back room reserved for the band during the break. Contemplated a double shot of Jack Daniels before facing them, but in the end walked out sober.

Liam lifted his glass in acknowledgment. 'Long time no see.'

Adrenaline surged through her system. If Liam wanted to play games, so could she.

'You missing The Styx's unique sound?' He had to have some excuse at the ready for being there.

'A happy coincidence. I'm speaking at a conference in Lorne and saw the band was playing.'

Damian wasn't giving anything away but she doubted he would buy that. She wondered if Liam had researched her current living arrangements. He might have been arrogant enough to assume she was still pining for him, if the last encounter was anything to go by. On the other hand, revenge didn't tend to factor in the other person's desires.

Damian leaned on the bar watching them.

'So what was the conference?' Natalie asked.

'Forensic science shindig.'

'I thought you'd be up to your neck in the Georgia Latimer hearing.'

'Tania's a big girl, she'll cope. Besides, we've got a solid case. Your patient's never going to get off on a bad luck defence.'

'Jacqueline Barrett may disagree.'

'Then may the best man...or woman...win.'

'I heard you were homicide now.' Liam turned his attention to Damian as he took a slug of his Guinness.

'Did you?'

'Grant MacArthur still there?'

'Nope. Retired early. I took his job.'

'He was a good cop. Pity he left.' Liam looked at Natalie. 'Always seems to me that older guys,' his gaze flickered over Damian, 'can teach younger ones quite a lot.'

Damian took a sip of his beer and refused to rise to the bait. If it was just baiting.

Liam's smile towards Damian as he excused himself was stiff, and Natalie was left to wonder about the longer look back at her, and whether it really did hold traces of sadness. But mostly she was left doubting her own judgment about what had happened the last time they were together and whether the evening in Apollo Bay would have ended differently if Damian hadn't been there.

After the last bracket she went to the bar. Unable to see Damian in the crowd as it broke up, she nursed a bourbon and wondered if it was a habit she was growing out of. She seemed to be losing her taste for it. Or maybe she was close to spiralling downhill. Nothing ever tasted as good when you weren't high, and being on an even level was a hard place to stay. She caught sight of Jasper, who now had two young girls with him. The one sitting on his lap looked like the daughter of the Malosevics' chef and driver. Both were focused on him in the way women focused on Frank. It was probably the eyes.

'O'Shea was watching you.' Damian came up on her other side, not looking at her, gesturing to the barman.

'People do when I'm singing. That's why I stand at the front.'

'He's still hot for you.'

'I doubt it. Likes to think he has some power over me, more likely.'

'Does he?'

Natalie caught his eye and held it. 'At a personal level? No. It's over. He was bad for me then and he's just as bad for me now.'

'Because he's married?'

'That too.' She didn't feel the need to elaborate. Damian

could work it out for himself.

Natalie nodded towards the young man who looked like Frank. 'Thought of grabbing his glass for DNA? I'm sure I can manage to get a sample from Frank.'

Damian shook his head. 'This isn't *CSI*, Natalie. I'd have to get…'

'Live dangerously,' she said as she left.

Damian followed her back. She took it for granted, and he no longer asked. Did it matter that they were using each other to forget their previous partners? Everyone moved on and who was to say the next partner, rebound or not, wouldn't be more suitable than the last. Anyway, part of her liked the reassurance of Damian's presence. And he wasn't entirely conventional. She saw when his bag fell open that he'd removed a glass from the pub. More genetic games, but it might help make sense of what had happened to Frank's wives. And, if not, of what was at the core of Frank's grief.

Sunday night Damian served a chicken casserole in her stilt house. He was heading back to town the next morning and neither had brought up the topic of what would happen between them after the case was closed. Damian told her his father's Spanish second wife had taught him to cook. The casserole was nothing like anything she had eaten in her childhood. Red and oily, rich with flavour.

'Your own mother had problems, right?' He'd never said, but it was a party trick she could do when she felt like it. Tell them their back-story from what she knew. She generally got the broad gist right; more accurate, deeper, the longer she'd known someone. She knew Damian well enough to have worked out he had a mother problem.

'The marriage certainly did.'

Natalie looked at him. 'She still alive?'

Damian paused. 'Yes. Actually, she's pretty good now. I'm so used to playing down her problems, minimising the effect they had, I kind of forgot I probably don't need to do that with you.'

'So are you repeating patterns?' Natalie didn't let him off, dared him with her eyes to break off contact.

'You mean are you like my mother? Or was Caitlin? Or both of you?'

'Any or all, I guess.'

'Sounds like a relationship-type question. But we don't have one, do we?'

Natalie grinned. 'It was a trick question. You passed.' She paused. 'Now answer it properly.'

Damian eased himself back in his chair. Thought. Really thought about what she had asked. 'With Caitlin I tried to pick someone as far away from my mother as I thought was possible.'

'Did you succeed?'

'Yes and no. Caitlin wasn't mentally ill, but she is every bit as self-centred as my mother.'

'If you'd had kids together you'd still be there.'

'Yes. But only because of the kids. I'd known for a while she wasn't interested in me, not the me that wanted to be a homicide detective, the me that pictured us driving around Australia with the kids in the back, camping every night, or the me who was passionate about making something of my life. Luke and she are a far better match.'

She debated asking and stopped herself, but he had seen the question on her lips, heard it in there at the start. He answered it anyway.

'You are nothing like Caitlin. You're both petite but she's blonde and controlling as all hell. She cooks a mean curry, would rather spend her day filing her nails, gossiping and watching soapies than ever helping anyone. Do anything.'

'But...you think I'm like your mother.'

He surprised her. 'A bit. You're unpredictable and I don't think that's just that I don't know you so well. Maybe it's the bipolar, I don't know. My mum? She had issues, but doesn't everyone?' He looked at her. She was sure he wouldn't have been able to interpret anything in her expression. 'I'm not a shrink Natalie,' he finally said. 'But this attraction is gut instinct and a lot of animal lust.'

'The two aren't mutually exclusive.'

'So you think you're bad for me and I need therapy?'

'Yes to the first. Probably no to the second. We're both on the rebound.' She regretted her words as soon as they left her mouth. The look of hurt wasn't about Caitlin, it was about Liam.

'So I'm just the fuck until you find the next doctor or lawyer?' He tried to make it sound light but failed.

'Only ever screwed one doctor, and that was a mistake I assure you. Before Liam it was a cop. Briefly.' Tom hardly fitted Damian's description, either. And Eoin, even if he had lived, was never going to be establishment.

'I'm sorry. I shouldn't have said that. Just raw after Caitlin.'

'Don't worry about it.'

A lot of time passed in silence, a meal finished, dishes cleaned up. She thought she would just go to bed. Without him. He could use the downstairs bed. Easier. Let him move on.

'You aren't like my mother, you know.'

241

She looked back from the frame of her bedroom doorway.

'I love her and she is...well was, impossible. Made me take on too much responsibility far too early. But it made me who I am and I'm okay with that. She tried; didn't drink like her mother did when she was growing up.'

'Do you know what bipolar means? Do you know I've gone totally nuts a couple of times? No of course you don't. Nearly got disbarred as an intern. Fucked Alison's boyfriend—the one and only doctor on the score card—in the art gallery moat. Only reason I didn't end up with a charge was because my psychiatrist said I wasn't responsible.' She didn't wait to hear his comeback or see his expression. She closed the door.

She was in the midst of a bad dream when Bob screeching, 'Call the cops!' woke her. It was still dark and she groaned, figuring it was probably a possum. Then the night sky lit up as a bang sounded from downstairs and flames shot up past the back deck. Natalie was down the stairs in seconds, colliding with Damian at the door. As they ran outside she saw the flames had taken over the front section, along the railings of the balcony where they'd eaten earlier.

'Is there a garden hose?'

'Around the corner.'

'Call the fire brigade.' As Damian disappeared to get the hose he added, 'And the police.'

Natalie raced back inside to get a phone. After making the call she grabbed the metal bucket by the fireplace and began to throw random buckets of water onto the flames. Luckily they were mainly in the tree. Judging from the smell, they were fuelled by petrol.

The CFA were there first. It couldn't have taken them

longer than ten minutes, but in that time the tree beside the balcony was ablaze and the balcony had caught. With Bob serenading them with screeches, they calmly and carefully made sure every ember was out.

Luckily none of the glowing debris that had fallen onto the neighbour's tin roof had taken hold, and the house itself, apart from being full of smoke and drenched in water, was untouched.

'You're damned lucky you have your house left,' the fire chief told Natalie. 'If the wind had been going in the other direction it would have been a different story. Winter or not, this whole area is like a tinder box.'

'What I think saved it,' said Damian grimly, 'was that whoever threw the Molotov cocktail had a bad aim.'

They all looked at him.

'I heard it hit,' he said. 'My guess he was aiming for the balcony, but it lodged in the tree.'

'So given this looks like arson,' said the police sergeant, 'either of you want to tell me who might have thrown it?'

It was 4 a.m. before the CFA finally left. Natalie was exhausted but so tightly wired she knew she wouldn't sleep. She was too tired to clean up, and the only room totally unaffected by water was her bedroom, furthest from the back balcony. They both looked at the bed and then each other. 'You're safe,' said Damian, sounding as tired as she was. But she wanted him there with her and he saw it in her look.

The bed sagged down beside her and she rolled into him, neither of them wearing more than underwear. Skin on skin sent tingles through her; she smelled the singed hairs on his arms and the sweat from his fire-fighting efforts and wanted him.

'Maybe I should sleep on the floor.' Restraint was going to be impossible for them both otherwise.

'Oh what the fuck,' Natalie said.

She kissed him, and any hesitation on his part disappeared. His hands went over her body, pulling her to him, and she felt enveloped in a gentleness that gained increasing force as his ardour took over. When he knelt above her she thought how very different he was in every way from Liam, and the next thought, as they both came, was that there was something to be said for survivor sex.

It was inevitable I would bump into Jasper, but it didn't happen in the way I expected.

'Now doesn't that just take you back.'

I knew Mala well enough to pick the sardonic lilt. It's subtle; few others would.

We were sitting in the living room enjoying the aircon. Both Reeva, late in her pregnancy, and Vesna had retired for an afternoon nap. I followed Mala's gaze. Outside the distant sea was a dazzling blue and we were far enough away to enjoy it without any hint of the tourist throng. But she wasn't looking at the sea. Her focus was on the boathouse and the two people trying to untie the small boat from the jetty. One was Senka, sitting in the boat looking up at the young man, her face hidden. Jasper was looking as much in our direction, as he was at her.

'You know him?'

'Eliza's brat.'

I looked self-consciously to my room off the mezzanine. The door was firmly closed.

'Has…' I didn't need to say more. Mala could always tell what I was thinking.

'No, and I'll make sure she doesn't.' Mala got up and poured us each a glass of white wine, rubbing my shoulders with the freed-up hand after I took the glass. 'You worry too much.'

Reeva picked there was something wrong when she joined us a half an hour later. Senka and Jasper were still on the lake and I forced myself to not look in that direction. Mala smiled at Reeva and offered to get her a cold drink. Pregnant was bad enough; pregnant and hot was worse. She was also hyper-vigilant. I had yet to make sense of her preoccupations at that stage. But I didn't want to give her cause for them to escalate.

Unfortunately Vesna did not have the same clarity of mind on the subject as Mala and me. When she emerged from her siesta in a drug haze, she saw him immediately.

'What's he doing here?'

Reeva started at the venom in Vesna's voice. 'What's who doing here?' She was looking at Jasper and Senka walking up the path. Reeva frowned and looked at me.

'His name is Jasper Carson,' I said. 'I used to go out with his mother.'

Reeva was quick, she kept looking at me, eyes narrowing.

'Eliza slept with someone after me. To upset me,' I explained. 'Unfortunately he looked rather like me. Give or take.'

She didn't believe me. But in the end it didn't matter. She was dead two days later.

Before Liam closed the prosecution case he called Wadhwa. Channel Ten news interviewed the psychiatrist afterwards.

'The woman has a clear case of dissociative identity disorder,' said Wadhwa, beaming at the reporter, oblivious that she had taken a step back and extended the arm holding the microphone as if to distance herself. 'Persons with this disorder are *not* responsible as I have reported in many articles!'

According to the print media he had said much the same in court. And more.

Professor Wadhwa seemed to be of the opinion that he was a defence witness and kept wanting to argue the merit of the legal case for dissociative identity disorder. Justice Miller, after a remarkable show of patience, admonished the OPP and excused the witness. Justice Miller had refused to allow the OPP to bring in experts who had used Meadow's Law or similar discredited statistics. Now he added, *and I don't want psychiatric hocus pocus either.* It might not have been a great step forward for psychiatry, but it made Natalie's day.

The nights that followed, she slept fitfully. The local police had no leads on who had tried to torch the place; nor did Damian.

'Why don't you stay back in Melbourne?'

She wasn't sure if he was hinting that they could still date. 'I'm thinking of it,' she said. She didn't tell him she had spoken to her manager at Yarra Bend hospital, where she usually worked, and was planning on going back there. Even if she did continue in academe, it couldn't be with Frank.

As she watched Damian leave, she felt a little as if a holiday romance was ending—that things wouldn't be the same once she was back living in her Collingwood warehouse. There was a lot she liked about him, a lot that might even have been good for her, but she'd never once felt the spark that fired her up every time she had ever seen or thought of Liam. Even now, half-hating Liam, thoughts of him energised her. Damian's calm influence was what Declan had recommended. It was what her mother had settled for, too. But Natalie didn't think she could do it. Better, in the end, to be single.

Her nights were still full of images of blood, of the Worm and the fire and dead babies in a line of cribs, each with Vesna's haunted look, creeping into the crevices of her thoughts, taunting her. On the night before she was due to give evidence in Georgia's defence, she woke up shaking. It took several moments for the balaclava man at the end of her bed to disappear. She knew her lithium had to be low, but at least that meant the nausea was settling a bit. She hadn't taken her second mood stabiliser at all last night. If she took it now she would be slowed down and Liam would annihilate her on the stand.

*

Natalie was at the court at 9.30 a.m. Jacqueline Barrett was waiting for her, looking immaculate as always. Hair coiffed into the perfect bob, tan stockings, figure-hugging suit, skirt just above the knees. She ushered Natalie into one of the rooms earmarked for lawyer–witness discussions. Her junior joined them, an attractive girl in her early twenties trying to channel Jacqueline with a less expensive outfit and not quite succeeding.

'We've scored a reasonable judge,' said Jacqueline. 'Fair and not taking any of O'Shea's bullshit.'

Natalie wished she could ask what bullshit, but kept quiet. She'd seen Liam screw over one of her vulnerable patients on the stand, after he'd petitioned for Natalie not to testify because of a conflict of interest. The girl had crumbled. Natalie had no intention of doing so.

'How's Georgia bearing up?'

'Nervous, which is understandable.'

'So you're still not going the "not guilty due to mental illness" route?'

Barrett shook her head. 'She is very clear that she didn't kill her children. The autopsy reports leave room for doubt. There is no solid evidence of what caused these children's deaths.'

Barrett's case didn't sound as solid as her tone was trying to convey.

'Any feeling for how it's going?'

'I never try to predict these things.'

'And you wouldn't answer even if you did know.'

Jacqueline looked at her sharply and Natalie cursed herself. There was no love lost between them but she couldn't let her real feelings show. She stretched her fingers and rolled her shoulders, realising how tense she was. If she felt irritable with this lawyer, there would be fire and brimstone when Liam cross-examined her. Was it tension, or worse? She'd now had three days of low-dose lithium and no quetiapine. But there were no odd colours on the edge of her vision. That had to be a good sign she wasn't going manic.

It didn't help that Natalie thought Georgia was most probably guilty, even if she had mixed feelings about the appropriate punishment. Ultimately, it wasn't up to her. And maybe there was reasonable doubt—it was Jacqueline's job to lodge this in the minds of the jury. But Natalie wished she could paint a real picture for the jury, not the black and white one they were going to get. Georgia wasn't the personification of evil. She'd had a shit life, and she was a survivor. Paul may have been completely innocent technically but he hadn't stopped her killing their three children. He would have to live with that. And Georgia would have to live with the deaths—probably behind bars for most of the rest of her life.

'Paul came across well,' said Jacqueline finally. 'The autopsy results will be brought up again with my expert and so I'm not too fussed about that yet.'

Natalie nodded. She just wanted this over.

'So if we can go through your testimony?' Jacqueline's voice was icy. Seemed like she still would have preferred not to call Natalie, but thought she could limit the damage by doing so rather than letting the prosecution bring her in.

'I think she dissociates, but not into different characters. The dissociation is a defence, but not a complete enough process to mean she could have killed each of her children at these times and then had no memory of it,' Natalie summarised.

'So she doesn't have dissociative identity disorder, right?'

'That's what I'm saying.'

'Then just say that. We've already heard from Professor Graves'—Natalie didn't recognise the name—'that she is legally and psychiatrically competent.'

'And O'Shea is going to let me get away with that?'

'He'll probably make you elaborate.' Jacqueline sounded as if she'd like a bus to run Natalie over on the way into court.

'You're going to bring up the self-harm?'

'Professor Graves said it's common in borderline personalities. We don't need to go there again.'

'How was Georgia when Paul presented?'

'Same as always, best I could tell.'

Georgia had probably dissociated.

'She's told you that he knew about the self-harm?'

'Yes,' said Jacqueline sounding impatient. 'But she isn't going to testify. It's not something I want to dwell on.'

Natalie shrugged as the door opened and Georgia's solicitor stuck his head around it. 'We're on.'

Natalie followed him, feeling Barrett's eyes boring into her. What she said probably wouldn't make any difference anyway.

Natalie had given evidence before. The court room no longer held her awe-struck as it once had. It was about rules and process more than the whole truth—justice rather than best outcomes. Yes, Georgia had had a bad life but there were people from worse backgrounds who didn't kill their children. Whatever the background history of any of the criminals who came before this court, they were now adults, responsible for themselves. Responsible for making up for the past, not using it as an excuse.

If she were judge and jury what would she do? Guilty

verdict, maybe, yes. Keep Georgia away from children, definitely, yes.

But prison? Years behind bars would hardly change her. Nor deter anyone else, not when the cause was psychological in origin.

She sat behind Georgia, Jacqueline and the rest of the defence team. At the next table she saw Liam and Tania Perkins in easy conversation with their solicitor. Liam briefly looked up but didn't look directly at Natalie. She was sure it was a deliberate avoidance and steeled herself. Behind them, Paul gave her a half smile before looking away.

They all rose when Justice Miller entered, a lean man in his sixties wearing a suit that looked like he'd bought it before a cholesterol test had inspired the diet and daily walk with his wife. He nodded to the defence and prosecution, and they all sat. There were a few moments of discussion about something from the previous day before they called Natalie and swore her in, then got her to go through her qualifications and dealings with Georgia, first as an inpatient at Yarra Bend, then as her patient after she was out on bail. Liam was looking at her, smiling. She felt herself perspiring in her suit jacket. It made her feel she was playing at being a grown-up.

Jacqueline got straight to the point. 'Do you believe the defendant has dissociative identity disorder?'

'No.'

'But you are treating her, is that correct?'

'It is.'

'Could you describe, then, just what you are treating?'

Natalie knew Georgia's lawyer was trying to make her sound more like a therapist to the 'worried well'—the neurotic, rather than the seriously disabled—and for a moment it unnerved her. She took a breath and went slowly through her diagnosis of a mixed personality disorder, referring to the DSM V, the psychiatrists' bible. She was aware out of the corner of her eye that something she had said had generated a lot of interest on the prosecution table. There were notes and frantic whispers.

'Dr King?'

'Ah, I'm sorry, where was I?'

The clerk read back her last statement 'the narcissism meant that in her relationship with her children it was important that she was seen as a good mother and that if this was put into question it might destabilise her.'

Had she said that? Judging from Barrett's glare, yes.

'Yes...it's possible.'

'Surely that is the case for all mothers?'

'It's a matter of degree.' Natalie kept looking at the prosecution table. Liam smiled back at her. She felt herself start to shake. Grabbed hold of the railing in front of her and took a breath. *He's out to get you. You're not safe. You'll have to get him first.* Her thoughts started to fire in all directions.

'Dr King? Did you hear the question?' It was the judge, frowning.

'Yes. I, um, no, can you please repeat it?'

Jacqueline did so, slowly. '*What* is a matter of degree, Dr King?'

'How much such thoughts really shake your foundation. What defences you have to answer them back.' *Attack first. Don't let him get to you.* She sneaked a look at him. His blue eyes bored into her. *He thinks he can win.*

She managed to ignore him for the next two questions, mindful of how hard she was gripping the railing. Yes,

Georgia had maintained her innocence throughout her therapy sessions.

'That's all at this stage for the defence,' said Jacqueline. 'I retain the right to re-examine this witness.' She looked at Natalie oddly. She hadn't asked about the self-harm.

Natalie looked to the prosecutors, steeling herself. To her surprise it wasn't Liam who stood. As Tania rose Natalie could feel herself sweating. *What had Liam told her? What game was he playing? That's why he slept with you again, he wants you to fear him. It was all a plan to make you look like an idiot. You shouldn't ever have trusted him.*

Natalie took a deep breath and looked straight at Tania, whose eyes seemed to say *I know all about you two.* Shoulders back, eyes blazing. Fringe flicked to the side.

'Dr King we have heard from Professor Graves that Ms Latimer has a personality disorder. You would agree, is that correct?'

'Yes.'

'Does she dissociate?'

'Yes.'

Tania frowned, made sure the jury saw her look of confusion. 'Can you explain what you mean by that? Didn't you just say she didn't have a dissociative disorder?'

'Dissociation is also an unconscious defence. A separation of the mind, separating it away from feelings and actions, like you look at yourself and what is happening as if it wasn't you.'

'I see.' Tania scratched her head theatrically, looking to Liam for extra effect. 'Like *no I didn't pinch that officer, I was just watching someone else do it?*'

There was a ripple of amusement through the court room.

'No, not like that,' said Natalie stonily. 'More like—'

'Have you seen Professor Wadhwa's report?' Tania interrupted.

'Yes.'

'Exhibit 24, your Honour.' Tania offered a copy to Natalie as the judge rummaged in his papers to find his own. 'To refresh your memory. So you agree with him she has a dissociative identity disorder?'

'No, I—'

'Sorry, so you think she has a personality disorder like Professor Graves, who doesn't think she dissociates, but you don't agree with Professor Wadhwa who thinks she does?' Tania was shaking her head, puzzled look in place. More flicking. 'Wadhwa, who is an expert on dissociative disorders, tell us that Georgia has D.I.D. Yet you are telling us she has a personality disorder, but also dissociates, is that right?'

'Yes, but—'

'Can I clarify, you don't think she has D.I.D.?'

'No, but—' She stopped, took a breath. Didn't trust herself to speak.

Tania raised her eyebrows, continuing to fake a surprised look for the jury. Natalie was giving the prosecutor exactly what she wanted to hear, but it was the truth. *Liam will never let you live it down. No defence lawyer will ever touch you again.*

Tania looked into her notes though Natalie was sure she wasn't reading them. 'I can't see a PhD here amongst your qualifications, is that right?'

'I have a fellowship of the Royal Australian...'

'Ah, here it is. You're thinking of enrolling in one is that right?'

Bitch. Natalie gritted her teeth. 'Yes.'

'Perhaps you'd like to tell us how someone who hasn't

even yet enrolled in further education thinks they are better qualified than Professor Wadhwa, who I believe was your boss until recently?'

Tania was using one psychiatric witness to tear down another and discrediting her in the process. Natalie could see the jury looked confused. Would Tania drop that Wadhwa was no longer her boss because she had been ill, but omit the fact that he had resigned under pressure because of incompetence? Would she mention Natalie's psychiatric illness? Natalie had to fight a rising panic.

'I never said I was more qualified, Miss Perkins. But *Associate* Professor Wadhwa has spent maybe six hours with her. I have spent more than thirty.'

'Of course, Dr King. And you'd be less qualified than Professor Graves too, would I be right? I suppose it'd only be, what six thousand or so hours to complete a PhD?' Tania walked closer to her. But her eyes were on Liam and she was picturing the Worm coming at her, motioning across his throat and smiling dangerously, and involuntarily swayed back. Liam stared at her, frowned and signalled to Tania.

'May I ask your Honour for a moment's indulgence to confer with co-counsel?'

'Make it quick Mr O'Shea.'

Liam leaned over to Tania. She looked up at Natalie, then back at Liam, frowning and shaking her head.

'Mr O'Shea the court is waiting.'

'Thank you, your Honour. Miss Perkins is ready to continue'

Co-counsel did not look happy with whatever she had been told. She continued with her questions, tone less strident; what evidence did she have that Georgia had borderline, sociopathic and narcissistic traits? Why didn't she have D.I.D? And of course, was she responsible for her actions?

'There's something in your notes I need clarified.'

Natalie's stomach turned. *Shit.*

'You say here that the defendant was receiving cards from her husband.'

'Yes.' In the corner of her eye she saw Jacqueline Barrett's expression. If looks could kill Natalie would have been relieved of the pain she was currently enduring.

'But then...' Tania made a great fuss of turning over pages. 'Here you say...Actually, could you read it out?' She thrust the page at Natalie and pointed.

Natalie stared at where Tania was indicating, mouth dry.

'There is a question mark. Then *Did Paul or Georgia send these.*'

'Objection.' Jacqueline Barrett was up standing before Natalie had finished. 'These are clearly the doctor's personal deliberations at the time, not anything my client said.'

Justice Miller looked to Tania.

'Your Honour what the *treating* doctor who spent *thirty hours* with the defendant was thinking is surely relevant to what was going on in the defendant's mind?' Tania flashed a look a Liam that Natalie couldn't interpret.

'I'll allow it,' said Justice Miller. 'Providing you get to the point.'

'Certainly.' Tania smiled but her eyes were cold by the time she had turned to Natalie. 'So Dr King. Can you read the other highlighted sections?'

Natalie looked over the pages. Three lines over several appointments. She took a breath. '*Why bunny cards? Could this be because I reacted? Is she feeding me what she thinks I want?*'

Tania smiled. 'Thank you Dr King. That will be all.'

Jacqueline Barrett was back on her feet. 'Permission to re-examine?'

The judge nodded, straightening his robe and eye on the clock. The lunch break was imminent.

'Those comments all had question marks, correct?'

'Yes.'

'Do you know who wrote those cards?'

'No.'

'So it could have been her husband?'

'Yes.'

'You testified earlier that you thought the defendant had a personality disorder, correct?'

'Yes.'

'Can you tell the court what factors are likely to tip someone with a personality disorder like Georgia's to dissociate *occasionally*?'

'Stress. Of any sort, but children are unique in that way because there is the psychological meaning, the raising of unresolved issues from one's own childhood. But also because they are a constant demand, twenty-four seven.'

'So are there things that can improve or ameliorate the stress?'

'The stress of children? Yes. Support. Particularly by mother and partner.'

'But Georgia didn't have a mother available did she?'

'No.' She saw Tania pushing a note angrily at Liam. *Don't trust any of them.*

'So what help was Paul?'

Natalie looked at Paul. He met her gaze in stony silence. 'Paul was part of the problem.'

There was an immediate objection from Tania. The

judge overruled her and instructed Natalie to elaborate.

'Georgia needed him to adore her.'

Tania smirked. She couldn't read Liam's expression.

Natalie pushed on. 'From therapy it was clear that Paul liked to control her emotionally.'

'Clear? How?'

Natalie flashed a look at Georgia but she was looking over her head into nothingness. 'Subtle things. Which is why I believe them to be true. The type of things that occur in abusive relationships. Looks, withdrawal of affection. Georgia was vulnerable.'

'Were there any indicators that might have alerted him there was a problem?'

Finally Jacqueline had got there. 'Yes. Georgia self-harmed.'

Jacqueline's expression said something like, 'Fuck with me now and I'll make sure you never practise again.'

She could join the queue with Tania and Liam.

'Objection, your Honour. We already know this from Professor Graves. Where is counsel going with this?'

The judge leaned forward. 'Ms Barrett?'

'One moment and it will be clear.'

He nodded, mouth in a grim line. He was a man who needed his lunch.

'Georgia cuts herself, quite severely and in intimate places.'

'Now—' Barrett took a moment to refer to her notes. 'We heard earlier from Mr Latimer that he didn't know anything about it or any hint of mental illness. What do you think of that?'

'Georgia had been doing it for years. If you look at her general practitioner's notes and the obstetric record carefully, there is evidence of it happening prior to the birth of her first child.'

Tania made a grab for her copy of the file and there was a murmur throughout the courtroom.

Liam stood up 'Your Honour, can I request a chance to look at this through the lunch break and return to question the witness then?'

Jacqueline was on her feet saying they had had plenty of time and that the court was chewing up a professional witness's time, but she was overruled. The judge was hungry.

The police have closed their investigations. There is a sense of anticlimax, rather like the time after the funeral when there is no longer anything to contemplate but absence. We have not talked about it but we do not have to. The atmosphere is no longer tense, and though Vesna still takes long naps, Mala and I both feel less obliged to ensure my mother is watched.

She suffered from postpartum psychosis after each of our births; was this on my mind as I watched my wives' bellies distend? Did I have a fear, however illogical, that in my family childbirth was fraught with danger? That Vesna would also be more unpredictable? Of course when I discovered Reeva's family history I realised that any concern I might have had was not illogical. She was dismissive about it. But postpartum psychosis is considered a form of bipolar disorder, and there is a familial link.

Lyuba, Vesna's mother, suffered after Vesna's birth. She told Vesna she had a Romani curse on her; she was an uneducated woman and knew little else that could explain the horrors she had endured. But those horrors never left her, and Vesna's bedtimes stories were more Grimm than fairytale. Vesna's birth was physically difficult and afterwards Lyuba was unable to have more children. Part of the curse, she believed.

Vesna believed it too.

When she was excused from court Natalie walked out and kept walking. She was vaguely aware of Jacqueline Barrett calling, of the junior lawyer running after her, but she was out of the building and around the corner before she could be caught. She took gulps of air and found herself in a car park gasping, trying to control her breath. What the fuck had just happened? She felt electricity like a live current through her limbs, and her head buzzed. Fury boiled up inside her and she smashed her fist into the car park ticket machine.

'Fuck.' Her hand hurt, badly, but she didn't care. She wanted to hit Liam or Tania or Jacqueline Barrett. But it was herself she wanted to hurt. Why the fuck hadn't she taken the medication? She hit the machine again, this time hearing a knuckle crack. She could see one of the attendants tentatively approaching her.

'Ah...are you okay?'

No she wasn't okay. The entire fucking legal profession were plotting against her. *No.* She took a breath, assured the young man she was fine and returned to the street to hail a cab. She texted Barrett: she was unwell and wouldn't be back.

Barrett tried ringing but Natalie let it go to voicemail. A minute later a text appeared. *Tomorrow?* She'd have liked to reply no, but for Georgia's sake she couldn't do that. At least tomorrow she'd be in better shape than she was now.

Okay.

She went home to the warehouse, took twice the usual dose of her antipsychotics and slept.

There were texts from Damian and Liam when she woke the next morning, as well as Barrett's junior asking for clarification of her health state at 8 a.m. She was tempted to write *fucked* but conceded after a strong coffee that, while her head was foggy and she was still irritable, she felt less shaky than yesterday. Highs were great, usually. The irritable paranoid variety? Not so much so. And of course when she was really manic she got herself into trouble. She was getting better at picking the warning signs, but could still be sucked into the wonderful feeling of being invulnerable. If only that were the reality.

She wrote *okay*, had another coffee and took the tram into court.

'Yesterday morning was a train wreck.' Jacqueline didn't mince words.

'Can you recover ground?' This wasn't her problem, Natalie told herself. But even she didn't believe it.

'No problem. Long as Paul confesses to topping the kids, I'll have her home for Christmas.' The lines on Jacqueline's face looked deeper etched than Natalie had noticed in the past. Whether she truly cared for Georgia or it was just about winning, Natalie didn't know. But this mattered to Barrett too. 'I left my paediatric experts until last, so there's hope,' she said a little less sarcastically. 'And to be honest,

Perkins was scraping the barrel going for the qualification thing.' She smiled. 'She actually lost the crying woman on the jury. She looked like she was going to jump over the gate and defend you.'

Natalie wanted to say she didn't need defending, but this wasn't the time.

'So vulnerable is good,' Barrett went on, 'but say as little as possible.'

'Perkins wouldn't let me get a word out,' Natalie said angrily, though part of her knew she was just doing her job. And doing it better than Natalie.

'She was good.' Jacqueline frowned. 'But O'Shea is better. I can't for the life of me understand why he didn't take the lead.'

'Because he was worried about the jury, probably.'

Barrett shook her head. 'He can get a jury to eat out of his hand—women in particular.' Her eyes narrowed. 'Is there any history between you two?'

'Previous case.'

'I mean personal'

Natalie remained silent.

'You know it's considered unethical to examine anyone on the stand if there's a relationship history?'

Of course. Liam would know that.

'He hasn't declared a conflict of interest,' Barrett continued hopefully. 'So if there is I could still...'

Natalie shook her head. 'We are not in a relationship.' No sense having their personal life splashed around, even if Lauren already knew about their affair. Liam had done the right thing by handing over to Tania, after all.

Jacqueline looked disappointed. She sighed and then went on to tell Natalie she had been able to put in two character witnesses the previous afternoon, which had brought the level of tension down. And the hearing hadn't been delayed. 'Which is just as well,' she said. 'Miller's a stickler for time.'

That might have been true but he seemed genuine when he asked after her health, before reminding her she was still under oath. She had vowed not to look at Liam, but to her surprise he wasn't even in attendance. No one else seemed to think this odd. She assumed he was needed elsewhere. Or was anxious that Jacqueline might go the ethics route and get a mistrial. She relaxed a little.

Tania started with Georgia's self-harm, suggesting the cuts were so small and discreet that they would have gone unnoticed. Natalie smiled at her. She felt calmer than yesterday. Not her normal self exactly; but she wouldn't lose it today. *No matter what.*

'I suppose that is possible. She would have bled after intercourse at times; maybe they just pretended she was a virgin.'

Tania looked at her in shock. Some of the members of the jury looked likewise but at least two had to fight down giggles. The crying juror looked like she wanted to pump her fist in the air.

'What if they rarely had sex?' Tania persisted. 'Or only in the dark?'

'You'd have to ask Paul for his version of their sex life,' said Natalie evenly. One of the jurors frowned, leaned forward. 'My understanding from Georgia was that it was quite robust. If you're talking hard evidence, they had sex at least four times we know of, and children aren't usually conceived on a single occasion.'

Jacqueline got to ask the final question. 'When Georgia was self-harming, would she have appeared well?'

'No. She might have been able to hide her distress at times, and maybe from those who didn't know her.'

'But not from her husband?'

'No, not from her husband.'

When she left the court she smiled at Georgia but the woman looked right through her. She paused, wanted to pat her shoulder, let her know she wasn't completely alone, but was aware of the whole court watching her. Sympathy might make it worse rather than better for Georgia, so she kept walking.

Outside the air was cold and traffic noises drowned out her thoughts. She leaned against a parked car feeling sick. It was over. She had nothing on now until she returned to Yarra Bend in a couple of weeks. Plenty of time to settle her mental state.

'What happened yesterday?'

She froze.

Liam. He had been waiting for her. He must have been in the foyer of the law court and seen her leave. He stopped when he saw her expression.

'I was...briefly...not well.'

'What sort of not well, Natalie?'

She straightened herself up. Liam had seen her on the border of full-blown mania, hadn't known what it was, but hadn't liked it. Then the Worm had sent him the records of her first admission. He had a pretty good idea. *He hadn't used it against her.*

'None of your business.'

'Jaysus Natalie, I'm trying to help you.'

She felt her anger surge, felt her fists clenching. 'Like you helped me when you came over last?'

Liam looked at her guiltily. 'We need to talk.' His hand

went to her arm and she pulled away angrily.

'Get your fucking hands off me.'

He stepped back, hands in the air. 'Relax. I'll buy you a coffee. Or something stronger if you like.'

'I don't want you buying me anything.'

Liam rubbed his forehead. 'I'm sorry about my jibe. When I was leaving your place, I mean. I hadn't realised I was still angry. At myself, not you.'

Natalie looked at him, steadied herself on the parked car. 'I can't have you in my life Liam.'

'You seeing McBride?' There was a tone she couldn't quite pinpoint. If her mind hadn't been so foggy she'd have said it was regret.

'I'm needing to repeat myself: none of your business.'

He looked like he was going to step in and grab her but thought better of it. 'Lauren and I were over the moment she knew about our affair.' So she had thrown him out. Poor Liam. She wondered if he got to see his children, whether Lauren had turned them against their father. The only one they had, for better or worse.

There was an instant where he let his vulnerability show, but he closed it down quickly, and shrugged. 'I moved out six months ago.'

She stared at him, overwhelmed with the implication of what he was trying to convey, then without saying anything turned and walked away.

She was only ten metres on when one of the parked car's doors opened. Damian stepped out and leaned across the car, glancing to where Liam was still standing.

'You okay?'

No, but she couldn't talk about it.

'You didn't answer my calls or texts.'

'Been busy.'

'Preliminary tests say that Jasper and Frank are related.'

'Ah. Guess that figures.'

Damian frowned. 'Natalie, you can talk to me.'

'Yeah?' She looked back towards Liam, who hadn't moved and whose expression was indecipherable.

'I see.' Damian's mouth was in grim line. 'I guess I'll be going.'

She watched him get back in the car, and had already started walking before he drove off. She didn't look back.

In the end she forced herself to see Declan and risked him telling her that it was too early to go back to work at Yarra Bend. Talking helped, as it always did, and when she left his rooms she felt more confident that she wasn't on the verge of a full-on relapse.

'You're only a few months out from a major depressive episode,' Declan reminded her. 'Someone has tried to kill you, or warn you off at the very least.'

To say nothing of her personal life. But Declan was more interested in another matter.

'What's happening with Frank Moreton? Is he still debriefing with you?'

'Truth is I've avoided meeting. Well, he cancelled one, I cancelled another.'

Declan sat still, pen poised. 'Why?'

'Why did Frank cancel? I don't know, but I had lunch with his sister, which he might not have liked.'

'His sister?'

Declan didn't look happy; maybe it was Mala he had in therapy. But Frank was not her patient so boundary issues weren't the same. There was no rule that said you couldn't see a supervisor's sister. Nor a peer's. Natalie's 'debriefing' of Frank, as Declan called it, was informal, friendly. She ate with Frank in restaurants. Her gut feeling was that Declan wouldn't like that either.

'Frank's family think I'm wanting to follow in Alison's footsteps. I can assure you I am not.'

Declan still didn't look happy. 'So why did you cancel?'

Now that was a more interesting question. No point giving a glib answer; he wouldn't let her get away with it. 'I don't know.'

Declan leaned forward. 'Before you get defensive, think on this for a moment. Carefully. You are in an awkward position with him. Confidant and peer, yet his junior. And you essentially work for him. You're also single and attractive.'

She nodded, didn't intend to let herself off the hook. But she didn't answer.

Declan hesitated. 'Does he intimidate you?'

Her eyes widened and she nearly gave her reflexive retort: *No fucking way.*

She caught herself. Declan was not diminishing her ability as a professional, or as a woman. She remembered Frank's subtle looks of pleading, mingled with entitlement and assurance. It was the same fertile emotional ground that had nurtured Georgia and Paul's relationship. She also thought of the gloss it had brought her to think she was smarter than Reeva—because then Frank would like and approve of her?

'No,' she said finally, her tone covering an uncertain territory of maybes. 'However...' She took a breath.

Declan watched as she organised her thoughts.

'There is sense I have with him of being...I don't quite

know. Roped in? That it would be easy to please him, rather than telling him the hard stuff.'

'And you want to please him?'

Did she? Yes, but when she'd cancelled the last appointment it was because part of her had rebelled. She recognised at a deep level her feet were in quicksand and she didn't like the feeling.

'Be careful, Natalie. And get him into therapy.'

Natalie walled herself up for the rest of the week, meditating by the sea. The media were engrossed in Georgia's trial so she was able to follow it online. They largely ignored both Graves and herself, for which she was grateful, but wrote pages on the paediatric testimony. Justice Miller might not have let Liam's dubious statisticians into his court room, but he had allowed Barrett's experts, and she clearly had some convincing statisticians arguing Georgia's case. Perhaps that was why she hadn't wanted to focus on the murky grey psychiatric side of things.

'*So what are the chances of three children dying of SIDS in one family?*'

'*It very clearly becomes more likely rather than less,*' Professor Larkins said. '*One in a thousand. But then it's more like one in a hundred after two or three. It simply suggests that there is a common underlying condition that we have been unable to detect.*'

The journalists had been at least partly convinced. Only one picked up what the prosecution had highlighted: '*Wasn't the oldest child, Olivia, at nearly two, too old for SIDS?*'

The arguments concluded at the end of the six-week trial and the jury was sent out to deliberate. It seemed it was going to be close. The final arguments for both sides were compelling. Jacqueline had pushed the notion of reasonable doubt and raised the tragedies of innocent women put in prison by false science and public opinion, rather than any actual evidence.

'*A woman who did well at school, who has had a ten-year marriage, who was a functioning member of society,*' Jacqueline was reported as saying in her final argument. '*She had a rough start in life but she was resilient. She had skills, as you have heard. She worked in a caring profession, as a nurse. Yes, she had some personality traits that came out under stress—but I ask you all to look deep within. Don't you all? Can you all honestly say you've never screamed at a child? Wanted to slap one? But it doesn't mean we do.*'

Natalie imagined the feeling in the courtroom would have taken a collective breath at this point. '*Did she have to harm her children to get rid of these frustrations? No, of course not. No more than any of us do. She had an outlet— Facebook. And in darker moments—darker than you or I have ever known, perhaps—she hurt herself, rather than them.*'

Liam had gone for the bruise on the older child's nose— some evidence at least—and the Facebook entries that had suggested anger.

'*The defence experts say one in a hundred. But that refers to SIDS in infants, not a two-year-old child. Whether the chance is one in a hundred, one in a thousand or one in a trillion*'—Justice Miller must have been glaring—'*it does not explain a two-year-old dying, let alone one with a bruise on her nose. When only her mother was there. No controlling husband, just Georgia Latimer. Georgia's mother killed. Georgia killed. Narcissistic rage, ladies and gentlemen of the jury.'*

Anger that Natalie's diagnosis, as well as Graves' and Wadhwa's, had explained. The same anger that underpinned dissociation and self-harm could also have caused her to kill.

There was nothing more she could do, so Natalie's thoughts went to Frank, and what Declan had said about him. Did Declan know, or had he guessed something? Intimating perhaps that Frank was more than a simple narcissist; rather, a malignant one, situated at the end of the spectrum where the disorder blurred with psychopathy and the person, incapable of empathy, used others to their own end.

She doubted she could get Frank into therapy, but it wasn't this that worried at her. She still owed Alison. Still had the pieces of a jigsaw in front of her and felt she was the only one who could put them together. Her own narcissism perhaps? Maybe, but Damian's tools, the methods of law enforcement, were too crude for this puzzle. He needed her help.

She thought about the tyres and the fire bomb. Eliza or Jasper warning her off? She wondered how much danger she was in.

Bob, sensing her anxiety, kept telling her to call the cops. All it did was remind her that a real relationship, with someone she could confide in, was missing from her life.

She thought about Liam, reanalysed the night in her warehouse, their last meeting. Any way she looked at it he was still bad for her, and it didn't matter if he was with his wife or not.

She'd blown it with Damian. As she always did, her life

script. Her father left her with what Declan had suggested was a 'narcissistic wound': if her own father hadn't loved her enough to stick around, then how could any other man ever love her? Easier to pick unavailable men, or reject them first.

Damian hadn't been bad for her, but she'd been bad for him.

My childhood was one of bad magic and secrets. How does one deal with such a heritage when one is intelligent and educated? Psychiatry offered me a way of making sense of both my worlds without relying on tarot cards, conspiracy theories or pills. The life examined. I could, I suppose, have achieved the same through my own psychoanalysis. An hour a day, on a couch three to five times a week. I could have unloaded my guilty secrets and desires onto a therapist, and unravelled the complex interplay of my desire to be loved by my mother and her need to be cared for; my need to glow golden before Antonije and my fear that because I was not an artist I would never be good enough. And the unnamed pain and longing that occasionally caught me when I least expected.

I saw an analyst for three months during my psychiatry training. I might have continued had I not chosen badly. It made sense to me to find a female therapist; have I mentioned that I get on best with women? There is none of the competitive drive that men arouse in me. And doubtless I subconsciously wanted the unconditional love of mother in the safe environment I had never had. But we are all driven by such subconscious longings; there was hardly harm in it.

Victoria had seemed a good choice from a limited field. Ten years older than me, she had only been practising in private for a few years. What I was still too junior to understand was that she was still undergoing her own analysis and supervision. I would not have willingly allowed any of my story to go beyond her and me: I did not come from a family that trusted easily.

For the first month I thought we progressed nicely. In the second month she seemed more withdrawn and less forthcoming with comment or interpretation. In the third it became clear that she was struggling with her own issues: the countertransference. Was it because she was single and found me attractive, or because she was gay and I challenged her ideas of sexuality? From wearing skirts that showed her knees and shirts that outlined her breasts rather well— perhaps too well—she started wearing trousers and loose jackets. She thought I wouldn't notice that she had moved her chair ever so slightly further away but the carpet marks betrayed her. She no longer leaned into me or gave the small secret smile as I left. At one stage I wondered if she was videoing us, so hard was she trying to present as the perfect therapist. When I asked, she looked so terrified for a moment that I thought I was right.

'No. Whatever makes you say that?' she asked, too quickly.

I knew I had hit on something. 'Have you spoken to anyone about these sessions?' I smiled at her, watching the twitch under her eye flicker three times.

'No. Well, yes. I...I get supervision. No names or anything.'

But it meant that someone else knew my story. Someone

I hadn't given permission for her to share it with, knew about it. I had revealed more than enough information to identify me. And I had named my grandfather, often.

'I expect that to cease.' I was pleasant; I haven't lost my temper since I was ten. 'And I would like the notes. All of them.'

Victoria was flushed; it made her skin an unpleasant mottled colour. She tried to argue that the notes belonged to her, but she knew she wasn't going to win that argument.

I didn't return. But I did pay my bill. I like loose ends tied up.

Georgia was Natalie's last patient of the day. The jury had been out for two days and the waiting wouldn't be easy for her: Georgia's capacity for denial would be stretched to the limit. Natalie wasn't expecting an easy session and she wasn't surprised that Georgia was late. But when she was fifteen minutes overdue and didn't answer her home phone or mobile, Natalie felt a twinge of anxiety.

'Yes,' said Jacqueline Barrett. 'I spoke to her around one o'clock when we were told the jury wouldn't be back today.'

Natalie stared at Georgia's file and replayed the conversation she had with Declan. What if Georgia had finally seen the reality of her life? If she was found guilty, which seemed likely, it meant a long time behind bars. Arguably, she deserved it. But the picture of Georgia, regressed to a child, wetting her pants, was firmly etched in Natalie's mind. Tempering justice with mercy wasn't easy. Maybe for a psychiatrist it wasn't meant to be.

It took thirty minutes in the peak hour traffic to get to Georgia's flat. The apartment block, a relic of the seventies in a leafy suburban street, was tired and out of place.

Predictably, no one answered. Curtains shrouded the windows. Natalie banged louder.

'What the hell you doing lady?' The head of a young black man emerged from the next door along the corridor. His accent was heavy Horn of Africa. It looked like he'd been sleeping. Or trying to.

'I'm worried about my friend,' said Natalie. 'I think something might have happened to her.'

The man groaned, stepped out. Six feet six of bone and muscle. Tracksuit pants longer than her height hanging around his butt. He flicked a knife out of his pocket. Natalie stared at it, too stunned to react. 'Locks here are shit,' he said. A quick jerk and Georgia's door was open.

'Can you stay here a moment?' Natalie asked, looking into the dark corridor, suddenly panicked. The knife-owner gave her a goofy smile, one hand hitching his trousers.

She called out and stood in the echoing corridor listening to her own heartbeat. The apartment was devoid of character in the dim light. She would have sworn no one had lived there for months. No pictures on the wall, no ornaments or little tables to put them on. In the kitchenette, as she walked past, there was a solitary cup on the sink; benches wiped clean of ownership.

Natalie had prepared herself for something gruesome. Blood, or the sight of the bulging tongue and eyes that result from hanging. She had treated slashed wrists, stabbings and gunshot wounds as an intern in the emergency department. But what dominated her memory was the team's urgency and efficiency; the equipment ready at hand to help save life.

What Natalie wasn't prepared for was the still, quiet reality of a lonely death.

Georgia was in her bedroom. Natalie had known

somehow that was where she would be. No blood. No bulging eyes to accuse. As yet, no smell. Just empty pill bottles and skin cold to touch. She looked, thought Natalie, strangely at peace. There was no note but Georgia hadn't needed one: the explanation was all around her.

The Sudanese lock-breaker called the police while Natalie waited with Georgia, both of them surrounded by the artefacts of the existence Georgia had wanted to believe in.

Every surface, including the ceiling, was covered in photos. All were of Paul and her. There was not one picture of their children; neither the three dead infants nor the one who'd survived.

Later Natalie recalled thinking over and over that things went in threes and that this meant it was all over. She was trying to explain that to Declan hours later, when he came out of his rooms and found her sitting on the porch in the rain. But nothing she said made any sense to either of them.

Georgia's suicide had opened the memory of her own depression; the terror she'd felt at the bottom of the pit when she had considered killing herself. She had despised herself for her weakness; yet doing so meant she had to despise Georgia and all her troubled patients who went to that place. She didn't want to be like them, and was ashamed at her own narcissism, the belief that she was superior. As she poured out her thoughts to Declan she didn't even know she'd been thinking that.

'You're angry,' Declan observed, and it horrified her that he was right. How could she be angry at Georgia, whose future, when she'd looked ahead, had been so bleak and so meaningless that death was preferable? She didn't want to be someone without compassion. But the anger was at herself, and not just for her weakness, for having thought of doing the same as Georgia. The anger was that Georgia had shown her up to be less than perfect. Less than even a good-enough therapist.

'You aren't her, Natalie,' Declan said. But for months now Natalie hadn't known who she was. The old Natalie kicked butt. She would never give up, or in. The passivity of the new one terrified her.

'I shouldn't have testified.'

'You were legally obliged and she knew that, Natalie. The perfect relationship she desired wasn't with you, it was with Paul. She killed herself because the fantasy couldn't be maintained: beneath the surface she was very fragile and without defences. And it wasn't despair that killed her, it was anger. Uncontrolled anger, the same that may well have killed her children, and then turned inward. This is the work we do. The risk we hold and have to bear. We won't ever be able to save everyone.'

'I failed her.'

'No Natalie. Her family failed her, the system failed her when she was a child. It was her illness that then killed her. You did more than anyone else.'

'It wasn't good enough,' Natalie said, mostly to herself. She needed to harness her anger, not turn it inward; if she did that, the black hole would reclaim her. Seconds turned into minutes. Natalie finally took a breath and sat up, looking directly at her supervisor. 'Georgia made her choice, now I want to make mine. I want myself back.' Natalie watched Declan's expression become wary. 'I've tried, but trouble attracts me, and vice versa. Honest truth? I like it that way.'

Declan rubbed his forehead. 'This isn't exactly news to me, Natalie.'

'I know, Declan. But I just can't settle for a life where I am constantly having to pull myself back. I am passionate about my patients and passionate about my work: the tough stuff, not research. Without that? I'm barely alive.' She'd just re-read bits of a memoir: a psychologist and professor of psychiatry (possibly the only academic she had any time for) who had bipolar disorder. Leaning in to Declan, she quoted: *'If I can't feel, if I can't move, if I can't think, and I don't care, then what conceivable point is there in living?'*

Declan looked thoughtful. He stood and went to his bookshelf. 'If memory serves,' he said, 'she abandons the idea of a life without mayhem, but—'

'Not mayhem. Without *storms*,' said Natalie. 'Because she preferred turmoil over a stunningly boring life.' Like a life in the country doing research.

Declan shook his head, leaned in as he sat. 'I doubt Professor Jamison would be happy to know that's all you took from the book.'

Natalie smiled ruefully. 'Yes I know, Declan. She thinks lithium saved her life.'

And Natalie was taking her lithium. Just a lower dose, to minimise side effects. It was hard to know which was worse: the black hole or the prospect she might never feel the wild energetic magic of a high ever again. 'Not just the lithium,' Natalie added. 'Also her psychotherapist.'

She wasn't normally one for sentimentality but now she smiled. 'What would I do without you?'

Natalie started reclaiming her life by throwing out the pastel-coloured clothing she'd tried for the demure-researcher look. Floral? She shuddered. One night down, and the nightmares were better. Telling her fears to fuck off was working better than meditation. As for the herbal tea, she'd thrown her Morning Dew to the cockatoos, who were as uninterested in it as she was.

The next day Jacqueline Barrett informed her that the jury had turned in a verdict. Natalie wondered if Georgia would have taken the same decisive action regardless of the jury's conclusion. She congratulated the lawyer, but neither of them felt like celebrating. Still not sure what she felt about Liam, she texted him: *Nobody won this one.*

Georgia might have been found not guilty, but Natalie felt guilty enough for them both.

'I have missed seeing you.' Wei came over as soon as she arrived, meeting her at the computer carrel. He looked her up and down. 'Had a makeover, have we?'

Natalie turned to face him, back in skin-tight black and her own bodyweight of silver jewellery, a heavy line of kohl around her eyes. It was a new look only to those who had met her for the first time since she arrived down the coast— now she was looking like the real Natalie. She hoped her inner sense of self would catch up soon.

Wei's expression suggested that he knew why Natalie was pulling all her papers out of the trays. 'I've done a lot of thinking. I want to finish off some things here and then I'm resigning.' She wasn't sure she actually had any arrangement formal enough to warrant a resignation, but it amounted to the same. A failed trial of sanity-on-the-sea.

For a moment Wei looked surprised, though she couldn't imagine why. It wasn't as if he would be there much longer either. 'Does Frank know?'

Natalie shook her head. 'Not yet.' She put the papers in her bag and slung it over her shoulder. 'I need to use the computer in the office.' She didn't wait for his response, just strode into the office that had once been Reeva's and Alison's, and fired up the machine.

She was determined to resolve this case, in her own mind at least. With any luck, she'd be able to give Damian some sort of proof as a consolation prize for helping her hold herself together in the past few months.

She felt decidedly unhappy, but the flip side was that she was *feeling*. Facing life, not running away from it. Perhaps Georgia's greatest gift, one Natalie didn't feel she deserved, was to show her how much she did want to live, and how grateful she was to Declan and the hospital team that had treated her and steered her away from ending up like Georgia.

She was feeling the normal—unpleasant—feelings of life not dealing you the cards you want. Much better than the grip of despair that could lead her places she didn't want to go.

And she felt adequately energised to try and re-deal the pack. In her own house, in her own job, after talking to the real estate agent about repairs to the stilt house. And after finishing what she had started with Frank and his wives.

She opened up the internet browser on Reeva and Alison's computer. This time she went through its full history. After staring at the browser and the genetic searches she couldn't believe she had missed it. Why would anyone risk their baby with an amniocentesis if there was no need? The baby needed checking only if one parent was positive. From her family history—lack of it—Alison had known she wasn't a carrier. It was *Frank* she would have checked.

She made some calls. The second lab found his test results for Huntington's. Done a week before Alison died, around the time she had rung her ex-boyfriend Oliver, when she didn't want Frank to know what she was up to. Natalie had to ask the technician to repeat the results twice.

Negative.

On the way back to the stilt house, she stopped in Lorne. Eliza Carson's gallery was closed but she made her way around the back where she could see Eliza in the breakfast room painting. She looked up when Natalie knocked, making no attempt to hide her irritation at the intrusion as she opened the door.

'I don't have anything to say to you.' Eliza's lips were pressed firmly together, faint creases lining her mouth. She was about the same size as Natalie, a little heavier, but not prepared for Natalie pushing past her.

'Out! I want you out of here.' She stood in the doorway as Natalie sat on a kitchen chair.

'After we talk.'

Eliza went to get her phone.

'If you want the police I'd be delighted. I'm sure they'd be very interested in my theory of who petrol-bombed my house. And let's not get started on the cost of an expensive pair of tyres for my bike.'

Eliza crossed her arms, digging into her fingernails into her own flesh. 'I don't know what you're talking about.'

'Really? Should we call your son, then?'

Eliza's fingers loosened their grip. For the first time she looked doubtful.

'Sit.'

Eliza reluctantly did so.

'So here's my theory,' said Natalie lying back in her chair. She put her bike helmet on the ground. 'Jasper may or may not know who his daddy is, but unless you have DNA evidence of someone other than Frank, he's going to be pretty sure he does know.'

'It isn't any of your business.'

'It became my business when Alison died because I have this odd characteristic. I like to pay for my mistakes. Balance the ledger. Don't care if someone owes me, happy to let it go. But if I owe them? I like to pay. I owed Alison because I behaved badly; I hurt her, and she died before I got to say sorry properly. She wouldn't talk to me back then, and more recently she had other things on her mind.'

'She's dead. If the Malosevics are responsible they'll get away with it. That's what happens when you are that arrogant and rich.'

'But it also became my business when someone targeted me. Any idea why that might be, Eliza?'

She shook her head. But she suspected something; she wouldn't look Natalie directly in the eye.

'You've been paid off, to keep quiet, right?' Eliza didn't respond, which Natalie took as an affirmative. She pushed ahead. 'So here's my wild theory. Jasper, a bit lost and fatherless, sees me in the band. Sees Frank checking me out. Maybe hears that Frank and I have a regular get-together in Wye River, it being a small town and all, and nothing like that would be hard to find out around here. Including where I've been staying. You still with me?'

Eliza nodded. Her eyes went to the clock.

'And just maybe you are on Alison's side, hell you've been there before, haven't you? And you were seeing it happen all over again, or so you thought. Even if Alison didn't.'

Eliza was shaking her head, now looking angry. 'No,' she said. 'Jasper wouldn't...'

'Wouldn't slash my tyres? Petrol-bomb the house? Really? Someone did.'

'He wouldn't. I haven't said anything to him about Alison or Frank or...Nothing.'

Natalie wondered if she could be telling the truth. If Eliza hadn't told him, he'd worked it out for himself. 'There is of course another possible motive along the same lines.'

Eliza frowned.

'What if Jasper thinks he's Frank's son—and wants to be his only son?'

Eliza's eyes widened.

'You came back to Lorne when Reeva was pregnant. Did you know about her and the baby?' Natalie watched her. Her money was on Eliza driving Jasper's malevolence. Older, with many more years to let bitterness and greed eat away at her. Once Reeva got pregnant the inheritance started to look more complicated. If her bitterness had worked on Jasper, he wouldn't have been hard to persuade. All Eliza would have had to say to him was, 'Wish this new doctor would leave town'.

Had Eliza also planned with him to get rid of Alison? Jasper was young and arrogant; he thought he'd get away with it, thought he was invincible. He probably hadn't covered his tracks well.

It was then that she heard the throb of the V8 coming down the lane beside Eliza's gallery.

'Worried, are you?' asked Eliza.

I was a young man faced with unreasonable circumstances. It is hardly surprising that I behaved with less dignity and care than I would today. I was trying to examine and make sense of my life; hadn't that been the purpose of seeing Victoria?

One of the first topics we discussed was Eliza. Though Antonije had handled the situation I felt a degree of involvement such that it was hard to distance myself entirely.

I say 'discussed' but of course psychoanalysis, even more than its half-sister psychodynamic psychotherapy, is more a soliloquy with an occasional one-liner from the analyst to show they haven't gone to sleep. To be fair, Victoria at least gave me her interpretations when I requested, as well as at the end of the session whether I asked or not. They improved as she got to know me. Or, as I later understood, as her supervisor got to know me. This was disturbing in retrospect. Victoria was young and relatively inexperienced. Her supervisor was older and male, with thirty years of practice.

What did they make of my heartless treatment of Eliza? Victoria didn't have all the pieces because I hadn't been foolish enough to trust her that much, and I did of course balance the facts of our splitting up and her pregnancy with Eliza's own behaviour, and what I had come to realise. The reasons why I had chosen to terminate the relationship.

She was a slut.

Victoria reacted to that: I could see the word on my lips left a bad taste on hers. 'Can I clarify? Didn't you tell me last session she was a virgin?'

'I meant slut in that she sought to sell herself, not that she had.' Though she did, of course.

Victoria looked confused. 'She wanted you to pay her?'

Victoria really wasn't very smart.

'She wanted it all. Marriage, kids. But most of all she wanted Mount Malosevic.'

'Did she tell you that?'

I laughed. 'Not directly. But yes, she said it.'

Unluckily for Eliza, women talk to me. I can be persuasive if I have to be but in this case, with her girlfriend, I merely had to buy her a drink.

'You've got it all wrong,' said Eliza abruptly.

The engine died and Natalie could see through the kitchen window as he got out of the silver Commodore, running his hand through a longer version of Frank's wavy hair. She was reminded of the Worm; a little taller and heavier. A good deal bigger than her. She felt her stomach tighten and she set her jaw defiantly.

'What's she doing here?' Jasper was talking to his mother but his eyes were on Natalie. He was taking up most of the doorway, a slab of beer tucked under one arm.

'Let me handle this.' Eliza looked pale. Worried, but about what? What he might do to Natalie? He was smirking at her. All Frank's arrogance without the charm. Or rather, charm not turned on for her now. Her stomach tightened further; she could feel her heart pounding as she repressed the anxieties that still lingered from the Worm's attack in the past, and the increasing possibility that she was at risk again. The link with the girl at Mount Malosevic gave Jasper the means to kill Reeva and Alison—he could easily be there visiting at any time. She hadn't until now thought it a real possibility that Jasper had been responsible for any more than the warnings. Now she was concerned she was looking at someone a good deal more calculating than an adolescent angry at his dad for not owning up to his paternal responsibility.

Natalie remained seated. Standing over her gave him the psychological advantage—but only if she let it. In any case she was going to be dwarfed by Jasper whatever she did. Let him think she was scared if he liked. That would give her an element of surprise; her only potential way out if things got ugly.

'Jasper.' There was an edge to Eliza's voice. Jasper shot her a look Natalie couldn't interpret.

'I was telling your mother,' said Natalie, 'that it would be a good idea to dissuade you from more stunts with Molotov cocktails.'

'Yeah? Am I meant to know what you're talking about?' He closed the door behind him, the soft click more ominous than if he had slammed it. He stood between her and it.

'Does Frank know about it?'

Jasper's eyes widened. She took that as a no. Yet there was something there she had touched on. Pleasure at having harmed someone he thought his father might care about? Pleasure that he was taking action while his father was a wimpy academic?

'Seems to me,' said Jasper, putting the slab down on the table, 'you're messing in stuff that is none of your business.'

'That was the message the fire bomb and tyre-slashing were meant to deliver? And let's not forget the attempt to run me off the road.'

He was standing closer to her now, close enough for her to make out the rash of acne on his cheek and a skull hanging from his earring. Eliza was stony faced: Natalie wouldn't rely on her to come to the rescue.

'I think you know jack-shit.'

'I think you should go.' Eliza moved to the door.

'I haven't finished.' Natalie didn't move.

'Tough.'

Natalie ignored Jasper and spoke to Eliza. 'When we talked last time you mentioned Antonije's *alleged* war heroism. What was that about?'

Eliza stared at her, confused. She looked quickly at Jasper who seemed uninterested in the conversational turn.

'I think he had a more comfortable war than some,' said Eliza. 'Ask Frank about his grandmother.' Lyuba, who had died young. 'And have a close look some time at the family's favourite photo of Antonije and his *wife*.'

Eliza shot another glance at her son. Was she worried his patience was running out? Or something else?

Natalie stood up slowly and picked up her bike helmet. She met Jasper's eyes and held the look for a moment before stepping around him. He immediately stepped into her path. 'Say please.'

Twenty-year-old bully, she thought. Insecure and dangerous—trying to prove himself.

'*Please* get out of my way. *Dickhead.*'

She knew she shouldn't have taunted him but at the moment anger was her only weapon against her fears. The threat of harm from him was less, in her mind, than the danger of giving into her anxiety. Eliza stepped forward and grabbed his arm. As he shook it off Natalie stepped around them both and walked out.

'Don't come back, bitch!' he yelled after her before the door slammed.

*

'I'm sorry, Frank.' Natalie had just told him that she wasn't going to continue with the PhD. Or at least not with him. This, as far as she was concerned, was the last meeting at Wye River. Frank looked like he was still trying to make sense of her new—to him—look. The previous night she'd experimented with blue streaks in her hair.

'Is there anything I can do to change your mind?'

Natalie shook her head. 'I don't really think I'm cut out for it. I'm missing my patients and the forensic work. And I'm just not a country girl at heart.'

'When are you heading back?'

'In a couple of weeks.'

Frank filled his wine glass; Natalie was sticking to water.

'Can I at least get you to accept an invitation to Mount Malosevic before you leave? You didn't see it under the best of circumstances. We're having an event there Saturday week. You'd be welcome to stay.'

Natalie tried to picture Damian's expression if he knew she would probably accept. Better not to tell him.

'I'll miss talking to you,' he added, large eyes staring luminously at her.

'You should see a therapist, Frank. There's a lot of grief to deal with.'

'I have my family. Maybe later.'

'I was reading about your grandfather. He sounds larger than life.'

'Antonije? Yes, an amazing man.'

'A war hero too. I gather he rescued your grandmother?'

'Yes, he was amongst the partisans that liberated Stara Gradiška. She was one of the few survivors.'

'Was she badly affected by the experience?'

'I never met her,' said Frank. 'She died when Vesna was young.'

'Because the camp affected her health?'

'Yes.' Frank looked at her directly.

'What happened to her?'

'She killed herself. Vesna found her hanging.'

So Antonije hadn't saved her in the end, just as Natalie hadn't saved Georgia. Natalie saw the sadness in his eyes and automatically her hand went out to his. 'Oh Frank. So much sadness and loss.'

Frank's fingers crept between hers, a subtle rebuttal of comfort and assertion of status. Natalie stifled her impulse to pull back.

'It must have made it hard for you, growing up.' Her voice didn't sound as light as she had hoped.

'It was, until we came back to Australia,' said Frank. 'In England my father was in denial about any problems with her. Vesna, that is. I was one of those parentified children who, in true British style, hid my emotions.'

'Do you still do that now?' She searched his face for signs of softness and they were there in the tiny lines at the corners of his eyes and mouth, the longing in his eyes. He would have been an appealing child.

'Don't we all?' There was something else in his eyes; Damian's voice in her head reminded her not to trust him.

'They tend to come out somewhere, Frank, you know that. Anxiety, trouble sleeping.'

'Sleep?' He looked at her. 'I'm so exhausted I sleep like...I sleep deeply.'

But hadn't Vesna said something about sleep problems? Or was that as a child? She could see he was being cautious.

She changed tack. 'I saw Eliza yesterday.'

'Do you like her art?'

His comeback was faster than she had anticipated.

'Jasper was there too.'

Frank, still smiling, pulled his hand from hers and poured some more wine.

'I had my tyres slashed, and the house fire-bombed. I rather think he did it.'

This got his attention. 'What? Are you sure?'

'That my tyres were slashed and I was fire-bombed, yes. That it was Jasper?' She shrugged. 'I'd put money on it.' She watched him. He was reacting as though he had known nothing about it. If he really hadn't then would he make the next leap as well? Only if he was innocent.

'But why on earth would he?'

'I don't know Frank. Do you?'

Frank shook his head. He looked weary. 'He was seeing Senka, who works for us.'

'Any chance he thinks he's in the running for an inheritance?'

Frank smiled, but without warmth. 'I see you also think he looks like me.'

Yes, but she also had the preliminary DNA. Now she knew how good a liar Frank was. She felt her heartbeat accelerate.

'I take it you're in no rush to adopt him?'

Frank looked suddenly irritated. But he wasn't looking at her. She turned, to see that Jasper had just entered the bar.

'Is he following you?' I kept my irritation in check.

'Possibly.' Natalie looked so tightly coiled that her grip on her glass was likely to end in bloodshed. 'Or is it you he's keeping an eye on?'

This was becoming irksome. I had avoided the lengths to which my grandfather had gone, but now it seemed I might be forced to follow in his footsteps in more ways than one. Ostensibly Eliza had returned to Lorne because her mother died, but her mother had been gone for two years before Eliza showed up. It was Antonije's death that she had been waiting for. The old man had kept an iron grip on us all and his family continued to feel the influence. For others it might need some reinforcement.

Natalie and I watched the boy take a stool at the bar, then swing around on his seat, one elbow on the bar, and toast us with a beer. Natalie could have been Reeva all over again. I wasn't sure what I was more bored by; the predictability of women or the macho posturing of my would-be son. That was until Natalie leaned into me. Her hand went over mine and she smiled.

'He's trying to play games isn't he?' Her lips now were

only millimetres from my ear. I could smell her, a hint of some herbal shampoo and a female scent I had been missing. 'Do you feel like playing too?'

I met her eyes. Rather than accusing, they were playful. I could feel the tension in her arm as my hand went around her but there was a steeliness to her that made my heart sing. As I kissed her I wondered if perhaps, finally, I had met an equal.

'I have a hypothetical for you,' said Natalie.

Declan waited. She suspected he knew what was coming.

'Let's say you hear something about a patient. From a therapist you're supervising, or in a peer review group you attend. And let's say you were able to identify him whether or not names were used, because the patient was a psychiatrist himself.'

Declan was sitting very still, face immobile. She wanted to yell, *Help me here*! Wanted to believe she was special enough to him that boundaries could be crossed: had to be crossed, otherwise she might be in danger.

'And then,' Natalie continued, 'your teenage daughter starts to see that psychiatrist as a patient. You've no proof, and the rules of confidentiality mean...but you know there is a chance that he'll seduce her.' Their eyes met; she fancied his were filled with regret. 'Do you suggest your daughter sees someone else?'

In the silence there was a clicking of the clock on the mantelpiece. A car drove past, too quickly for a suburban street.

'In your hypothetical,' said Declan slowly, 'my daughter is a minor, and as a patient, also vulnerable.'

'And I'm not?' A rare occasion when she wanted someone to see her that way.

'You're a psychiatrist, Natalie. Bipolar disorder is something you live with; it doesn't make you a victim.'

'But was Frank?' she asked. 'And if he was Antonije's victim, what does that make him now?'

And who kissed who in the pub?

Frank had given her the name of two psychiatrists he had 'dated'. Why? Because he couldn't resist being a smartarse? She'd thought it was to draw attention to the fact that he knew about her problems with Jay Wadhwa, through mentioning Gillian, another academic. But if so, he wouldn't have needed to mention Victoria Moore. She had to be older than him. Frank would know he was safe because Victoria would never tell her if he had been her patient, any more than Declan was going to tell her if he supervised Victoria.

But that wasn't the question she was going to ask.

'Dr King? Victoria Moore returning your call.'

'Thanks. This is kind of awkward.'

'Yes?' The pleasant tone became cautious.

'And I don't usually do checks on my boyfriends,' Natalie continued, 'but honestly, my psychiatry radar is making me paranoid. Maybe too many bad internet dates.'

'I can't tell you...'

'Not about patients,' Natalie pressed on at full steam, 'Mine are generally incarcerated and I'm not about to go there. No, it's about your previous boyfriend and our colleague. Frank Moreton. Anything I should know about him?'

The gasp was faint but she'd been listening for it. 'I didn't...' Victoria stopped herself. 'He's bad news,' she said quickly. 'Don't ring again.' She had hung up before Natalie could respond.

She had three days before the Mount Malosevic Music on the Mount open day, planned for the first weekend of spring. With no commitments in town or in Geelong, Natalie focused her attention on the emails and browser details she had forwarded to herself from Reeva and Alison's computer. She started with two fresh sheets of paper; *Reeva* headed one, *Alison* the other. She wanted proof—or at least something stronger than suspicions—about what had happened to them. The coroner's court had left it open but she was certain in her own mind that suicide hadn't been part of the mix. And if Jasper was involved, how involved—and who was he working with?

Reeva. Reported to be psychotic, and constantly on the internet according to Frank. Yet her emails right up to the week before she died were businesslike and matter-of-fact. Natalie had seen it before: the psychosis delineated, cut off from the rest of the sufferer's life, making them appear normal in every way—except in their separate delusional world. Was this the case with Reeva? Perhaps because she had been accessing her account from home, she'd used this account for some of her final business dealings. A polite refusal to talk at a conference: *I'll be on maternity leave*, the words chilling in light of what happened next. A journal asking for an article review, which she had done. An exchange with Wei about ethics.

Only one email that Natalie couldn't explain straight away. It looked like an academic tiff: *I'm sorry but I thought you should know*. Scott Beamish from Manchester University. There was another earlier one from him, in which Wei was mentioned. She nearly let it pass but then did a quick search on Beamish, assuming he was a medical researcher. He wasn't: department of history. What had he thought Reeva should know? Was Wei the connection between them? Not expecting anything, she sent off an email to Beamish, copying Wei.

Next Reeva's browser. Or rather Reeva's and Alison's, depending on dates accessed. Nothing about genetics. Nothing about psychosis or neurodegenerative diseases. But there was one overlap with Alison: the Bethlehem. Had Reeva also wanted to deliver there? It was in Caulfield, an inner suburb of Melbourne, as Oliver had said. Natalie quickly checked out its website. Oliver had also been right that it was palliative care. No obstetrics. Natalie went back to the browser history list she had made and stared. She had spelt Bethlehem differently. Not Bethlehem but *Bethlem*. The Bethlem Royal Infirmary. A psychiatric hospital in London. Why on earth had both women been searching this?

She thought about asking Damian, but it would be easier and quicker to get in unofficially, although she might have only one chance at it. She emailed a British colleague, the only one she knew well enough for a favour. Charlie, another psych registrar, had been in Australia for a six-month term and they had done regular pub crawls together. She typed a light message. Hoped she was asking the right question.

Next she rang Damian to update him, but he was the one with the information.

'They finished the autopsy on Georgia Latimer,' Damian told her. 'I thought you'd want to know.'

'That she OD-ed? Kind of expected that. Doesn't matter

on what, really.' Patients sometimes showed their anger at their therapist by overdosing on what they had prescribed. At other times they deliberately shopped for drugs other than what their therapist had given them, to show the opposite. Natalie hadn't prescribed any medications for Georgia.

'Not that.' Damian cleared his throat. 'It was early, so she may not have known.'

'Known what?' If Natalie hadn't been so preoccupied she would have taken more note of Damian's reticence and been better prepared.

'She was pregnant.' After a moment of silence he added, 'The pathologist was the same one who re-did the autopsy on one of her kids. He cross-checked the DNA.'

Natalie stared into space, knowing just where Damian was taking her. Georgia's relationship had always been pathological, albeit in a way that had worked for both her and Paul. At least until they had children. Paul had portrayed himself as an unwitting victim, but she had always wondered—surely the pathology had to be two-way?

'The baby,' said Damian, 'was a full sibling.'

The charity crew were at Mount Malosevic in force; a group of teenagers supervised by an older man were stringing fairy lights down the driveway. A crew of men in shorts, more optimistic about the season change than the current temperature warranted, were erecting a tarpaulin while being served coffee and tea by flustered middle-aged women.

'Hope the weather holds,' said one of the men, contemplating the task ahead.

'Storm's forecast.' Natalie tilted her head at the marquee. 'That going to hold up okay?'

The man looked up instinctively, though there were no

clouds in the sky. 'We should have it down again before it hits.'

Frank appeared from the house and greeted her with a kiss on the cheek. She could almost convince herself it was as innocent as it looked. 'Do you want me to have Drago put your bike around the back?'

Frank insisted on a tour of the grounds, telling her all about the house as they walked around it, both sipping champagne. Wherever possible she tipped a little out; she wanted her mind to stay clear. He spoke as if the patriarch Antonije was still alive, and his influence certainly was. Frank's pride was evident in his description of the time, money and sheer work that had gone into first the structure that dominated the hill, and then the painstaking landscaping of its surrounds.

'The drought caused huge problems,' Frank told her. 'We ended up boring water to use about ten years ago, and the lake almost dried up completely. Plumbers had a lot of tunnelling to do through the hill to ensure we got water as well. But the tanks are full now so we have enough water for several years, I should think.'

They paused at the giant tree house Antonije had built for Vesna. The man didn't do things by half.

'It was their special place,' said Frank, and Natalie caught a hint of envy. That Antonije hadn't built him one too, or that Wendell hadn't? It had a staircase that wound around the tree trunk, and a tiny veranda. Natalie doubted Enid Blyton had ever imagined anything as elaborate.

The stables had never seen horses. 'He had seen a mansion in his home country,' Frank said, 'one he could never have afforded. This had to be bigger and better in every way.' Narcissism clearly ran in the family.

There was a lattice of paths between the exotic plants and sculptures, some of which caught her unawares on corners and seemed to glare ominously in the dimming light. The pet cemetery with its three small, white crosses reminded her of war graves. Pets? She couldn't see this family with a bounding red-setter chewing their shoes and digging holes in the garden. A disdainful Persian, maybe. She pictured Vesna clutching it like a Bond villain.

'It's spectacular,' Natalie said. She might have added, for a mausoleum. 'But right now, I need to get out of my bike leathers.'

'Of course, how remiss of me. You look…charming… in whatever you're wearing.' Frank's hand brushed her hair behind her ear and for a moment, thinking he was going to kiss her, she wondered how she should react. But Mala saved her.

'I'll show her to her room, Frank,' she said slipping her arm through Natalie's. Mala looked stunning in a green cat suit. In heels she was at least twenty centimetres taller than Natalie. She led Natalie through the kitchen entrance. A half dozen women were busily cutting sandwiches and heating sausage rolls. Natalie paused in the main living room, looking at the painting that had left her so uneasy. The feeling was back immediately, but it was hard to pinpoint its origin.

The painting was in the characteristic shades of black and grey; looking harder, she could pick five people partly blurred within the Mount Malosevic landscape. The scene was shrouded in mist, and both trees and people seemed to be emerging from a dream. Two were children. Mala and Frank, she assumed at first. But as she squinted she could make out that there were actually three children, all female.

One was clearly Mala. Were the other two Vesna and Lyuba as children? Both had Mala's large luminescent eyes. Another figure, a late-adolescent Frank, was on the edge of the forest, slightly removed. The only adult—Antonije?—was in the background. He had the look of a man presiding over his kingdom.

'Interesting isn't it?' Mala was watching her reaction.

'Interesting? Yes,' said Natalie.

'The spare room is this way. I trust you don't mind using it?'

The room where Reeva died? Better than the boatshed, all things considered, but only just. Mala threw open the door. If Natalie had expected the room to retain any traces of Reeva she was disappointed. There was a bed with a plain fawn bedspread, beige carpet and little else. For a moment she sensed a hesitation before Mala left the room. As if she wanted to hang around while Natalie changed, or had perhaps had been about to say something, then thought better of it.

It only took her a few minutes to exchange her bike leathers for a black-and-red steam-punk bodice and a leather mini skirt. She wasn't likely to upstage Mala, but Natalie felt more herself dressed like this and to hell what anyone else thought.

Glancing out the window, she saw people were starting to arrive, among them Wei. Tonight he was paying homage to his Chinese background, with a high-necked satin jacket in pink and silver, dragons twisting around on the back. It looked like Natalie wouldn't have to wait until he or Scott Beamish returned her email; she might be able to get to the end of that mystery tonight. She texted Damian quickly to let him know where she was—and who else was also likely to be there. She had the sense of venturing into the unknown; it seemed wise to have a back-up plan.

Outside the room, the corridor was empty. Further down, the door to Frank's study was ajar. Did she dare?

The study was lined with bookshelves but the photo of Frank's grandparents was where she recalled seeing it when she was last in the room—with Damian, on the night Alison died. There were no photos of Reeva or Alison; no other photos at all. Look closely, Eliza had said. It was a faded black-and-white shot: a bear of a man posed with a rifle, his chest criss-crossed with ammunition, dwarfing the childlike woman next to him—wasted, undoubtedly, from the concentration camp. Natalie looked closer at what Antonije was wearing. She'd probably read too many books or seen too many movies. Maybe he hadn't been partisan at all: maybe he was one of the Ustaše fascists that had run the camp. He wasn't wearing a uniform, so how would she know? But judging from the size of him, wherever he spent the war he had been well fed.

The letters on the building in the background were presumably Croatian—they weren't English—so they were a mystery too. She'd googled Stara Gradiška. It was a women's and children's camp, at least as horrific as Auschwitz. But from the photo she couldn't even confirm that was where it had been taken.

Her eyes kept coming back to Antonije; it was hard not to. The camera lens begged you to. He was a very good looking man. She held the photo at arm's length. What wasn't she seeing? Lyuba looked terrified. She stood stiffly, as if she was afraid to look at the camera. Or afraid of...Natalie looked at the ground. It was hard to make out because the photo was slightly torn. She removed it from the frame. Part of the torn section was bent over, so she straightened it. It took a moment to understand what she was looking at because of the angle. Antonije had one hand around Lyuba. His other was on a rifle that stood upright next to him. This she now saw, had some kind of bayonet attached, and it was piercing the chest of a man in a black uniform lying on the ground in front of them. Antonije's foot was resting on what was left of the man's abdomen. The Ustaše, Natalie imagined. Still didn't mean he wasn't one of them. She tried to put herself in Lyuba's shoes. Had she been thinking she'd been saved by someone just as bad either way?

Music started up outside, and Natalie figured Frank would soon come looking for her, so she slipped out of the study. Rather than exiting via the front door, she followed a corridor into the kitchen, through which she'd passed earlier. It was larger than she'd thought, one end a glass wall that looked into the cellar. Another wall had a double stove and sinks opposite a long marble bench. It was cluttered with urns, paper plates and sandwich-making ingredients. Wei was standing there, trying to take charge but mostly the women were ignoring him.

'You moonlight as a caterer?' Natalie asked in disbelief.

Wei as usual was hard to read. He smiled tightly. 'Just helping out.'

Natalie waited until he looked as if he was about to disappear with a plate of mini quiches and followed him towards the door. 'Wei, could you clear up something for me?'

Wei adjusted his collar with his spare hand and smiled politely.

'Who is Scott Beamish?'

Whatever Wei had been expecting her to ask, it wasn't

this. He opened his mouth then closed it. Leaning in to her, he hissed, 'None of your business,' and walked off without looking back. Natalie stared after him. She thought about his CV and his year of birth. British. A researcher. And he was ten years younger than Frank.

Behind her, someone spoke.

'You're the latest doctor.' There was a strong trace of an accent, though the words were clear. Gordana, the chef. Sitting on a crate of wine, smoking and peering through the open door of the glass-walled cellar.

'Natalie.'

The woman was stick thin, with the bony hardness you saw in the smokers who hung around outside cancer wards. She looked older than Natalie imagined she was, and the yellow tinge to her eyes suggested that if cancer didn't get her, her liver probably would.

Natalie moved to sit on a crate next to her. She didn't seem to care if Natalie stayed or not.

'You knew Reeva and Alison.'

Gordana took a drag and said nothing.

'Did they fit in here?'

'How would I know?'

'I imagine you know quite a lot.' Natalie looked around. Behind her was the Chablis, in front the Bordeaux, all carefully labelled. There were a lot of empty spaces. Antonije's collection was being drunk and not replenished. 'Like how fussy they were when they got pregnant. No salami, no seafood?'

'Yeah, the second was like that. Blamed me, like *I* set the menu.'

So if she hadn't wanted to push Alison's listeria hysteria button, who had?

'But Reeva wasn't?'

Gordana laughed. 'Who knows? She used to eat in her room.'

'She didn't like your food?'

'Wasn't that.'

Evidence of the psychosis that Frank talked about... unless there was a basis for her fears.

'Do you know Jasper Carson?'

'You with the pigs?'

'No. Just curious. He doesn't seem to like me being here.'

Gordana picked up a beer that Natalie hadn't noticed until then. 'Jasper was seeing Senka.'

'Not now?'

Gordana shrugged. 'The boy likes being around here. Not sure it was Senka he was after.'

'When was he last around?'

'He'll be here now,' said Gordana. 'He never misses any public event.'

Jasper had the motive, however warped, and the access via Senka. But he was only twenty. Would he have had the knowledge or skill to inject Reeva with insulin? Perhaps with Senka's help. Had he just been lucky? Not twice, surely. Unless Mala and Frank had covered for him because at the end of the day he was a blood relative...

Then of course there was Wei, who might also have had access to the house via both Frank and Mala. And to both previous wives. The son of the woman Wendell Moreton had killed was a researcher, according to Damian. And hadn't Mala said Wei was raised by his father? He was the same age as the baby saved in the crash—she would have to re-check the CV to see if he was born on the same day. Or better, get Damian to. Wei was hard to read; but he could have sabotaged Frank's research team if he was intent on destroying the family that had killed his mother. Would he have killed Frank's wives with this as a motive?

Outside the music and applause suggested the event was getting under way. Some gentle classical piece that meant nothing to Natalie. She didn't pay it much attention; she had to be quick, or the family would wonder where she was. This was her last chance to make sense of the Malosevics, and possibly the deaths of Reeva and Alison: she wanted to find Antonije's paintings, the ones that only the family had seen.

There was noise in the kitchen as Natalie stole up to the landing. She spotted the master bedroom, Frank's, through an open door. It was a big room, with an ensuite. Wooden panels to waist height, walls above painted in off-white. Windows made up one entire side and looked out across the garden to the ocean in the distance. Dark clouds were gathering on the horizon.

She turned back to the room's contents. A large bed was covered in a quilt that matched the upholstery of two chairs; blue and gold, tasteful; straight out of an interior designer's portfolio. The carpet was in neutral tones, the chest of drawers a pristine low-key antique. On the walls were two small paintings of Australian scenes that could have been expensive originals or cheap prints, as far as Natalie could tell. They were clearly not Malosevics. Nothing in the room gave any hint of the character or mood of the owner.

It had been a little more than two months since Alison died. If she'd left her mark on the room, it was hard to know where it might have been. Natalie looked at the bedside tables. The only sound she could hear was the soft drone of the heater. No footsteps on the landing.

She went to the right side first. Bare, it suggested that the book Alison had been reading, the glass of water, the tissues and the anti-reflux meds had all been swept into a bin. Or maybe into the cupboard below.

But that was empty. So were the wardrobes where she imagined Alison's clothes would have been. They held only suits and men's shoes. Alison had been erased.

On the left side of the bed were some pens and what looked like a thesis Frank was marking. The cupboard below was stuffed with books. Only one stood out: a text on pregnancy. The rest were a mix of philosophy and history.

The bathroom was no more illuminating. No prescription medications, just the usual array of analgesics, anti-histamines and antacids. A packet of condoms suggested he was hopeful: but they could have been there for a long time.

Natalie walked back into the bedroom and stood, trying to see what she wasn't seeing. She walked over to the only wall that would have been large enough for a substantial piece of art. The Australian landscape—a print, she could now see—was a Streeton. She lifted it off, and did the same with the other landscape. Both were on fairly heavy-duty hooks that could have taken a far larger object. And very faintly, when she got up close, Natalie could see the difference in paint colour. One much larger piece had hung there once.

As she slipped out into the corridor the noise from the kitchen was still all that she could hear. From the mezzanine, the living room below, when she peered over the rail, was empty.

The next bedroom was dominated by a queen-size bed

with a red and green bohemian velvet quilt. In the lamplight the walls glowed a soft, deep pink. Rugs and cushions were scattered over the floor. Chairs and heavy drapes covered the wall of windows. Vesna trying to get in touch with her Romani ancestry, Natalie suspected. But she doubted Lyuba had ever lived like this. Not with her own mother, anyway.

Natalie glanced around. It was hard not to see the pill boxes in disarray. Diazepam, amitriptyline, olanzapine—and those were just the ones she could make out. She knew them all. She wondered about the last. It was an antipsychotic that could be used as a mood stabiliser, sometimes as a sedative. Why was Vesna on it? The painting on the wall opposite the bed was obviously a Malosevic, even to her untrained eye. Antonije, daughter and granddaughter. The dark swirls against the white skin of the women were startling in the dim light. But there was something far more malevolent about the picture. Somehow, she decided, he had managed to capture innocence and knowing in one look of inescapable sadness.

The last room off the landing was Mala's. Natalie made the paintings her first priority, and sure enough there were two. One that was hung as it had been positioned originally and one that had, presumably, been on the wall of Frank's room. Now it was propped below its companion.

It was all there for Natalie to put together. It was only a matter of who knew what; the answer had always been within the family.

She was trying to make sense of all of the possibilities when she heard a new sound. Footsteps, and already along the landing. If it was Mala she had no more than two seconds; the first got her to the walk-in wardrobe, the second had her pressed behind the disarray of designer-label dresses, her feet edging under a pile of carelessly tossed-in shoes.

The door opened and there was silence. Natalie pictured the woman standing there, sensing the intrusion. After a few moments there was a sound as she moved into the bathroom. Cosmetics dropped into the sink, then Mala came back into the main room and opened the cupboard door a metre to Natalie's left. Shrinking back, Natalie could make out the flash of green as the cat suit dropped to the floor. She was changing.

Natalie felt her heart pounding in her ears, willed her breathing to slow. Time seemed to stretch, each second more like a minute. Her phone pinged from where it was tucked awkwardly into her belt, and the bottom dropped out of her stomach. Had Mala heard it over the outdoor music? Natalie couldn't hear anyone. Prayed Mala had disappeared into the bathroom.

Natalie found her phone and switched it to silent. She wondered if was Damian texting her and checked the messages. Not Damian. Charlie, her British colleague. *You owe me! I'm thinking all rounds on you your first night in London, if you ever get here. Yes. Admitted for three months when he was ten. Can't get the notes sorry.*

Ten. When Mala was born and his father died. When Frank himself had survived the car crash that killed his own father but which another child, maybe Wei, had survived. Three months in hospital, but not with a physical injury. Bethlem was a child psych unit. So just what had been going on with Frank Moreton then? And did it have any bearing on what was happening now?

There had been no sound of Mala leaving. Cautiously, Natalie found another crack to look through. Mala was standing in front of the bed wearing nothing but a thong.

313

Long, tanned limbs. A model's slimness. She turned, pouting and posing as if she knew she had an audience, kicking off her shoes. She threw the dress down and returned to the cupboard, tried another. It reminded Natalie of herself as a teenager, prancing around, pretending she was Buffy about to slay the latest guy she was hot for.

Mala finally settled on a white gown with a neck line clasped at the waist with a gold belt. A heavy gold chain dangled a medallion between her breasts. One item to go. *Shoes*. Natalie looked down in dismay.

Natalie's leathers were in a pile on the floor, the contents of her bag spilling out over the bed. I would have looked anyway. It is illuminating to see the contents of a woman's handbag. Reeva had journal articles, drinks and snack food; during the pregnancy, diabetic test equipment. Alison carried a diet book and *Who Weekly*. Natalie? Lithium. How disappointing. Not entirely surprising, though. I have to accept my own responsibility in this attraction. Obviously the chaos of my childhood has resulted in my being drawn to women who need help. Reeva with her paranoia and chilled reason who trusted no one else. Alison and her neurosis. And now Natalie. I had wondered what it was in Melbourne she was escaping from; had it not been for my own more pressing issues I would have had time to check her out more thoroughly. Never mind. All information is useful, and never more so than now.

'You look divine.'

Mala was swirling around in front of her mirror when I found her. She laughed and kissed me on the cheek. 'You look rather dashing yourself. Very Darcy with that frown.'

'Have you seen Natalie?'

'Brother dearest, don't tell me you've lost another one?'

'Not funny, Mala.'

'You're far too serious. Celebrate seeing the last of those dreary policemen. How is it so much brawn and good looks can be so dull?'

'So are you looking good for anyone in particular tonight, Mala?'

'Is it a problem if I am? Don't even try and tell me you don't think your little shrink is hot.' She giggled. 'I certainly do.'

'Mala, Alison has only been dead...'

Mala interrupted. 'You're a man. You need to...You were sleepwalking again last night you know.'

I felt a headache coming on. I had suspected as much. I had been well for so long and then after Reeva left our bed I started to find my slippers were dirty in the morning. I thought it had settled before I married Alison. Given all that has happened with her it looks like it may need attention again.

Mala winked at me as she went to her shoe cupboard.

There was a fragment of silence in which Natalie, expecting to be exposed, wondered if she should pop out of the cupboard and say *surprise*. Mala opened the door wider, and Natalie pressed herself as hard as she could against one end, unable to see for the fur coat her face was buried in. Mala moved some shoes around carelessly, then she and Frank laughed and a moment later Natalie heard the door click. She breathed out slowly.

After five minutes had passed she edged herself forward, listened, then eased herself out of the cupboard. Her mind started thinking again, as the fear slowly thawed. What was it Mala had said? *Sleepwalking…again.* The music outside was now louder; several strings and wind instruments.

She checked her phone again, still nothing from Damian, but an email caught her eye. It was from BeamMeUpScotty and she nearly deleted it as spam until she realised it came not from a random *Star Trek* fan, but from Reeva's Scott Beamish. His gmail, not his university account. The man that Wei knew and was keen for her to stay away from.

You asked me about my relationship to the Malosevics, he wrote. And he said he'd told Reeva what he now shared with her. Was that what had got her killed? Natalie returned the phone to her belt, hand trembling.

Creeping down the back stair, she was about to take the door out through the garage when she heard her name.

'Dr King. Are you looking for my son?'

Natalie hadn't noticed Vesna who, dressed in white, almost blended with the settee. Champagne in hand, she rose and walked to the selection of bottles on the sideboard.

'Do stay and keep me company for a while.' Vesna selected the champagne bottle from the ice bucket, topped up her glass and held out another that had been standing on the sideboard. Natalie reluctantly accepted it. The bead was still strong, so it hadn't been sitting long. It was intended for Mala, presumably, who had passed on staying with her mother. So if Vesna had seen Mala, had she also seen Natalie coming out of Mala's room? From where she had been sitting, probably not. Vesna's smile suggested this might not be her first glass for the day; perhaps she was beyond monitoring anyone's movements.

'What do you think of Mount Malosevic?' Vesna asked, resuming her seat.

Darkness was starting to fall. Natalie sat opposite, sipping champagne. She put her phone on the arm of the sofa next to her, in case Damian texted. A soprano was singing faintly in the background. *Madame Butterfly*. There had been a baritone before that, singing something from *Carmen*. On the lawn in front of Natalie shadows danced as the winds picked up. The path to the boathouse was primarily lit by the house lights. Fairy lights strung along the path were swinging in the wind, clinking. It should have been beautiful but Natalie found herself looking for danger in the darkness.

'To be perfectly honest,' said Natalie, 'I find it too imposing. I can't imagine living here.'

Vesna didn't look as if she had heard.

'It's designed for grandeur rather than comfort,' Natalie went on, thinking of the young Frank arriving here, traumatised after his father's death, his own near miss. The sleepwalking was surely a response, the burying of the underlying trauma coming out in his dreams.

'Comfort?' Vesna looked at her as though the concept was one she had never considered. 'We have every possible comfort.'

Except the one they needed. A place of safety, of acceptance without the need to perform. Unconditional love. 'I don't think Frank did as a boy.' Natalie wouldn't have pushed a patient like this, but Vesna had answers she needed. 'Was his sleepwalking a big problem?'

Vesna frowned. 'Frank? Sleepwalking?' She took a long sip, savoured it, her mind elsewhere.

'Like, did he ever...do things in the night he couldn't remember?'

Vesna's free hand moved up and down her leg, picking at her clothing. 'I don't know what you mean.'

But she did. Natalie was sure Vesna knew exactly what she meant but wasn't sure if telling the truth would get her son into trouble.

'I'll get us some food.' Vesna stood up, stiff and disorientated for a moment, then disappeared into the kitchen.

Natalie was in no hurry to join Frank and figured staying with his mother was as good an excuse as any. The weather was looking more ominous. She doubted the guests would finish the evening without a soaking. She wandered over

319

to the window and was looking out across the lake to the boathouse when Gordana, rather than Vesna, came through the kitchen door.

'You're a real doctor, right?'

'Yes. Why?'

'Vesna's had a fall.'

Not surprising, given the alcohol and the meds. This much general medicine she could manage. Natalie followed Gordana back into the kitchen where the numbers of middle-aged women fussing had dwindled to one. There was no sign of Vesna.

'She went down to the cellar,' said Gordana, leading Natalie out towards the garage.

'Cellar?' Natalie frowned. 'I thought that was...'

'They keep their good stuff under the house.' Gordana's look suggested *so I can't get it.*

What the hell was Vesna doing down in the cellar? She didn't need any more to drink. Natalie was feeling light-headed after half a glass.

Her Ducati was standing at the back of the garage. Beyond it she found a trap door propped open, revealing steps that descended steeply into darkness.

'Vesna, are you all right?' It was impossible for Natalie to see anything in the hole. She took a couple of steps and hesitated. 'Vesna?' She took another step and bent down. Had the sudden feeling that it would be prudent to let Gordana go first, but made the decision a fraction too late. She couldn't be sure who pushed her—but there was no doubt about the shove that sent her tumbling down into the darkness. Nor the slamming of the trapdoor that left her in the pitch black.

*

It took her a few minutes to make sense of what had happened. She had fallen probably less than a metre but the dirt floor was hard, and she had landed on her shoulder. She knew the feeling: in a day or two it would sport a large bruise. The rest of her seemed intact. She felt around for the stairs, crawled back up them and banged on the door. It didn't budge. Solid timber, and no one likely to hear her over the music. Even less likely that anyone would come to the garage.

Natalie closed her eyes, steadied her breathing. She was safe for the moment. She just had to work out why Gordana—or Vesna—had put her down here. They'd have to let her out eventually. Wouldn't they? No one, not even Damian would think to look for her here. A coldness seeped through her. It was several degrees cooler than it had been upstairs. Her arms and legs were bare. It wouldn't be the first time she'd counted the cost of vanity.

Vesna had to think she was protecting Frank, and must have roped Gordana in to get Natalie to the trap door. Paranoid, yes, but not necessarily because Frank really needed protecting. But would she tell him what she'd done, or was she so high on pills that she might even forget Natalie was down here? Would Gordana remember either, after the next bottle of wine? She felt her pulse rising, had to stop the images of the Worm, images from her nightmares surfacing. She would *not* let this beat her. Or *them*.

Her phone. It was still sitting on the arm of the sofa. Frank would see it, would look for her. Unless they were all in it together. Surely they couldn't possibly explain away another dead doctor. But maybe they wouldn't have to. Would the woman in the kitchen have noticed her? Probably not. The only other people who had seen her were Malosevics...and their loyal retainers. Damian could trace her phone, but they could dispose of that any way they wanted.

She started to crawl around, getting the feel of the space. It didn't seem to be used as a wine cellar. The wall behind the stairs that would, if she had orientated herself correctly, be facing the driveway was lined with empty boxes. To the right, away from the house, she encountered what felt like strands of spiderwebs, and drew back. Opposite, towards the house, there was only the gritty surface of concrete. The final wall, the one towards the lake, was full of clutter. She felt around it and a box fell on her, the contents spilling out. She stumbled back and slipped, hitting her head on the edge of the stairs, falling to her knees with glass crunching as she fell. She put her hand to her head, then her mouth. Tasted blood. Hoped the gash wasn't too bad.

Natalie sat carefully on the bottom stair. Why the hell had Antonije built a tiny room underneath his garage? Part of his own paranoia, the legacy of his war experiences? She rubbed her arms, cycled her legs in an effort to keep warm.

'Fuck you, Malosevics, all of you.' She repeated it, louder. She didn't expect anyone could hear but it made her feel better. She wondered what time it was. Strained to hear the music and found she couldn't. Just silence. She closed her eyes. It wasn't as if she could see anyway. Pictured Antonije and his family, the house and gardens Frank had shown her so proudly. *Had to be bigger and better in every way.* Would that have included escape tunnels, maybe? Given their history? She sat up again, staring ahead into the darkness towards where she imagined the lake was. Where the boat shed was, the one that Antonije had used as an artist's studio. Could he have connected it underground?

Natalie edged cautiously across the room, pushing aside

the broken glass, and struggled with some boxes, feeling for the back wall. It was there, but it felt smooth like clay, not the abrasive touch of concrete. She edged along it, and as she did another box fell. This one, heavier, landed on another full of glassware which shattered, by the sound of it, out across the floor. Working systematically she tried to feel for a gap. Hoping, but as she covered most of the wall, no longer expecting to find one.

She kicked the wall in frustration, reiterating her opinion of the Malosevics, and her foot failed to connect. She recovered her balance and knelt down, trying not to knock over any more boxes. Sure enough, there was a hole. Hardly the escape passage she had hoped for, but bigger than a wombat hole. Big enough, she figured, to shimmy along; probably even crawl on all fours. If it went anywhere.

She decided to wait and see if someone arrived to rescue her rather than venture into a dark tunnel without a light or any idea of where it went. Time passed slowly. She tried to keep moving, and huddled under cardboard when she wasn't. Half an hour. An hour, maybe two. No one was coming. She felt back around the rim of the tunnel, thinking she'd have to try or she might freeze. But before she had made a decision she heard a sound above and the trapdoor eased open, a shaft of light revealing that the hole behind her disappeared for as far as she could see. Sitting perfectly still she remained obscured by boxes, trying to make out who her rescuer was.

'I know you're down there.'

A man's voice. Not Frank's. As his boot came onto the first step, Natalie had only a split second to decide. With a small man like Wei she might have had a chance. Jasper? No way. She turned and started crawling, as quietly and as quickly as she could.

For the first thirty metres Natalie focused on getting away. She could hear Jasper in the room behind her, throwing boxes around and crunching over glass. It would only be a matter of time before he found the hole. Question was whether a man his size would be able to come after her.

The torchlight, probably from his phone, didn't reach her but she couldn't be sure if he could see her in the shadows beyond. She froze. There was low chuckle.

'Think you can get away, bitch?'

Natalie kept moving, slower now. Still watching the light, mostly blocked by Jasper's bulk, as she tried not to bang against the pipe that had clearly been the reason for the passage's existence. Bore water, Frank had said. Tunnelling through the hill. Presumably to the lake. Was there some sort of maintenance access further in? She hoped so.

'Hope you have agoraphobia bitch.' *Moron.* The light suddenly went out. She heard the slam of the trapdoor and stopped. Took a deep breath. Immediate danger gone.

But she was now back in the dark, and there was still, by her reckoning, at least three hundred metres to negotiate. *If* the tunnel went direct to the boathouse or lake. Unhelpful thinking: she pushed on. She needed to get there before Jasper worked out where it might go. Would Vesna know? Not Vesna. Gordana. It had to be Gordana and Senka working with Jasper. Maybe Eliza was the driver behind them. Probably a promised share of the future inheritance at stake.

Her knees were quickly grazed and bleeding. The cut on her forehead had started dripping blood into her eyes and couldn't be stopped. The tunnel floor was getting rougher, rocky and uneven. And, she suddenly realised, wet. The surface above her was dripping. She might well be under the lake, crawling in a place built temporarily for workmen years earlier; she blocked out the thought that all her banging around might cause a cave-in.

The tunnel seemed to go on for ever. Natalie had no idea if it was straight or not, no idea, any longer, what direction she was travelling. Which became a problem when she rammed straight into a wall and found, feeling around her, trying not to panic, that the tunnel branched into two. Above her a sound like a distant gunshot shattered the silence. Natalie stifled a scream and took another deep breath. What the *hell* was Jasper doing? The sound came again, this time longer and rumbling. Thunder. The storm that had been coming all afternoon had arrived.

The dark silence of the tunnel was broken only by the blood and water dripping onto her face. Not fucking tears at least. She used the same mantra that had got her through her accident and months of physio; bottom line was to harness some anger and refuse to believe she could be defeated. She wouldn't let up on herself now any more than she had then. Left or right? Right, surely, would take her to the lake. She went left. Hoping.

Her progress was slow. Pain and fear intermingled with a feeling of wooziness. Shit. Was there a problem with oxygen? She tried to take deeper breaths, struggled and couldn't work out why. *Nearly there. Don't stop. Don't let them win. One hand in front of each other. Keep going.* But the need to close her eyes, to rest, began to dominate. She wasn't certain she was still moving. Was there a light somewhere ahead? A noise? She no longer had the luxury of waiting to work out if it was Jasper or not.

'Help.'

Had she made any sound? She tried again, feeling

lightheaded, nauseated. Pushed herself further, sure now that up ahead was the faintest of lights. The tunnel widened out and she could just make out a change in the tunnel floor. Stairs. *The boathouse.* And someone was in it, moving around. She crawled the last two metres to the foot of the stairs but something stopped her going any further. She stared and reeled back. Through the gaps in the stairs was a skull. A tiny human infant skull—with a large hole in the side where it had been crushed.

'Where the hell is she?'

Mala looked at me. 'Whoever do you mean?'

'I'm not playing games.'

Mala frowned. 'Really? I rather thought she was.' Seeing my expression she softened, ran her hand over my shoulder, digging into the muscles that were now set to give me a migraine. 'Well I know where she *was*. I just assumed she'd follow us down when the coast was clear. I...' She bit her lip.

'What?'

'Well, I told Vesna to expect her.'

'Vesna?'

'You don't think...?'

'No I don't.' Or did I? Vesna had been known to act on her conspiracy theories before. Usually just by abusing people on the phone. Occasionally taking the Bentley to the council, where she now had her own personal liaison officer. She had already taken it upon herself to visit Natalie. What had she done this time?

I took the stairs two at a time, banged on Vesna's door and entered without waiting for an answer. My mother was out cold on the bed; I shook her but it merely induced her to hit out at me. I wasn't about to get anything sensible from her.

Mala watched me return.

'I'll search the grounds. If she turns up, text me.'

Mala waved her champagne at me. 'She's probably waiting for you in the centre of the maze or something terribly romantic.'

Mala knew perfectly well she wasn't. The question was whether she knew where Natalie really had disappeared to.

We both turned as thunder rumbling overhead sounded, in time to see lightning open up the sky.

'What the hell?'

Another crack of thunder and the sky lit up, a white crack dissecting the heavy black clouds, as ominous as the shadows. The air was still, waiting for the heavens to open. Natalie could see Frank, standing in the doorway, stop and listen; he had heard her gasp.

He looked astonished as Natalie emerged from the trap door in the floor of the boathouse. She didn't stop to worry whose side he was on. She had to have a better chance if she wasn't in a tunnel, particularly one containing a dead baby. Never mind it had been dead for some years. Frank helped hoist her up. She lay panting on the floor and watched his face. If she was reading it right, she looked even worse than she felt.

'Can I get you something to drink?'

Natalie nodded, slowly sitting up and taking a glass of water from him.

'If it isn't too stupid a question, just what do you think you were doing?' There was a terse edge to his voice.

'Trying to avoid getting killed.'

'Killed?'

'Yes, you know. Strangled, beaten, maybe smothered.'

Frank turned back towards the sink, wet a cloth, and returned with it. 'You're bleeding.'

Her knees and hands were raw, and the cut on her head had closed her eye and filled one ear. She took the cloth but it was soon evident that it wasn't enough. Frank helped her over to the sink and watched as she tried her best to make herself look less like she'd crawled out of a First World War trench.

'Sit,' he said. 'I'll make you some tea.'

'Tea, Frank?' The level of her voice was rising. 'Didn't you hear what I said? Someone tried to kill me. Aren't you a tiny bit interested who? And why? Also, that there's a dead baby down there?' She looked to the trapdoor, half-fearful that the baby would emerge.

Frank lit the heater and filled the kettle as she looked around the room, baffled. There were two wide armchairs, and a sofa was pushed against the wall. Paints and canvases were stacked in one corner, an unfinished portrait on the easel. The gas heater—the one that had killed Alison—was working flat out. Already the room felt hot. Outside another bolt of lightning split the sky. A shiver went through her—it was as if Antonije, godlike even in death, was fulminating at what she was about to do: uncover his world for all to see.

'Of course.' Frank's voice was measured, polite. And disbelieving.

'You don't really think I'd have crawled through a half kilometre of tunnels without a good reason do you?'

'I'm sure you think there is and I'd be happy to hear your theory.'

'What?' Natalie stared in disbelief.

'Have you been taking your lithium Natalie?' Frank was

330

trying to look concerned. It took Natalie a moment to be able to put words together coherently.

'You condescending bastard.' Natalie gripped the edge of the bench to steady herself. 'You don't really think you're going to be able to get away with blaming all this on me being ill do you?'

'You do seem rather emotional.'

'Emotional?' Natalie screamed. 'I've been locked up by your mother and threatened by your son, and I'll have nightmares about small enclosed spaces stacked with skeletons. So yes, you could say I'm a bit fucking emotional.'

'Natalie...please. I didn't mean to...please sit down. I need to hear what happened.'

Natalie eyed him suspiciously, moved away to the windows, peering out into the darkness. It was hard to see anything. No reason to believe that Jasper knew where the tunnel finished. But what if he did? She rubbed her temples, suddenly feeling very tired. It made no sense that Jasper and Frank were working on this together. Frank would protect her from his bastard son, even if he was treating her like she was unstable. Wouldn't he?

'How did you know I was on lithium?' she asked suddenly.

'We couldn't find you so I checked your room.' Frank poured water into a teapot. 'Your pills were on the bed.'

Natalie shook her head. It didn't really matter, she supposed. She wasn't going to work with Frank anyway. But it didn't make her feel any better.

'The secret family recipe.' Frank handed her a mug and sat down in one of the armchairs, sinking deep into the faded fabric splattered with paint.

Natalie took a sip. This concoction had a little more

taste than most of the herbal infusions she had tried lately, but it was bland nevertheless. She felt herself shaking. Frank was right—she was cold and in danger of going into shock. The tea would help.

'It must be the British part of me,' said Frank. 'I've always enjoyed tea.'

Was he trying to calm her, or to distract her? Natalie took a breath. The dead baby was foremost in her mind, but that wasn't what was putting her at greatest immediate danger.

'Did Jasper kill Reeva and Alison?'

Frank didn't seem to hear the question. 'I used to sit here and watch my grandfather paint.' He looked around the boathouse and gestured to the artwork. 'Not mine. My mother and Mala both paint when it takes their fancy.'

'Frank, Damian McBride is going to listen to me. He's not going to think this is my imagination or mental illness no matter what you say.'

'No, I don't suppose he will.' Frank fiddled with his cuffs. 'Humour me. I need to tell you about my grandfather, so you can make sense of it.

'Antonije.' Natalie thought of the *Family* paintings she had seen, and let Frank speak. Her hand was trembling as she held the teacup.

'Wendell hated Antonije,' said Frank. 'My father wouldn't let me study art, it was all about maths and science and sport. But I didn't have the talent anyway.'

'Why did he hate your grandfather?'

Frank smiled. 'The eternal question as woman marries man: does her husband usurp her father in her affections, or will he always be second rate?'

'They were rivals?'

'Well, let's just say…' The smile held stories that he had no intention of sharing. 'My grandfather always won in the end. We all adored him.'

'Your father died.' Natalie felt increasingly tired. The heat was oppressive.

'We all do eventually.'

Despite the heat Natalie felt cold inside. Frank sounded more sad than threatening, true; but in the shadows it was hard to read him. She thought of Eliza. *Beware Eliza* Vesna had told her. But apart from being paranoid, Vesna would ultimately be concerned to protect her family. That was probably why she had told Gordana to lock her up. But who had told Jasper she was there? Not Vesna surely.

She needed to stop herself from falling asleep. How could she be so tired? She pulled herself up and moved to the canvases; Vesna's, she assumed. The eyes were haunted. After seeing Antonije's *Family* Natalie knew why.

'Eliza imagines the camps haunted your grandfather's work, I think. Here they seem to haunt your mother's as well.'

'I don't think my grandmother ever recovered, nor Vesna from her death.'

'And Antonije?'

'Antonije was a partisan. He wasn't incarcerated in the camps. He liberated my grandmother. But I think what he saw, yes, that haunted him.'

'Your grandmother was at Stara Gradiška, you said?'

'I rather think she was at Sisak.'

'Sisak?' She couldn't recall this from her reading. Her hand went to the wall to steady herself. Outside the ominous low grumbling continued. Frank stood. Took an arm and guided her back to the armchair.

'A children's camp,' he said, after he watched her take another sip of tea. 'I rather think they liked to pretend she was a little older than she actually was.'

Frank was watching her. Like a cat, she thought randomly, and wondered why. The tension in his hands? The feeling he was about to pounce? And why did she just feel tired rather than wanting to flee? It occurred to her that the mouse rarely got away.

She stared back, feeling he knew she had pulled the photo out of the picture. Or else believed that Eliza had told her more than she had, perhaps the information that Eliza had shared with Alison the night she died. The information that had revealed the family secrets, rather than the red herring Alison had been chasing with the negative genetic tests.

'The Ustaše had escaped Stara Gradiška before the partisans arrived. I think Antonije told Lyuba that story because she couldn't remember her mother. It comforted her.'

'How old was she when he rescued her?'

'Does it matter? My grandfather was her saviour. They fell in love and married. Emigrated to Australia. We have photos. My grandmother was tiny. We were told it was because of the malnutrition. She couldn't recall her mother, let alone her date of birth.'

'Could she remember if Antonije was actually a partisan, or one of the Ustaše that ran the camp?'

Frank didn't skip a beat. 'Eliza's paranoia? She can't prove that. Antonije was not a stupid man. And he was lucky. I'm not saying he didn't find a way to souvenir some of the spoils of war, but who are we to judge? We weren't there. He was investigated. In the end there was no one left alive to say one way or another.'

But Natalie knew he knew: either he'd guessed or Antonije had told him. In the end Frank had admired him as a survivor, regardless of what he had done along the way. 'What about how old Lyuba was?'

'It's not like there were a lot of records.' Frank shrugged. 'She was Romani so her birth probably wasn't recorded anyway.'

'Too young to become a mother?'

'Too young and too traumatised.' Frank bent over and picked up one picture then another. 'Life was very different back then.'

'What about with Eliza, Frank? Was she young and traumatised?'

'Eliza?' Frank's expression hardened. 'Eliza always knew exactly what she was doing.'

'Really?' Natalie took a deep breath. 'She was what? Eighteen? Your grandfather was a hero to her. You don't think he wielded power over her?'

'He wielded power over us all.' Frank was smiling but there was no warmth in his eyes.

'How was that for you?'

Frank smiled, a faraway type smile. Chilling.

'What about five words for your relationship with him when you were a child, Frank?'

'Five words?' Frank looked at her calmly. 'Magnificent. Powerful. Challenging—but always because he wanted the best of me and that was what I wanted to give. Frightening.' He noted at Natalie's peeked interest and laughed. 'No, he didn't frighten me. I was only scared—then—that I might not be worthy of him.'

'And fifth?'

'Perfect.'

Except it wasn't of course: Frank's relationship with Antonije was idealised, even in the face of him knowing, as an adult, how much pathology was there between them. Between all the family members. Watching her reaction, Frank grimaced. 'I know it wasn't perfect Natalie, I'm not stupid. That was what I thought *then*.'

Yes, he'd rationalised. He thought he'd worked it through; Natalie could see he hadn't. But she couldn't be sure how much of his knowledge of the family secrets was conscious, how much subconscious. He must have suspected an incestuous relationship between Antonije and Vesna. She certainly had, when Frank had spoken of Antonije expecting too much of his daughter after her mother had died; when the sexual undercurrents in his painting left Natalie uneasy. Vesna had been six when her mother died; somewhere in the intervening years, probably by the time she was eight if statistics meant anything, Antonije had replaced Lyuba with their daughter.

'What about the dead baby under the floor Frank?'

'But...' Frank frowned and rubbed his temples. 'Before my mother went to England...she was...I don't know if anyone knew about them. No one ever knew she was pregnant.'

Denial of pregnancy. Uncommon but not unheard of. Natalie had seen it once: a young girl panic-stricken when she went to the toilet with gastro, so she thought, and instead delivered a baby. The child had been lucky to survive.

'Really?' Natalie watched him closely. She replayed his words. *Them.* 'How many?'

'Three.'

Three times Vesna had conceived before she gave birth to Frank. Three times she had killed the child. Were the other two skulls below, with the one she had seen? Natalie suppressed a shudder. The police could look. 'It is uncommon to occur more than once. And usually in religious families, with poor sex education.' And in strong patriarchal households where emotions weren't discussed.

'Lyuba died when Vesna was a child. I doubt she had any sex education.' He looked directly at her, clear eyes. 'And she was terrified of my grandfather.'

So much for them all adoring him. In Frank's ambivalence, some true feelings surfaced from beneath his determination to paint the perfect family picture. Antonije. The patriarch. With his own set of rules and values. *Family* he had titled the series of paintings where he had shown just what his values were clearly: one absolute dominance.

'So she escaped to England.'

'Yes. She told Mala the babies never cried, that she thought they were dead, but I imagine she dissociated and just left them.'

Frank clearly hadn't seen the skull. That baby hadn't died of starvation.

'So when I arrived,' Frank continued, 'and did not die, the guilt resurfaced and fuelled her psychosis. The medication treats that—but the guilt and fear have always remained.'

And the paranoia. Justified, Natalie would argue. 'So when did you find out? Was this what Reeva and Alison discovered?'

He leaned forward and spoke so softly she barely heard him. 'Why are you here, Natalie?'

'Because you invited me.' She put her cup down, aware that her shaking was risking it spilling all over her.

Frank stood up abruptly. 'My sources tell me you are not quite as demure as you make out. Alison certainly didn't think so.' He stood over her, and now in his voice she heard the anger. 'Your current attire seems to attest to that.'

Natalie rose slowly. Standing made her feel dizzy. She shook her head. Frank looked at her oddly. She didn't think he would hit her, but what did that prove? Neither Reeva nor Alison had died as a result of direct physical violence. She didn't know what this man was capable of.

He stood only centimetres from her and she willed her body not to tremble, steeled her mind to block out thoughts of the Worm. Of the immobilising powerlessness. She gritted her teeth and let her anger bubble—if anything could activate her, anger would.

'I could tell you weren't attracted to me.' Frank's hand strayed carelessly up her arm. 'Not initially, anyway. Which made me wonder what you were up to.' She wondered if those middle-aged women were still packing up. The music had stopped long ago. Would anyone hear her if she screamed? Even if they did, would the staff and family just ignore it? Perhaps they'd all grown to accept that what happened here had its own set of rules. Her head felt fuzzy, tiredness and the heat almost overpowering the adrenaline that was starting to pump through her. Had he put something in her tea?

'Which was a relief on one level.' His hand now was stroking her cheek. 'I certainly don't want another wife.'

'But a fuck wouldn't go astray, right?'

She had surprised him. He laughed, hand frozen mid-air. 'Now that you mention it...'

She never got to find out how seriously he would have tried. Whether sex was even on his radar at that moment. Whether she would have reacted or would have been overwhelmed with the tiredness that was creeping up on her from nowhere. Part of her wondered if he would have tried at all. There was menace and threat, but there was also some kind of resignation. Perhaps that, in the end, he wasn't alpha enough. That try as he might, Grandpa was always going to outdo him.

She never got to find out because they were both stopped in their tracks, frozen by a sound. A sound she didn't recognise until it came again, louder, and with it a rush of flames and heat as the door to the boatshed exploded. This time, the aim was better.

I hit the water and it knocked the breath out of me. Then I was on the bottom of the lake tangled in weeds, my chest straining for air. The instinct for survival is strong so I must have fought first to make it to the surface, first thought of air and the need to breath, done so automatically and without question. Other things came later. There was no pain from the burns to my face and torso, no awareness of the blood I was losing from where some debris had punctured my abdominal wall. Instead, the first thing I recalled was not the boathouse on fire, not Mala's shriek, but an intense rage. A murderous rage that I hadn't felt since I was ten years old—wanting to kill Vesna for telling Wendell who my real father was, but instead becoming catatonic.

Then, my rage incapacitated me. For years the memory had been confined to nightmares and my sleepwalking searches. The white walls of the Bethlem adolescent unit and the studied caring of its staff were the only memories I retained of those three months. I was silent when I felt rage, hit out when I longed to be touched; refused to eat even when hungry.

I never recalled those nights when I was found in odd

places, but I assumed in retrospect that I was trying to get home.

I never remember what I do when I sleepwalk.

'The loss of his father,' said the soft voices of those stupid enough to think they could see inside my head.

'The shock of a new sister,' said others.

Yet when they finally brought Mala in, she was the one thing that soothed me, that made sense of the furious torment inside me.

My mother knew; knew what I had heard. Knew what my father—Wendell—had discovered and why a man who was normally teetotal had drunk himself into oblivion and then tried to kill us both.

Now my rage felt targeted and controlled. But murderous all the same.

There was another explosion. I saw the debris coming towards me but was too slow. Everything went black.

The noise rang in her ears and Natalie felt herself flying through the air. Watching, as if in slow motion, the floorboards travelling with her.

The first sensation was relief as she hit the water: a balm for her overheated senses. But it was brief. She didn't have an easy relationship with water, had always hated submerging her face even for a second. As a child it had made her panic.

She struggled to swim to the surface and take in the situation, aware that she was still in danger, uncertain if she had been hit by the debris. She thought the figure on the bank was Frank.

Another bang sent more flames across the lake and she reluctantly dived back under, reflecting that he couldn't possibly have got to the edge so fast. When she surfaced both the figure and most of the boathouse had disappeared.

Gulping air, she heard debris falling around her. She dived back under but the reeds tangling around her legs impeded her movement. If Frank was there, finding him was not going to be easy. She looked around her, trying to judge how far he might have been flung, using the floating debris as a marker.

The chill of the water cleared the fuzziness in her head, but waves of exhaustion were pushing back against the adrenaline and fear that surged through her. She knew her body; knew it didn't feel right. She thought of the tea. Had he drugged her? His wives had both had temazepam in their system. It wouldn't affect her quite the same, though—with the amount of meds she used, two or three sleeping tablets wouldn't have that much effect. But Frank knew she was on medication—had he calculated for it?

She took a deep breath and dived under the largest chunk of wood, but couldn't stay down for long. Nothing. Further along she did the same, but she was struggling to stay under. The feeling was the same panic she felt when dreams of the Worm woke her.

If Frank was submerged, time was critical. She didn't think about whether she wanted to save a killer or not. She fought back her fear of putting her head under water and took herself, for a moment, to the balcony of the stilt house, replayed her morning mindfulness. Smelled the salt in the air, heard the waves.

The next time she dived, she went deeper. And found Frank.

Swimming had always seemed a frustrating activity to Natalie: cold, wet; the release of explosive movement perennially muted. Pulling Frank out of the reeds only added to the frustration of working against the water itself. Her lungs felt like they were going to explode. It had been less than three minutes, though, she was sure. He appeared to be unconscious but there was still hope if she worked quickly.

Then she discovered it wasn't the reeds pinning him. There was a large piece of the boathouse on his leg, too big to lift. But the lake floor was soft. She dug with one hand and pulled his leg with the other. On the third attempt it came free. She used her last remaining strength to pull him up with her to the surface.

She didn't have to go far before she found that she was able to stand. Half-swimming, half-walking, she pulled herself and Frank through the reeds. Slipped; lost her footing. In the corner of her eye she caught sight of the figure she had seen earlier. He was wading into the water. There was a chance he wouldn't notice her crawling out on her own; zero chance if she had to pull Frank out and try to revive him.

Frank was too heavy for her to do more than prop him on the edge of the lake. She thought she found a faint pulse, banged him hard on the chest anyway, then half-rolled him over to clear the lake debris from his mouth. He coughed. Coughed again, this time bringing up fluid. In the dark it was hard to know how much was lake water and how much was blood.

As she breathed slower and relaxed a little, she took a better look at him. Even in the shadows she could see that, while she might have saved him from drowning, he was far from being out of danger. The entire right side of his body was severely burnt; all that remained of his clothes was the right arm of his shirt. Natalie didn't need light to know these were first-degree burns. The chances of him surviving were limited. And the scarring…She thought of how beautiful he had been and wondered if he would prefer to die.

Frank coughed again. He opened his eyes and saw her. 'What…?'

'There was an explosion.' Natalie kept her voice low, eyes darting to the other side of the lake. 'Someone tried to kill us.'

Frank's breathing was shallow. 'You okay?'

Natalie nodded. Enzymes and adrenaline would counter any sedation that was running around her system. She was starting to think more clearly. Whatever Frank had been planning, it didn't include the explosion.

'Jasper?'

She nodded again.

'How am I doing?'

Did he catch the slight stillness before she spoke, or had he smelled the burnt skin? It was down to bone on his right hand. He would soon be feeling excruciating pain. But he might remain conscious, even if his body started to shut down. Burns like these could lead to a long, slow, agonising death.

'Might take a while before you're as pretty as you used to be.'

Frank tried to put a hand to his face but she stopped him.

'I need to call an ambulance.' She moved but didn't get far, his left hand grabbing her wrist tightly.

'First...' he coughed. 'I...'

'Later Frank.'

He shook his head, eyes staring right into her. He had always had the ability to make her feel like the only person in the room. Now she felt as if she was the only person in the world. She saw in that look that Frank knew he was going to die.

'Did you drug me, Frank?'

It was hard to make sense of his expression in the shadows. He coughed.

'Olanzapine,' he said. 'In the tea.'

A sedative antipsychotic. Vesna's. She'd had it a couple

of times and hated the fact that it made her want to eat constantly. But her body was well practised at metabolising these drugs. She was fighting it okay.

'You thought it would kill me?'

There was a moment of hesitation but she couldn't see his face well enough to try and read his intent. 'No. There was going to be a motorbike accident.'

No one would have thought twice about olanzapine being in her system. Even Declan knew she was prone to self-medicating—he might have figured that if this was all she could get, she'd have made do, even though she hated it. Would he ever have wondered about where she had got it from? Unlikely. And she'd had suicidal thoughts not so long ago, ones she had mentioned recently. They'd all just think it was a sad tragedy. Put it down to her illness.

'Why, Frank?'

He looked at her and it was hard to believe he was a cold calculating psychopath. But that was what had made him so successful. She'd picked narcissist, yes. But he'd never made the hair on the back of her neck rise, the one feeling that had never let her down before when she met someone without remorse. Only the subtle hints about him from Declan. That, and her feeling of being pulled in.

He'd fooled Alison and Reeva too, but it irked her all the same. They weren't psychiatrists. And she'd been looking hard for it.

'You wouldn't let it go.'

She frowned. 'My being here tonight?'

'Wei told me you'd been at the computer.'

'Why did Alison think you had Huntington's, Frank?' This was one bit that she hadn't worked out.

'My father.'

'You know you don't have it?'

There were now a number of people. She could pick out Drago and Senka standing at the other end of the lake. Mala, still in white, was standing near what remained of the boathouse shouting for her brother. The figure in black was nowhere to be seen.

Frank nodded. He was struggling to speak, shock beginning to set in. She felt for his pulse. Racing. His breath shallow. 'She was wrong.'

His eyes started to glaze, voice fading.

'Thought my father had tried to kill me because we were both...sick. A genetic illness. My mother's...Alison thought there had been miscarriages because the baby was genetically abnormal, abnormal because of the gene from Wendell. I...let her think it. Told her he had tried to kill me at the same time as he killed himself.'

Let her? Or maybe even encouraged her. Because it was better than the truth. If Wendell had tried to kill Frank, Natalie knew it wasn't because of the Huntington's gene, but because he was a child of incest.

Denial of pregnancy. Vesna's three pregnancies and three dead babies, also products of incest, killed or left to die under the boathouse. But Alison couldn't ever have known that.

Natalie had wondered about a house with a pet cemetery but no pets. A pet cemetery with three crosses. 'What did Alison think happened to the babies Frank?'

Frank coughed. It took a moment for him to breath evenly again. 'That they died at birth.'

'And were buried here? In the cemetery ?'

Frank started to speak then stopped. 'The pet cemetery

crosses, just for show. For my mother to mourn. She visits it often; Alison worked that out.'

And Alison must have misread Frank's narcissism as fear of some familial disorder that had caused his mother to miscarry; found out about the Bethlem admission and Wendell's murderous intent, sending her even further along the wrong trail of a genetic psychotic disorder. At least until the end, when the negative test result must have reassured her. Poor Alison; great with text books but here in the real world she'd added two and two to get five.

'Alison didn't understand you or your family, did she Frank?'

His grip on her tightened. 'Antonije was a great man... flawed...but he saved me. Us.'

'But Reeva didn't think so did she? She found out the true story, didn't she?'

She watched Frank fight his body, trying to survive. She saw Mala by the boathouse, stood up and yelled out. Frank should have his family by him. If he did pass out he might never regain consciousness.

'Alison knew in the end, some of it. About Jasper. Reeva was...smart,' Frank whispered. 'She was going to tell. I couldn't let that happen, you see.'

Natalie knelt back down as Mala started to run towards them around the edge of the lake.

'You killed both of them, Frank? Reeva wasn't psychotic, was she?'

'She wouldn't listen...'

'She was going to leave you, right? And Alison too?'

Poor Alison, who had dreamed of a prestigious husband and a baby, and instead had married into a family with a warped and dangerous paternal legacy.

'I tried to control my temper,' said Frank, coughing again. 'But...I don't always know what I do at night.'

Sleepwalking.

Natalie had heard of it being used as a successful defence once before and Frank had the perfect history. Early childhood sleep problems, terrors and bedwetting as an indication of unresolved conflict. Then major childhood trauma in an accident that killed the father who had been intent on murdering him at the same time. Finally a documented psychiatric admission at ten. It would probably reveal that his suppressed rage and unresolved conflict came out in sleepwalking.

'Do you remember doing it, Frank?' Had his wives even known?

If he answered Natalie she didn't hear it. Thunder, so loud it seemed to shake the ground, was followed by the largest and brightest lightning bolt she had ever witnessed. An arm stretched down so close that she half imagined it was the wrath of Zeus himself. In front of her, to the right of the house, where fireballs from the boathouse explosion had already taken on a life of their own, the bolt struck the huge tree that had supported the treehouse of Vesna's childhood.

In its flash of illumination, Natalie realised Jasper was standing beside her. Staring at her and Frank. Natalie stiffened. Checked, in the dimmer light after the flash, that she hadn't imagined him.

'Back off Jasper,' she said, standing slowly. 'You got what you wanted with Frank. You don't need another murder charge.'

Jasper walked towards her, stopping about a metre away. Close enough for her to size him up and know that if he chose to attack, she was history. 'The whole fucking family should die.'

'I'm not one of them, Jasper.'

'Yeah?' He gave a nasty laugh. 'Not for want of trying, I'm told.'

They both turned towards a new sound—not as loud as the thunder but accompanied by, Natalie imagined, the sorrowful groan of the dying Malosevic legacy. Embers from the boathouse explosion had taken hold in the roof and trees around the main house, all now ablaze. The roof of the garage buckled and crackled as it crashed down onto the Bentley. And her Ducati.

Jasper might have intended just to kill her and Frank, but the fire was likely to do much worse—including destroying the inheritance he had his eye on.

She watched in horror as the flames laid claim to the remainder of the house. Drago, who had been heading towards her, saw it too. He yelled something to Senka and ran inside. To call the fire brigade, Natalie hoped.

Jasper was still gazing in disbelief, stunned at the unfolding demolition, when Mala arrived. She glanced briefly at them both before sinking down beside her brother. Jasper was looking around wildly, agitated. If he knew Frank was still alive he might still act. If it was a family vendetta perhaps Mala was more at risk than Natalie.

'Mala?' Jasper looked from the house to Natalie and then to Mala. Natalie wondered if he was on drugs or if the sheer adrenaline had sent him over the edge. Now he looked around wildly, confused. Staring at the woman whose gown was now clinging to her, drenched in blood from Frank's abdominal wound, the hem muddy and torn.

Mala turned away from Frank to meet Jasper's eyes.

'You should have gone,' she said coldly, and turned back to her brother. Natalie wasn't sure who she was speaking to.

She remembered how Jasper had looked at Eliza in the kitchen and made an instant assessment, hoping she'd guessed right. He was dependent on the women in his life. He presented as a bully, but underlying his anger was a fear of rejection.

'Find your mother, Jasper,' Natalie ordered. 'She'll know what to do.'

Jasper took another look at Mala; then, staring at Natalie, seemed to return to reality.

'Hurry,' said Natalie, keeping her voice even. 'Before the police come.'

He left without saying anything. After a few metres he started to run.

Frank hadn't moved.

'I'm going to ring for an ambulance,' Natalie told Mala. She thought about Vesna and yelled over her shoulder, 'We need to get your mother.'

In her mind she was trying to work out how to get Frank to a car, if any had escaped the fire, and whether that would be quicker than an ambulance. The olanzapine wasn't helping her think, but the adrenaline was working on her side. 'Burn faster,' she willed her enzymes, aware of the irony.

Drago was stuffing the contents of a cabinet into a bag. Gordana emerged from Frank's study with another bag filled with stuff, Natalie felt sure, that would be deemed to have burnt with the house.

'There's no time,' said Natalie. 'Where's Vesna?'

'Don't know.'

'We need to get Vesna and Frank out.'

'Let them all burn in hell,' said Gordana defiantly.

351

Natalie found her mobile, still on the arm of the sofa, called triple zero and asked for an ambulance. Mentioned the fire before she hung up. She didn't entirely trust Drago to have called the CFA.

The main room was filled with smoke. The roof above her was glowing and the smoke was heavy around the spiral staircase. Half of the wall behind it was missing. She went back to the main staircase, knowing it was the smoke that killed you. The mezzanine was still intact; most of it anyway. Vesna's room was at the end furthest from where the flames had taken hold.

Natalie burst in and found Vesna, heavily medicated, drunk or both, fast asleep.

Natalie shook her hard and she stirred. In the bathroom she found a small plastic rubbish bin, tipped out the empty pill packets, filled it with water and threw the entire contents over the older woman.

She woke disorientated. Pulling away from Natalie in fear.

'We have to go, now,' said Natalie. 'There's a fire.'

Vesna looked panic-stricken, curling up tighter under the bedclothes. Natalie grabbed her arm and pulled her hard, but made no headway against the woman's dead weight.

'Shit.' Natalie heard a car starting up. She tried to sound calming, the way she spoke to her patients. 'Come on Vesna.'

'I want Frank. Where is he?' If she was surprised that Natalie wasn't still locked up she didn't show it. Maybe she'd forgotten.

'Mala's with him. We'll meet them. I need you to come with me, Vesna.'

She took the woman's hand and pulled again. Vesna tentatively edged forward, bare legs slipping over the end of the bed.

'We need to be quick, don't look, just run.'

Vesna nodded, but when they made it to the landing she stopped and cried out. Above them, leaping flames licked down across the ceiling. The smoke was thick now, sealing over them as a death trap.

'Down on your knees.' The smoke was slightly less at floor level but made it impossible to pull the older woman. Natalie saw immediately that Vesna wasn't following.

'Vesna!' Her voice was firm, a command: mother to child. Or perhaps, in Vesna's case, father. 'Move. Now.'

For a moment she wasn't sure it would work. 'Antonije would want you to leave, Vesna.'

This time Vesna started to crawl and Natalie fell in behind her, pushing gently, all the way to the main staircase. Vesna took her hand again, cowering against her as they went down one step at a time. They got to the bottom and had made it to the hall when Natalie heard the car pulling away. She left Vesna and ran to the door, but too late. Drago and his family were heading out in what looked like Frank's car. *Shit.* Pushing Vesna out the door, she guided her to a bench far enough away to be out of immediate danger.

Then she heard something. Someone moving around inside. She froze. Jasper?

Natalie headed back to the front door, from which smoke was now billowing in large black waves. She started coughing as she called out. No response. But there was the unmistakable noise of someone banging into furniture. Natalie took a deep breath, and against her better judgment, ran back inside.

Mala was standing in the living room, just visible, in silhouette. The calm of the dead, floating Ophelia. No sense of hurry or alarm. As if in slow motion, she looked at Natalie, then moved towards the staircase.

'Mala, your mother's with me,' Natalie managed to say between coughs.

Mala kept walking. Natalie saw her smile. She went after her and grabbed her arm. 'We need to get out *now*.'

'No. I have to get something first.'

'No possession is worth dying for,' said Natalie.

'This is.'

Mala pulled her arm away and Natalie watched in despair as she went up, towards the flames.

As soon as Natalie left I opened my eyes. 'I told her. About the sleepwalking. And the olanzapine. I said it was in the tea I gave her.'

Mala looked at me with the same perfect eyes she had as a newborn. She smiled, her hand caressing my head.

'Make sure Jasper gets put away for this, promise me.'

'You'll be there Frank, to see it for yourself.'

I shook my head. Already that was difficult. 'You'll be fine Mala; you're a survivor. Start afresh, let the house burn and start a new life.'

We both looked up at the house of our childhood, the one we had thought would be there for our old age.

'I need the paintings.' She pulled away from me.

Antonije had won. Again.

Fuck. This whole family seemed determined to put her out of action one way or another. Maybe the last of them would finally achieve it. Natalie watched Mala disappear into the smoke. Wait or go after her? Natalie didn't trust Mala's judgment, but as she followed, she knew her own was also in question.

Mala went to her room. When Natalie got there they were both coughing but Natalie was faring better, crawling at floor level. Mala was pulling the picture off the wall. Rather than argue, Natalie grabbed it out of her hands. At least a metre wide and a little higher with a heavy gilt frame, it wasn't light. But Natalie wasn't worrying about scratching anything. She dragged it after her, onto the balcony and threw it over to the room below. Mala was behind her, dragging the matching picture, which had been propped next to it. She looked on in horror as Natalie hoisted the second.

'We can get them from below, let's go.'

Mala didn't have to be told twice. Unlike Vesna, she now seemed to understand the danger. The two crawled quickly and then ran down the staircase. In the main room there was still a metre or so of air that was largely free of smoke. They dragged a picture each and made it to the front door, where Natalie dropped hers just as the front door burst open.

Damian. She'd never been more pleased to see anyone in her life.

The hospital wanted to keep her overnight but she refused. They had done blood tests, rehydrated her, patched the cuts and scratches and prescribed antibiotics. The CFA were still containing the fire Jasper had started at Mount Malosevic. They were winning the fight now, largely because the heavens had finally opened. The fireballs from the boathouse explosion had done their work, however, and the house was gutted. Jasper was being charged with arson. As a starting point. Drago and his family had vanished. Vesna and Mala had booked themselves into a local hotel and Frank was still alive; just. He was in an induced coma and had been given a fifty–fifty chance. The Ducati was history.

Damian arrived at the stilt house late morning, as she knew he would. She had waited up, watching the sunrise.

'You know you're fucking crazy, right?'

She nodded.

He shook his head wearily. 'It'll be days before we can interview Frank. We got Jasper at Eliza's and he isn't making much sense, except he seems to have been under Mala's influence. Can you explain? Because no one else seems to be able to.'

Natalie looked out across the ocean and wondered if anyone would believe what she had deduced.

'Have you seen the paintings?'

'The ones you and Mala nearly died getting?'

She nodded.

'Sick.'

Yes, they were certainly that.

'It's the same old story in many ways,' said Natalie. 'Antonije liked children. You knew I suspected that he had an incestuous relationship with his daughter? But it went further.' In the paintings his wife, daughter and granddaughter were all in their early teens. Wife and daughter pregnant—with his child, as Natalie now knew—and the other? Mala's expression in the painting, as represented by her grandfather, had been hard to fathom. 'Underneath the boathouse...well where the boathouse was...look for the remains of a dead baby.'

'What?'

'Frank knew about three dead babies. Babies Vesna had to her own father. Hidden pregnancies, the babies left to die. I thought it possible when I saw the paintings and reflected on the pet cemetery. When Frank said there were three, and there are three crosses, it seemed even more likely'

'You thought they were buried there?'

Natalie nodded. 'I imagine Alison thought so too— except she thought that they were miscarriages due to a genetic abnormality.'

'The DNA test.' Damian rubbed his head.

'You got the final result?'

Damian nodded. 'Eliza didn't lie. Frank isn't Jasper's father.'

'No, Antonije was. But she escaped. He couldn't control Eliza like he could his family. I suspect she told Jasper about it the night he tried to kill Frank and me.' Natalie paused. 'Did the DNA suggest Antonije was Frank's father too, as well as grandfather?'

Damian smiled. 'How did you know?'

Natalie shrugged. 'I couldn't be sure. I imagine Antonije liked the idea of Vesna pregnant; his own virility perhaps. But there was the awkward reality of babies and whose they were, which he couldn't allow. I think it's what Wendell Moreton found out and why he tried to take his son with him when he killed himself. Well, the boy he'd thought was his son up until then.'

'Does this tie in with why Frank killed his wives?'

She paused a long time before nodding. 'You need to get the records from Bethlem hospital in the UK. He sleepwalks.'

Damian groaned. 'You aren't going to tell me he can use a sleepwalking defence are you?'

'Okay, I won't, but I'm sure his lawyers will. Narcissistic rage against the perfect baby he wasn't. Or against the baby that survived the crash that his father had died in.'

It was a week before she was allowed in to talk to Frank. She found him in his hospital bed, the table beside him overflowing with flowers, more on the windowsill. On the floor she noticed the bag that had been in his office fridge, the one that she had never seen him use. She wondered what was so important that he needed it now. It still looked empty. His face was bandaged and she felt a pang of sympathy for him. He had been beautiful. Mala was at his side. She looked so perfect that it would surely make it all the harder.

Mala held Frank's one good hand as they both watched her; she saw wariness in Frank's eyes but Mala was impossible to read.

'I understand the police are involved again,' Natalie said. 'I told them what you said to me.'

Frank nodded. 'I know.' His voice was a hoarse whisper, probably also damaged in the fire.

'I've been thinking, Frank, and something doesn't make sense.'

She watched for a reaction. The bandages and burns hid any expression that might have given Frank away. And Mala?

Natalie thought over Scott Beamish's story. He'd been in a relationship with Mala during her brief stint at Oxford. She'd met him and his friend Wei at the same time, and both had adored her. *I thought she was the most beautiful woman in the world,* Beamish said. *But I never knew her.*

And when Mala told Beamish she was pregnant, he never knew whether the baby was his, either. He had been prepared to marry her, believed he loved her. He had no idea that Wendell Moreton, the man driving the car that had killed his mother, was Mala Malosevic's father: Mala told him as a parting gift. Presumably she shared this with Wei as well. *She laughed. Said I had survived, but no way was this baby going to.* She returned to Australia—with Wei, who, like many men and women in her life, she used as she needed to—dumped Scott and told him she'd had a termination.

First Wendell Moreton had killed Scott's mother, albeit inadvertently. Now Mala had deliberately killed his child. If indeed it was his.

Beamish still sounded bewildered by the whole encounter. Mala had set him up, no doubt. But of course in all pathological relationships both partners contributed. Natalie thought briefly of Georgia and Paul. In this relationship, though, Mala was the dominant one: a consummate psychopath with no need to hide guilt because she felt none. She was the type who passed lie detector tests effortlessly and played with people for the fun of it.

Natalie was still looking at Frank. 'You see, I always knew you were a narcissist,' she mused. 'And I knew you thought you were dying. So why on earth would you confess? A narcissist would rather die thinking they had outsmarted everyone. Particularly me; you needed to be smarter than me. Unless...'

'Unless what?'

Mala was beautiful, but her beauty was on the surface. Underneath she was envious and outraged that Frank had been preferred by Antonije. Frank was the great man's child while she was only his grandchild—and a woman to boot. Which in that family meant a chattel to be used.

And Mala would not want to be owned and used. The more Natalie had thought about the toxic atmosphere at Mount Malosevic, the more she had been sure that, while it had originated with Antonije, it was Mala who kept the evil alive.

'Unless, Frank, you were protecting the perfect relationship. And Reeva and Alison were never perfect, were they Frank?'

Never perfect; but he would not have killed them. Any more than he had drugged her. When she thought of the timing it was obvious. It takes oral olanzapine some time to work, particularly in someone with enzymes that are well able to metabolise it. It had been in the champagne, not the tea. Mala had known she was in the cupboard, had poured the champagne and told her mother to give it to Natalie. It was Mala, not Vesna, who had told Gordana to lure Natalie to the garage, Mala who had organised the menu that so antagonised Alison. Mala who pulled Jasper's strings. Frank had guessed and tried to cover for the sister he adored.

Ultimately Natalie had been right; Frank was narcissistic,

and not the malignant variety that blurred into psychopathy. His love for Mala was not one a psychopath felt, and he did care what others thought about him. Mala, on the other hand, was devoid of feelings for others and had little concern for what they felt or thought about her. 'You were Frank's perfect relationship weren't you Mala?'

Mala snickered. 'You have a vivid imagination.'

'Perhaps, but try this. Frank was surprised when I told him about the baby under the floorboards. And he thought there were three, but there weren't, not there at least. Frank let me think the baby I found was Vesna's, but it couldn't have been. The underground tunnel was a late addition, long after Vesna had returned from the UK. I think her dead babies are in the pet cemetery. The babies she left to die, or maybe suffocated. But the child I saw—barely a child, maybe twenty-eight weeks?—had its head caved in. Your baby, Mala. Was it yours and Scott's? Or yours and…?' She looked at Frank. Wondered.

'I never wanted a baby. Ever.' The smile that accompanied Mala's words made Natalie feel a sliver of ice had pierced her insides and then twisted like a knife.

She wondered what it was like being brought up by a paranoid mother, knowing that her father had killed himself and tried in the process to kill her brother, a half-brother who was also an uncle. In a family where secrets like the suicide of an adolescent grandmother and multiple miscarriages or self-induced terminations were mere icing on the cake.

For Frank, Antonije had offered a role model; but for Mala? An abuser and a master one at that. One who taught Mala to be an even greater manipulator. Right down to being prepared to kill Frank's wives so they could not bear the heir she wasn't permitted to.

I never wanted a baby. Ever. If her baby had been Frank's child, it was only to show that she could. That the power was hers. She wouldn't have shared the power with an heir.

Mala, Natalie thought, was Frank's weakness, but the reverse was not true. Mala had Frank's measure. She had only ever failed once—and that was where her vulnerability lay. Natalie thought of Antonije's painting and the expression on Mala's face she hadn't been able to work out. Now it came to her with a clarity that was startling: Antonije had been a narcissistic abuser, but he had also been a keen observer. She gambled on his observation—and her intuition—being accurate.

'Really Mala?' Natalie heard Damian's voice in her head: *just keep her talking.* But Mala wasn't her patient, and was not only not stupid, she was frighteningly brilliant. Could she be goaded? Maybe. But Natalie's instinct said she had one chance, and one chance only.

'You never wanted a baby,' Natalie repeated slowly, never taking her gaze from Mala. 'But you and I know that's not true, don't we?'

Frank eyes went to his sister. 'No, Mala...'

Mala's smile was supercilious, smug.

'But it wasn't Frank's baby you wanted was it?'

There was a flicker of uncertainty in Mala's expression. Frank's was impossible to read, his eyes never leaving his sister.

'You wanted Antonije's.' Natalie leaned in towards her. Thought of the painting where the only female who wasn't pregnant was Mala. 'But he rejected you didn't he? To him you were tainted. The offspring of the man his daughter had left him for.'

The slap was so fast Natalie didn't see it coming, and powerful enough to send her reeling back against the wall.

'He never rejected me!' Mala screamed, as Frank's hand gripped around her forearm in an effort to restrain her. 'He was just too old, that's all.'

'So you got pregnant to show him you were the new generation's life blood, didn't you?' Natalie continued, standing upright. 'But he died before you could tell him, so the baby no longer mattered and you killed it.'

'I never wanted that baby! I'd smash its head in again if I had to. '

'You couldn't bear Alison and Reeva having what you couldn't—or wouldn't—have could you?' Natalie wondered. 'Did Frank know?'

Frank let out an anguished moan as Mala, now cool and in control, said, 'Antonije was wrong. He thought Frank would look after the family. But it was always going to be me. I am the one who doesn't let emotion rule me.'

Because she didn't feel like most people. Maybe genetic, but it was also because in the toxic family she had been born into, it was the only way to survive. Put herself first and use others with one goal in mind: to meet her own needs. She had undoubtedly targeted Wei and Jasper and Scott Beamish, largely because she could. She needed to be adored to fill an emptiness in the soul that even Frank's adoration, if the glow in his eyes was anything to go by, didn't come close to satisfying.

Mala looked at Natalie with an unwavering stare. 'You wanted his baby too, I could tell. They all did, like bitches on heat.'

Mala had shaken free of Frank's hold and walked towards her. 'But you got pregnant anyway didn't you?'

Natalie felt no fear, though she had a second to think *how does she know?*

'That's why I wanted Jasper to kill you; when the stupid bastard found out from Eliza that Frank wasn't his father he wanted to kill you both.'

Natalie didn't wait to listen to any more. As she left she removed the wire the police had placed under her shirt and gave it back to Damian in the next room. Then she kept on walking. She was at the end of the corridor before Damian caught her.

'What did she mean about you being pregnant?'

Natalie stopped dead and took a breath before looking at him. 'They did a blood test last week after the fire. When I was hospitalised. I didn't know before that. I put the nausea down to my meds.'

He stared.

'I'm about eight weeks.'

He kept staring, refusing to make it easy for her.

'I'm sorry, Damian.' One in a million, he had said. But he'd been eating better, drinking less, was less stressed. Maybe his fertility had improved. 'I don't know whose it is. Because we weren't using...' She faltered, watched the pain in his eyes. 'It was only once and I...' No, she hadn't looked for it. But she hadn't stopped it either.

'O'Shea.' His mouth was hard. 'Does he know?'

'No.'

'Are you going to keep it?'

She had been thinking *no* for the last week. She still had time to make a decision. She had no religious beliefs about it and had never wanted to raise a child without the child's father—repeating her mother's mistake. Yet here she was, contemplating that exact course. Repeating patterns. She thought of the dead infant under the boathouse, of Vesna's children in the pet cemetery. Of Reeva and Alison's babies. Of Georgia's dead children and the foetus that had died with her. She took a breath.

'Yes. I am. I just can't...I don't have the stomach for any more death. When the DNA results come through I'll let you know if it's our mistake. Or...'

Much later that night she was still ruminating about something she had missed, and a thought came to her. The bag Frank had with him. The one he had hidden in his office fridge, the one she should have examined more closely. She'd ring Damian in the morning, or maybe text him. She was probably wrong anyway.

'Let it go!' she told herself out loud, wanting this case to be behind her. There were more important things to worry about.

She looked up, across the ocean and thought of Liam. Liam who had now left his wife, who had tried to back off her in court. Who had wanted her, and maybe still did. Liam, who when she was honest with herself, she still longed for. She texted him.

EPILOGUE

We expected the police of course, but there was no rush. The hospital would need to keep me for several weeks at least, and even after that I would need to return regularly as part of the long, slow process that would never truly see me heal. And the police needed to brief the prosecutor to decide if there was enough evidence to charge Mala.

I have had plenty of time to reflect, to remember walking in on Antonije and Eliza. Her look of shame. She had followed him, rubbed up against him, wanted to show me that I was nothing and that she would submit to the master after rejecting the student.

But I thought most about Mala. How I had stood by waiting for Antonije to die, so that I would be the one that she would come to rather than him. I was always about protecting her, because from the moment I saw her I loved her.

I have so many regrets, and one of the last is Natalie. I met my match in her. Perhaps we could have made beautiful babies. Perhaps with her I could have left my ghosts behind and moved on.

But I also know that there could never be anyone for me except Mala. My Achilles heel.

I never meant it to happen, but we both learned at Antonije's side that sex was about comfort, and about power. And Mala likes power. We slept together just one time before she went to Oxford. I was drunk; not an acceptable excuse I know, but Mala orchestrated it. She had been waiting for the moment all her life. She wanted power to wield over everyone, whenever she chose. I knew this; and yet, even so, without her I felt incomplete. No one could ever quite measure up. Separated by thousands of kilometres, I hoped to grieve and move on. I didn't expect anyone ever to be as perfect. But without her there, and with no constant reminder of the specialness of my soul mate, I could have made a life with Reeva.

At Oxford Mala had any number of lovers of both sexes but I imagine they were all too easy for her. I am not stupid; I know that she doesn't have empathy for others. Except, I like to think, for me. If it was my baby she would have kept it.

I will never know whether she and Jasper were still working together when he ignited the gas tank. She says not, but she is such a beautiful liar.

She thinks now that she will get away with it, with killing my two wives as well as her own child, that nothing she said was damning enough, that there is no real proof. I have underestimated Natalie in the past and I will not do so now. My poor darling sister. The only woman I ever truly wanted. Our perfection blinded me to her paranoid rage.

Did I suspect her, after Reeva died? Perhaps at the edge

of my mind it niggled; something made me pack up my wife's insulin so there would be no further risk. And I did warn Alison, after all. I told her to go and stay with her parents.

Mala knows I have the insulin; it was she who found the little bag for it, the one I kept in my office. She knows I am not prepared to live as anything except perfect. I will ask her to lie with me, for what more fitting way to be seen out of this world? But I could never leave her alone. We will go together. We will have a final drink and I will use the insulin I have there, sewn into the side pockets of the bag, well away from prying eyes, carefully refrigerated all this time. I will have to roll over onto her, subdue her and inject her with the first syringe. She will think as I am preparing it that it is for me. I wonder if she will protest, or if, in the end, she will see that I really did understand?

We were perfect. Now, in death, we always will be. And, finally, I win.

ACKNOWLEDGMENTS

Apologies to Professor Michael Berk, his wife Lesley and the rest of the (full) research team in Geelong (they do exist)— they bear no resemblance to my fictitious characters!

Also, apologies to the Lorne police and those who know the Great Ocean Road well: I have taken some small liberties with the geography around Lorne, for which I hope I will be forgiven; and in normal circumstances the local police wouldn't need the Melbourne homicide guys interfering. There were some amazing storms in Victoria in the last couple of years but the timing of the one in this book may not correlate accurately with the exact date. This is set in the winter of 2015, before the devastating bushfires of Christmas 2015 destroyed much of the area. The pub and the stilt house did survive.

This is a work of fiction and all the characters are fictitious: where real cases are mentioned, I had no involvement in any capacity.

My thanks to all the people who helped make this book possible:

Victoria Police Media and Corporate Communications department were very helpful with details around Damian's job, even if the more senior officers were a little shy.

Tania Evers, who reviewed the legal aspects for me. My first readers, who had wrestled previously with *Medea's Curse* and told me they liked this more: Sue Hughes (who also loaned me her house to write in—the inspiration for Natalie's stilt house), Karin Whitehead, and my daughter Dominique Simsion and son Daniel Simsion. And to the intrepid readers who helped me make it stand alone: May Ralph, Angela Collie and Robin Baker.

The team at Text: you're all so enthusiastic, it's a pleasure to work with each and every one of you. Mandy Brett is an author's dream of an editor (well, mine anyway), Lea Antigny and Jane Novak are fabulous publicists and Chong—I never got to thank him for the amazing cover of *Medea's Curse* (a last-minute change!) and now another thanks for this one.

The helpful suggestions and encouragement from Antoni Jach and his masterclass were again much appreciated— thanks Erina Reddan, Emilie Collyer, Anna Dusk, Tasha Haines, Clive Wansbrough and Rocco Russo.

The sources Natalie refers to are the Adult Attachment Interview by George, Kaplan and Main—the gold standard for adult attachment—and Kay Redfield Jamison's autobiography, *An Unquiet Mind*.

As always my husband Graeme, soul mate, mentor, sounding-board, inspiration...and tough editor, has been a key component to helping this book get written, at every level. I hope we survive as many books together as we have years of marriage. And keep surprising each other.